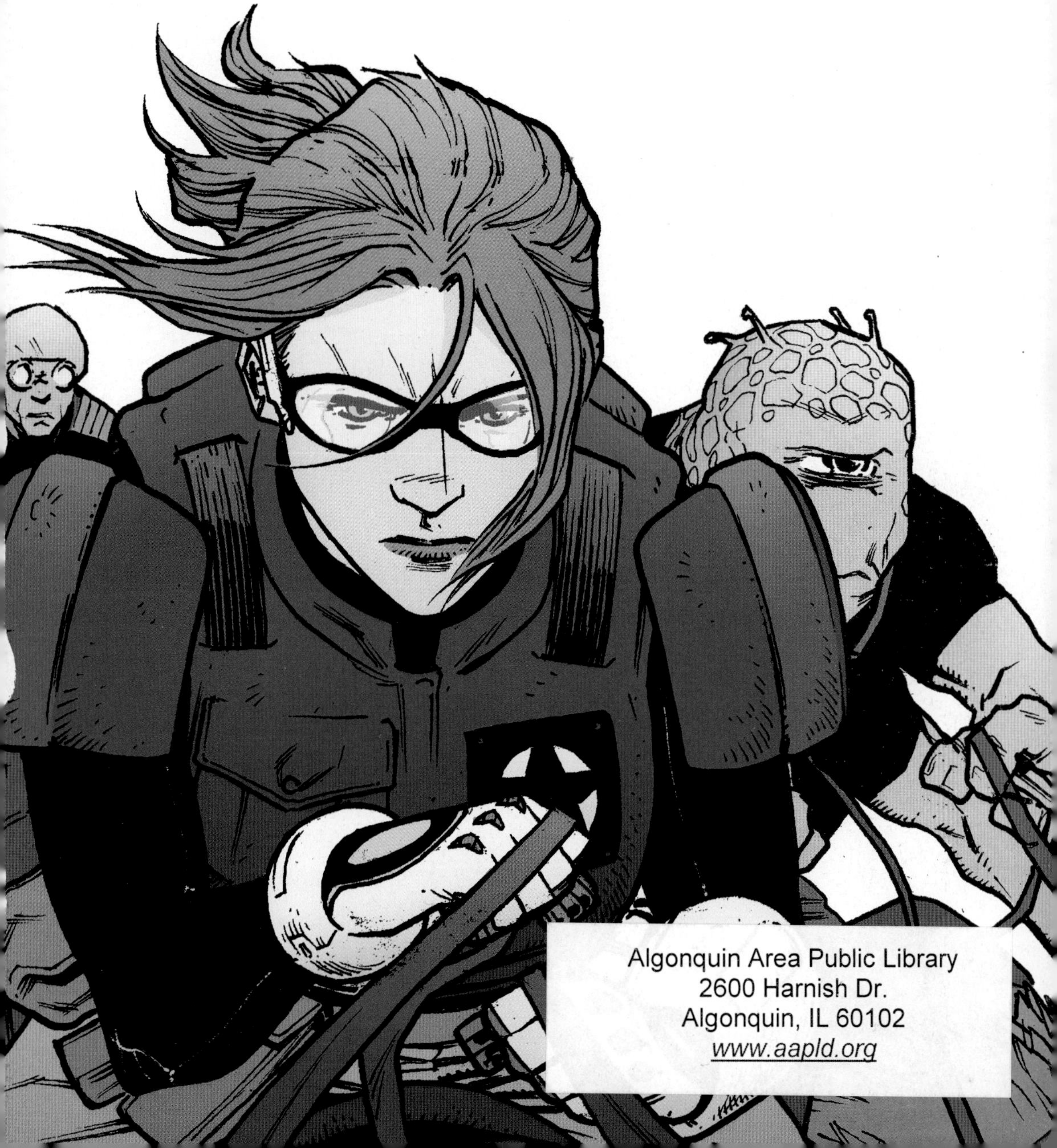

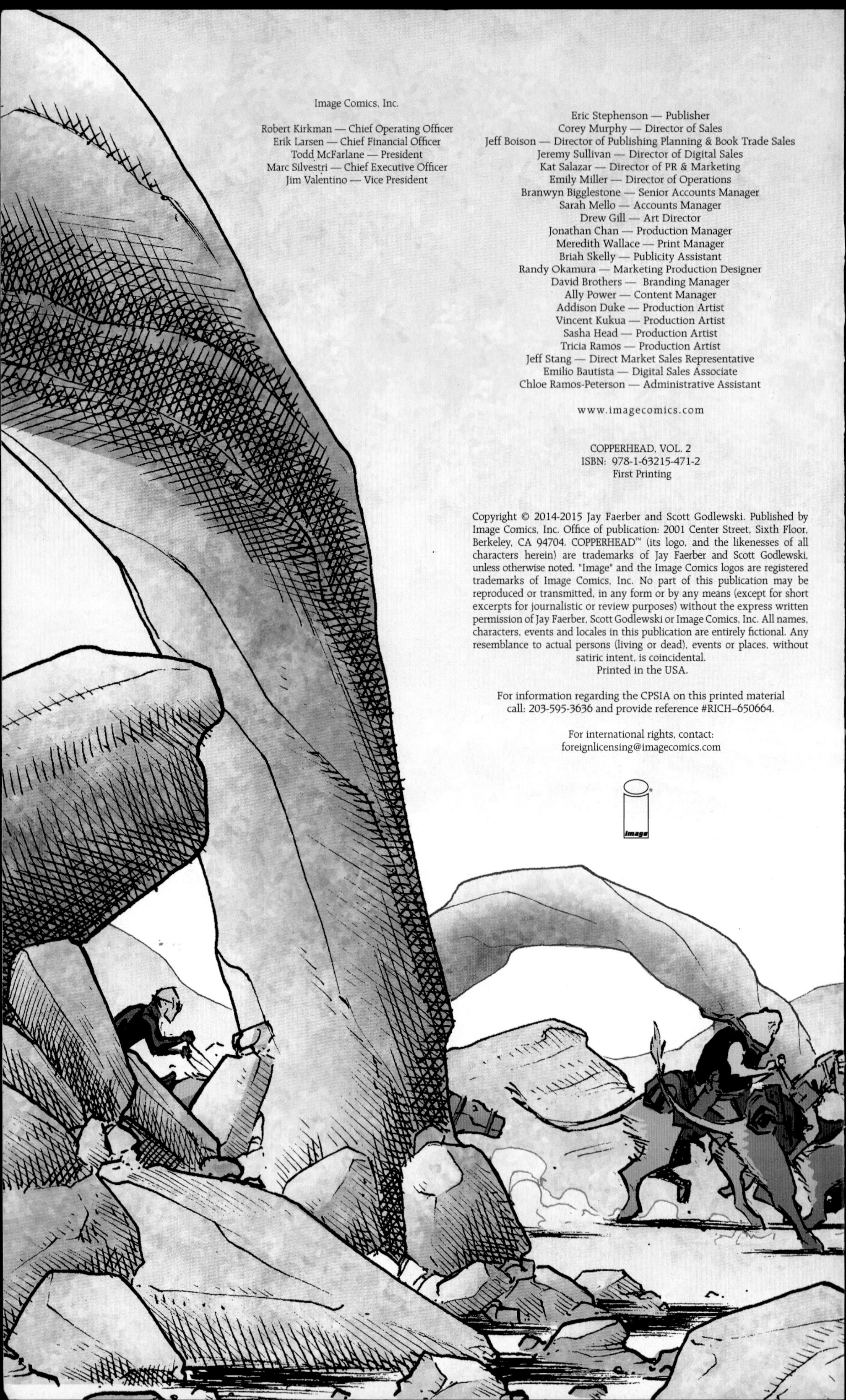

Image Comics, Inc.

Robert Kirkman — Chief Operating Officer
Erik Larsen — Chief Financial Officer
Todd McFarlane — President
Marc Silvestri — Chief Executive Officer
Jim Valentino — Vice President

Eric Stephenson — Publisher
Corey Murphy — Director of Sales
Jeff Boison — Director of Publishing Planning & Book Trade Sales
Jeremy Sullivan — Director of Digital Sales
Kat Salazar — Director of PR & Marketing
Emily Miller — Director of Operations
Branwyn Bigglestone — Senior Accounts Manager
Sarah Mello — Accounts Manager
Drew Gill — Art Director
Jonathan Chan — Production Manager
Meredith Wallace — Print Manager
Briah Skelly — Publicity Assistant
Randy Okamura — Marketing Production Designer
David Brothers — Branding Manager
Ally Power — Content Manager
Addison Duke — Production Artist
Vincent Kukua — Production Artist
Sasha Head — Production Artist
Tricia Ramos — Production Artist
Jeff Stang — Direct Market Sales Representative
Emilio Bautista — Digital Sales Associate
Chloe Ramos-Peterson — Administrative Assistant

www.imagecomics.com

COPPERHEAD, VOL. 2
ISBN: 978-1-63215-471-2
First Printing

For information regarding the CPSIA on this printed material call: 203-595-3636 and provide reference #RICH–650664.

For international rights, contact:
foreignlicensing@imagecomics.com

image

COPPERHEAD

Volume 2

writer
JAY FAERBER
artist
SCOTT GODLEWSKI
colorist
RON RILEY
letterer & designer
THOMAS MAUER

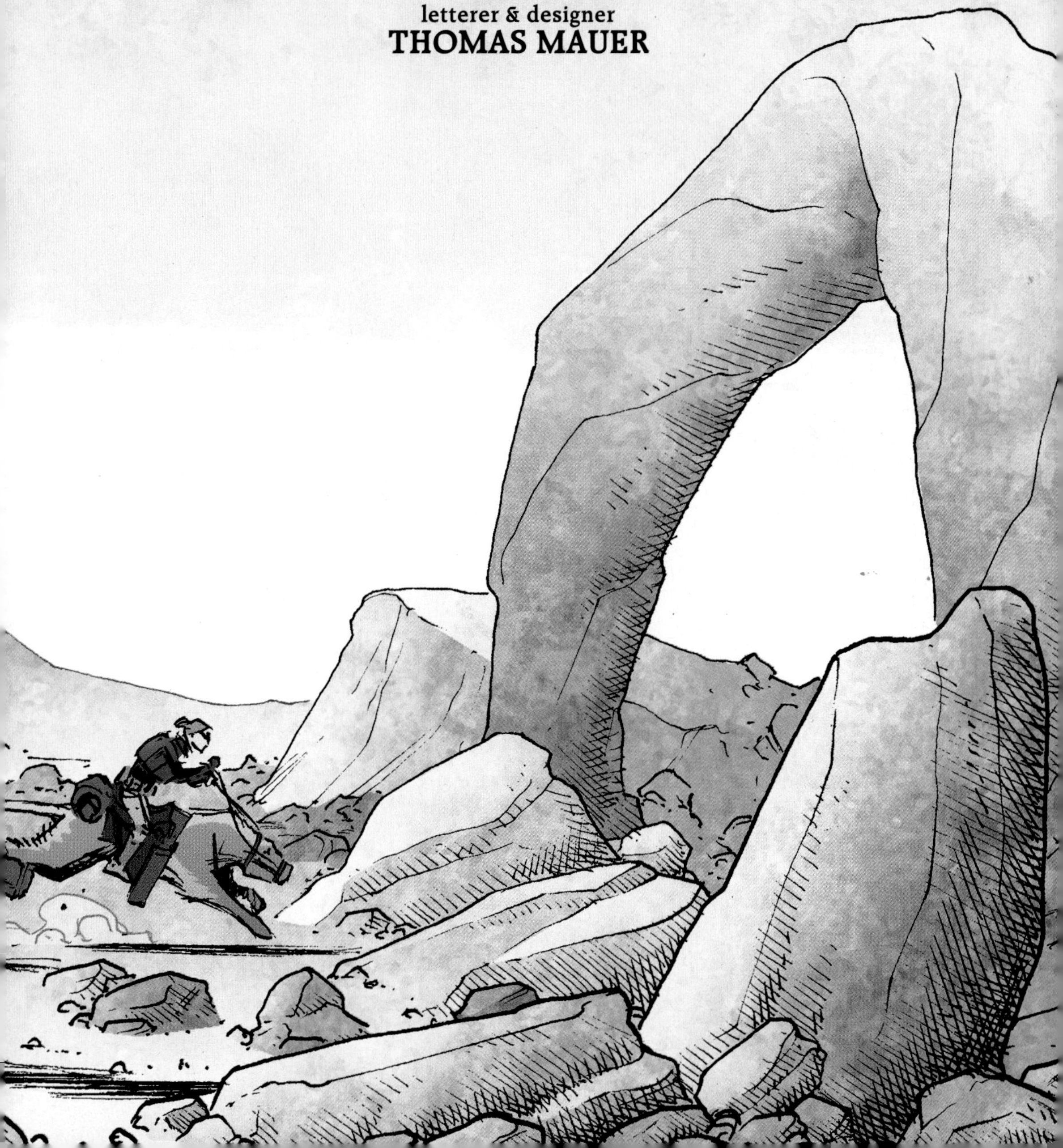

CHAPTER I

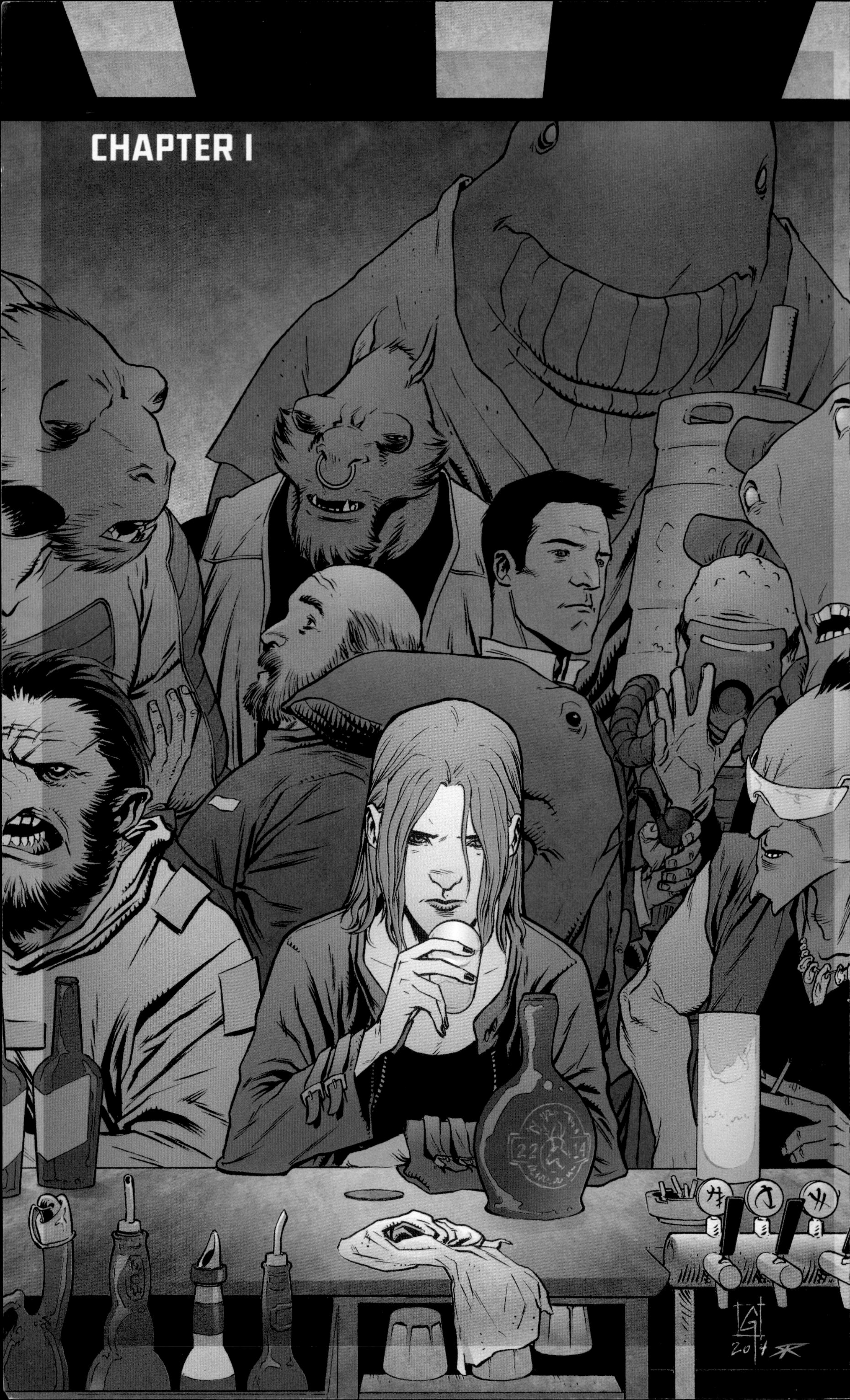

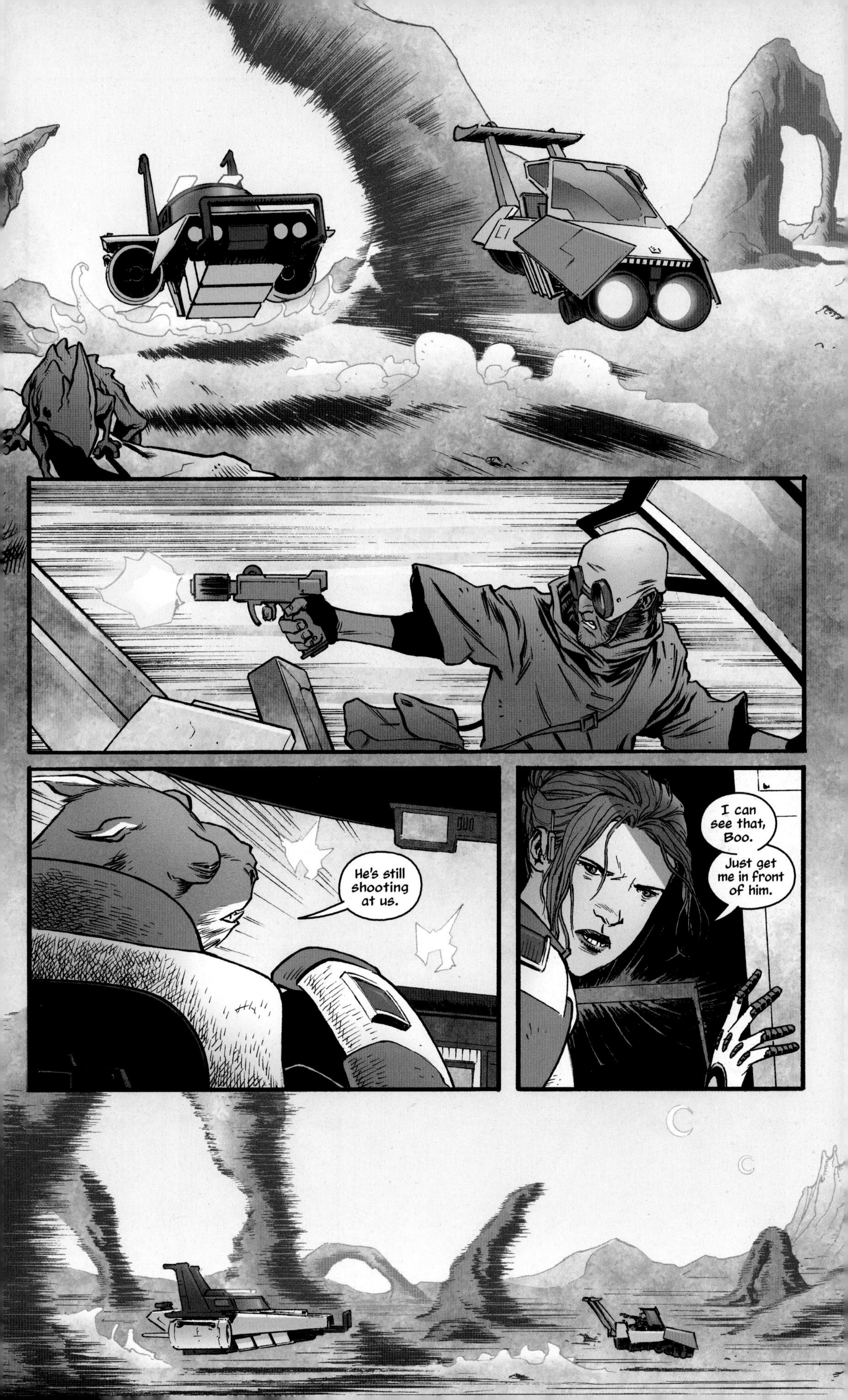
He's still shooting at us.
I can see that, Boo.
Just get me in front of him.

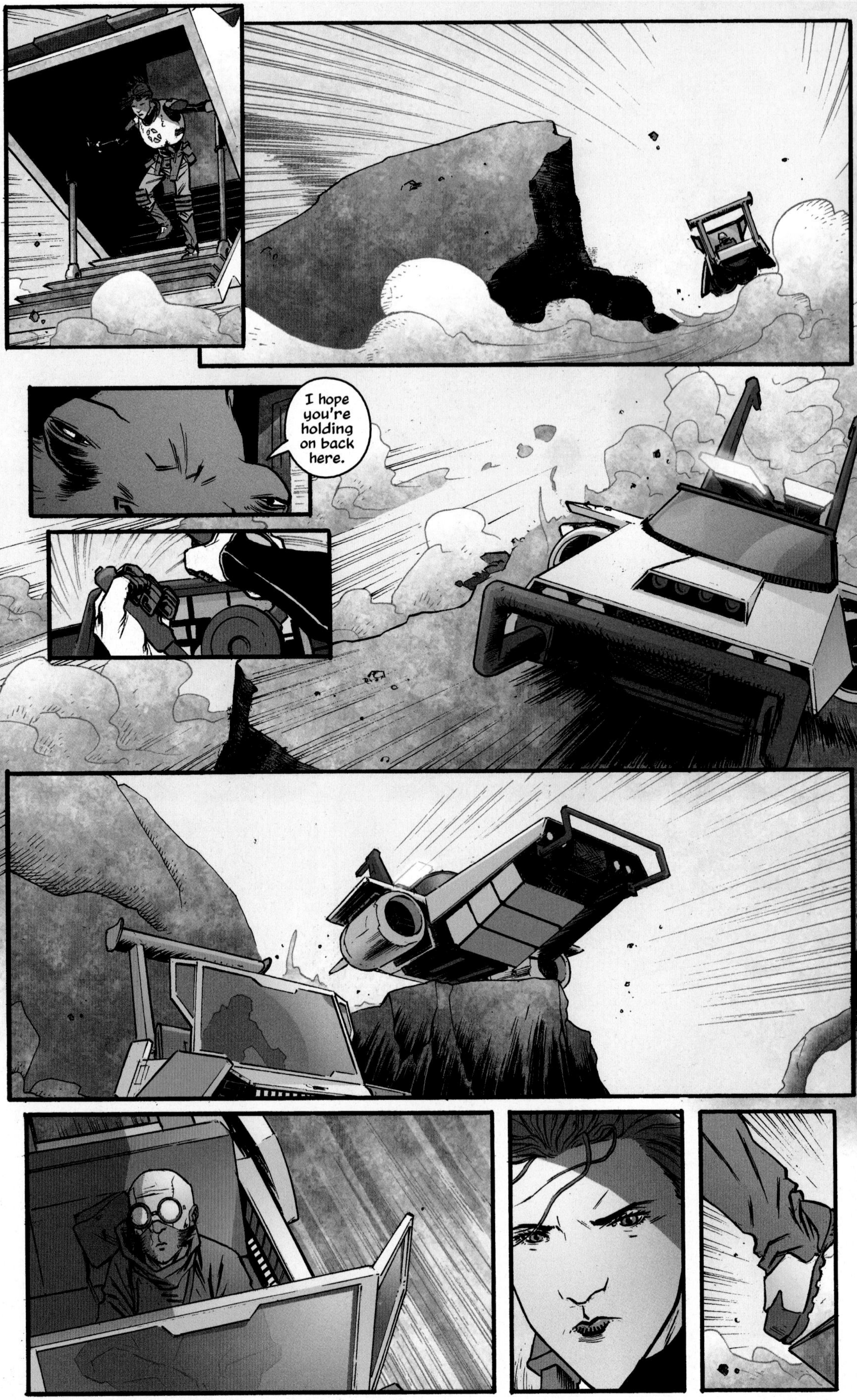
I hope you're holding on back here.

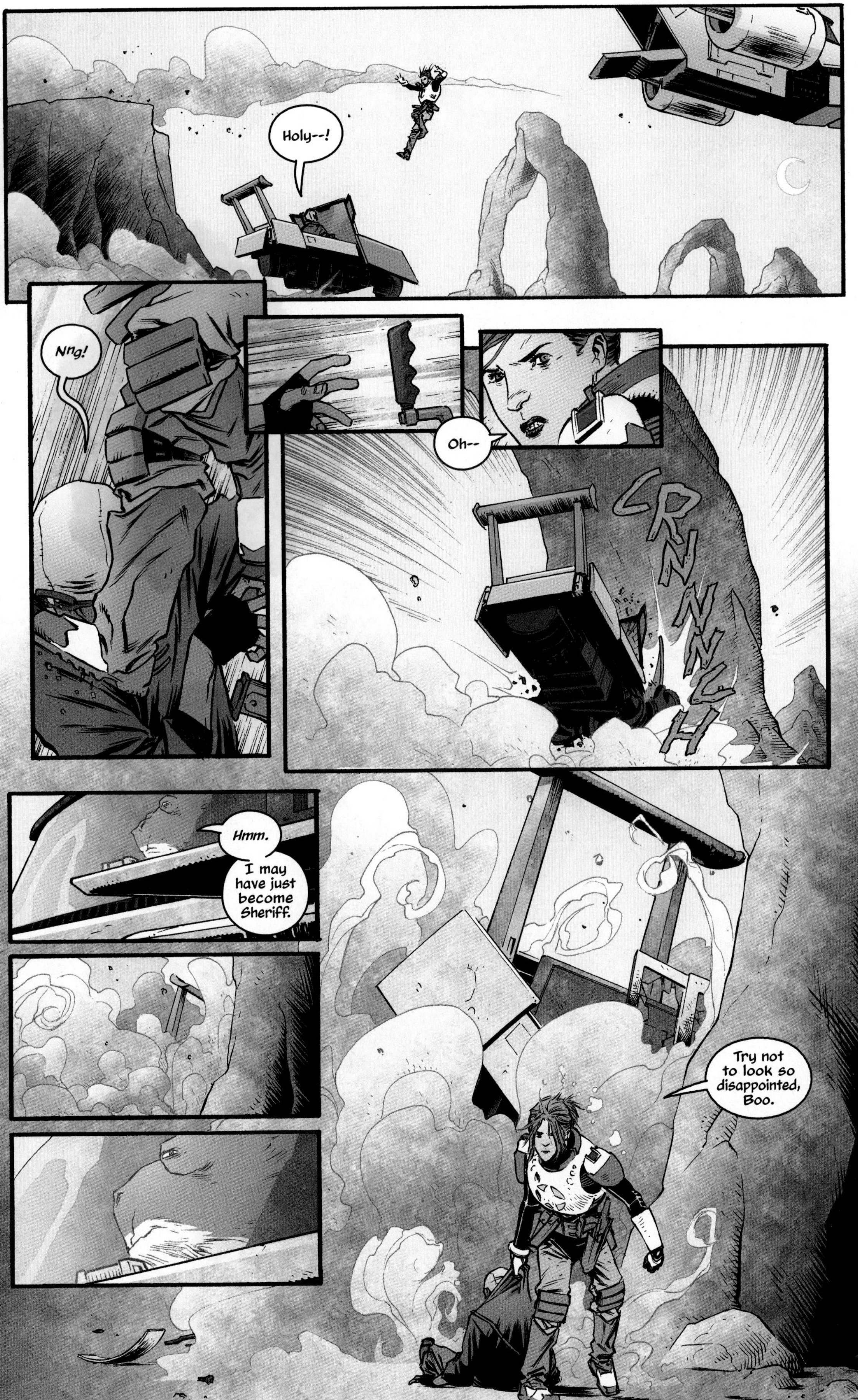
Holy--!
Nng!
Oh--
CRNNNUH
Hmm.
I may have just become Sheriff.
Try not to look so disappointed, Boo.

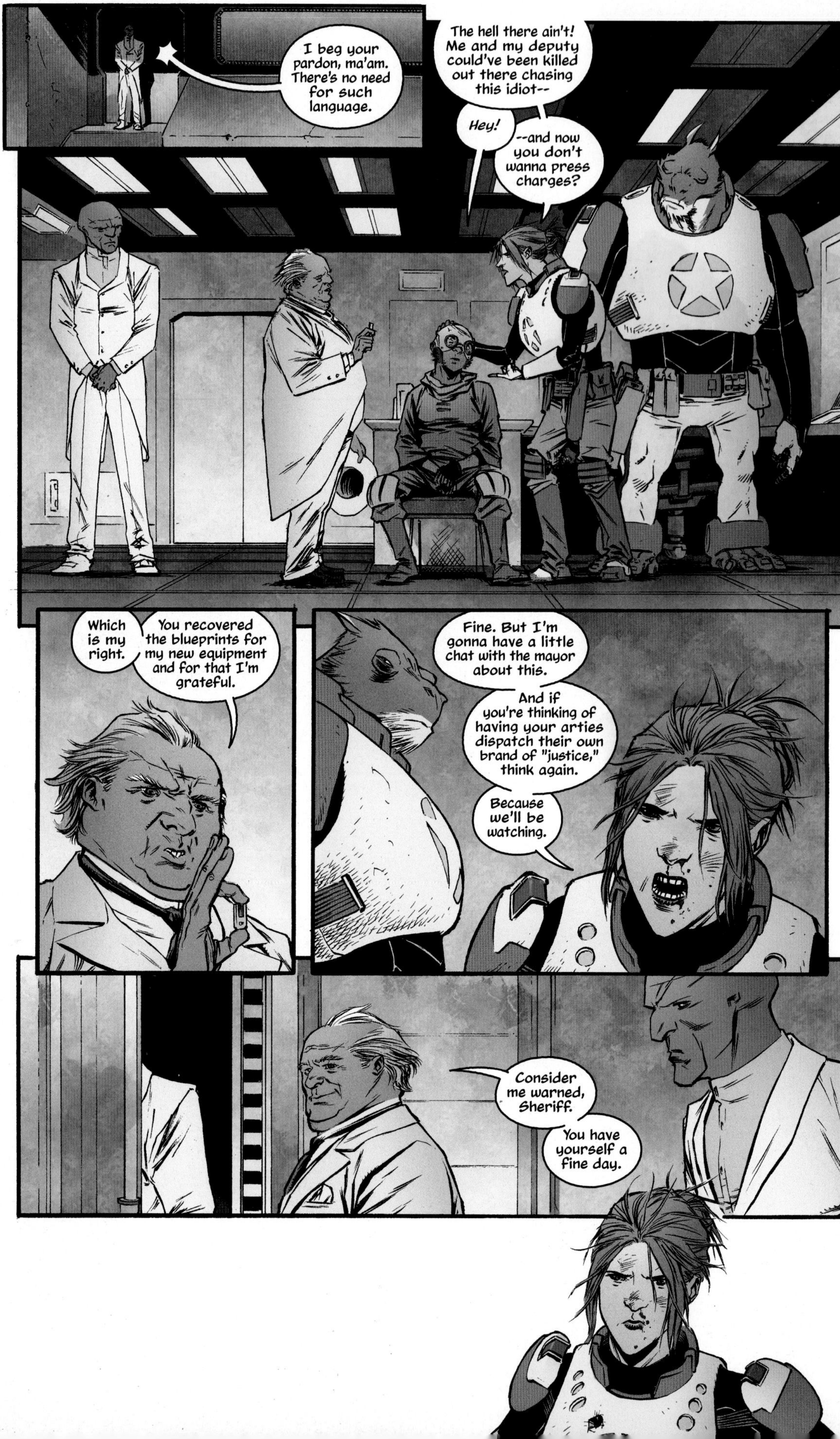

I beg your pardon, ma'am. There's no need for such language.
The hell there ain't! Me and my deputy could've been killed out there chasing this idiot--
Hey!
--and now you don't wanna press charges?
Which is my right.
You recovered the blueprints for my new equipment and for that I'm grateful.
Fine. But I'm gonna have a little chat with the mayor about this.
And if you're thinking of having your arties dispatch their own brand of "justice," think again.
Because we'll be watching.
Consider me warned, Sheriff.
You have yourself a fine day.

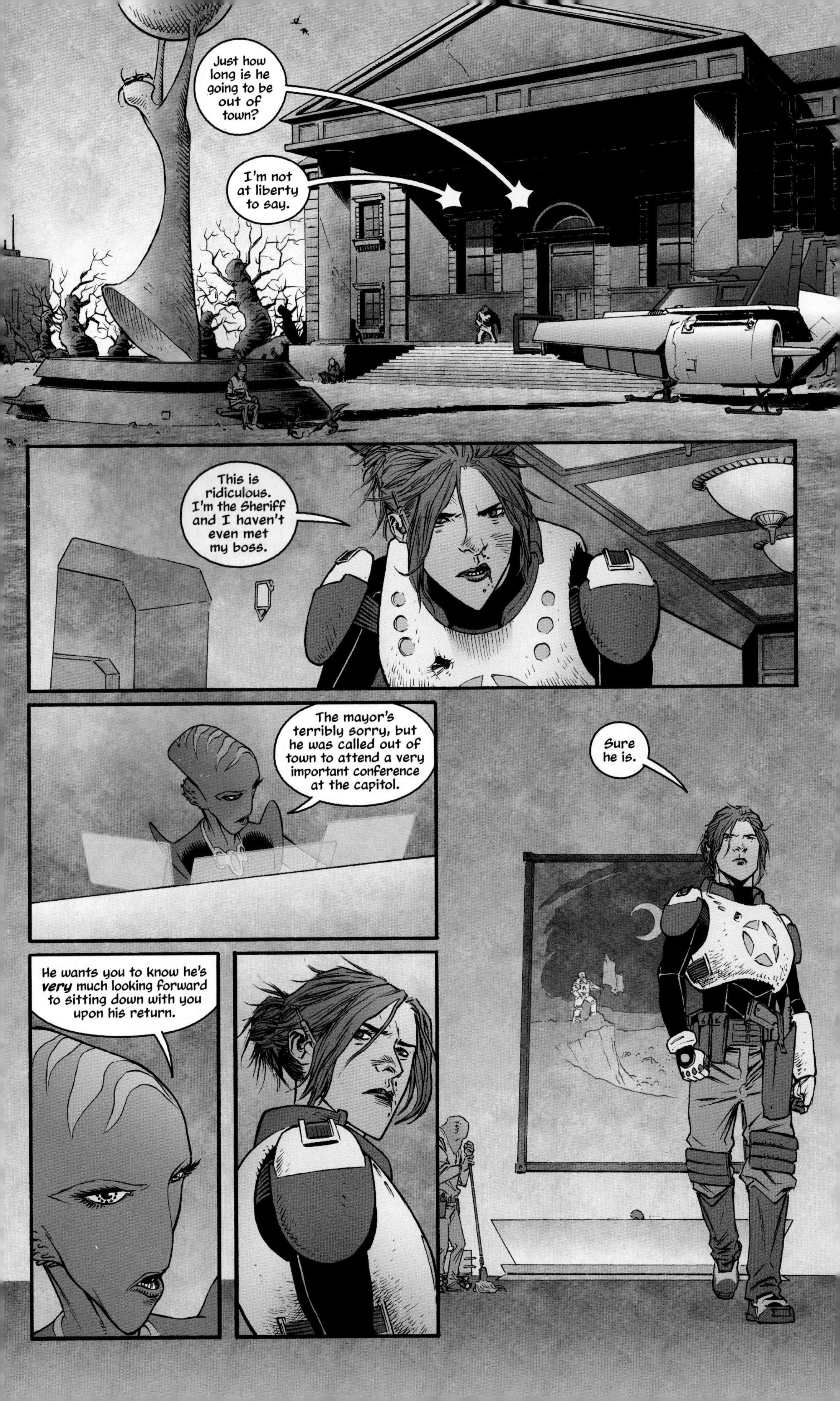
Just how long is he going to be out of town?
I'm not at liberty to say.
This is ridiculous. I'm the Sheriff and I haven't even met my boss.
The mayor's terribly sorry, but he was called out of town to attend a very important conference at the capitol.
Sure he is.
He wants you to know he's *very* much looking forward to sitting down with you upon his return.

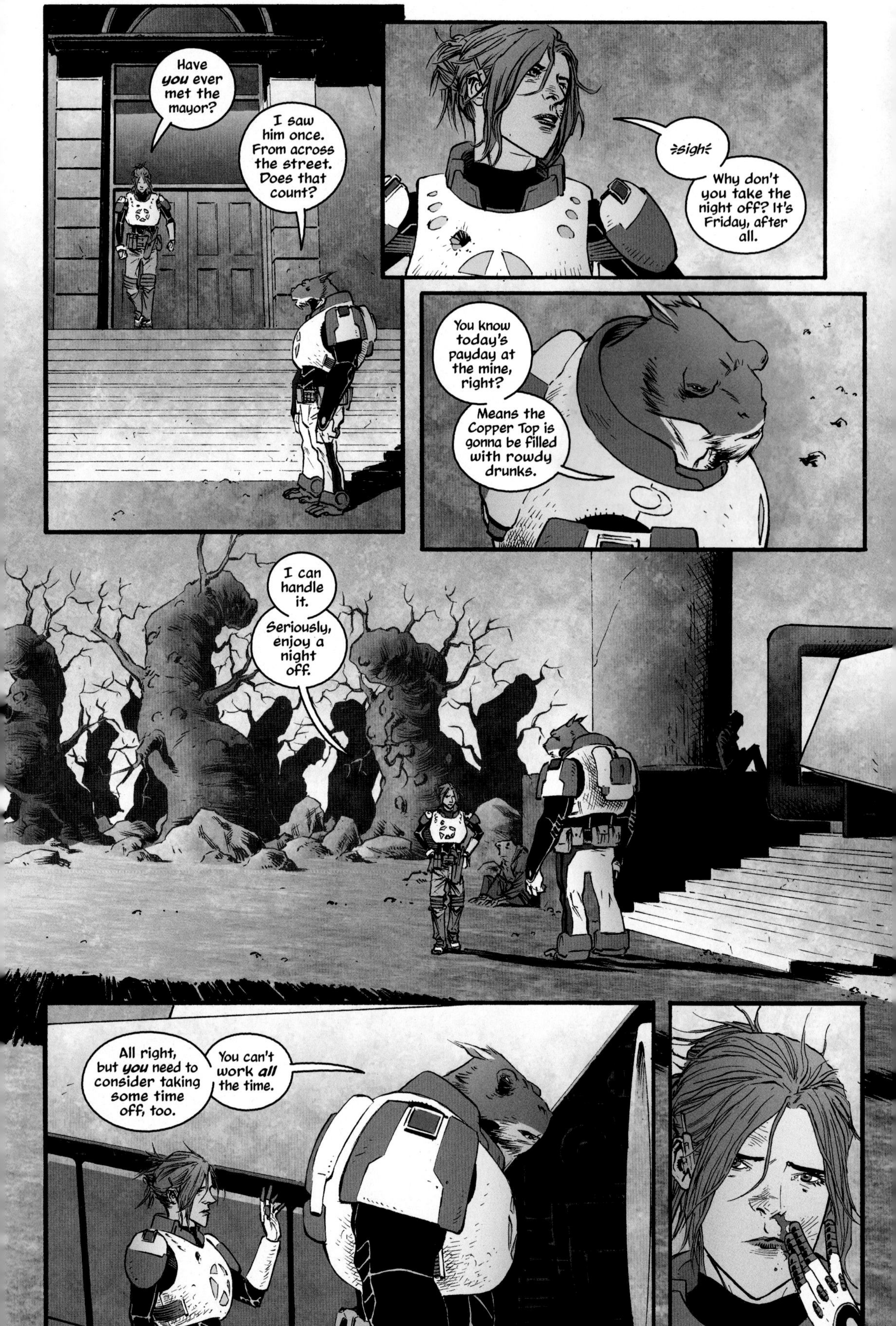
Have *you* ever met the mayor?
I saw him once. From across the street. Does that count?
≈sigh≈
Why don't you take the night off? It's Friday, after all.
You know today's payday at the mine, right?
Means the Copper Top is gonna be filled with rowdy drunks.
I can handle it.
Seriously, enjoy a night off.
All right, but *you* need to consider taking some time off, too.
You can't work *all* the time.

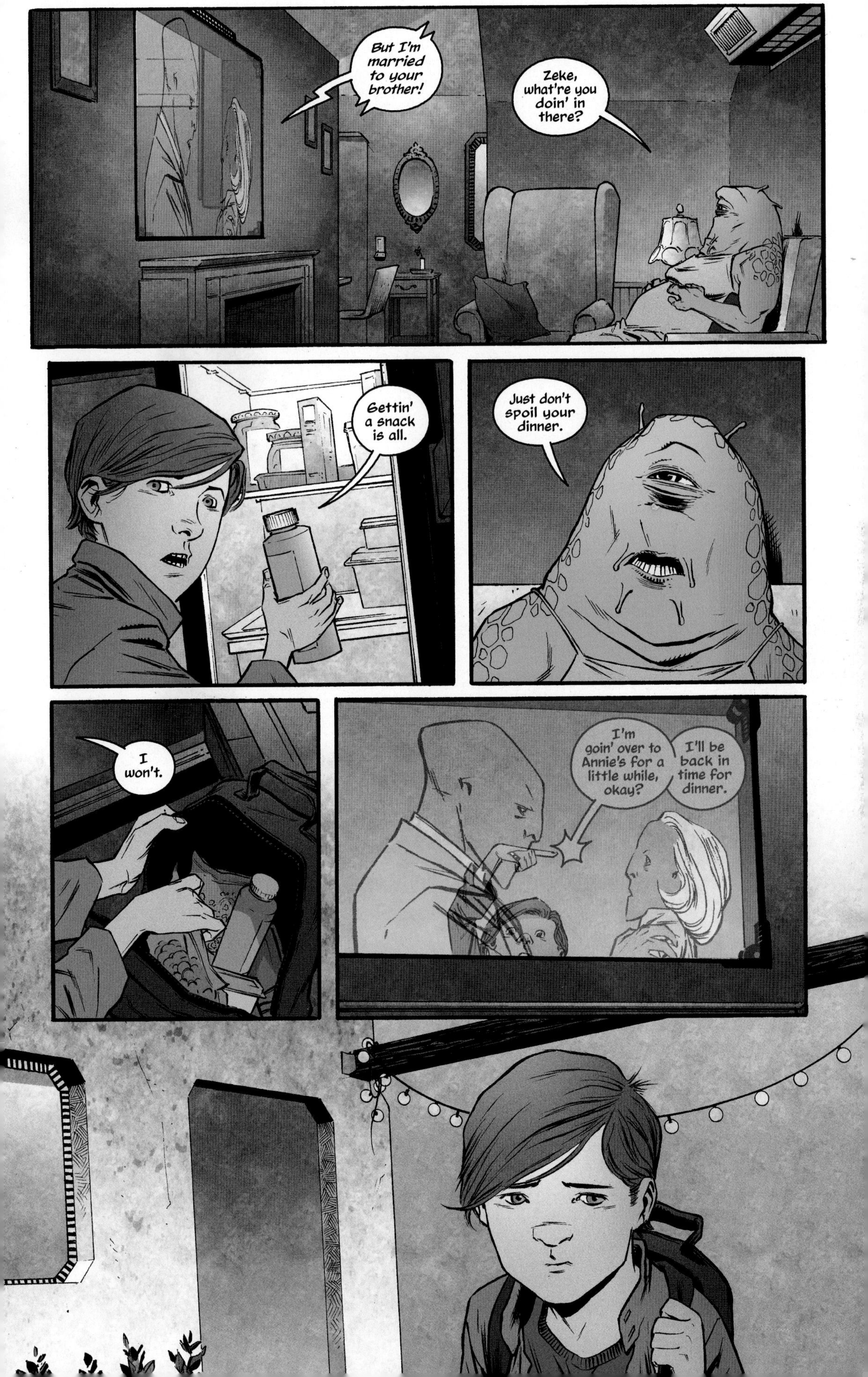
But I'm married to your brother!
Zeke, what're you doin' in there?
Gettin' a snack is all.
Just don't spoil your dinner.
I won't.
I'm goin' over to Annie's for a little while, okay?
I'll be back in time for dinner.

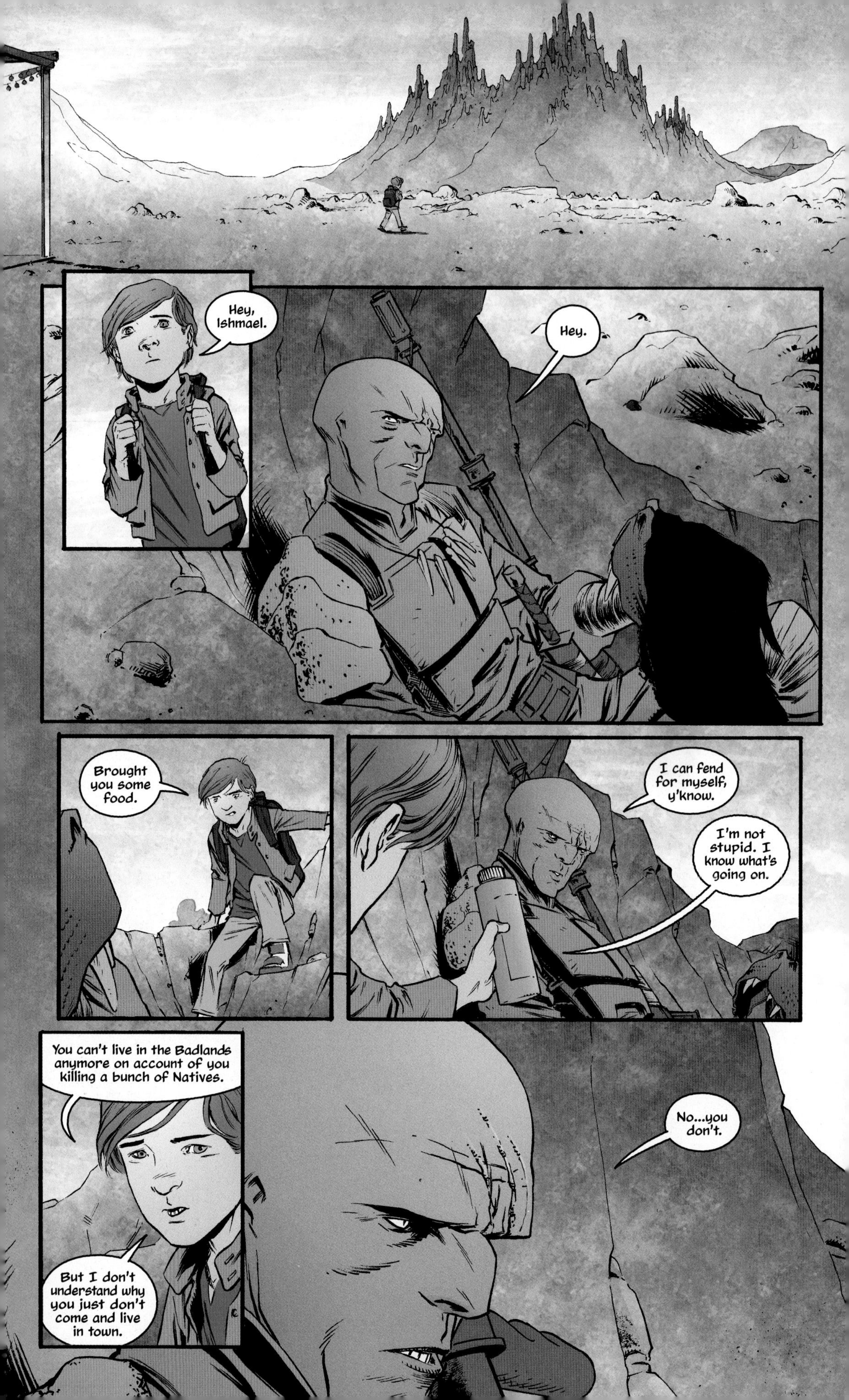
Hey, Ishmael.
Hey.
Brought you some food.
I can fend for myself, y'know.
I'm not stupid. I know what's going on.
You can't live in the Badlands anymore on account of you killing a bunch of Natives.
But I don't understand why you just don't come and live in town.
No...you don't.

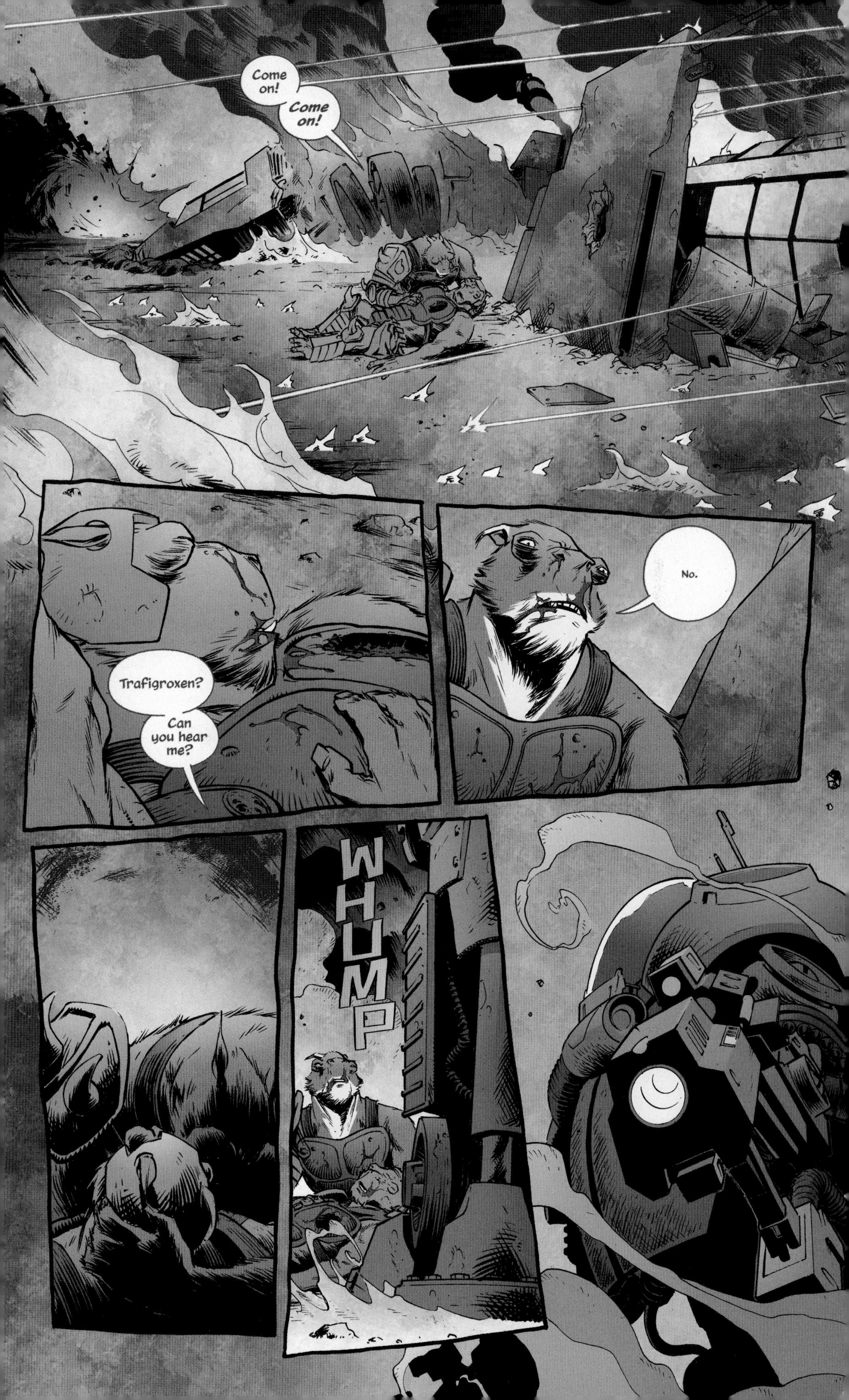
Come on!
Come on!
Trafigroxen?
Can you hear me?
No.
WHUMP

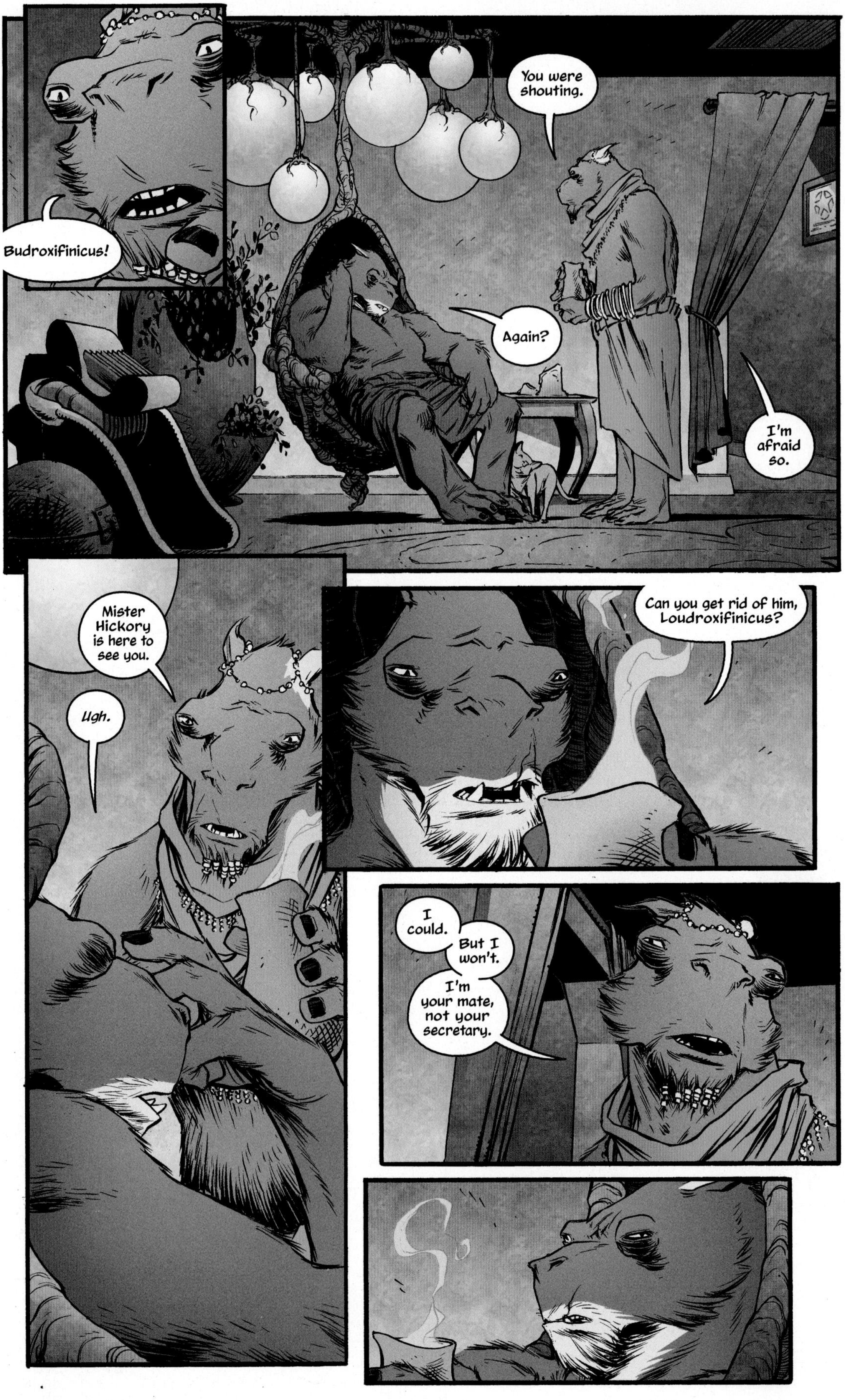
Budroxifinicus!
You were shouting.
Again?
I'm afraid so.
Mister Hickory is here to see you.
Ugh.
Can you get rid of him, Loudroxifinicus?
I could.
But I won't.
I'm your mate, not your secretary.

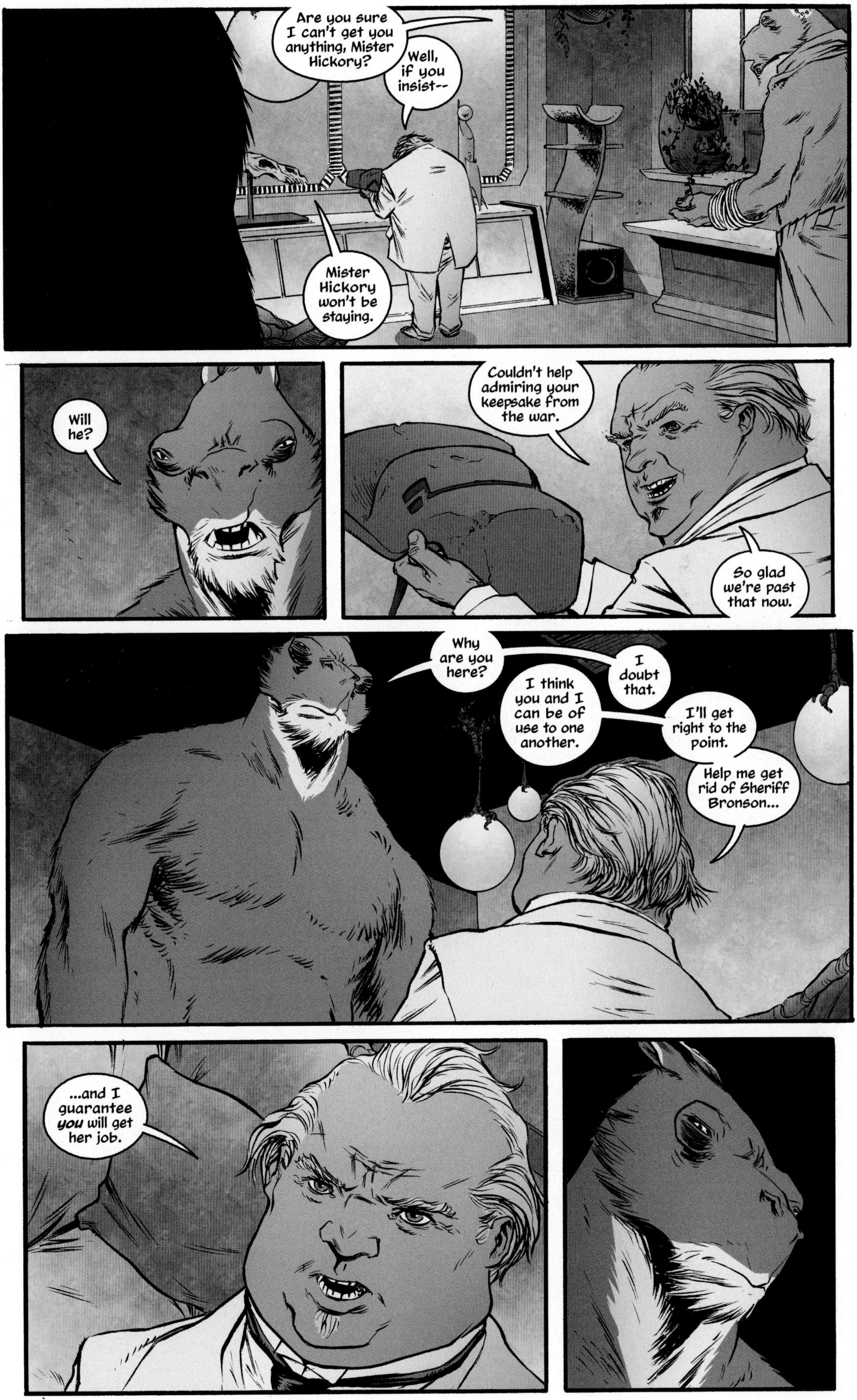
Are you sure I can't get you anything, Mister Hickory?
Well, if you insist--
Mister Hickory won't be staying.
Will he?
Couldn't help admiring your keepsake from the war.
So glad we're past that now.
Why are you here?
I doubt that.
I think you and I can be of use to one another.
I'll get right to the point.
Help me get rid of Sheriff Bronson...
...and I guarantee *you* will get her job.

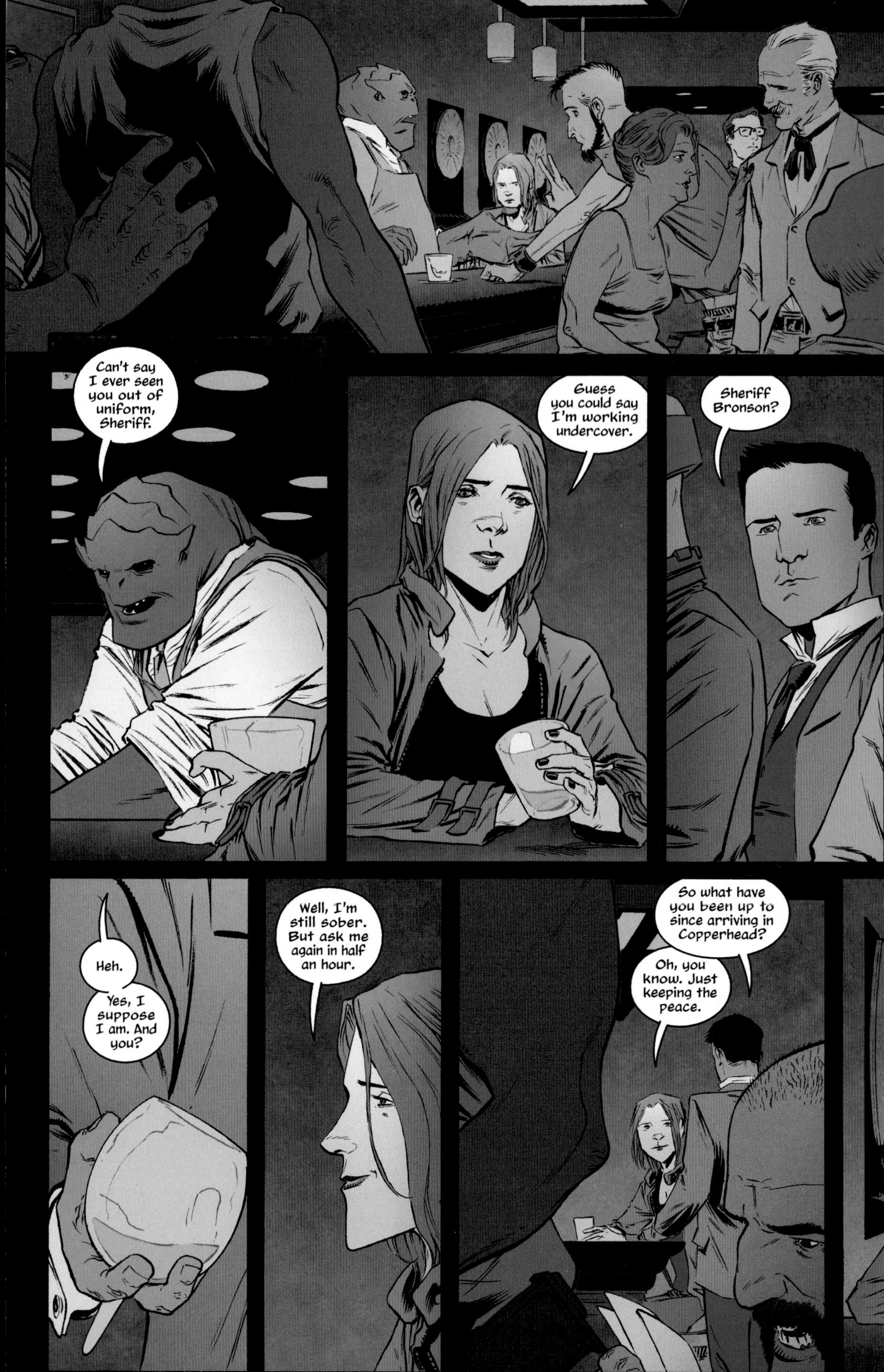
Can't say I ever seen you out of uniform, Sheriff.
Guess you could say I'm working undercover.
Sheriff Bronson?
Heh.
Yes, I suppose I am. And you?
Well, I'm still sober. But ask me again in half an hour.
So what have you been up to since arriving in Copperhead?
Oh, you know. Just keeping the peace.

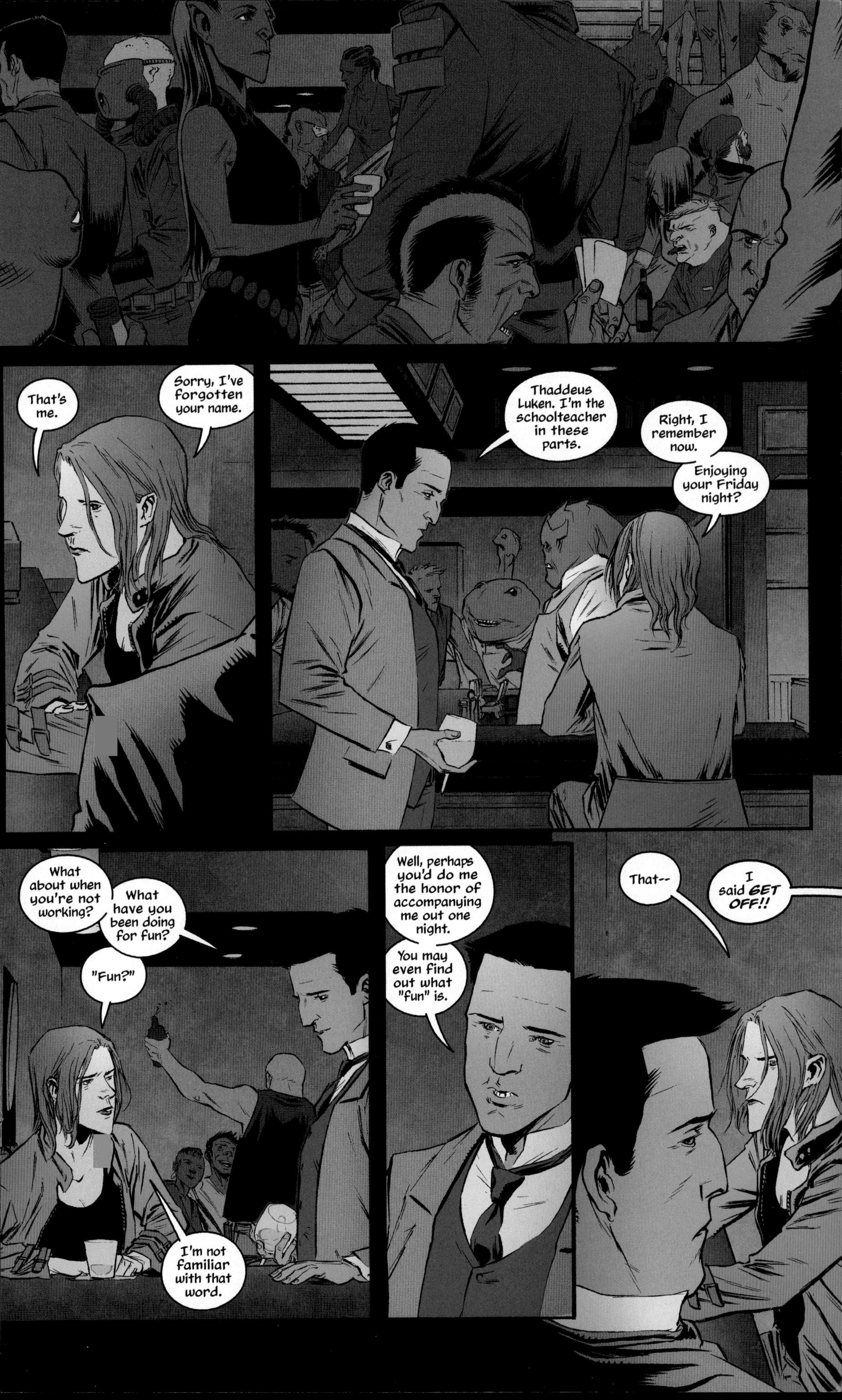

Sorry, I've forgotten your name.
That's me.
Thaddeus Luken. I'm the schoolteacher in these parts.
Right, I remember now.
Enjoying your Friday night?
What about when you're not working?
What have you been doing for fun?
"Fun?"
I'm not familiar with that word.
Well, perhaps you'd do me the honor of accompanying me out one night.
You may even find out what "fun" is.
That--
I said GET OFF!!

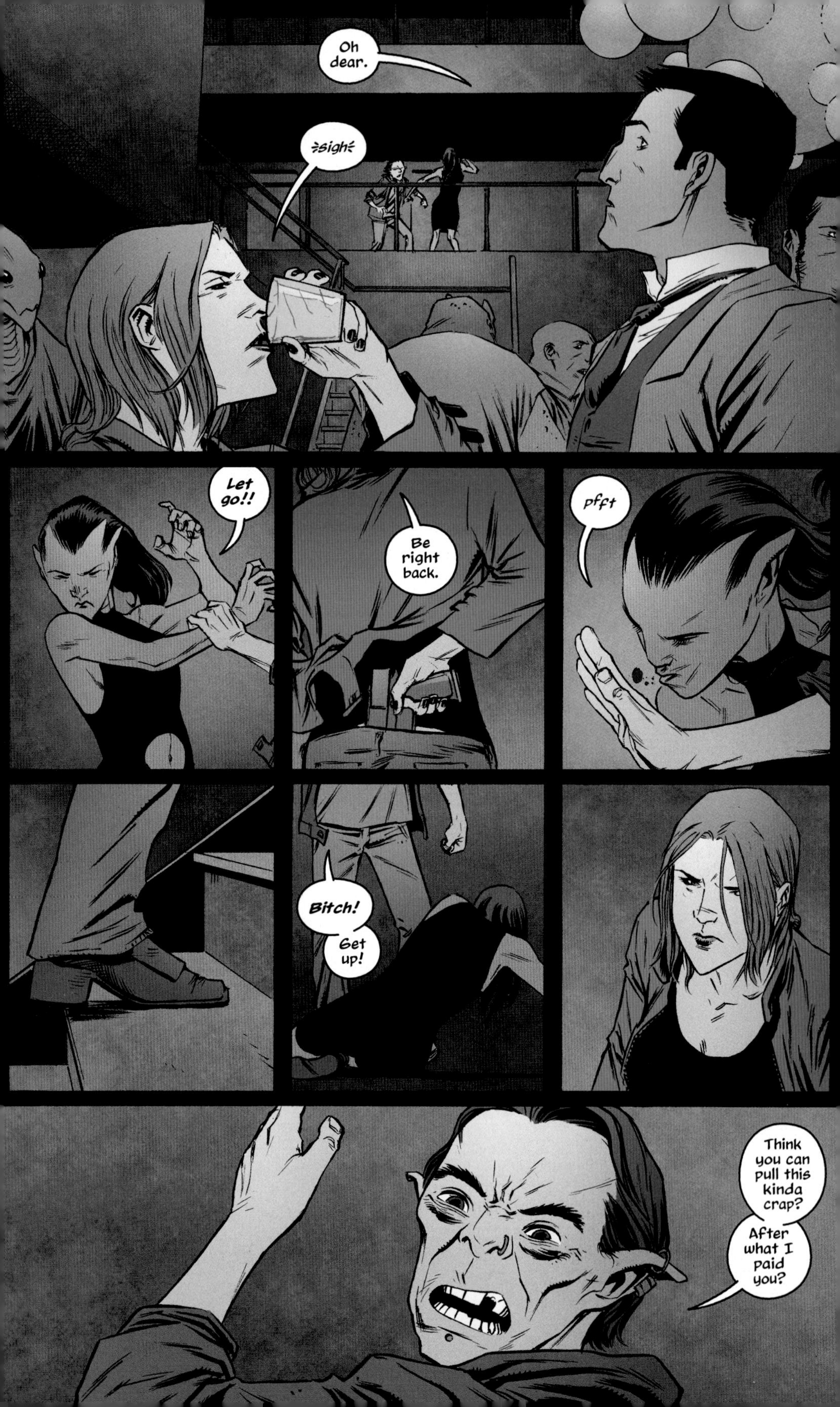
Oh dear.
sigh
Let go!!
Be right back.
pfft
Bitch!
Get up!
Think you can pull this kinda crap?
After what I paid you?

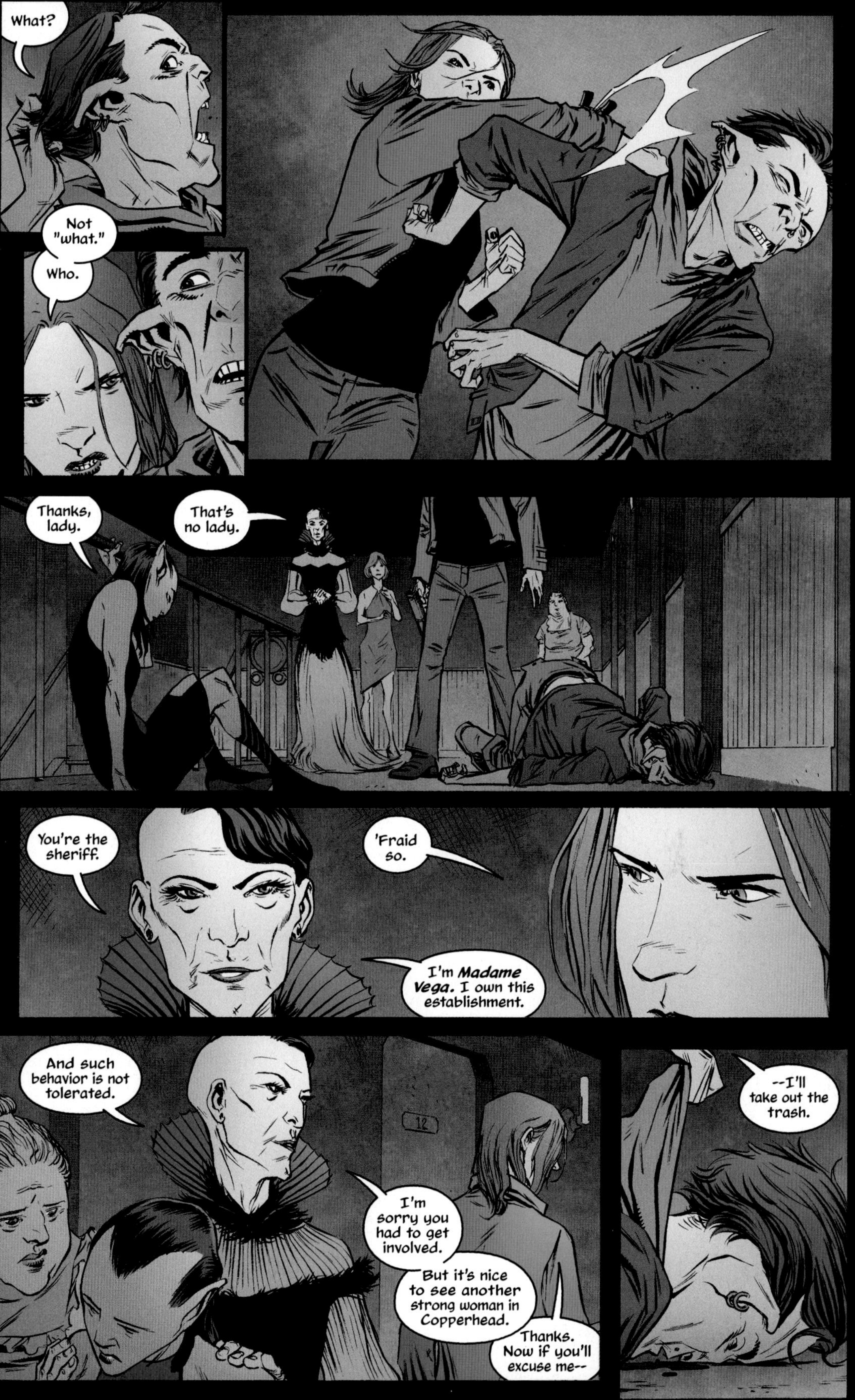
What?
Not "what."
Who.
Thanks, lady.
That's no lady.
You're the sheriff.
'Fraid so.
I'm *Madame Vega.* I own this establishment.
And such behavior is not tolerated.
I'm sorry you had to get involved.
But it's nice to see another strong woman in Copperhead.
Thanks. Now if you'll excuse me--
--I'll take out the trash.

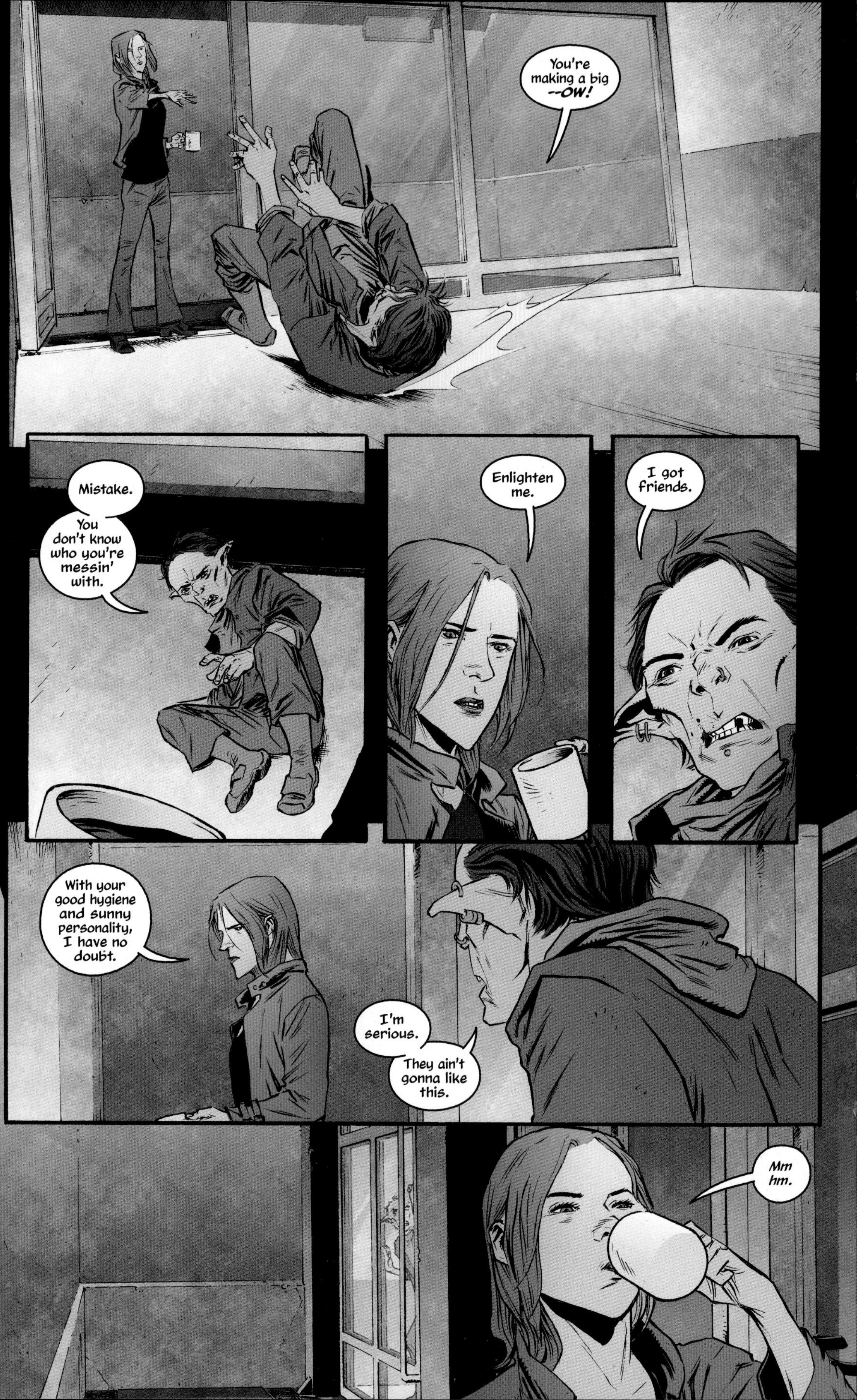
You're making a big --OW!
Mistake.
You don't know who you're messin' with.
Enlighten me.
I got friends.
With your good hygiene and sunny personality, I have no doubt.
I'm serious.
They ain't gonna like this.
Mm hm.

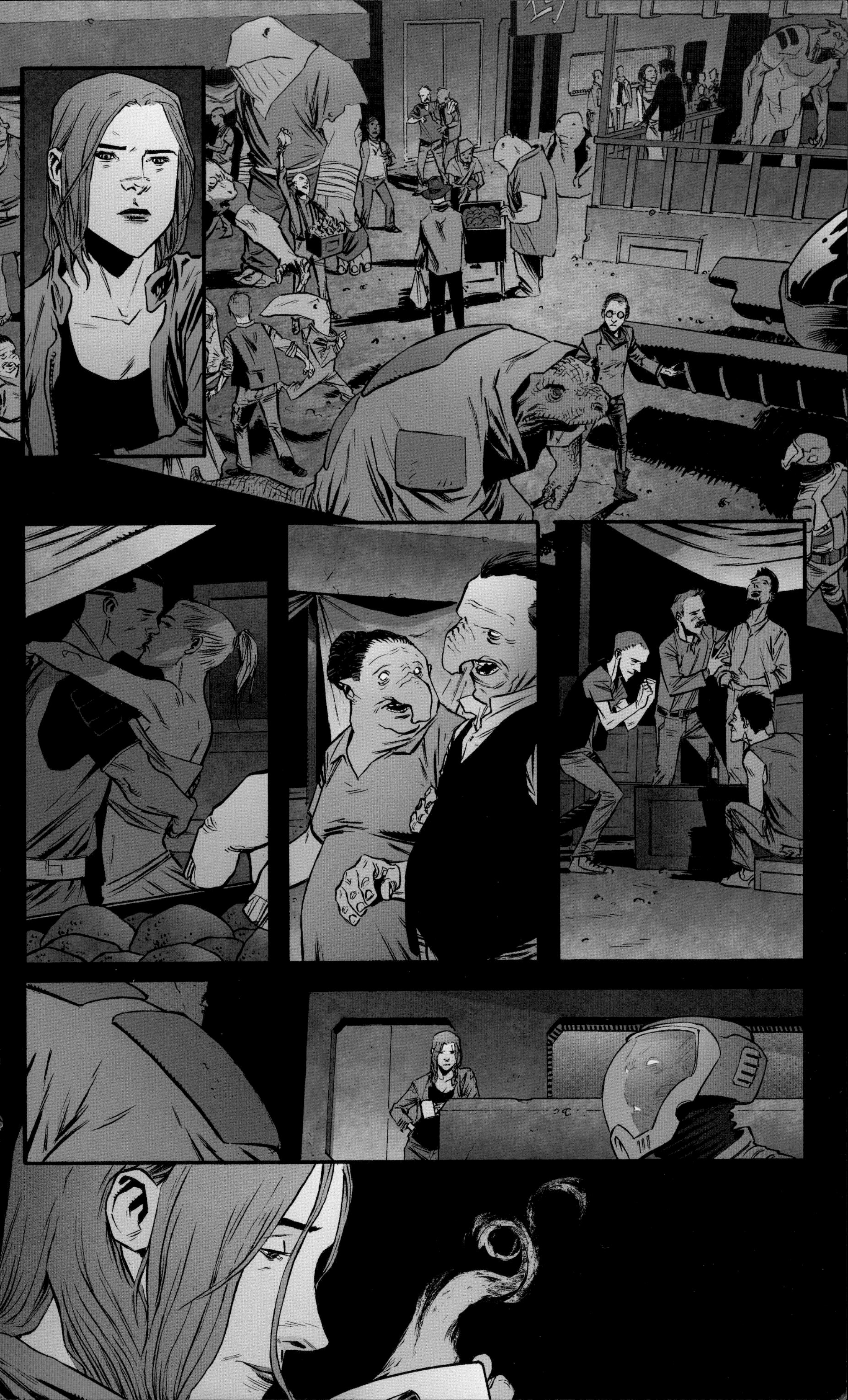

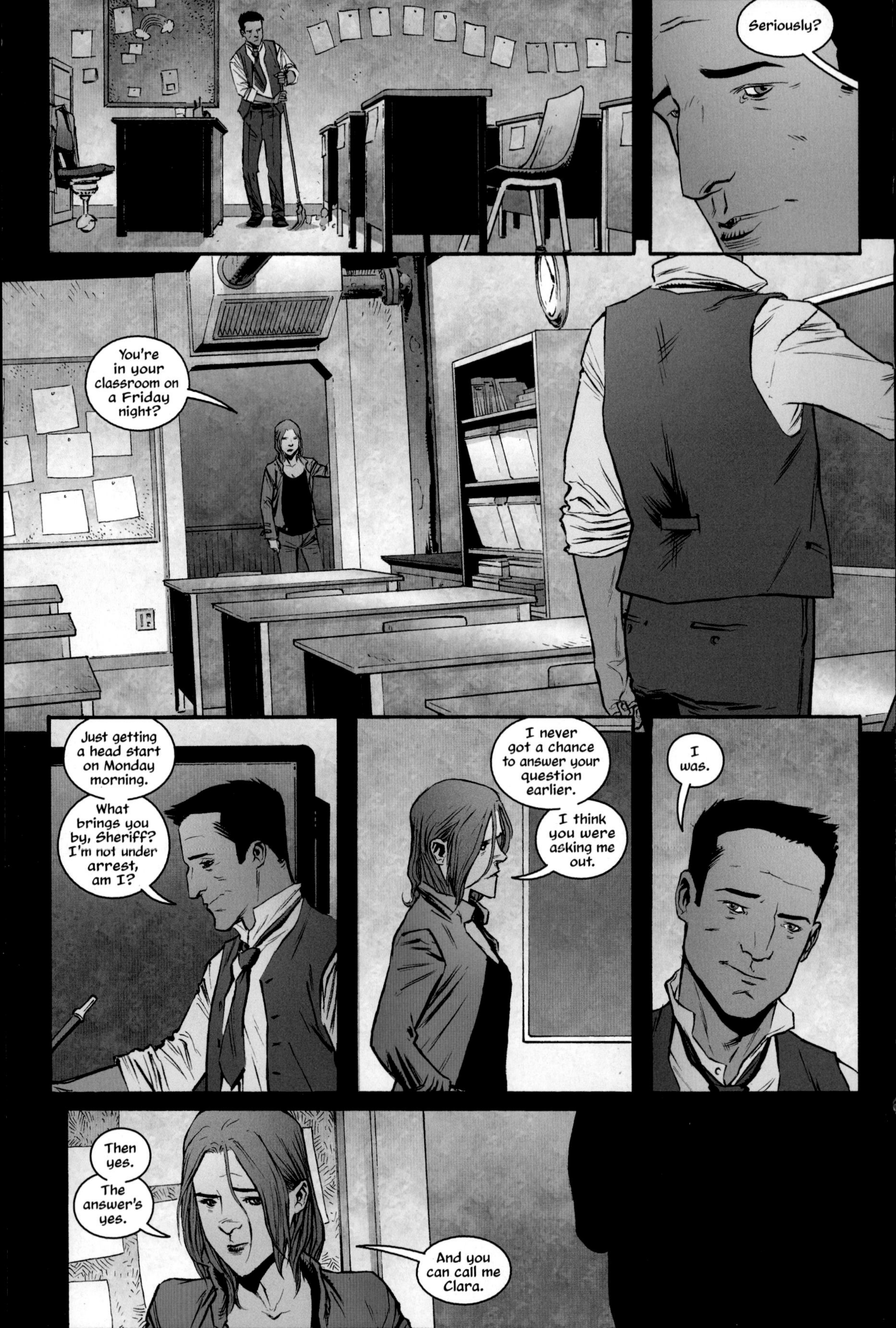
Seriously?
You're in your classroom on a Friday night?
Just getting a head start on Monday morning.
What brings you by, Sheriff? I'm not under arrest, am I?
I never got a chance to answer your question earlier.
I think you were asking me out.
I was.
Then yes.
The answer's yes.
And you can call me Clara.

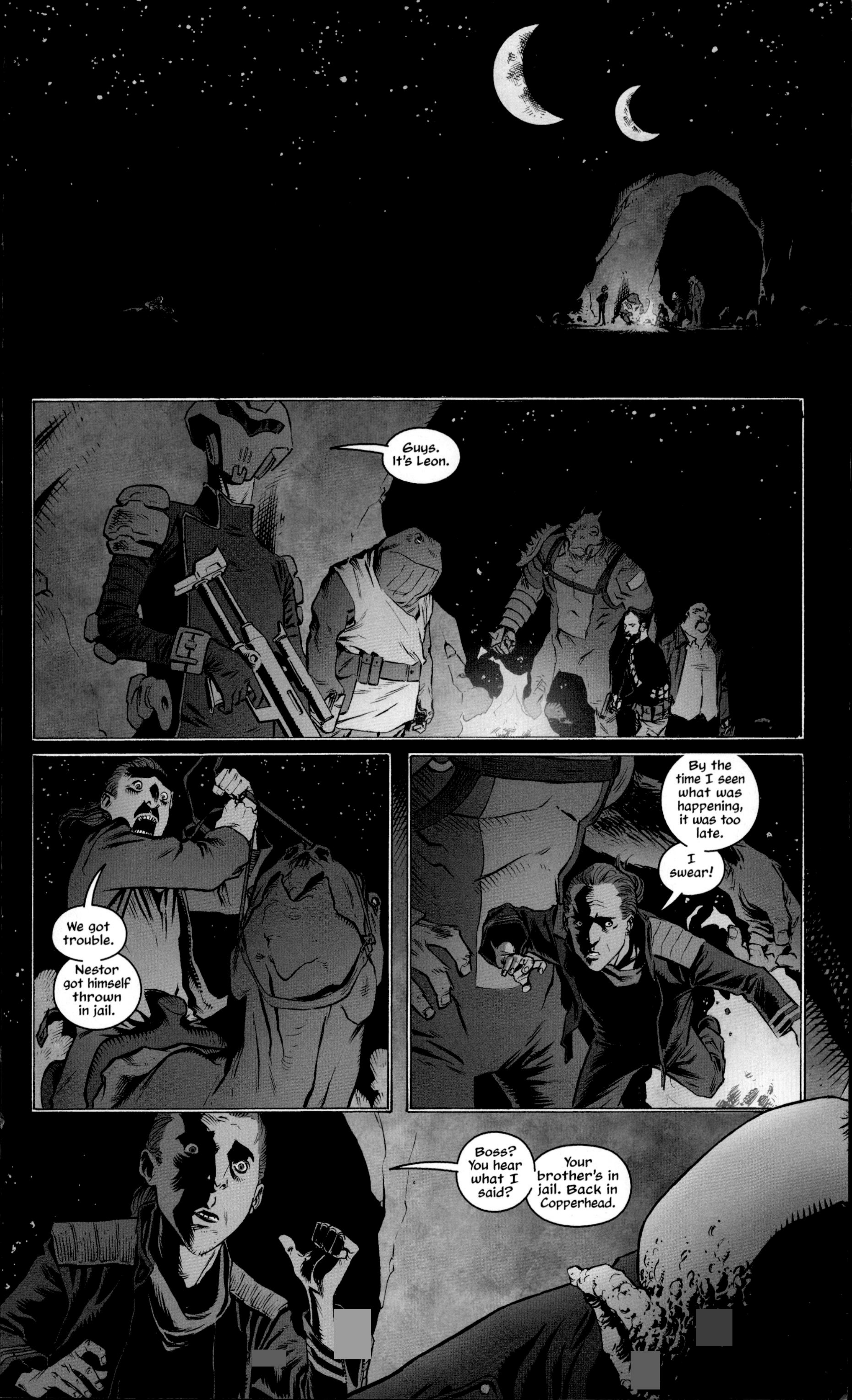
Guys. It's Leon.
We got trouble.
Nestor got himself thrown in jail.
By the time I seen what was happening, it was too late.
I swear!
Boss? You hear what I said?
Your brother's in jail. Back in Copperhead.

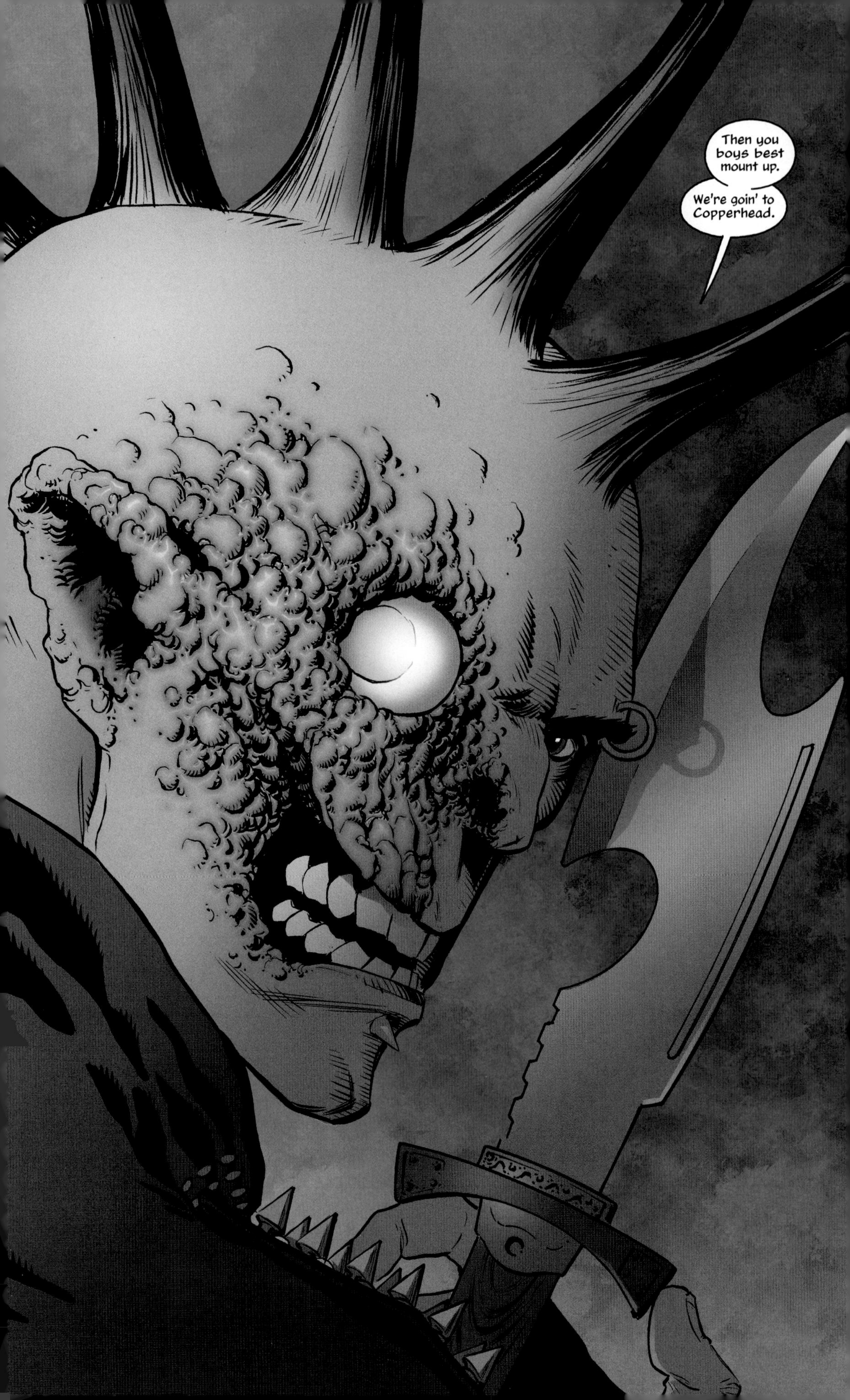
Then you boys best mount up.
We're goin' to Copperhead.

CHAPTER II

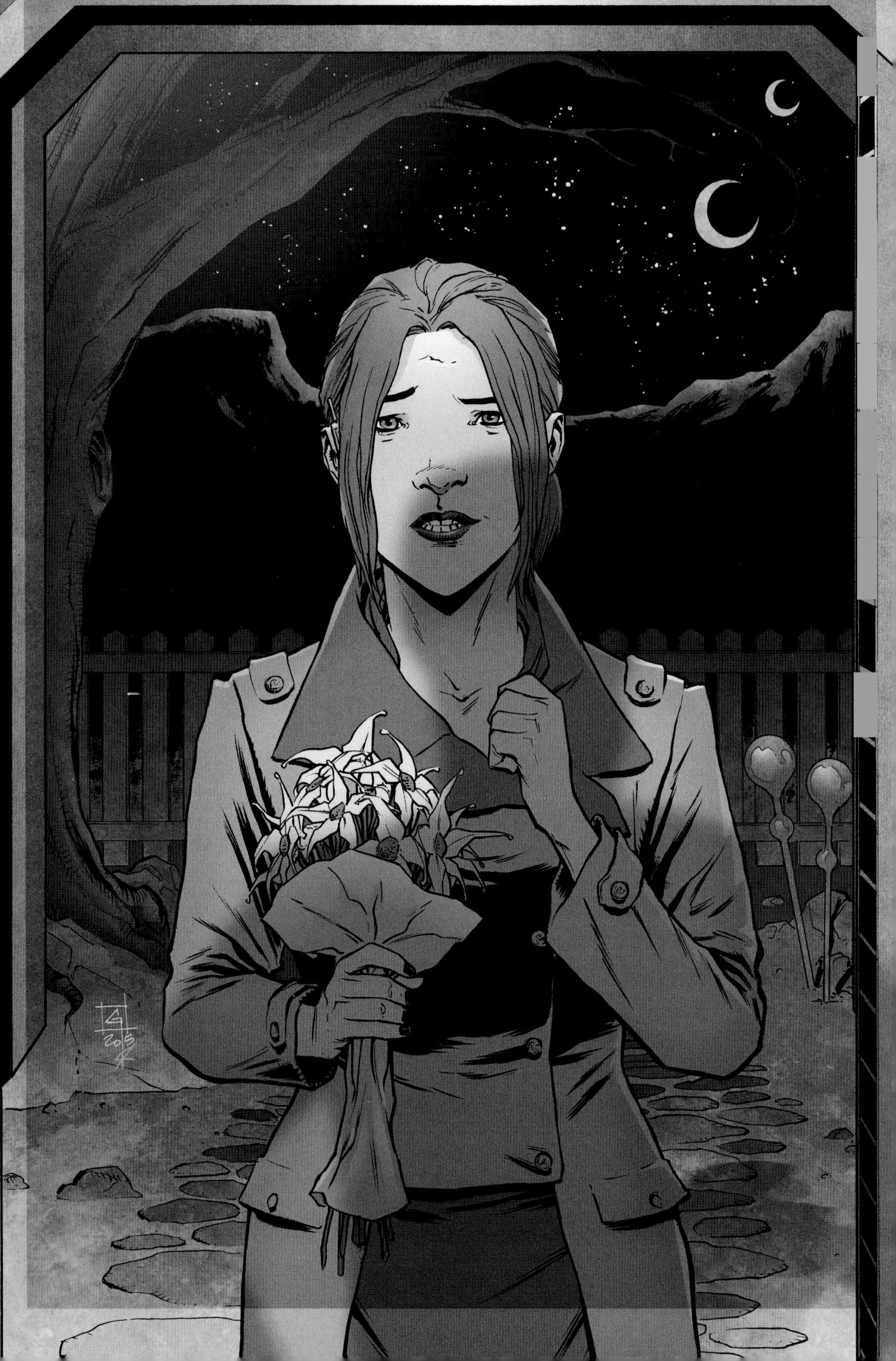

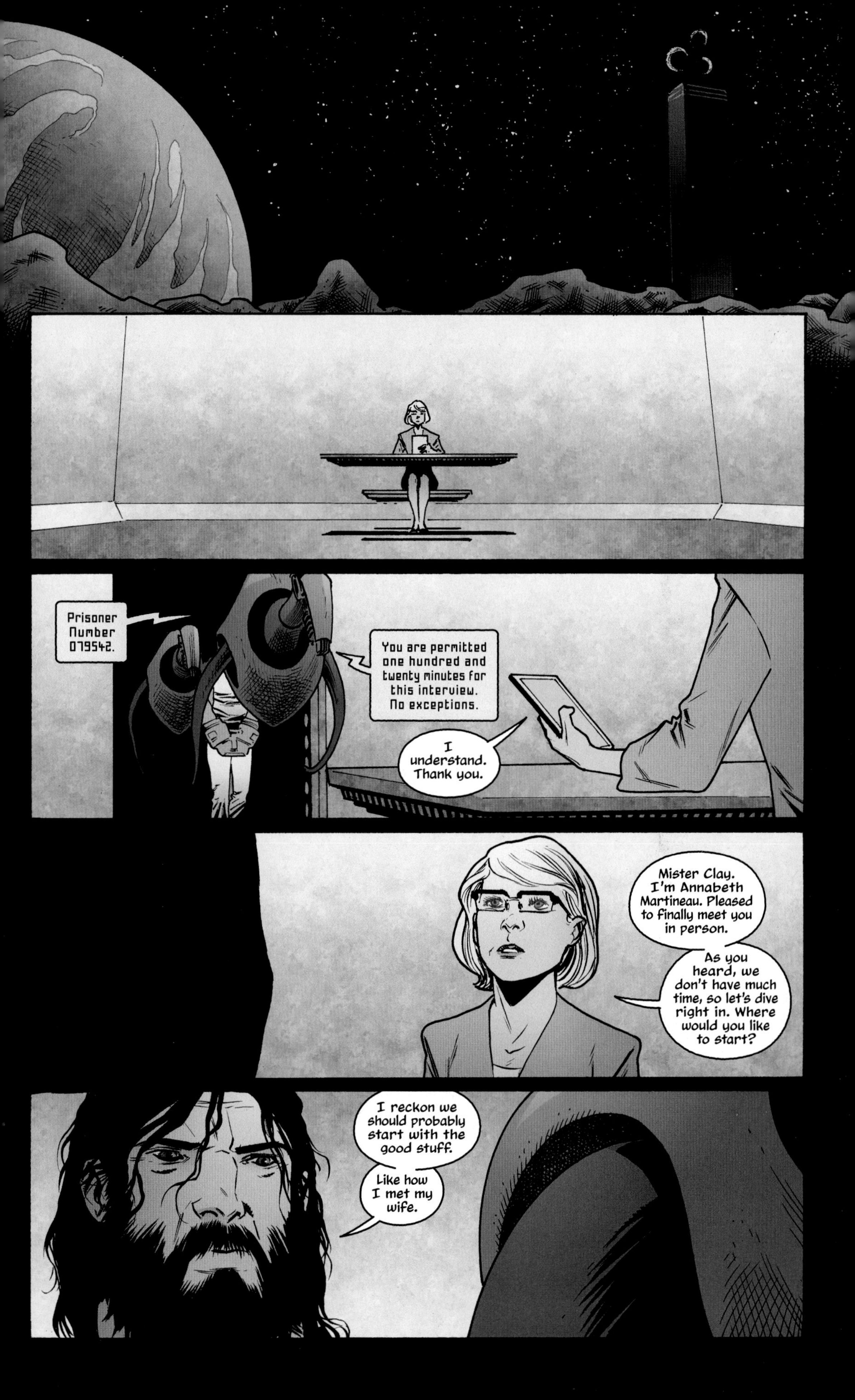
Prisoner Number 079542.
You are permitted one hundred and twenty minutes for this interview. No exceptions.
I understand. Thank you.
Mister Clay. I'm Annabeth Martineau. Pleased to finally meet you in person.
As you heard, we don't have much time, so let's dive right in. Where would you like to start?
I reckon we should probably start with the good stuff.
Like how I met my wife.

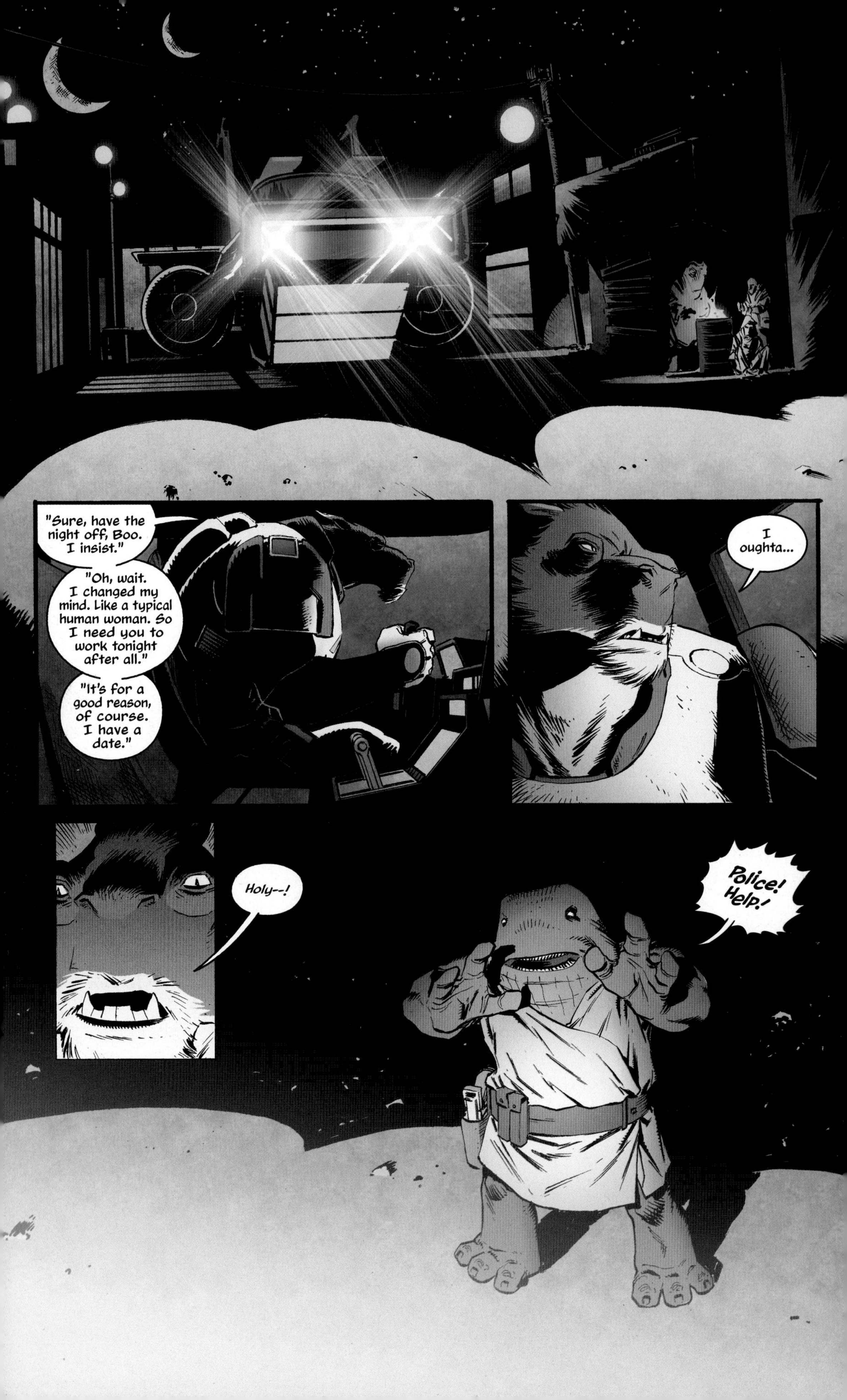
"Sure, have the night off, Boo. I insist."
"Oh, wait. I changed my mind. Like a typical human woman. So I need you to work tonight after all."
"It's for a good reason, of course. I have a date."
I oughta...
Holy--!
Police! Help!

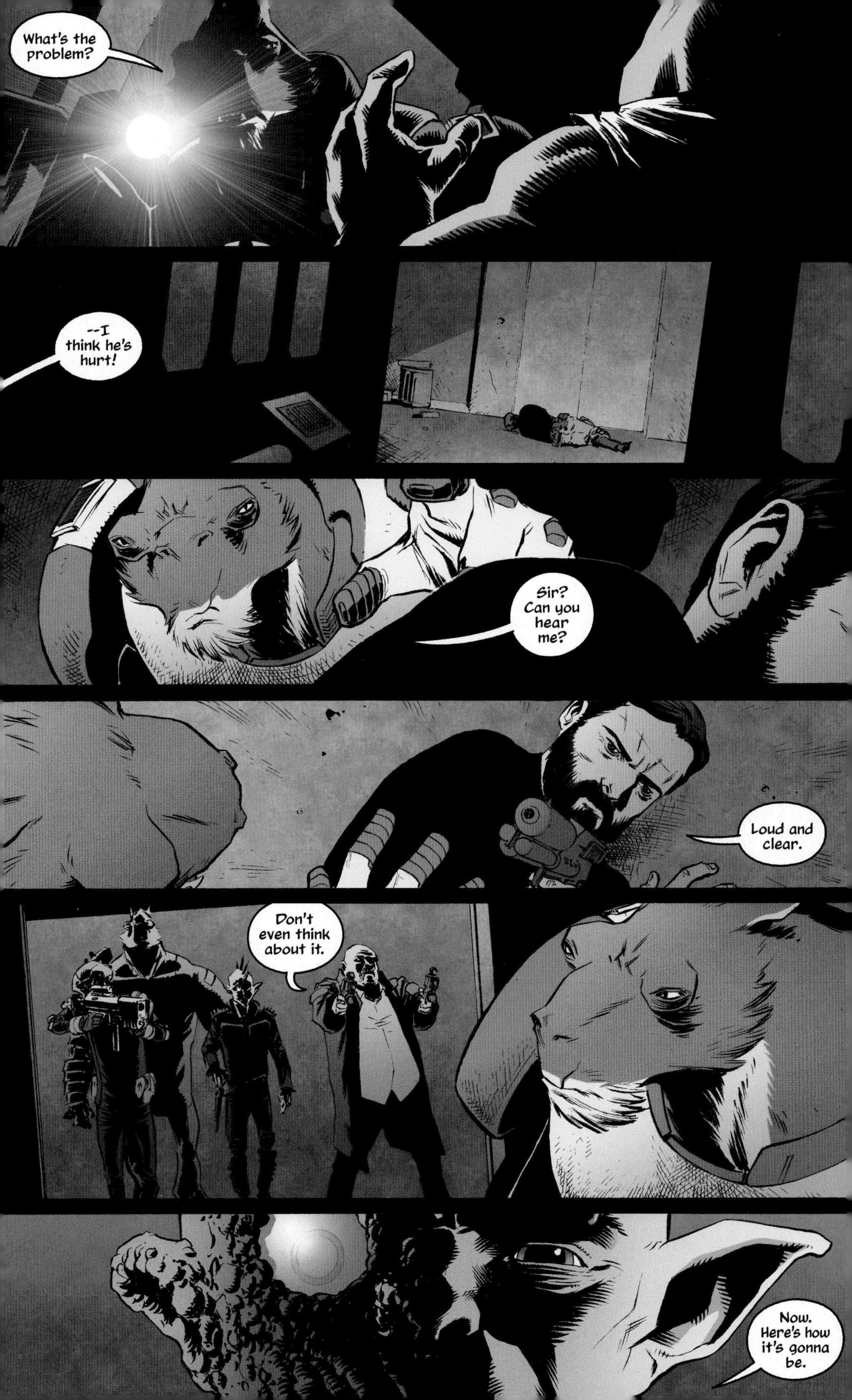
What's the problem?
--I think he's hurt!
Sir? Can you hear me?
Loud and clear.
Don't even think about it.
Now. Here's how it's gonna be.

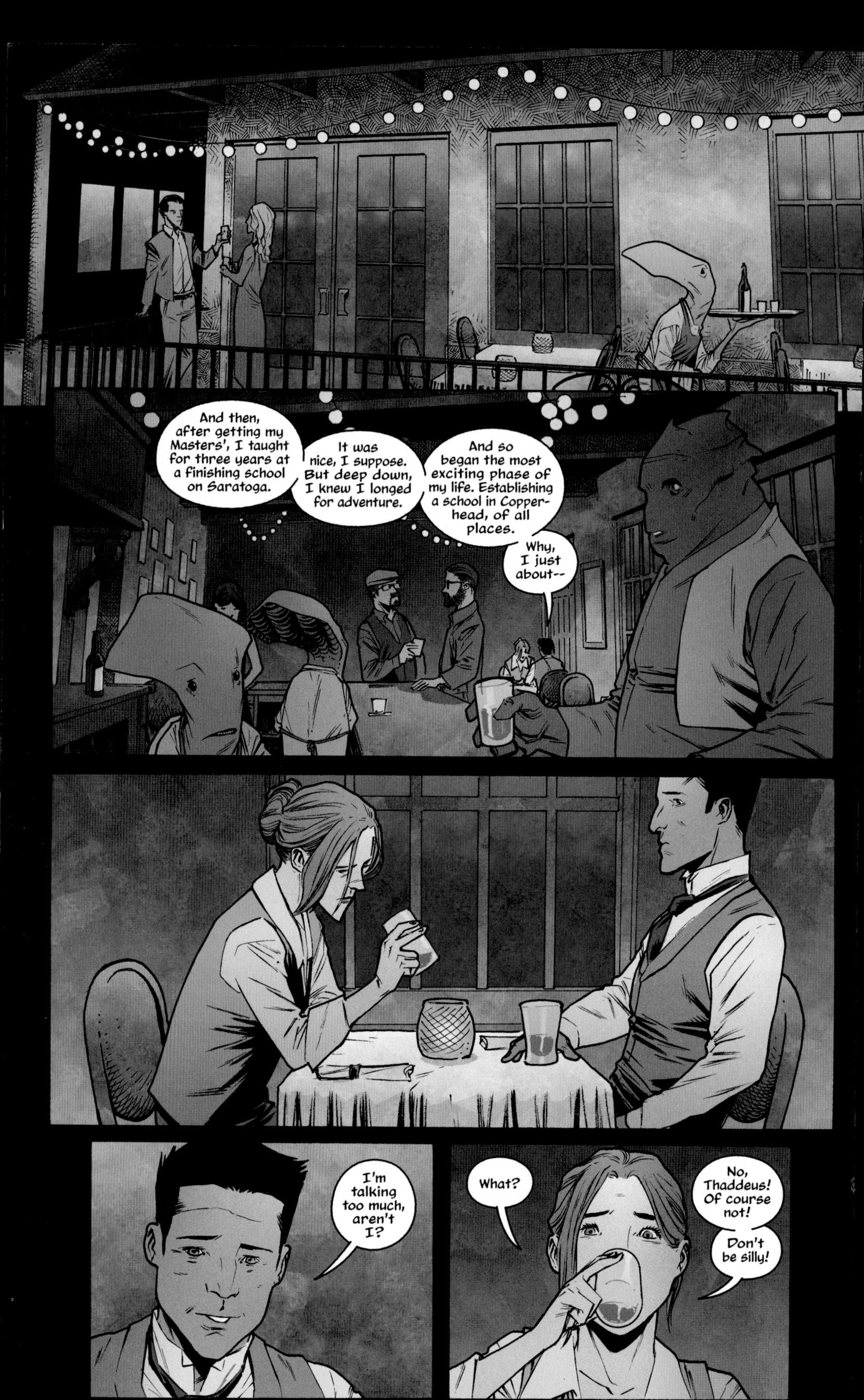
And then, after getting my Masters', I taught for three years at a finishing school on Saratoga.
It was nice, I suppose. But deep down, I knew I longed for adventure.
And so began the most exciting phase of my life. Establishing a school in Copper-head, of all places.
Why, I just about--
I'm talking too much, aren't I?
What?
No, Thaddeus! Of course not!
Don't be silly!

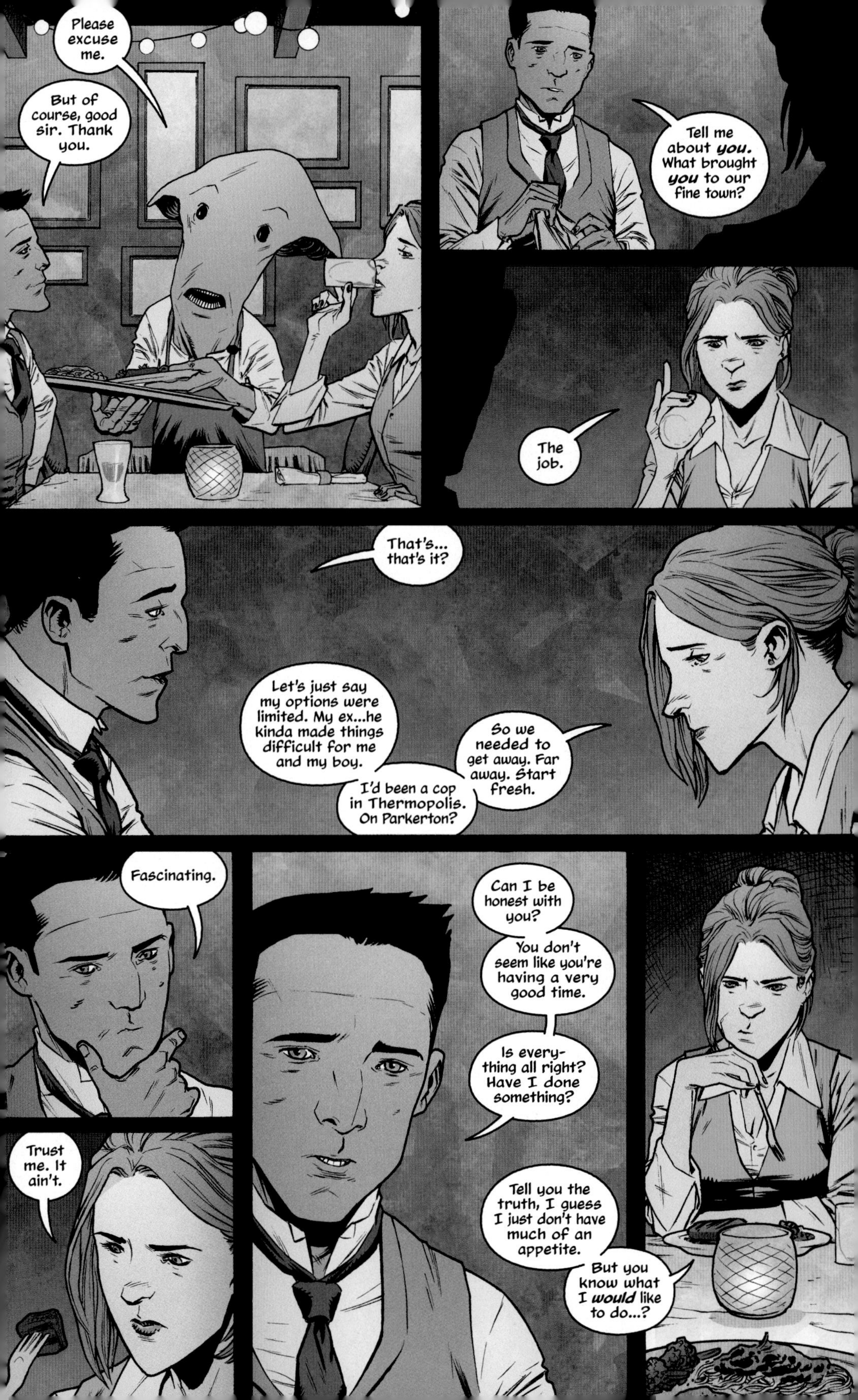
Please excuse me.
But of course, good sir. Thank you.
Tell me about *you.* What brought *you* to our fine town?
The job.
That's... that's it?
Let's just say my options were limited. My ex...he kinda made things difficult for me and my boy.
I'd been a cop in Thermopolis. On Parkerton?
So we needed to get away. Far away. Start fresh.
Fascinating.
Trust me. It ain't.
Can I be honest with you?
You don't seem like you're having a very good time.
Is every-thing all right? Have I done something?
Tell you the truth, I guess I just don't have much of an appetite.
But you know what I *would* like to do...?

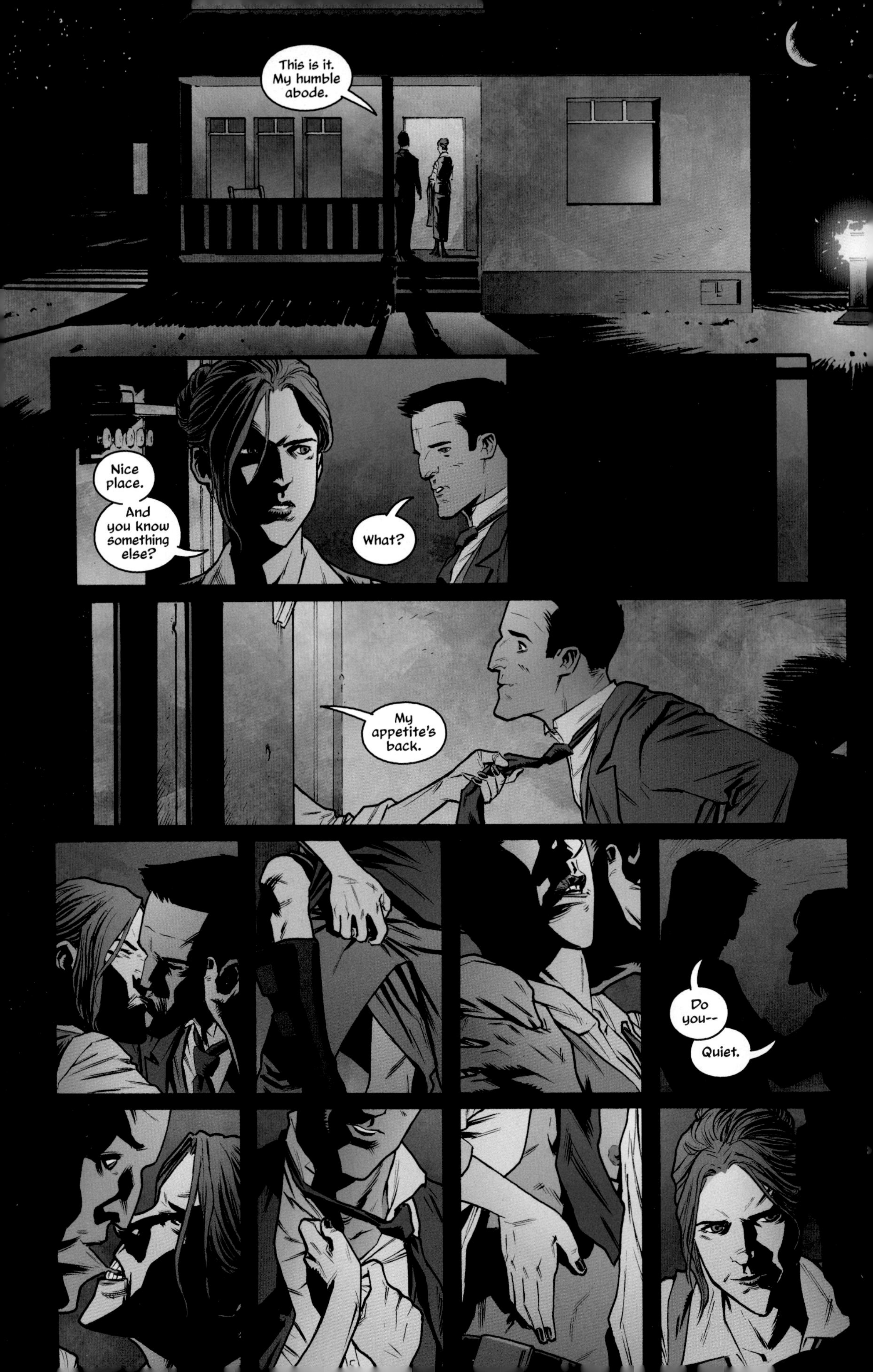
This is it. My humble abode.
Nice place.
And you know something else?
What?
My appetite's back.
Do you--
Quiet.

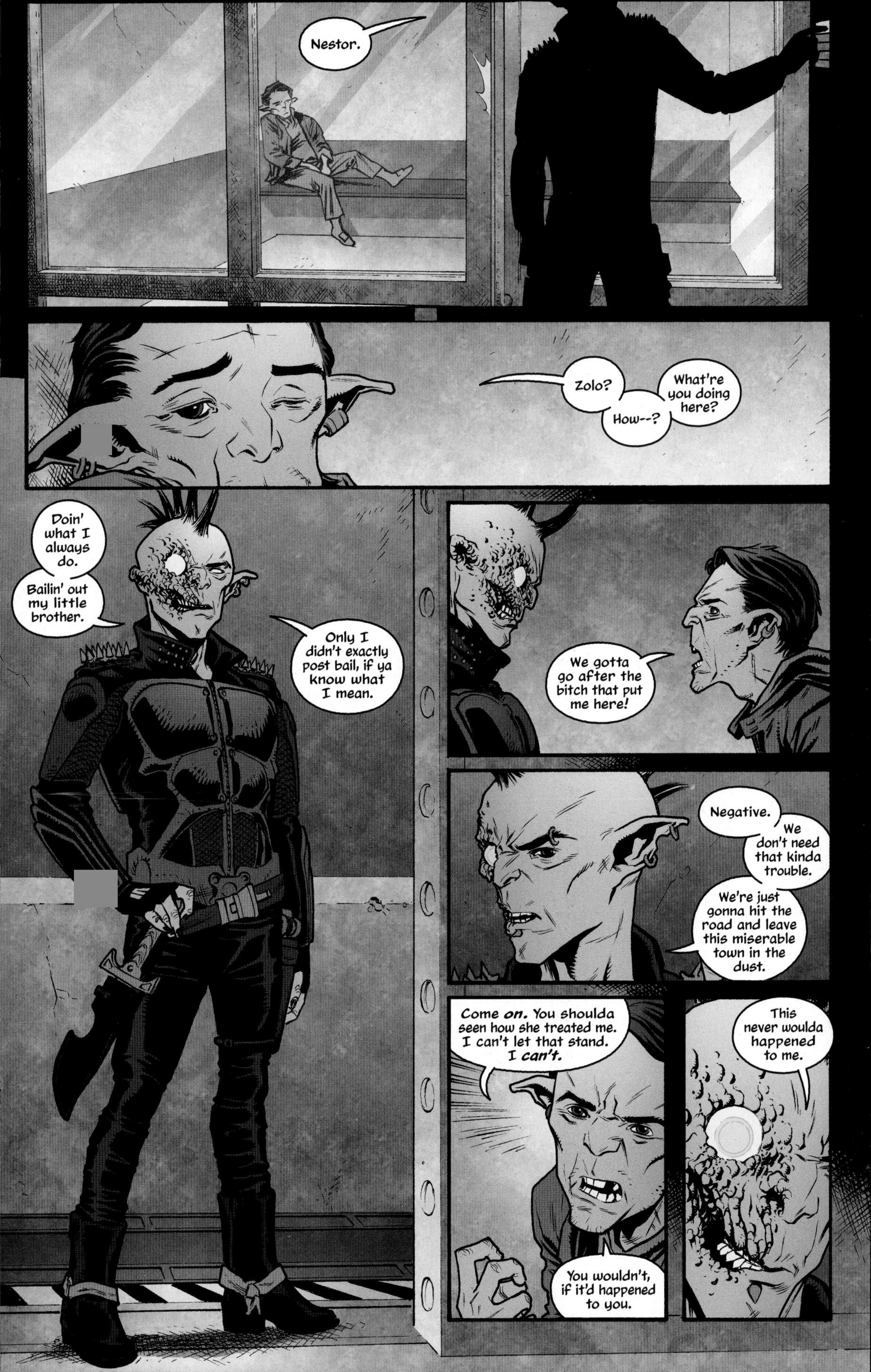

Nestor.
Zolo?
How--?
What're you doing here?
Doin' what I always do.
Bailin' out my little brother.
Only I didn't exactly post bail, if ya know what I mean.
We gotta go after the bitch that put me here!
Negative.
We don't need that kinda trouble.
We're just gonna hit the road and leave this miserable town in the dust.
Come *on*. You shoulda seen how she treated me. I can't let that stand. I ***can't***.
This never woulda happened to me.
You wouldn't, if it'd happened to you.

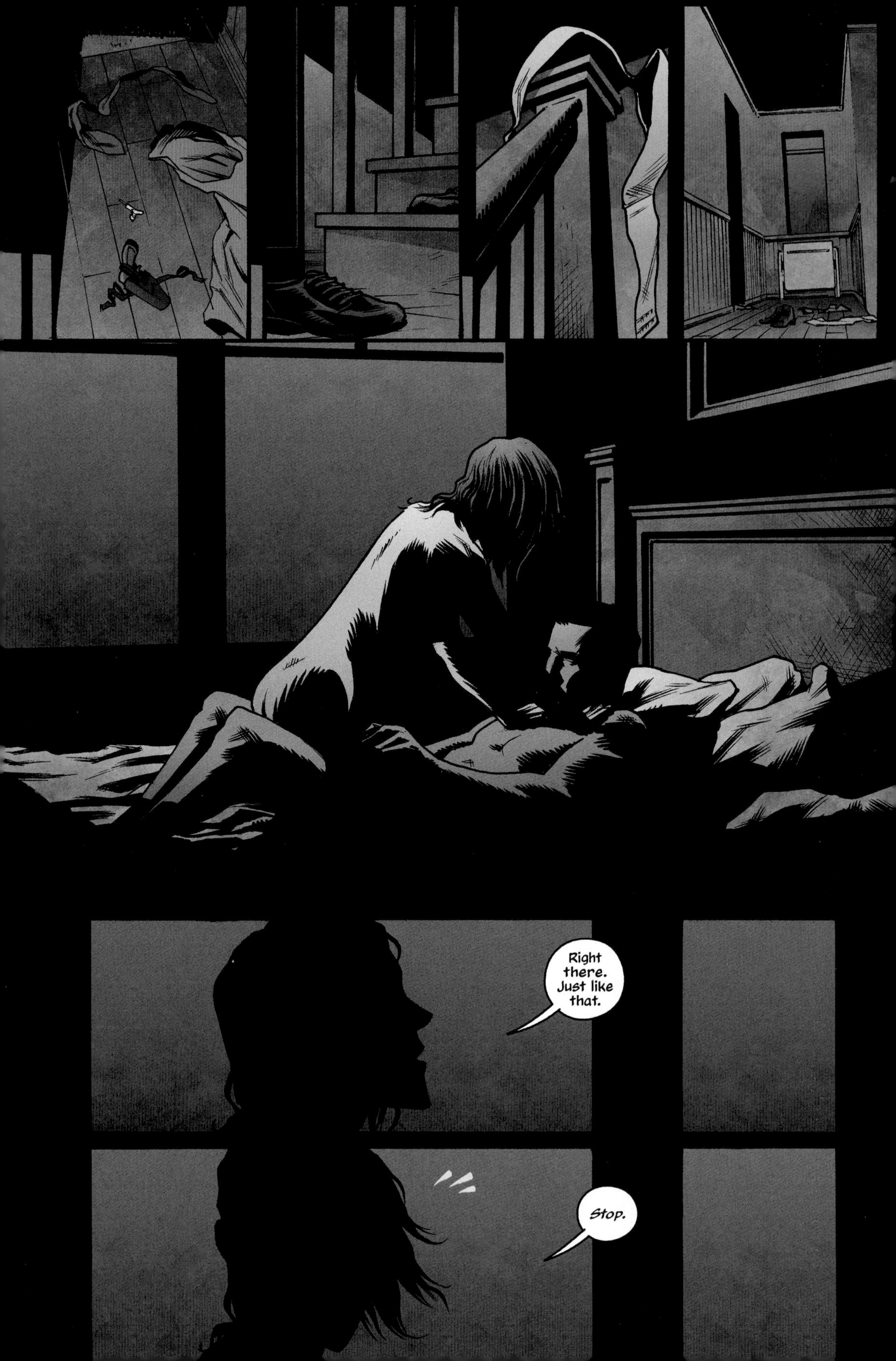
Right there. Just like that.
Stop.

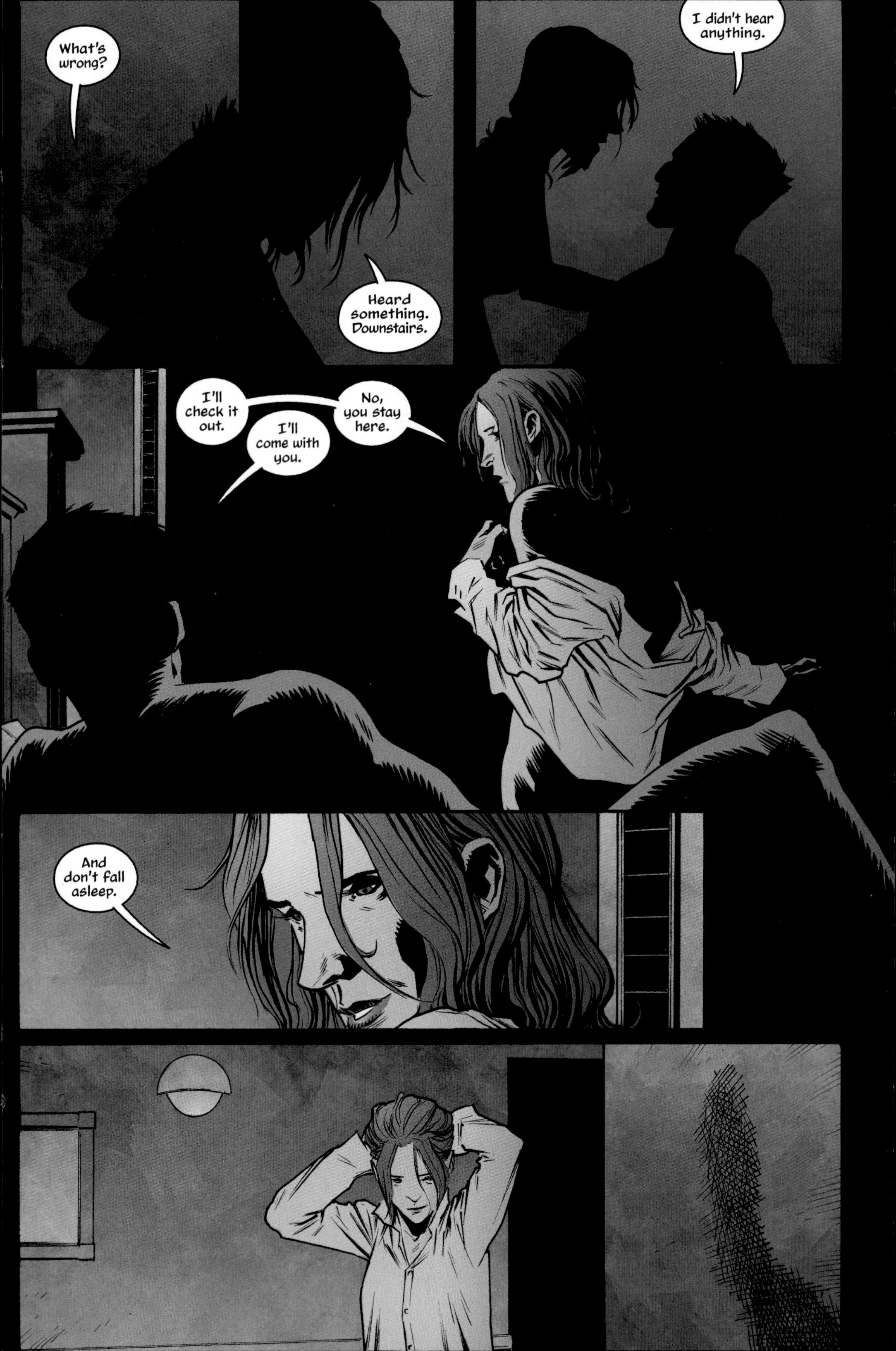
What's wrong?
Heard something. Downstairs.
I didn't hear anything.
I'll check it out.
No, you stay here.
I'll come with you.
And don't fall asleep.

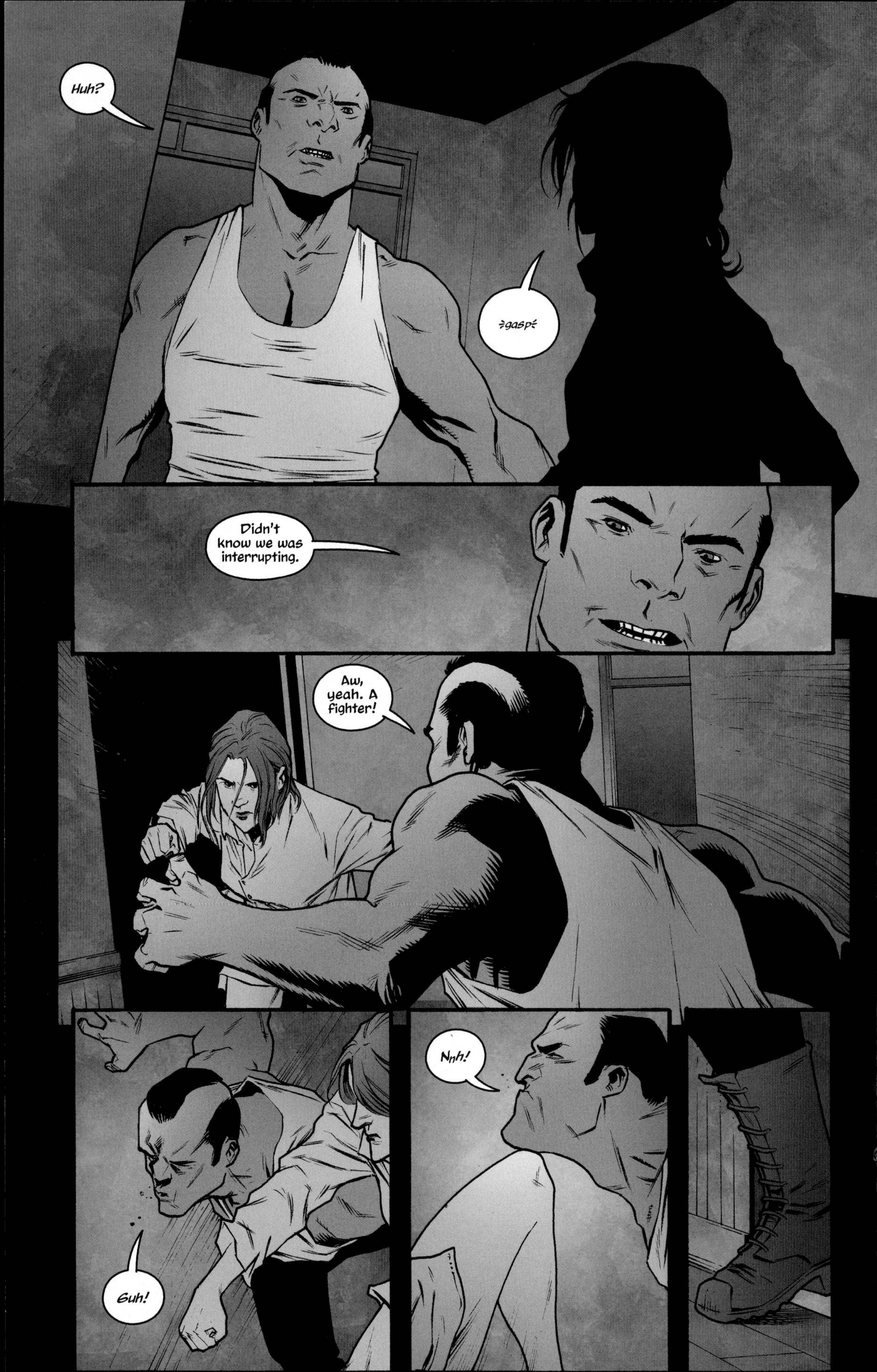
Huh?
≈gasp≈
Didn't know we was interrupting.
Aw, yeah. A fighter!
Guh!
Nnh!

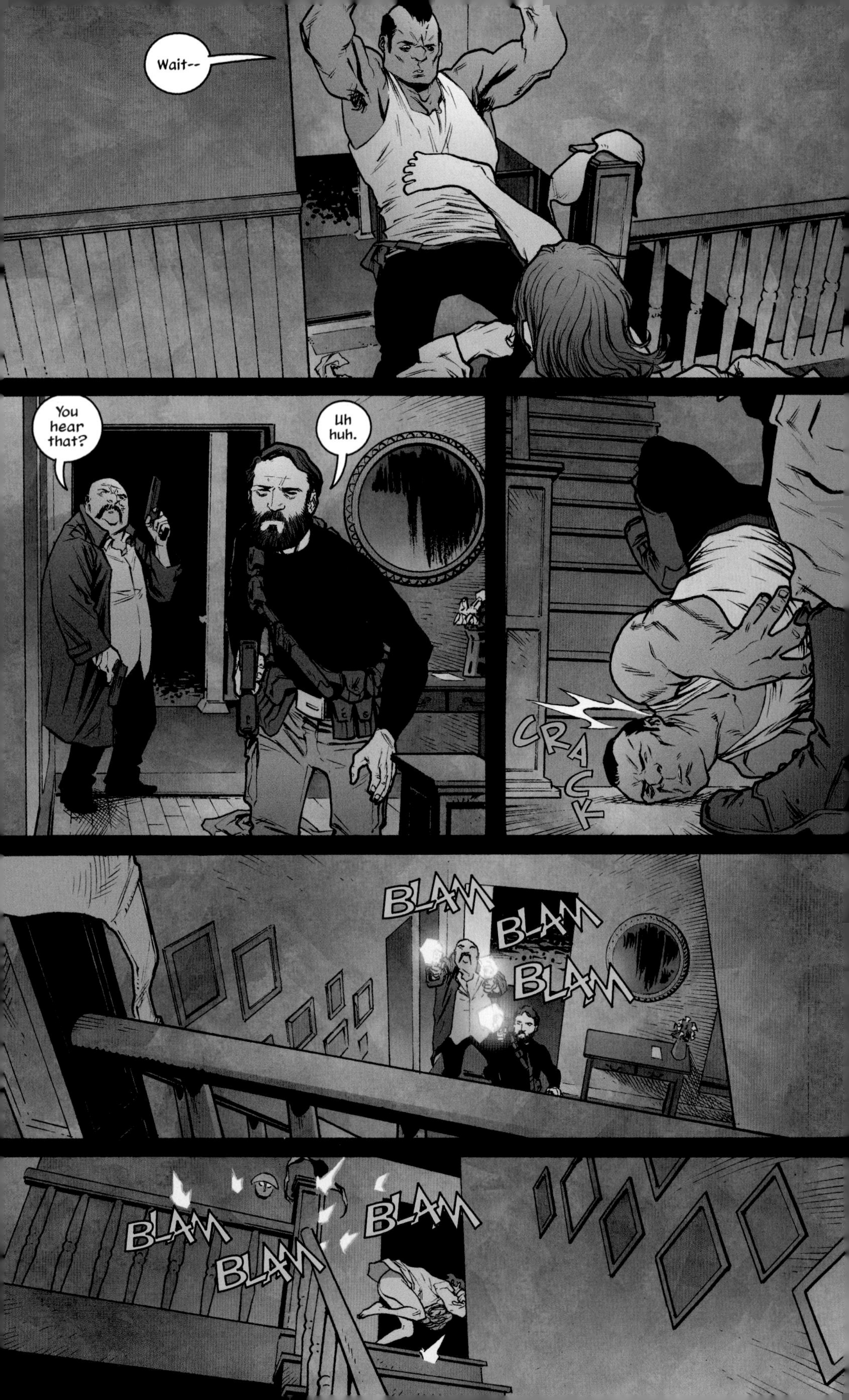
Wait--
You hear that?
Uh huh.
CRACK
BLAM
BLAM
BLAM
BLAM
BLAM
BLAM

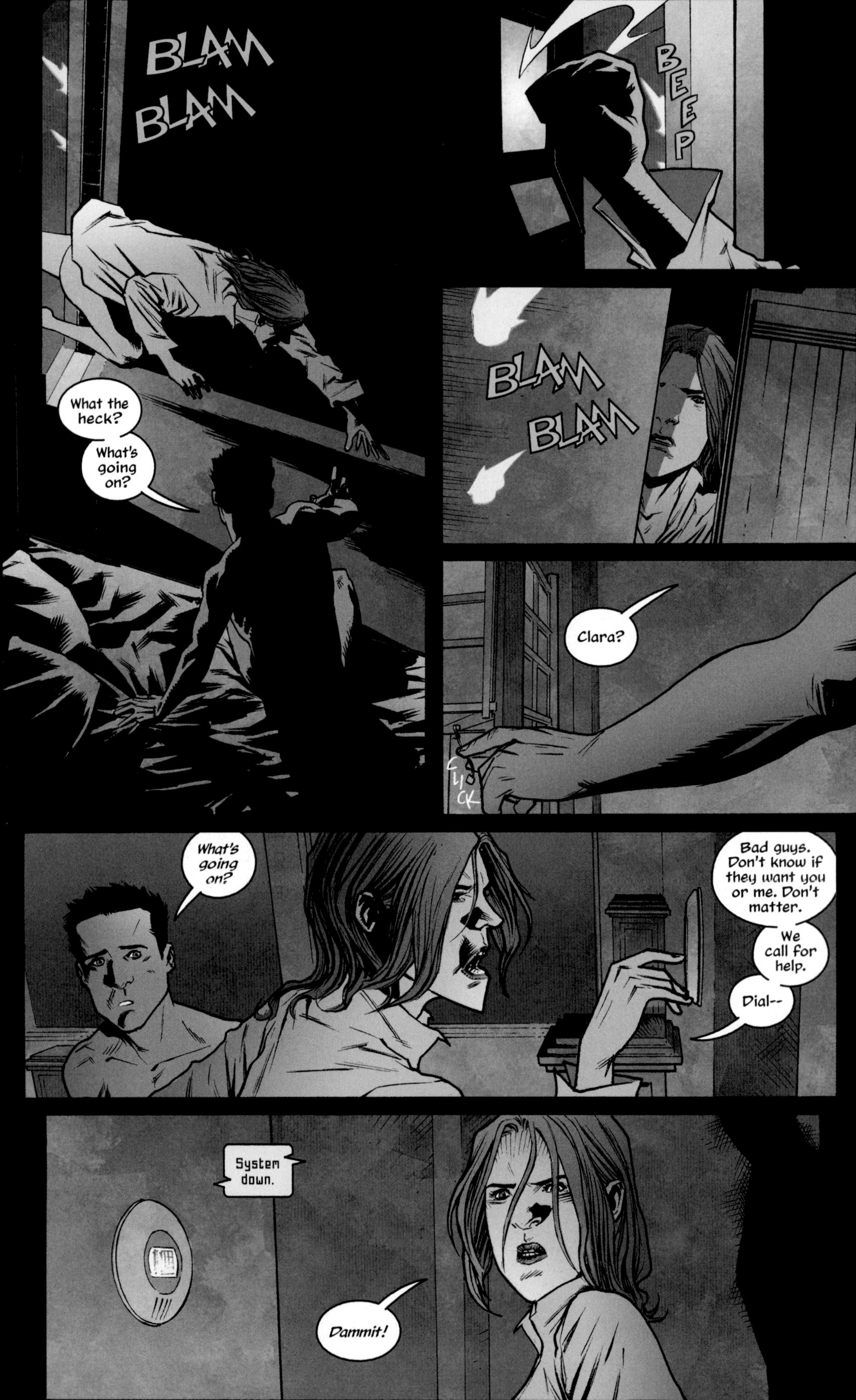
BLAM
BLAM
BEEP
What the heck?
What's going on?
BLAM
BLAM
Clara?
CLICK
What's going on?
Bad guys. Don't know if they want you or me. Don't matter.
We call for help.
Dial--
System down.
Dammit!

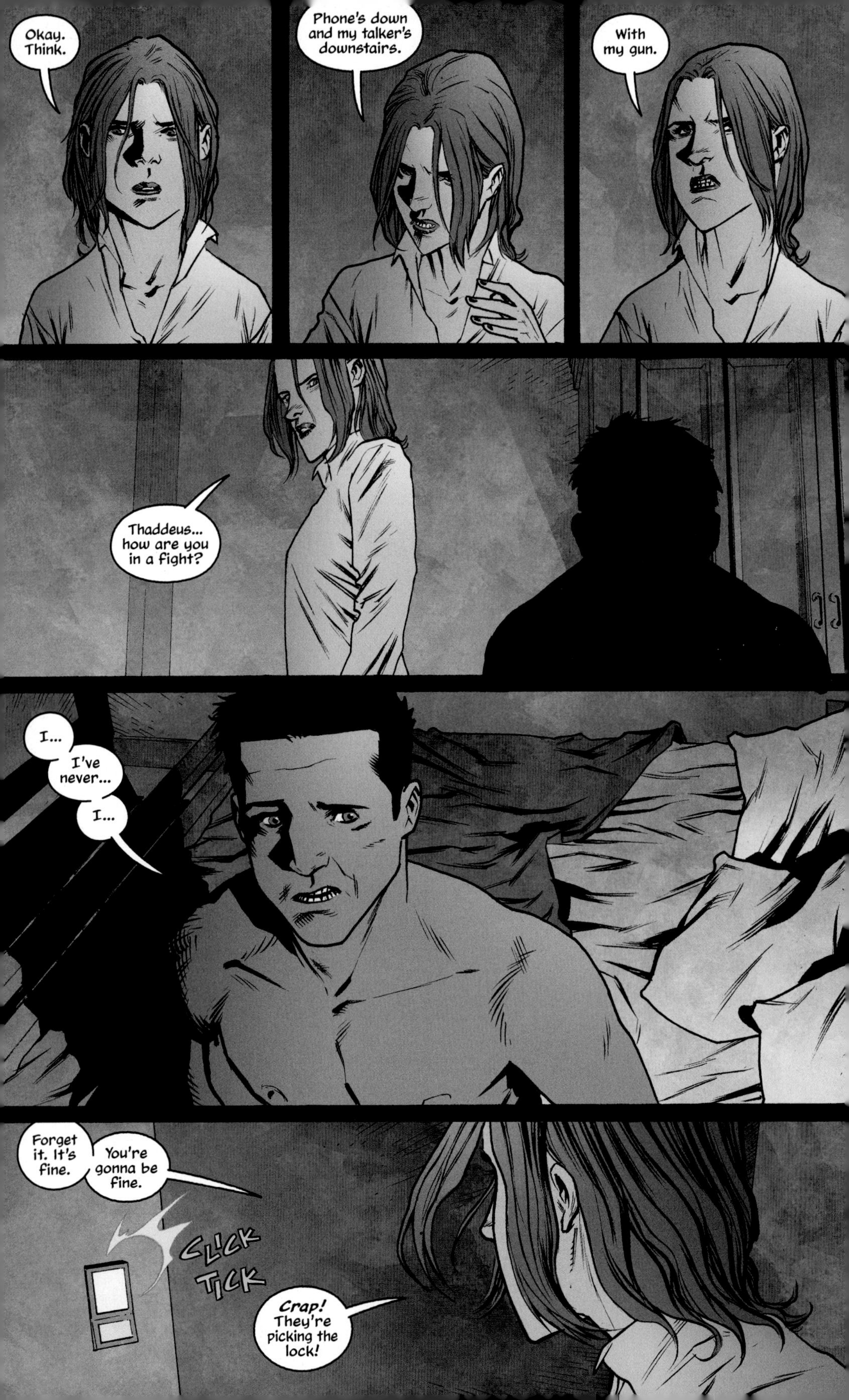
Okay. Think.
Phone's down and my talker's downstairs.
With my gun.
Thaddeus... how are you in a fight?
I...
I've never...
I...
Forget it. It's fine.
You're gonna be fine.
CLICK
TICK
Crap! They're picking the lock!

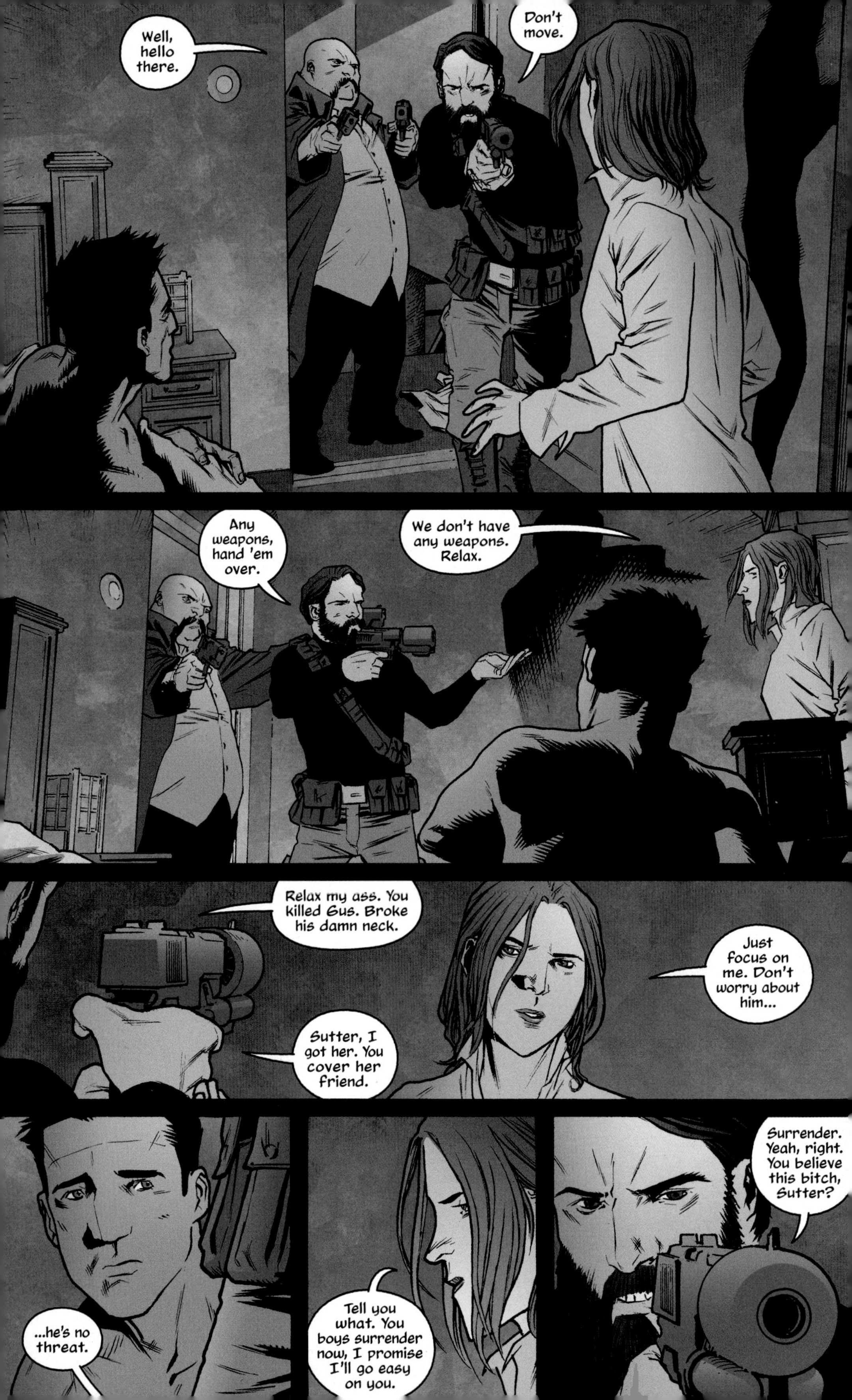
Well, hello there.
Don't move.
Any weapons, hand 'em over.
We don't have any weapons. Relax.
Relax my ass. You killed Gus. Broke his damn neck.
Just focus on me. Don't worry about him...
Sutter, I got her. You cover her friend.
...he's no threat.
Tell you what. You boys surrender now, I promise I'll go easy on you.
Surrender. Yeah, right. You believe this bitch, Sutter?

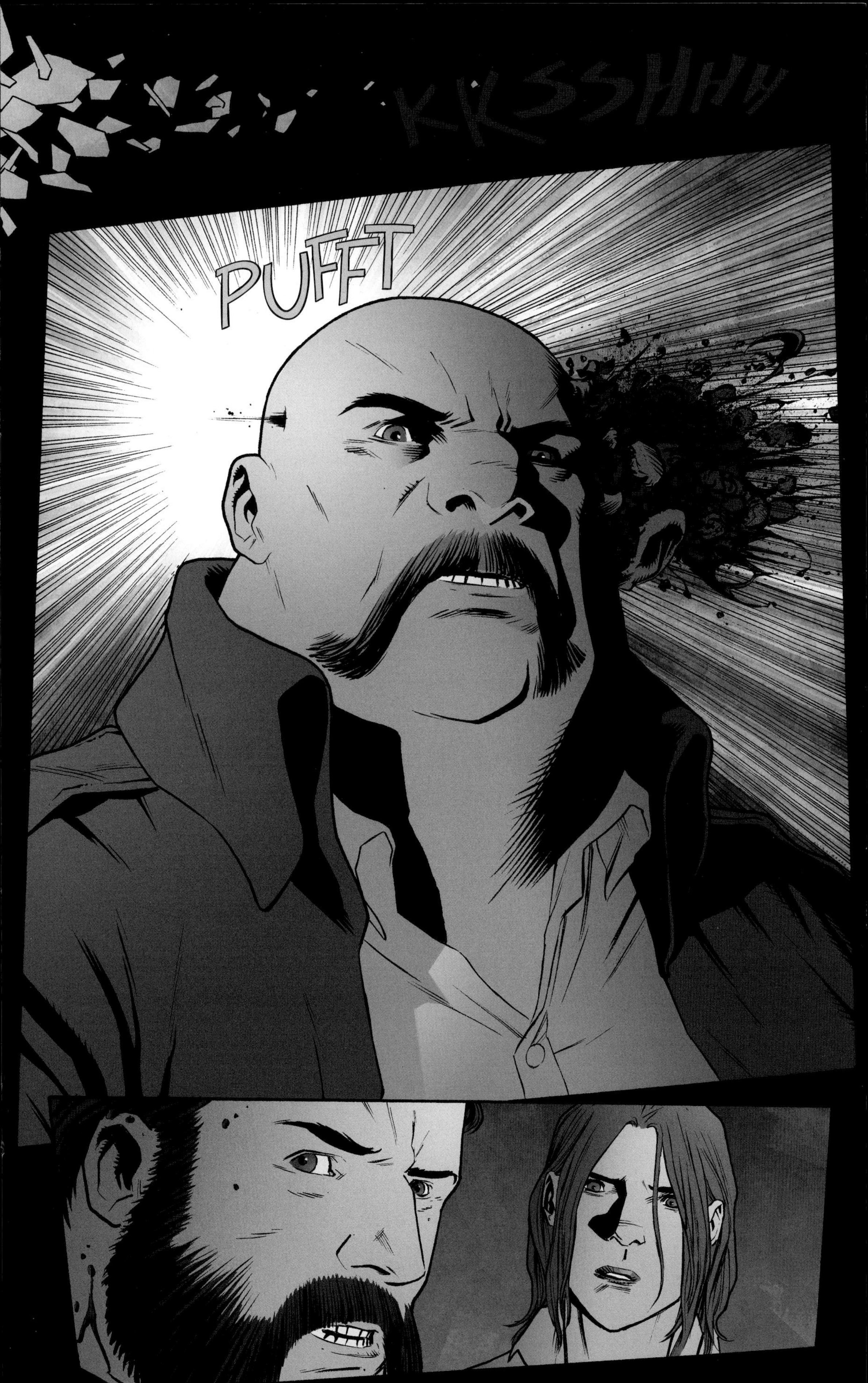
KKSSHHH
PUFFT

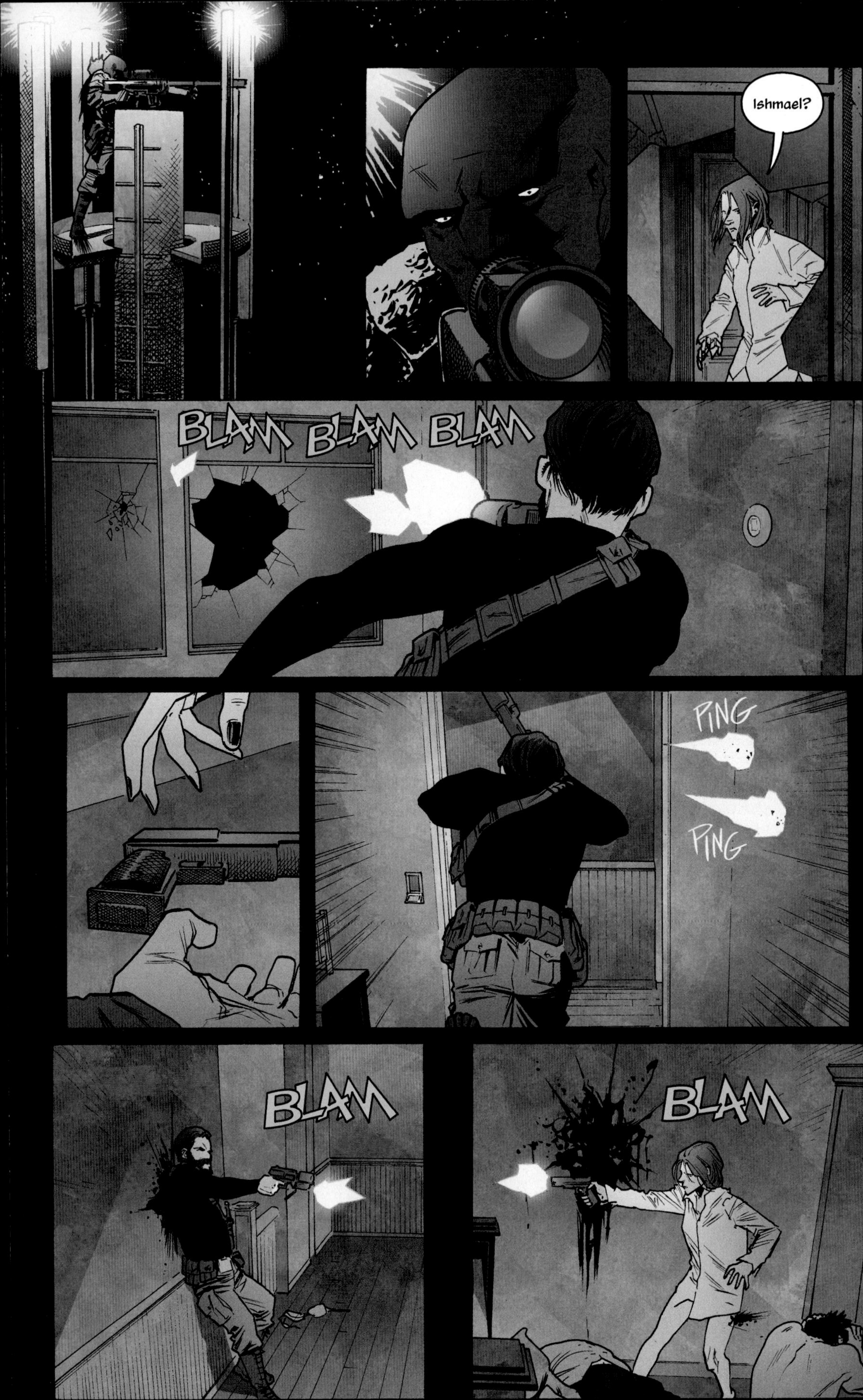
Ishmael?
BLAM BLAM BLAM
PING
PING
BLAM
BLAM

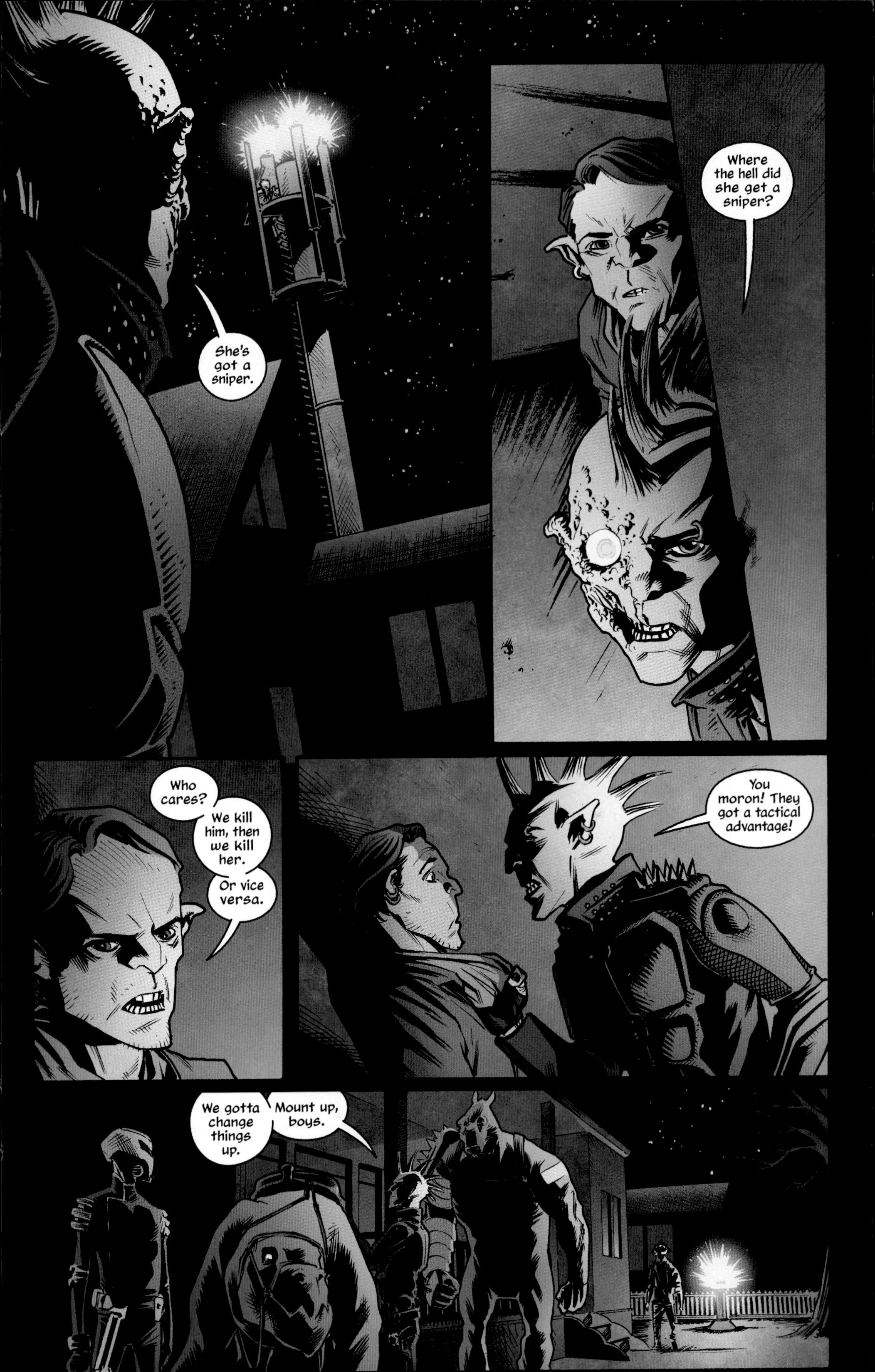
She's got a sniper.
Where the hell did she get a sniper?
Who cares?
We kill him, then we kill her.
Or vice versa.
You moron! They got a tactical advantage!
We gotta change things up.
Mount up, boys.

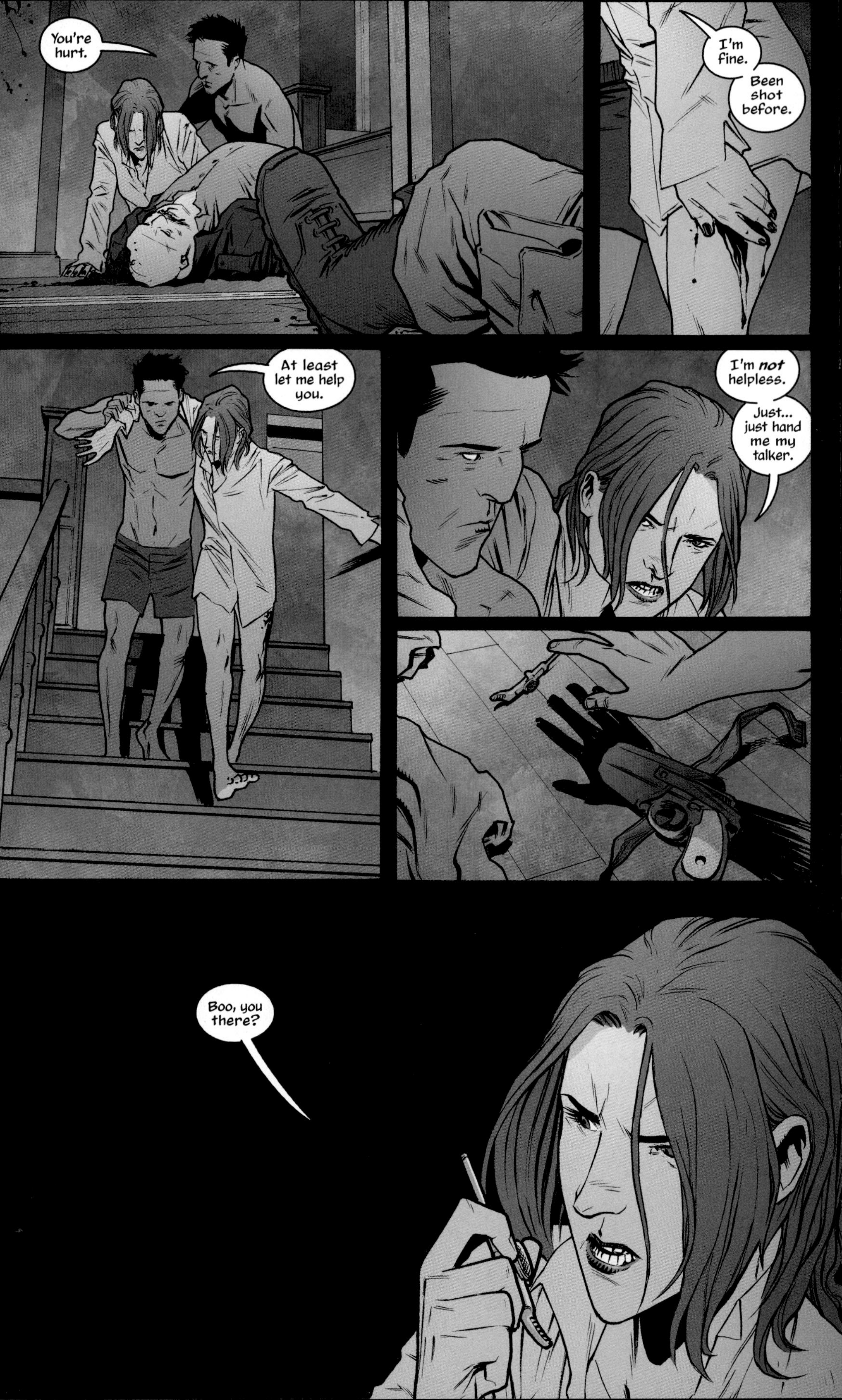
You're hurt.
I'm fine.
Been shot before.
At least let me help you.
I'm *not* helpless.
Just... just hand me my talker.
Boo, you there?

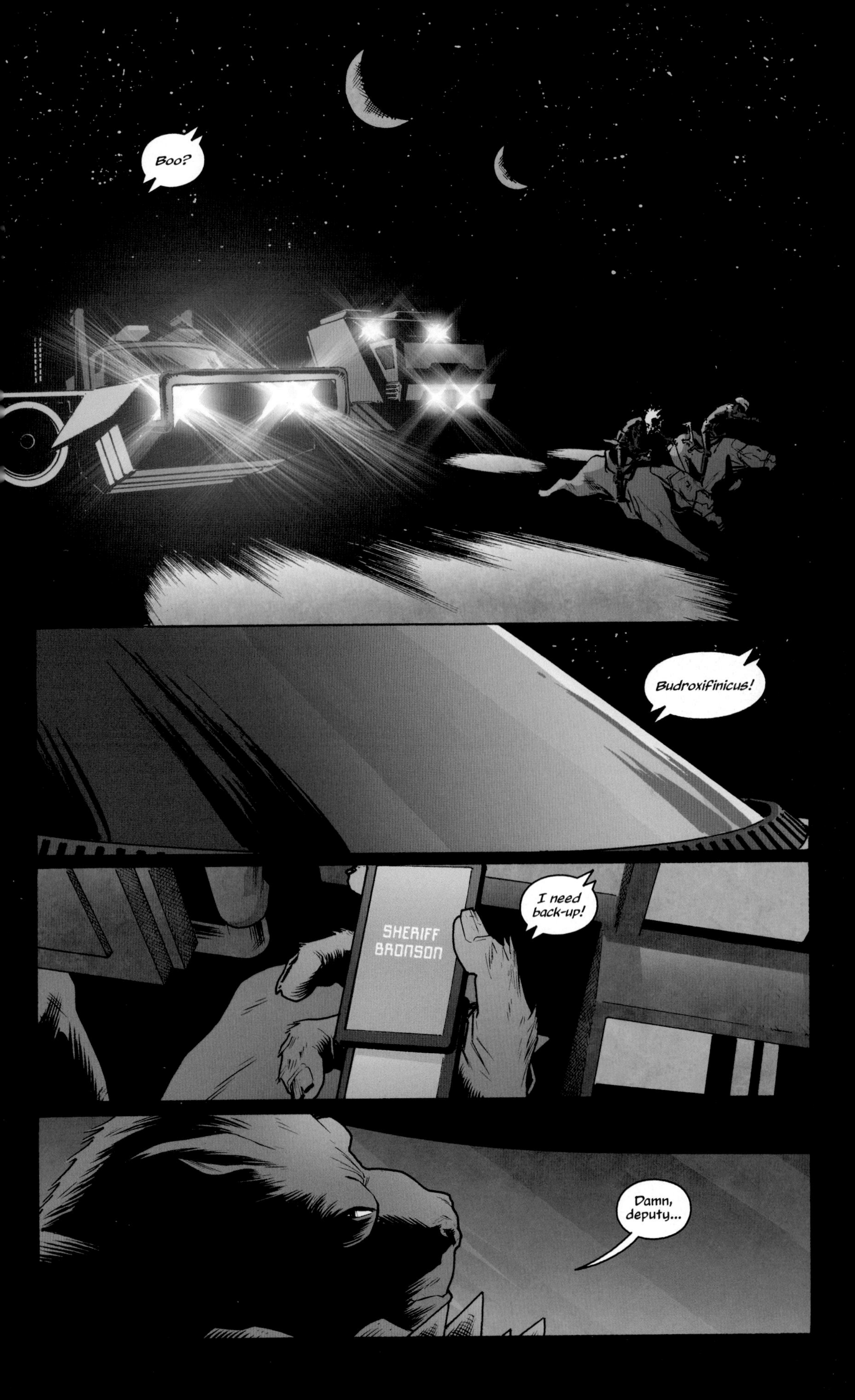
Boo?
Budroxifinicus!
SHERIFF BRONSON
I need back-up!
Damn, deputy...

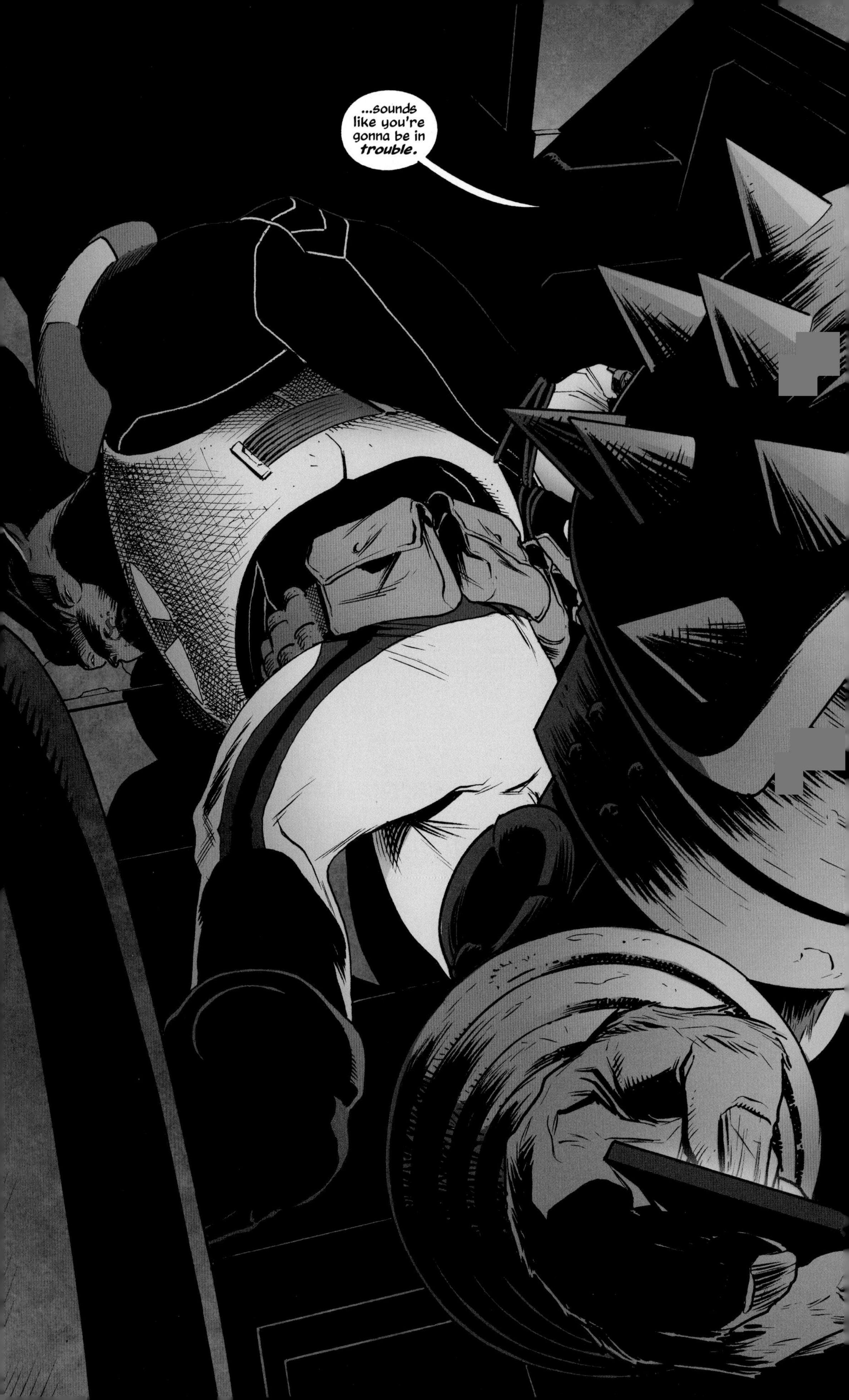
...sounds like you're gonna be in *trouble.*

CHAPTER III

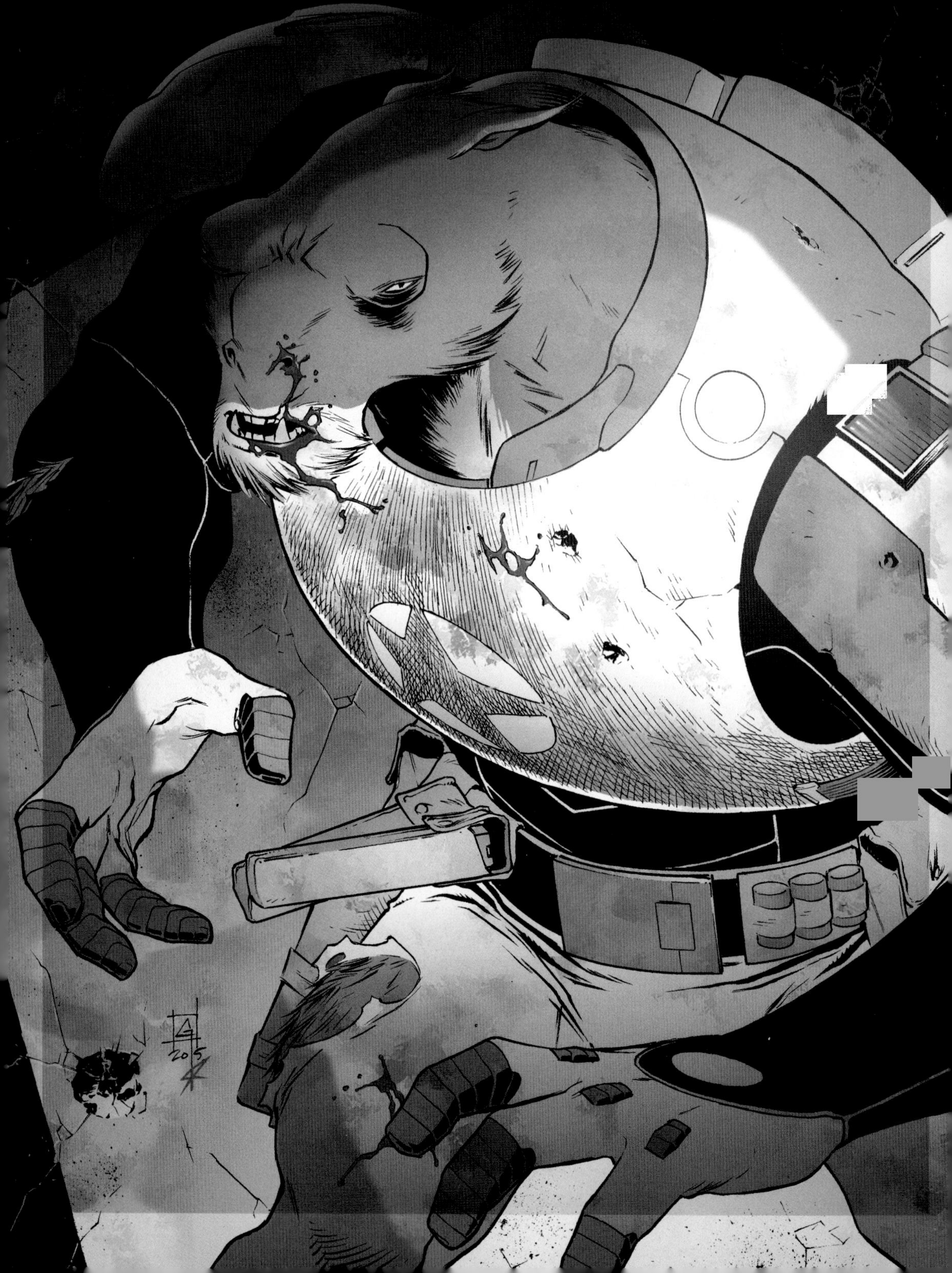

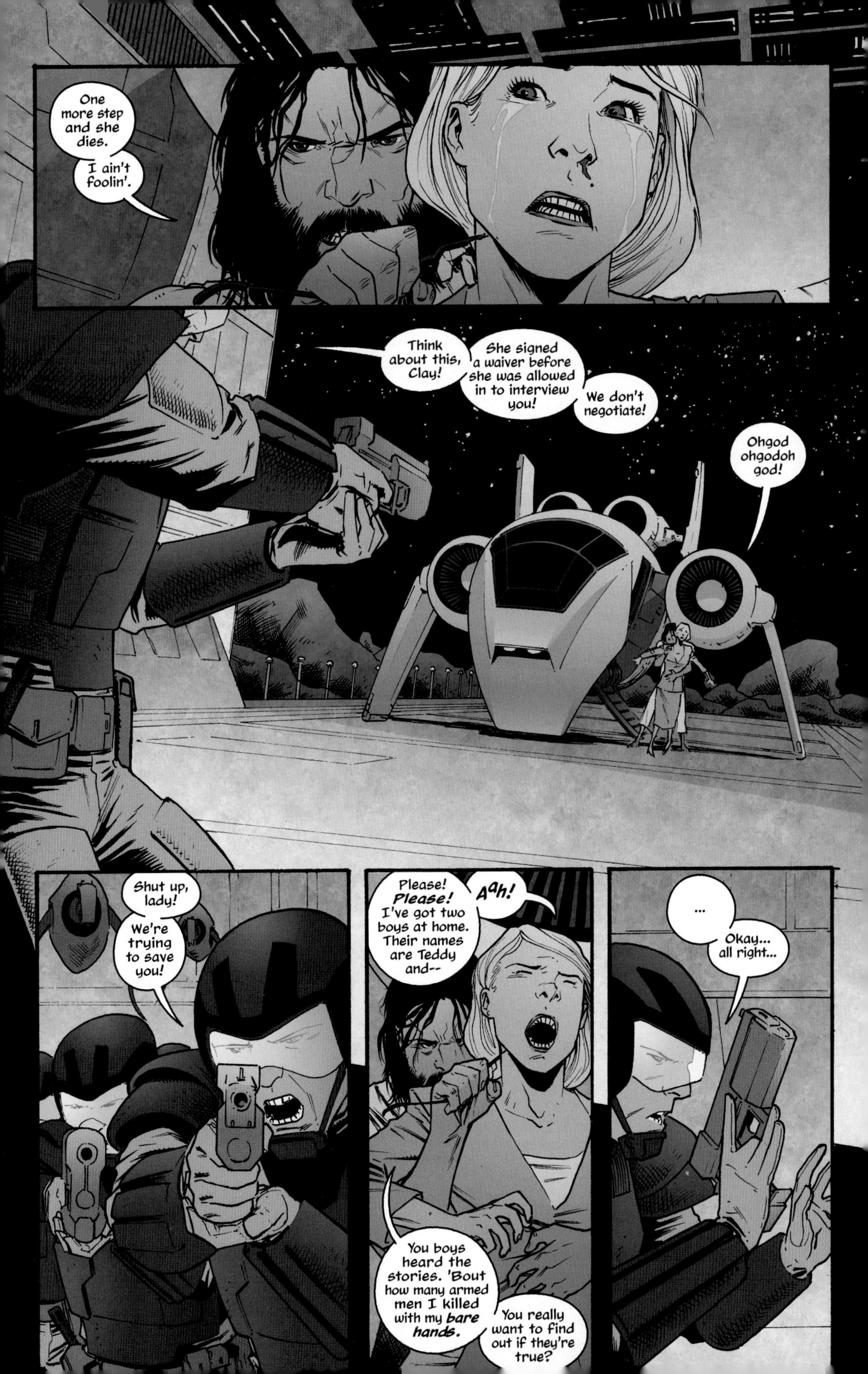

One more step and she dies.
I ain't foolin'.
Think about this, Clay!
She signed a waiver before she was allowed in to interview you!
We don't negotiate!
Ohgod ohgodoh god!
Shut up, lady!
We're trying to save you!
Please! ***Please!*** I've got two boys at home. Their names are Teddy and--
Aah!
You boys heard the stories. 'Bout how many armed men I killed with my ***bare hands.***
You really want to find out if they're true?
...
Okay... all right...

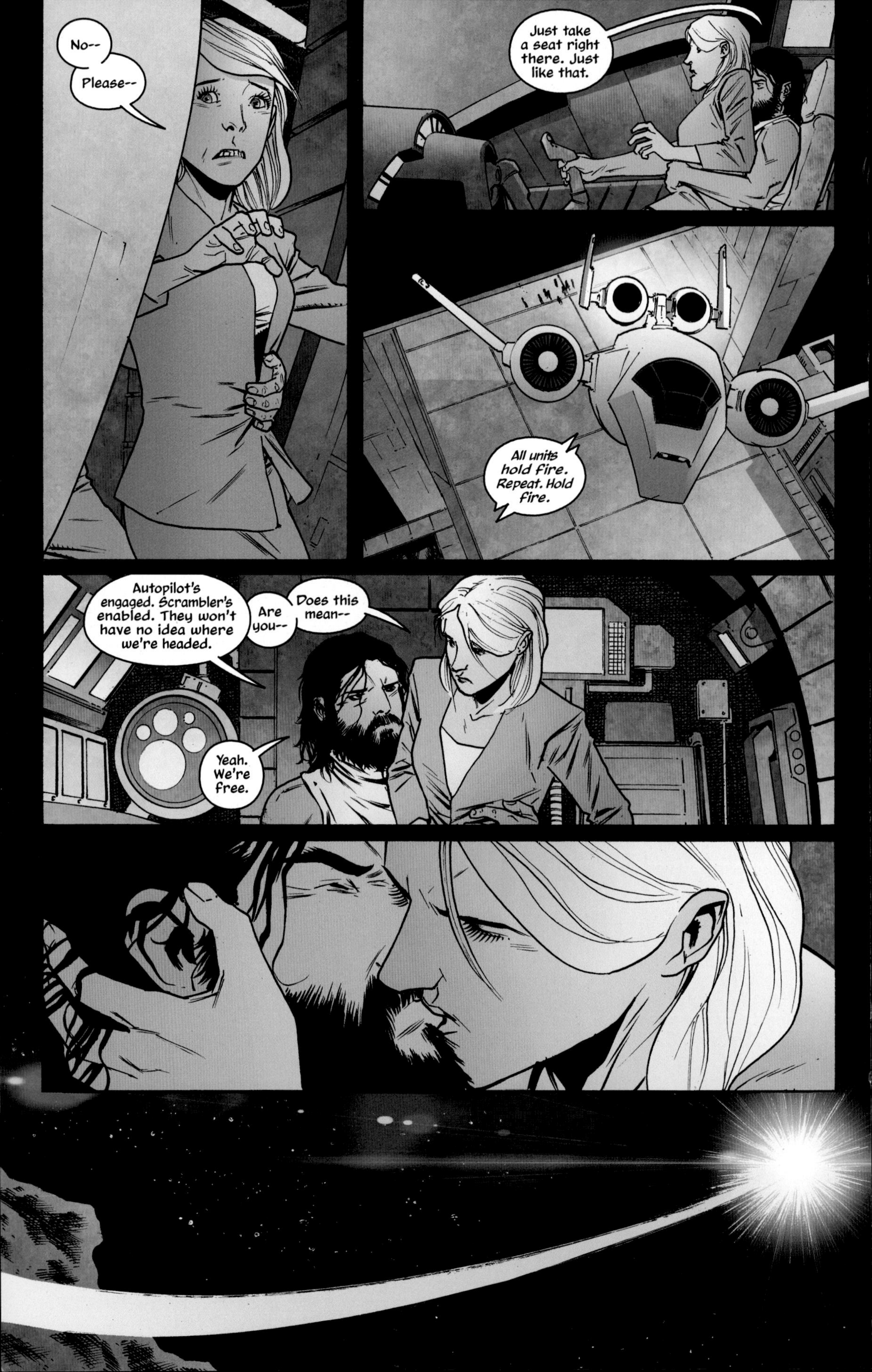
No--
Please--
Just take a seat right there. Just like that.
All units hold fire. Repeat. Hold fire.
Autopilot's engaged. Scrambler's enabled. They won't have no idea where we're headed.
Are you--
Does this mean--
Yeah. We're free.

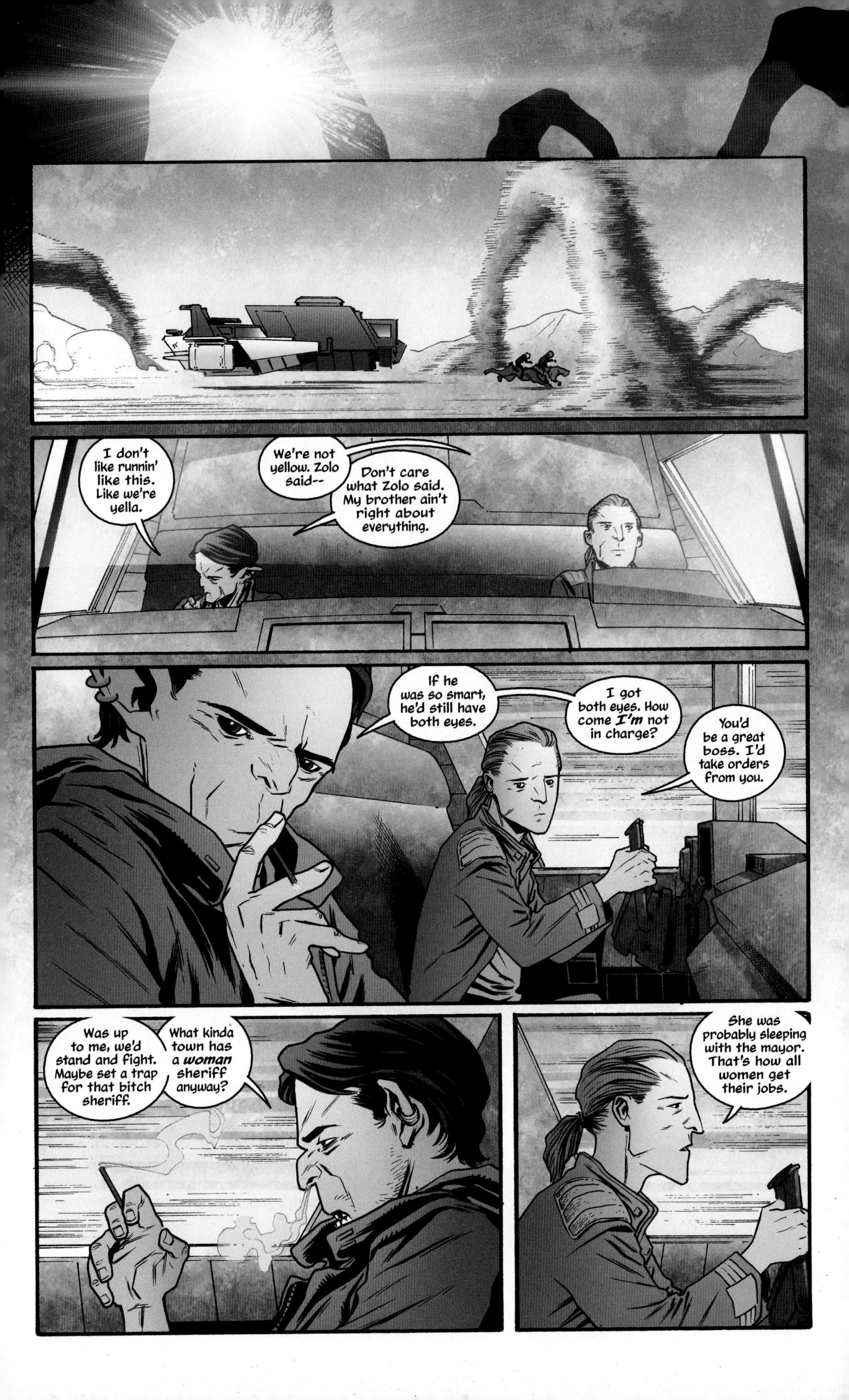

I don't like runnin' like this. Like we're yella.
We're not yellow. Zolo said--
Don't care what Zolo said. My brother ain't right about everything.
If he was so smart, he'd still have both eyes.
I got both eyes. How come I'm not in charge?
You'd be a great boss. I'd take orders from you.
Was up to me, we'd stand and fight. Maybe set a trap for that bitch sheriff.
What kinda town has a woman sheriff anyway?
She was probably sleeping with the mayor. That's how all women get their jobs.

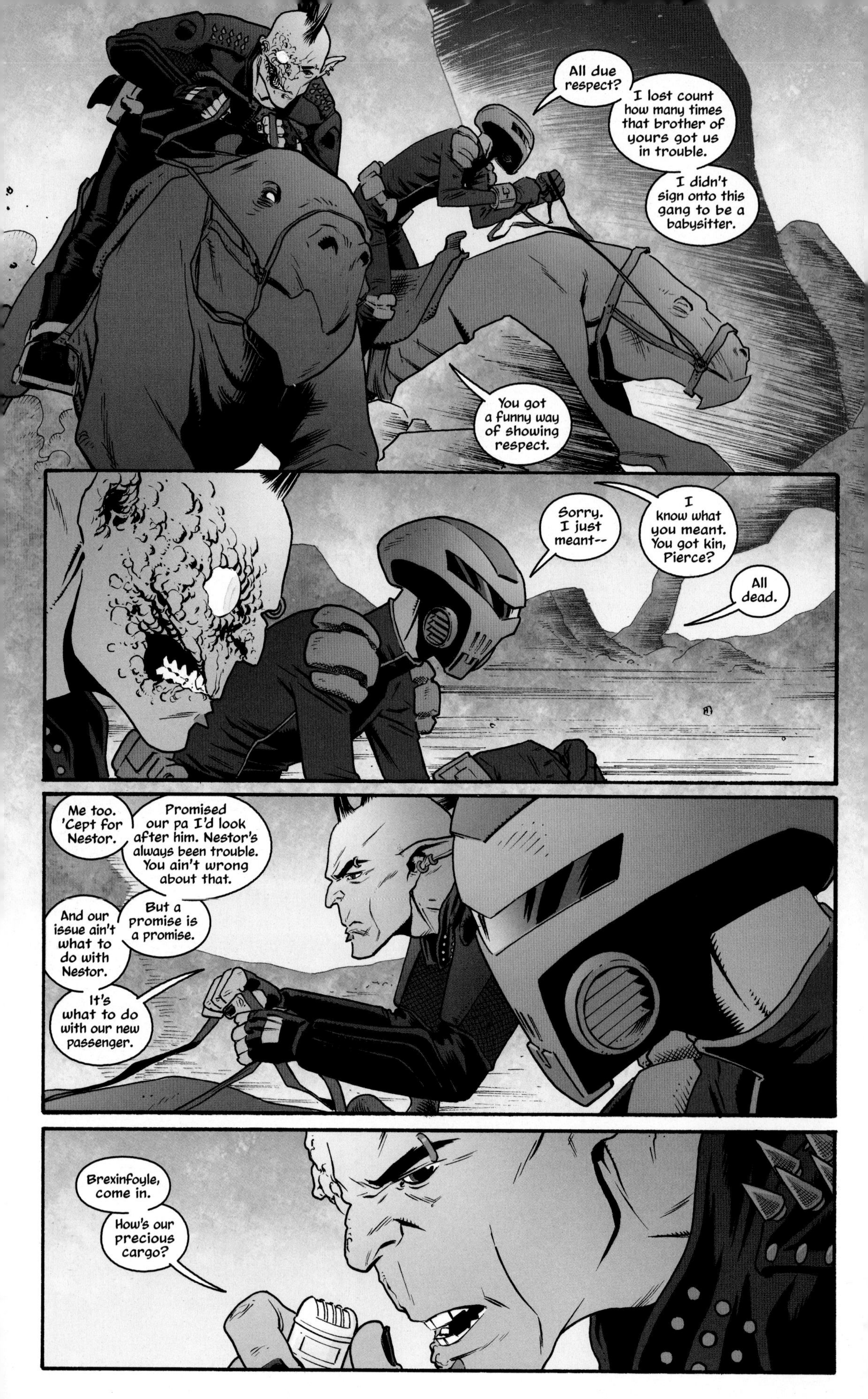
All due respect?
I lost count how many times that brother of yours got us in trouble.
I didn't sign onto this gang to be a babysitter.
You got a funny way of showing respect.
Sorry. I just meant--
I know what you meant. You got kin, Pierce?
All dead.
Me too. 'Cept for Nestor.
Promised our pa I'd look after him. Nestor's always been trouble. You ain't wrong about that.
But a promise is a promise.
And our issue ain't what to do with Nestor.
It's what to do with our new passenger.
Brexinfoyle, come in.
How's our precious cargo?

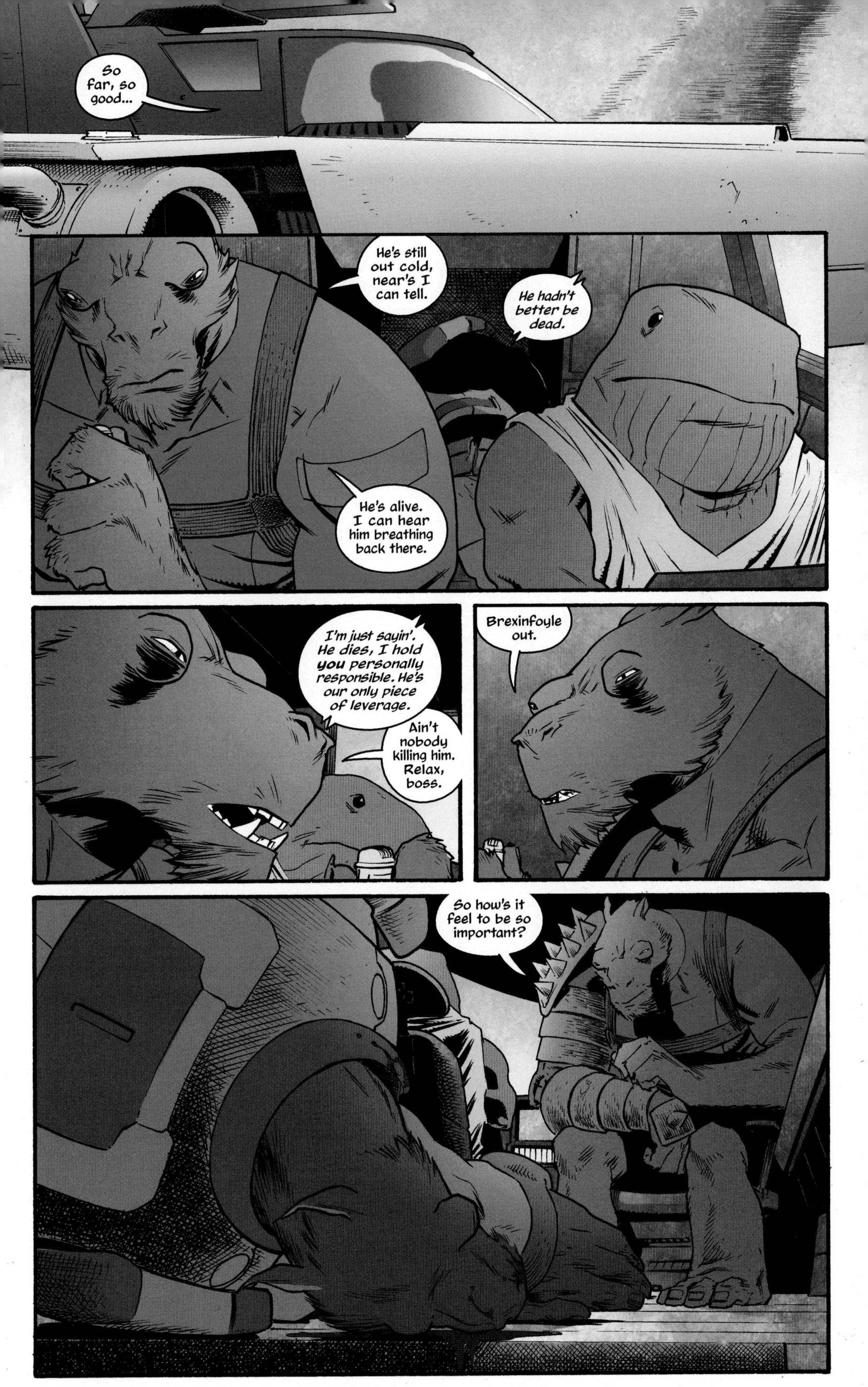
So far, so good...
He's still out cold, near's I can tell.
He hadn't better be dead.
He's alive. I can hear him breathing back there.
I'm just sayin'. He dies, I hold **you** personally responsible. He's our only piece of leverage.
Ain't nobody killing him. Relax, boss.
Brexinfoyle out.
So how's it feel to be so important?

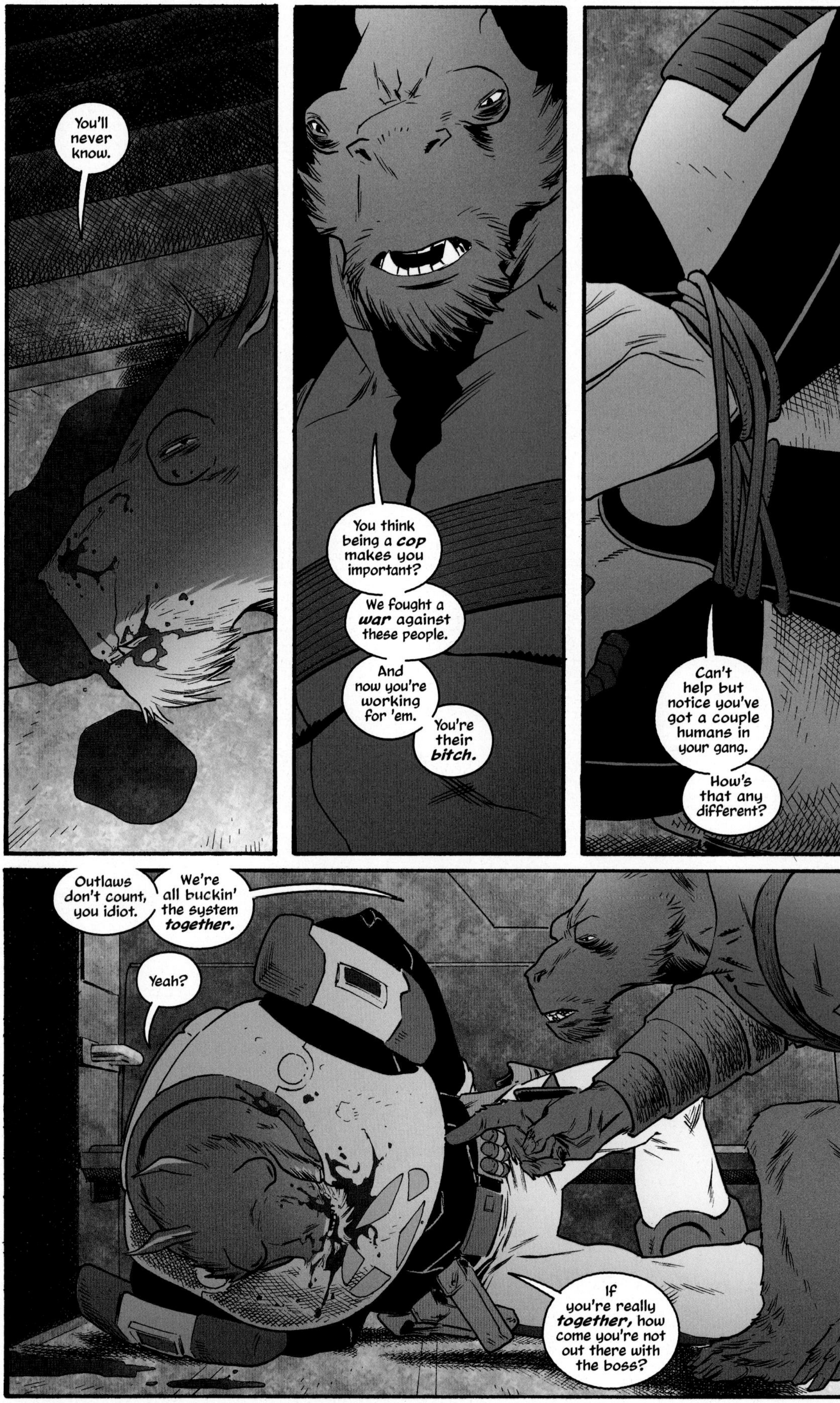
You'll never know.
You think being a *cop* makes you important?
We fought a *war* against these people.
And now you're working for 'em.
You're their *bitch.*
Can't help but notice you've got a couple humans in your gang.
How's that any different?
Outlaws don't count, you idiot.
We're all buckin' the system *together.*
Yeah?
If you're really *together,* how come you're not out there with the boss?

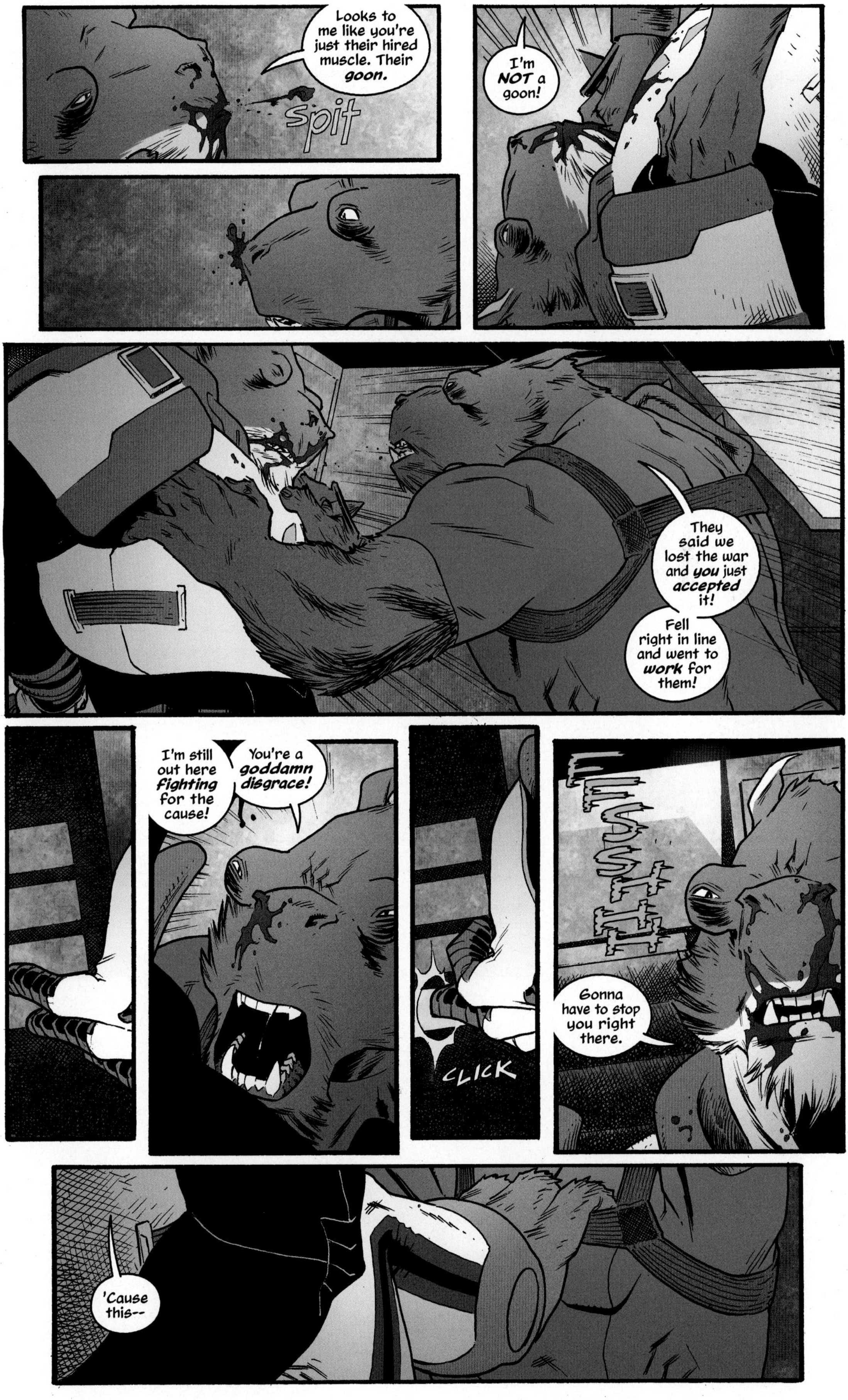

Looks to me like you're just their hired muscle. Their *goon.*
spit
I'm *NOT* a goon!
They said we lost the war and *you* just *accepted* it!
Fell right in line and went to *work* for them!
I'm still out here *fighting* for the cause!
You're a *goddamn disgrace!*
CLICK
Gonna have to stop you right there.
'Cause this--

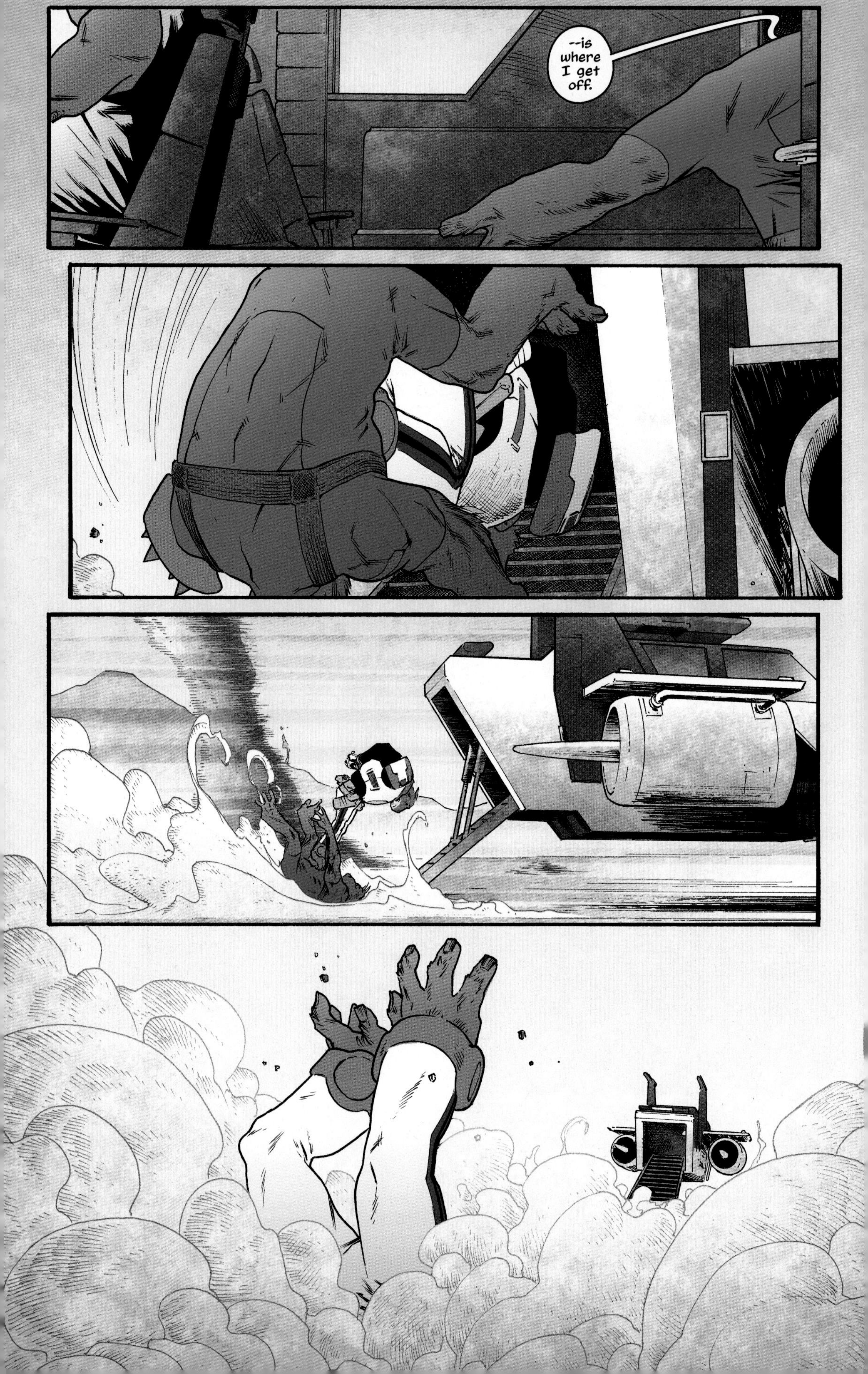
--is where I get off.

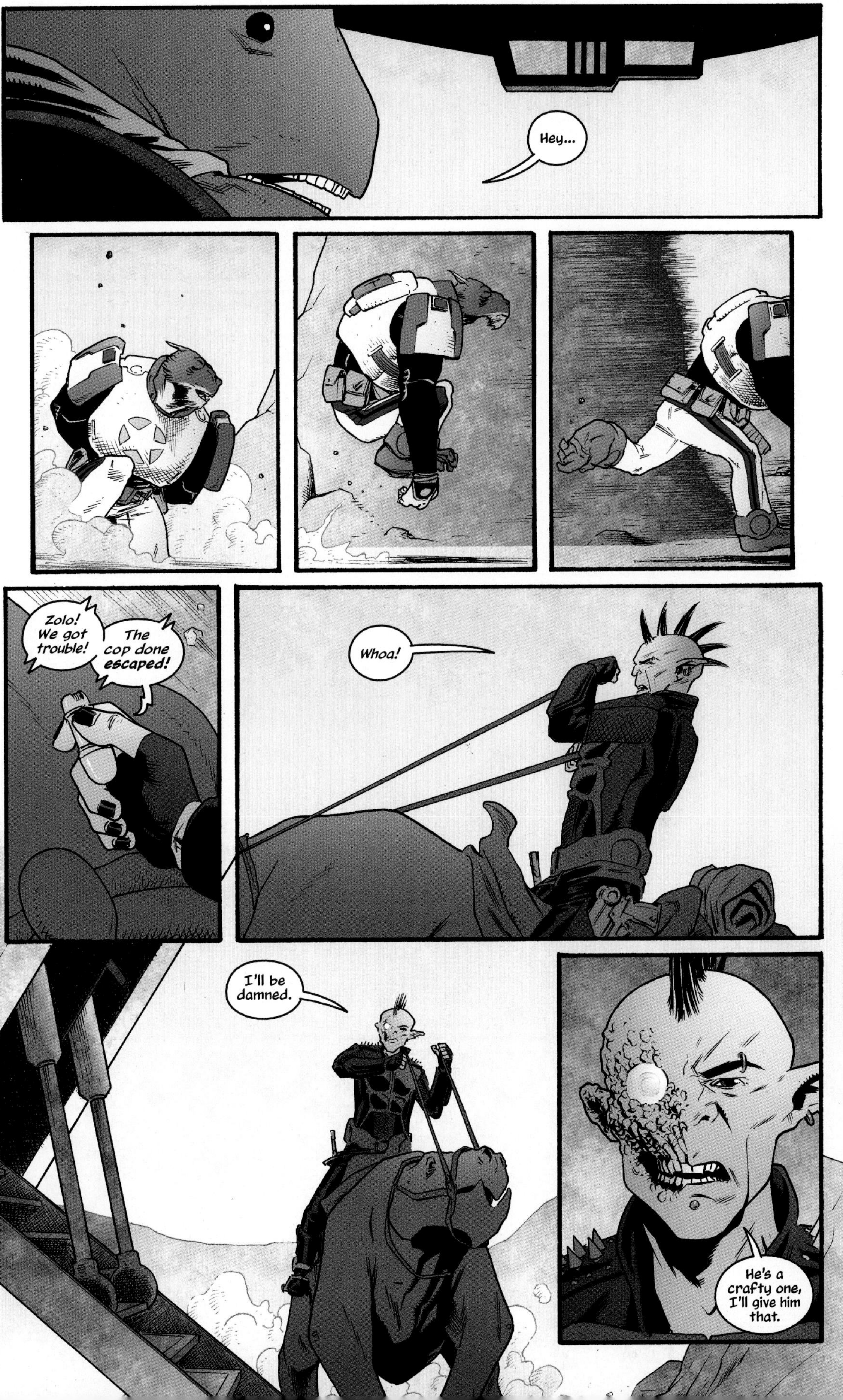
Hey...
Zolo! We got trouble!
The cop done escaped!
Whoa!
I'll be damned.
He's a crafty one, I'll give him that.

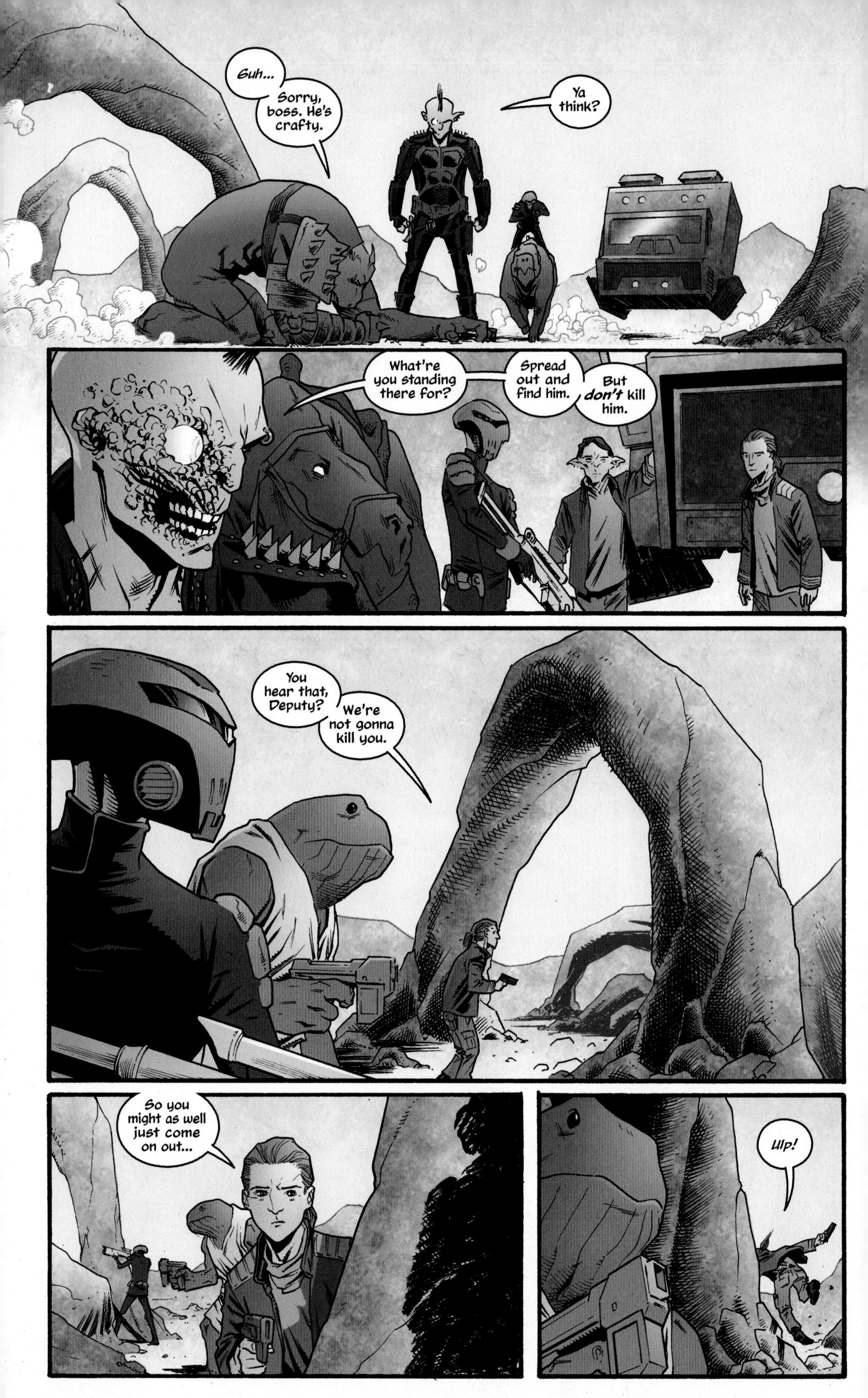

Guh...
Sorry, boss. He's crafty.
Ya think?
What're you standing there for?
Spread out and find him.
But *don't* kill him.
You hear that, Deputy?
We're not gonna kill you.
So you might as well just come on out...
Ulp!

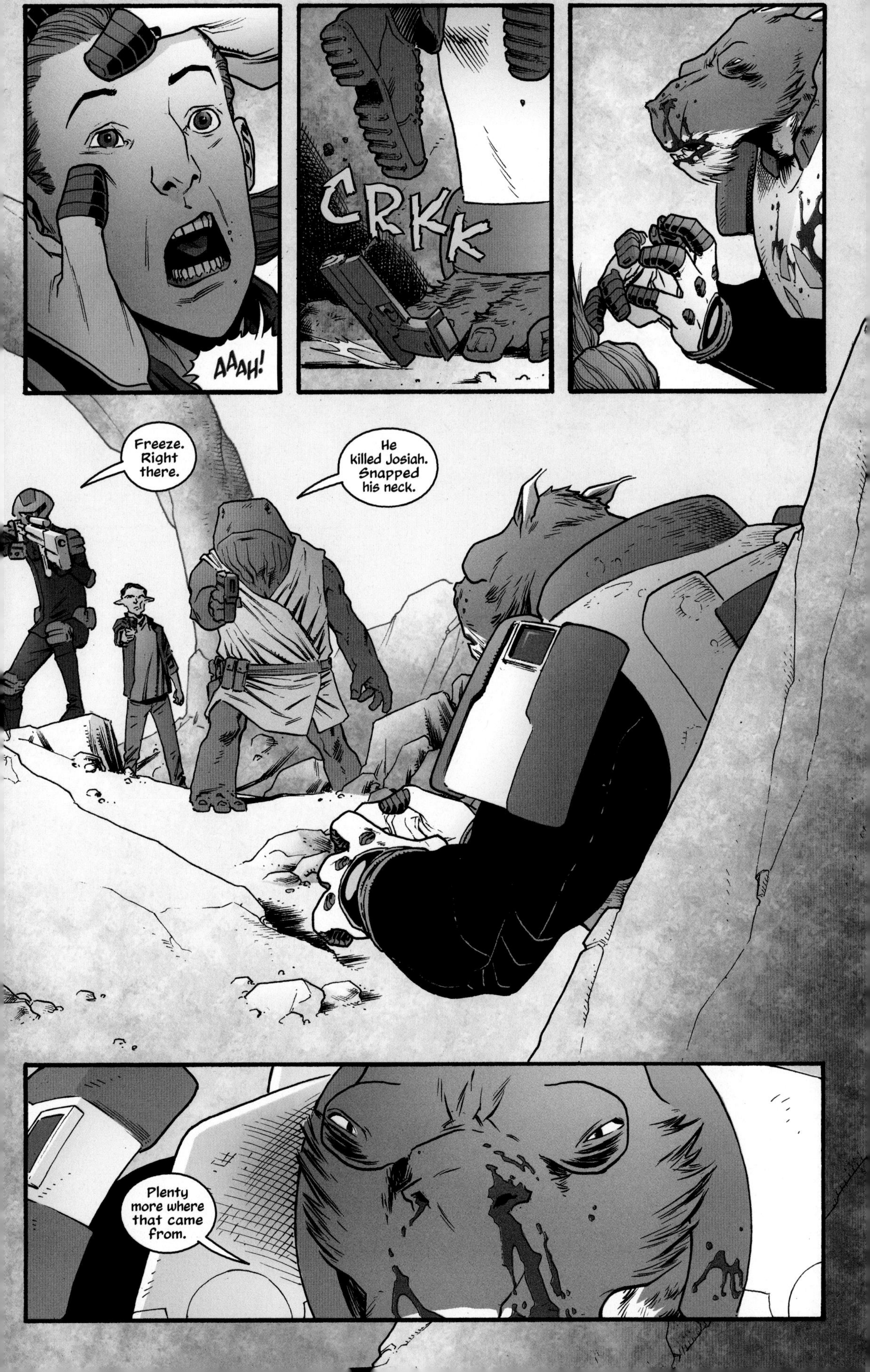
AAAH!
CRKK
Freeze. Right there.
He killed Josiah. Snapped his neck.
Plenty more where that came from.

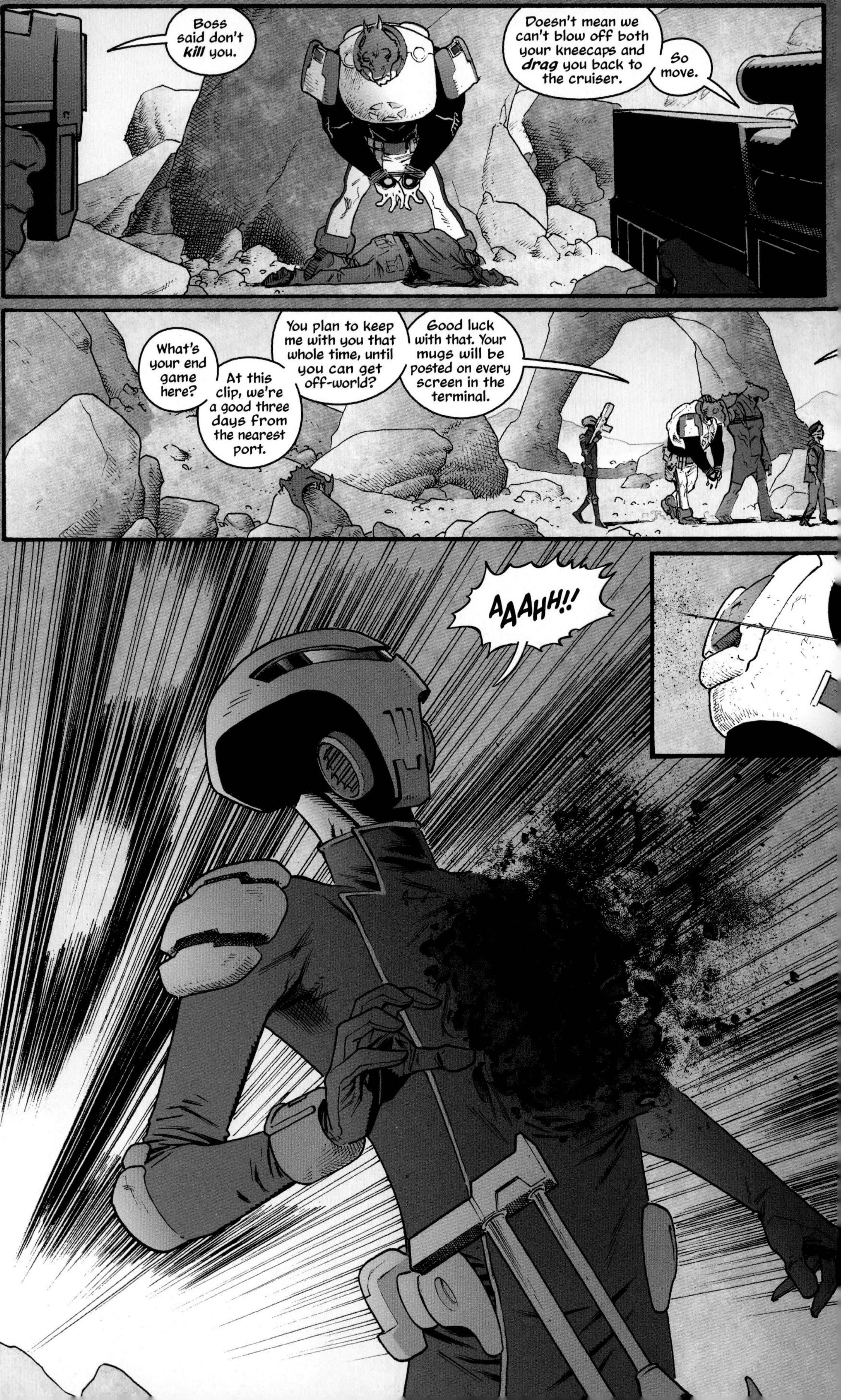
Boss said don't **kill** you.
Doesn't mean we can't blow off both your kneecaps and **drag** you back to the cruiser.
So move.
What's your end game here?
At this clip, we're a good three days from the nearest port.
You plan to keep me with you that whole time, until you can get off-world?
Good luck with that. Your mugs will be posted on every screen in the terminal.
AAAHH!!

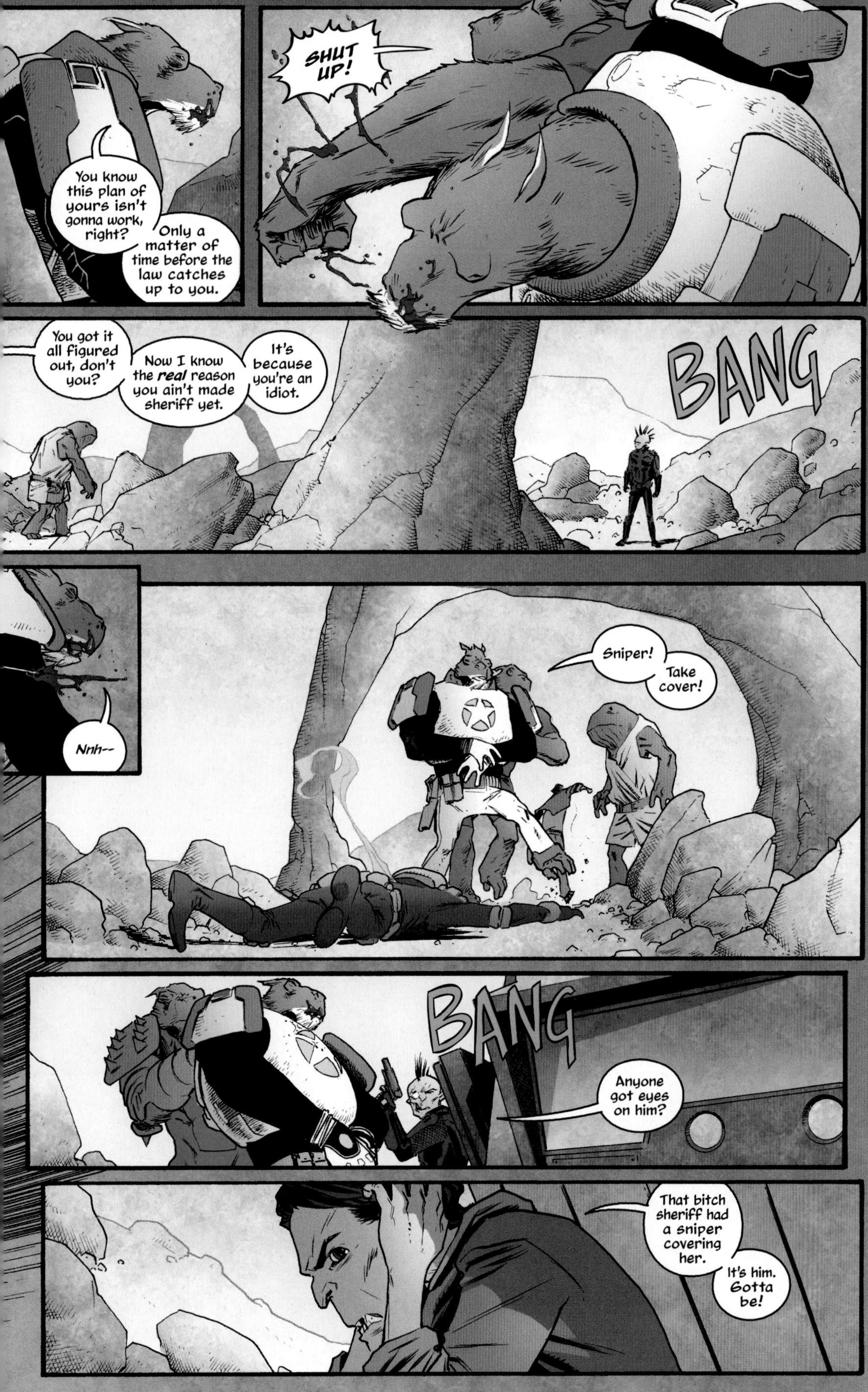
You know this plan of yours isn't gonna work, right?
Only a matter of time before the law catches up to you.
SHUT UP!
You got it all figured out, don't you?
Now I know the real reason you ain't made sheriff yet.
It's because you're an idiot.
BANG
Nnh--
Sniper!
Take cover!
BANG
Anyone got eyes on him?
That bitch sheriff had a sniper covering her.
It's him. Gotta be!

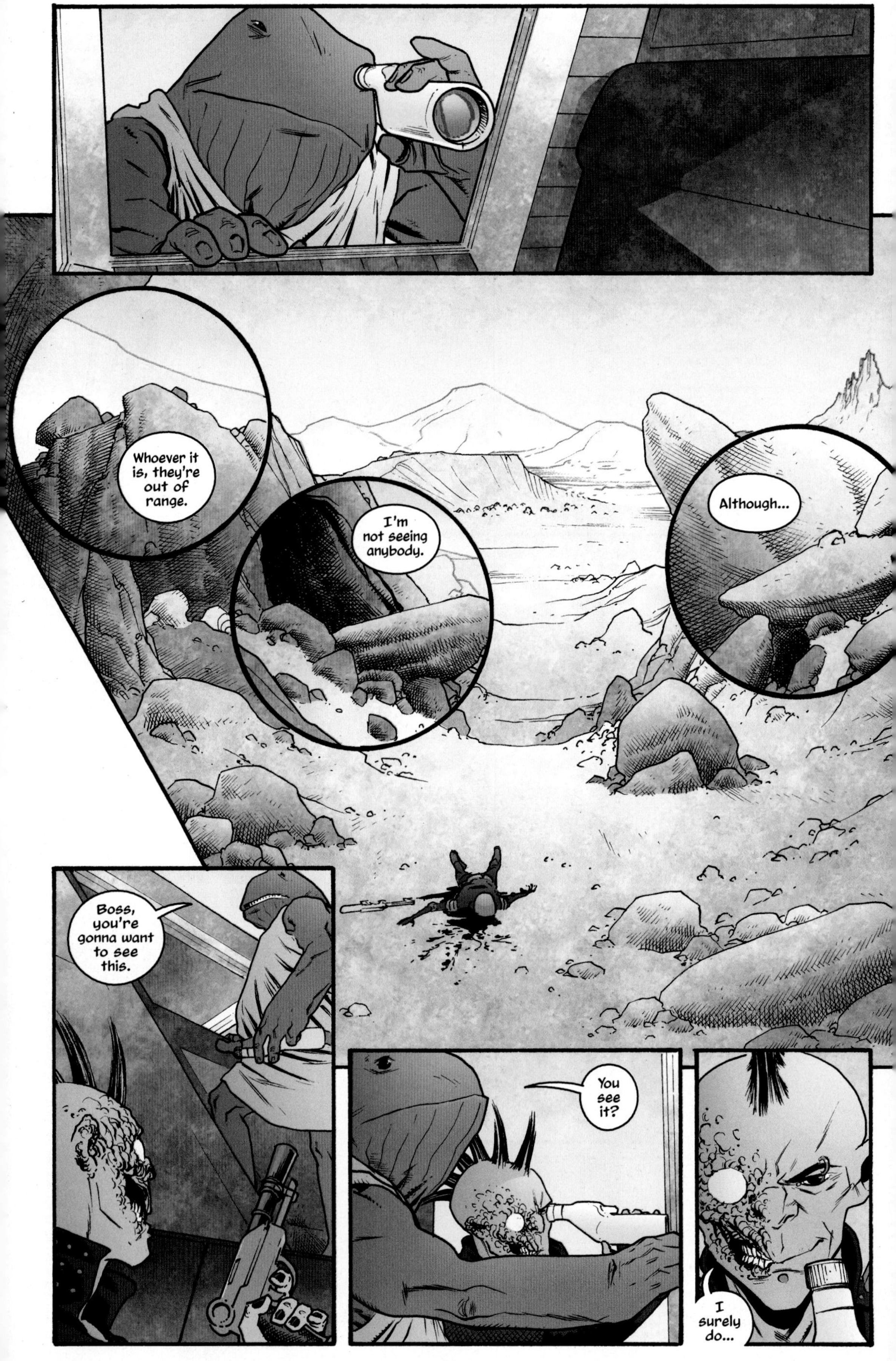
Whoever it is, they're out of range.
I'm not seeing anybody.
Although...
Boss, you're gonna want to see this.
You see it?
I surely do...

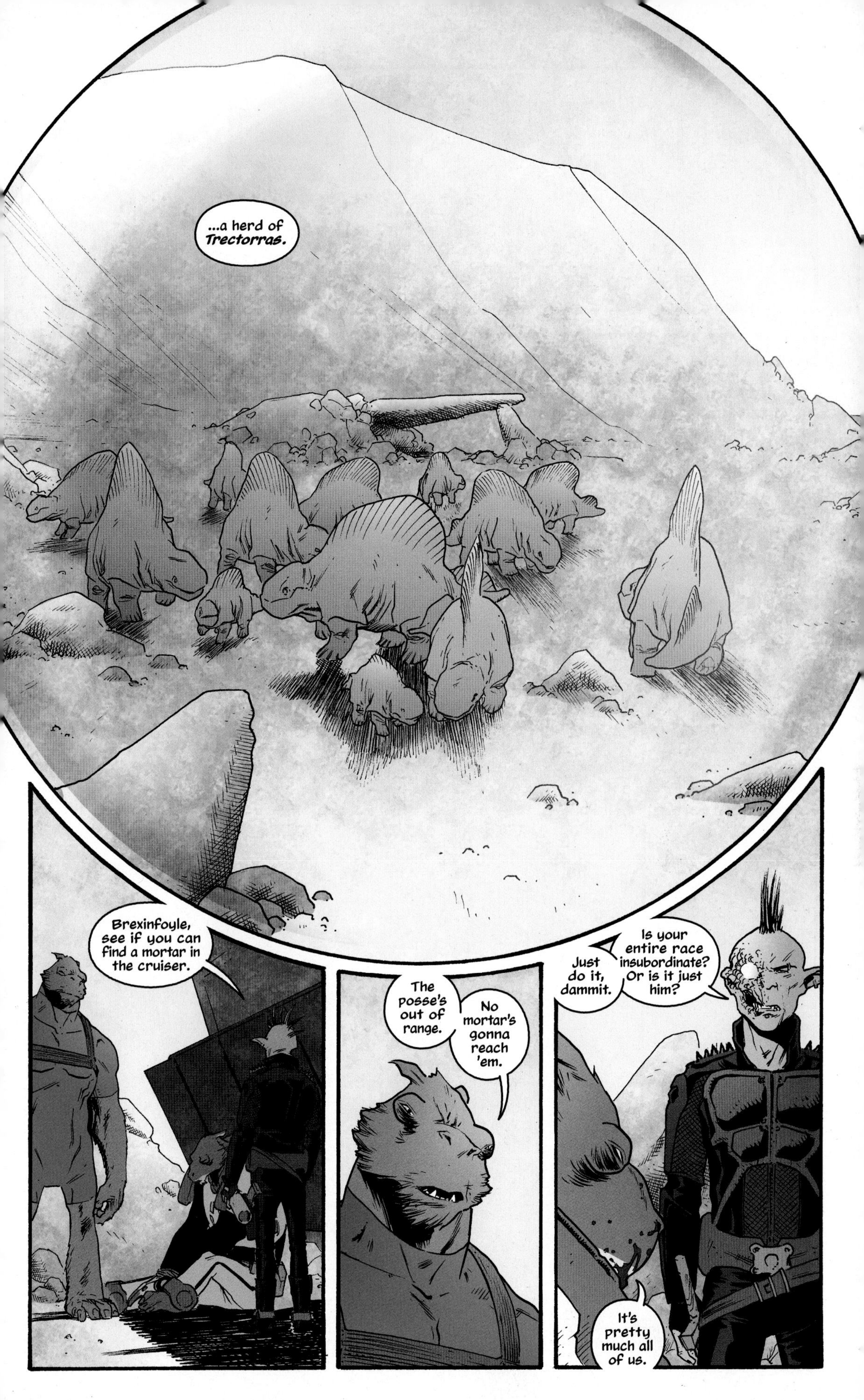

...a herd of *Trectorras.*
Brexinfoyle, see if you can find a mortar in the cruiser.
The posse's out of range.
No mortar's gonna reach 'em.
Just do it, dammit.
Is your entire race insubordinate? Or is it just him?
It's pretty much all of us.

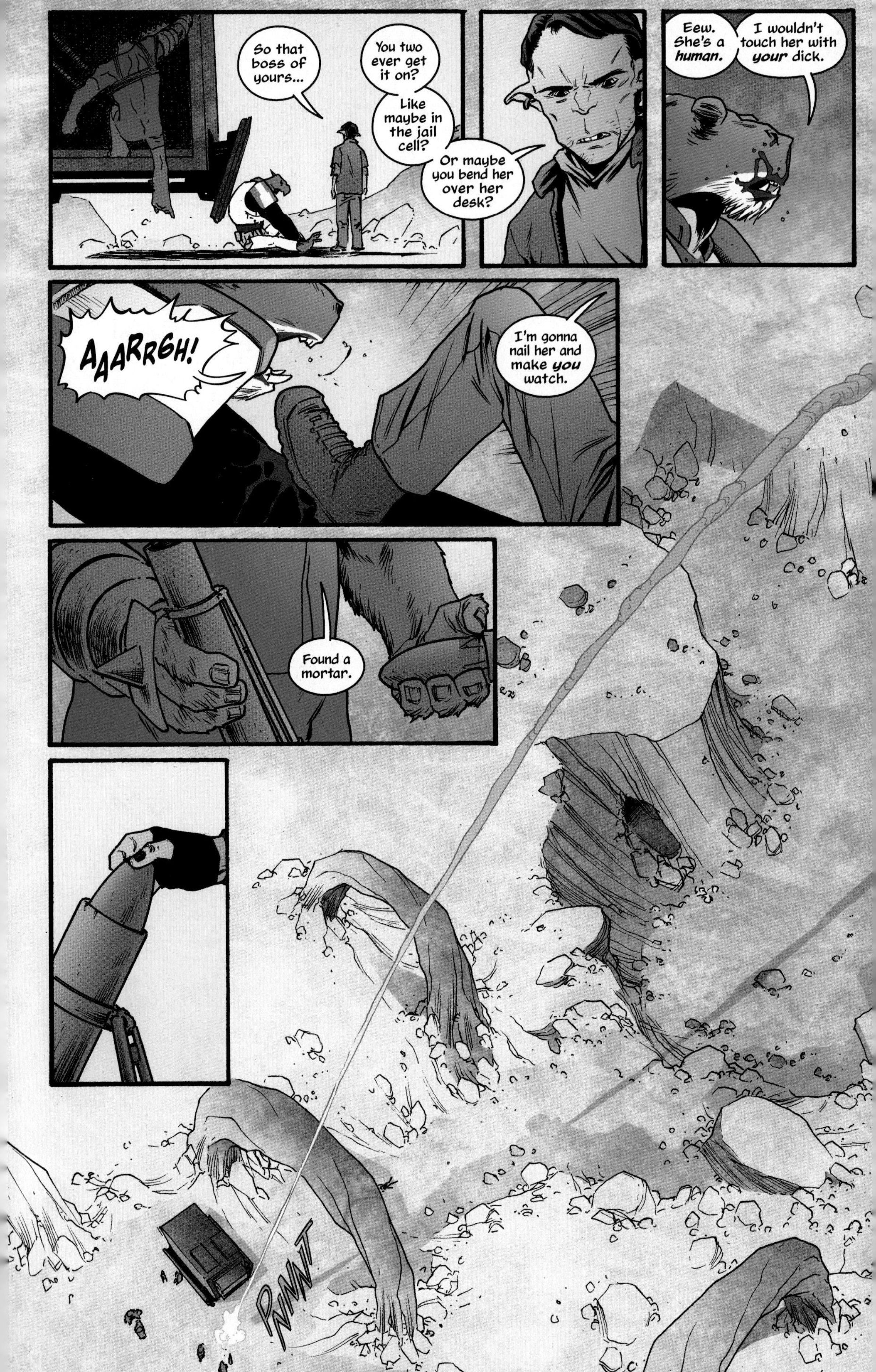
So that boss of yours...
You two ever get it on?
Like maybe in the jail cell?
Or maybe you bend her over her desk?
Eew. She's a *human.*
I wouldn't touch her with *your* dick.
AAARRGH!
I'm gonna nail her and make *you* watch.
Found a mortar.
PNNNT

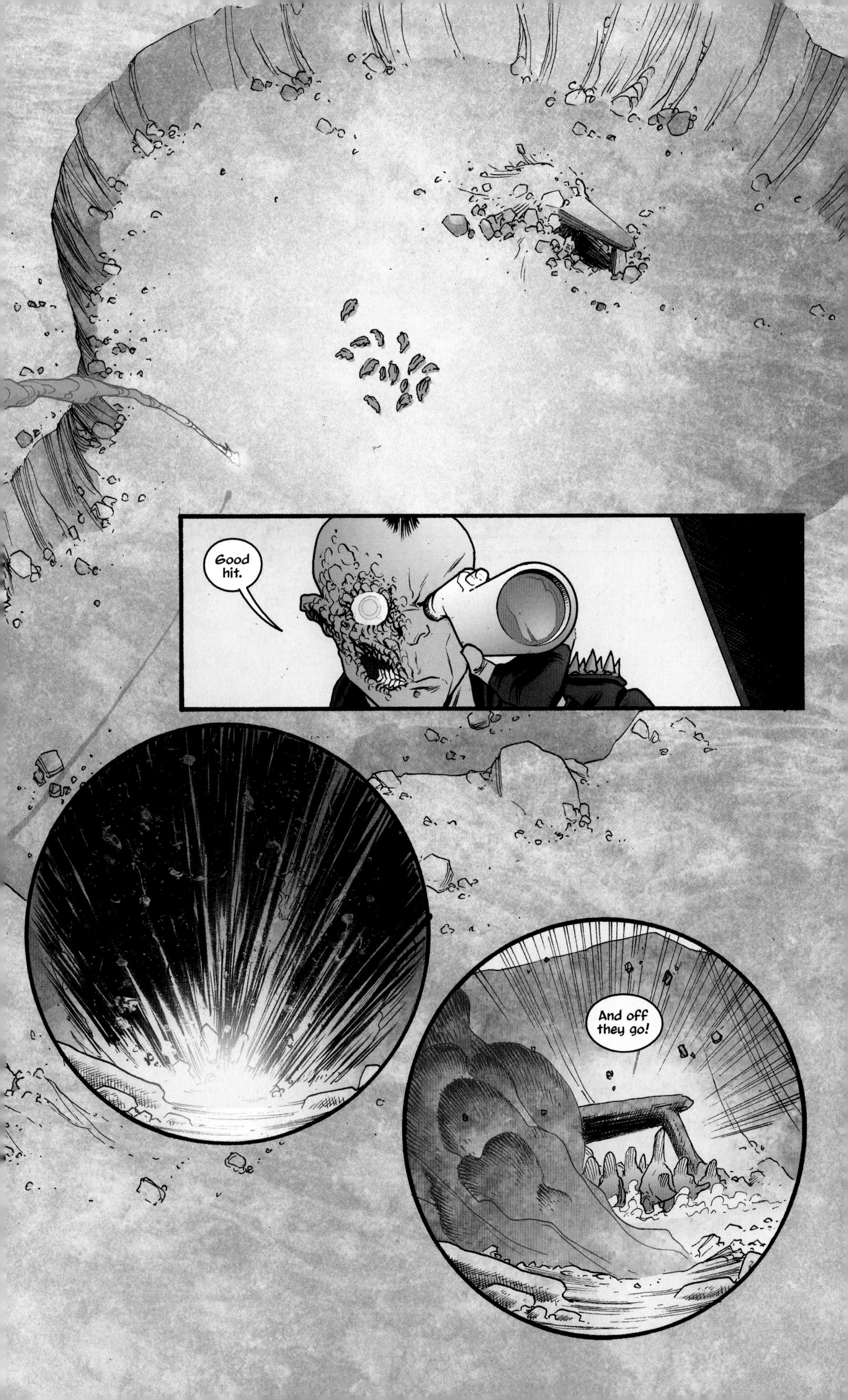
Good hit.
And off they go!

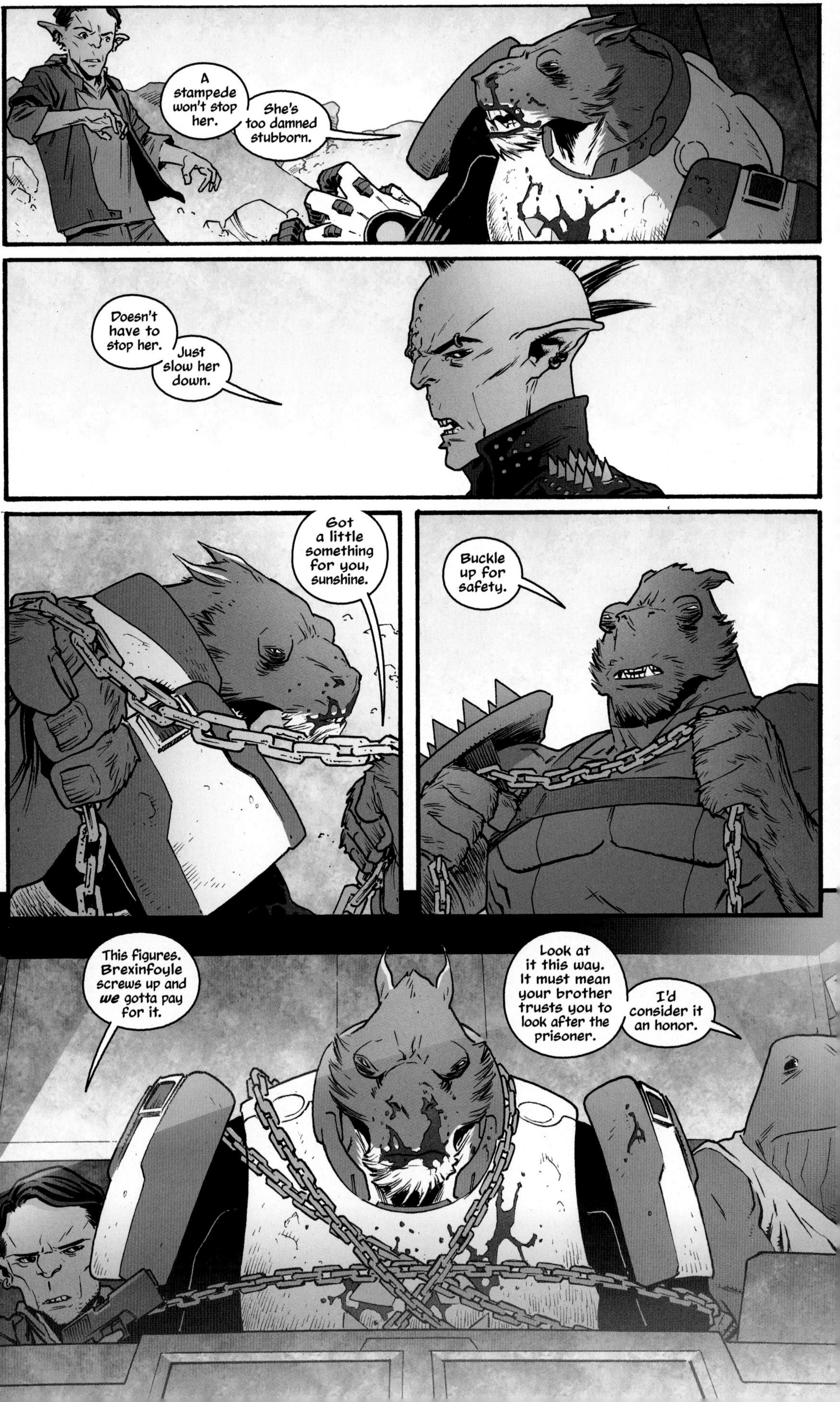
A stampede won't stop her.
She's too damned stubborn.
Doesn't have to stop her.
Just slow her down.
Got a little something for you, sunshine.
Buckle up for safety.
This figures. Brexinfoyle screws up and *we* gotta pay for it.
Look at it this way. It must mean your brother trusts you to look after the prisoner.
I'd consider it an honor.

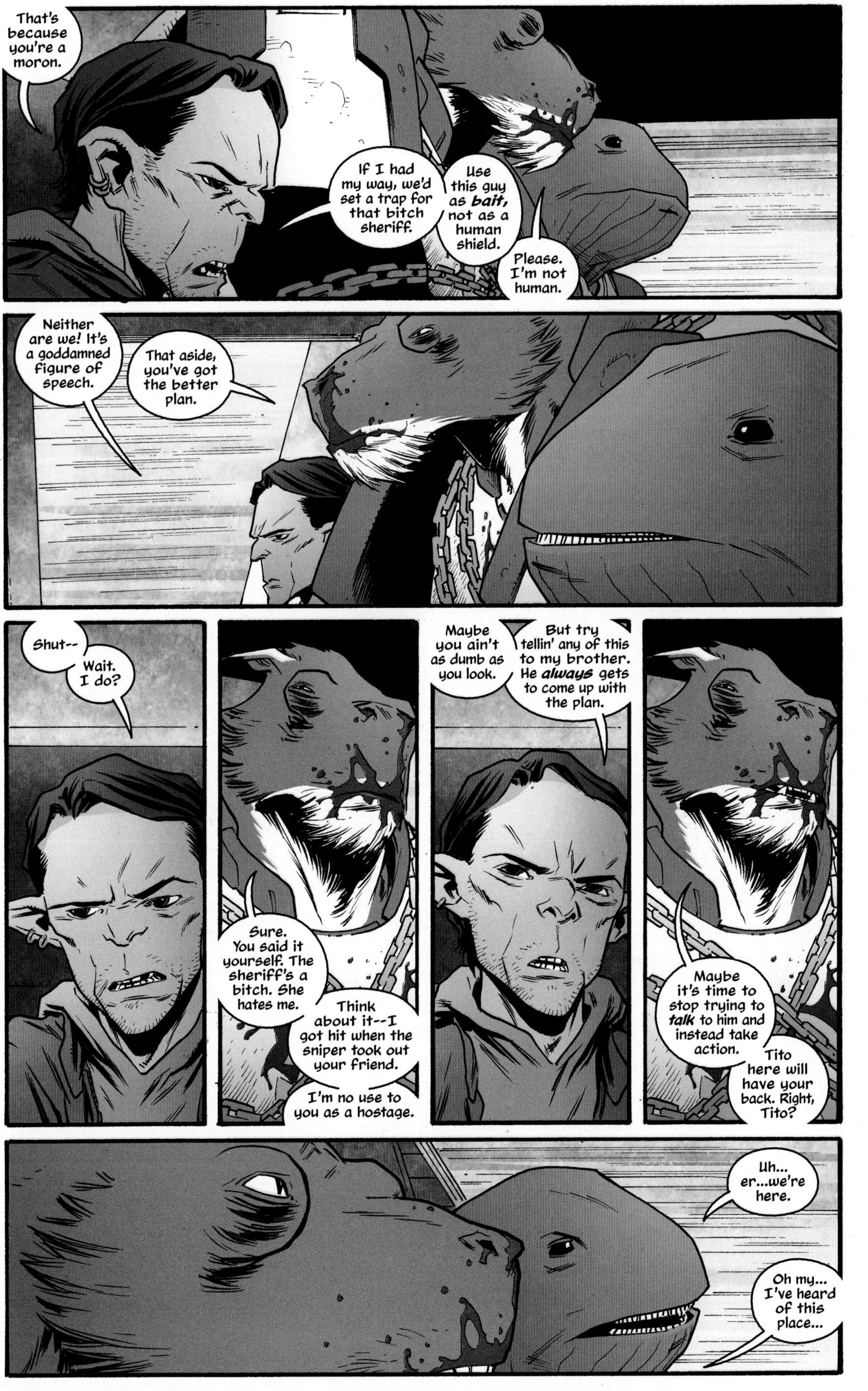
That's because you're a moron.
If I had my way, we'd set a trap for that bitch sheriff.
Use this guy as **bait,** not as a human shield.
Please. I'm not human.
Neither are we! It's a goddamned figure of speech.
That aside, you've got the better plan.
Shut--
Wait. I do?
Sure. You said it yourself. The sheriff's a bitch. She hates me.
Think about it--I got hit when the sniper took out your friend.
I'm no use to you as a hostage.
Maybe you ain't as dumb as you look.
But try tellin' any of this to my brother. He **always** gets to come up with the plan.
Maybe it's time to stop trying to **talk** to him and instead take action.
Tito here will have your back. Right, Tito?
Uh... er...we're here.
Oh my... I've heard of this place...

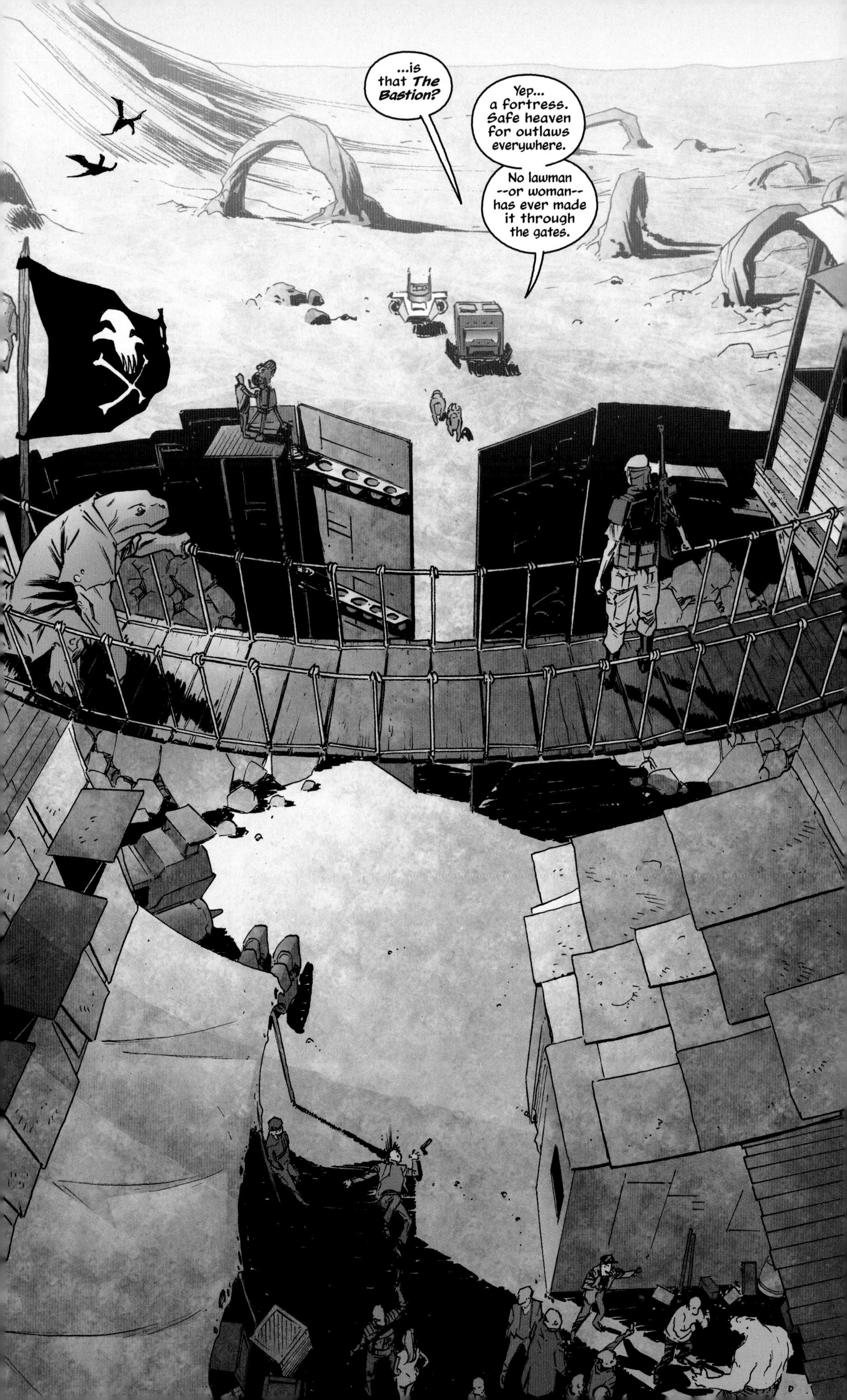
...is that *The Bastion?*
Yep... a fortress. Safe heaven for outlaws everywhere.
No lawman --or woman-- has ever made it through the gates.

CHAPTER IV

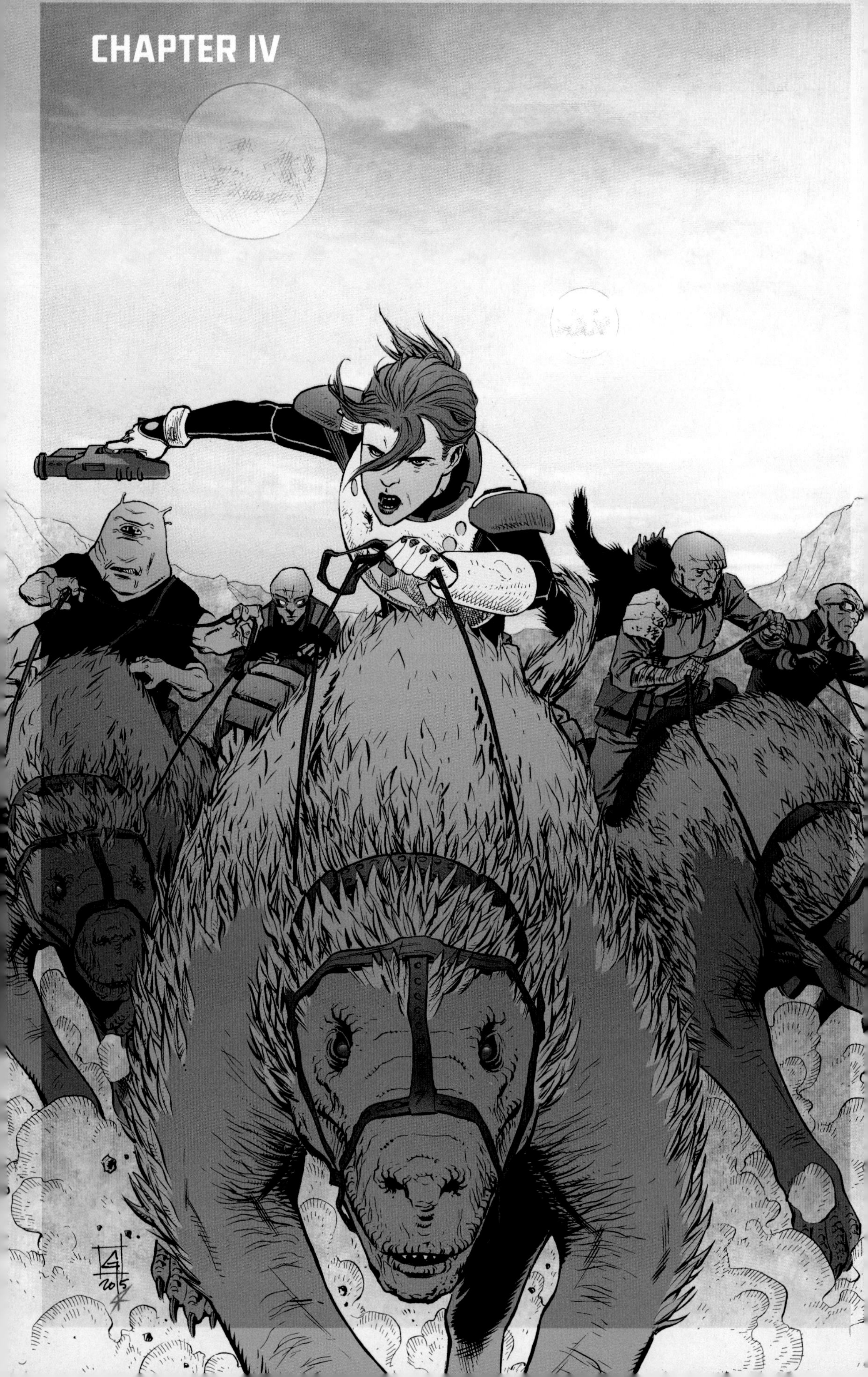

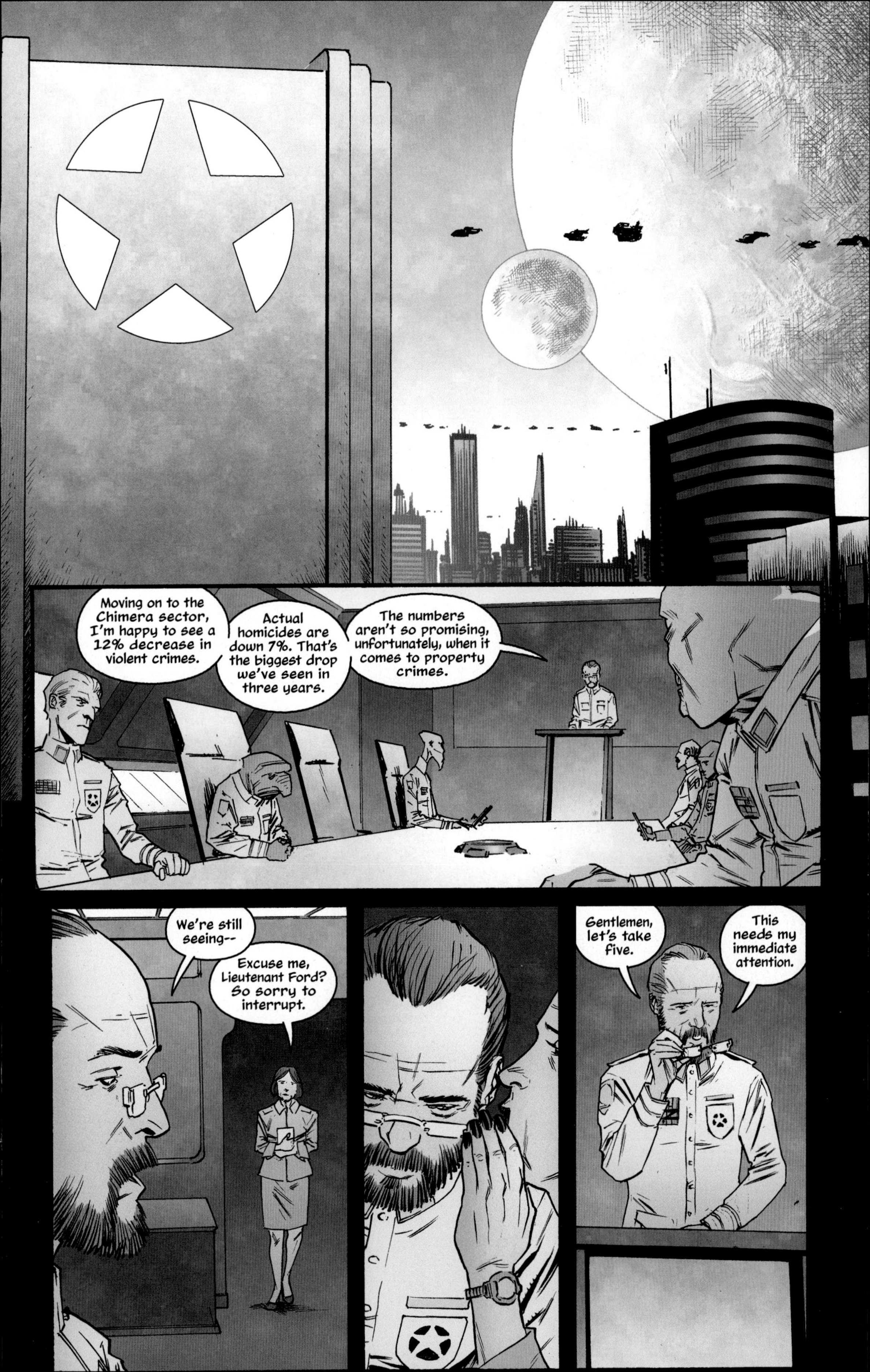
Moving on to the Chimera sector, I'm happy to see a 12% decrease in violent crimes.
Actual homicides are down 7%. That's the biggest drop we've seen in three years.
The numbers aren't so promising, unfortunately, when it comes to property crimes.
We're still seeing--
Excuse me, Lieutenant Ford? So sorry to interrupt.
Gentlemen, let's take five.
This needs my immediate attention.

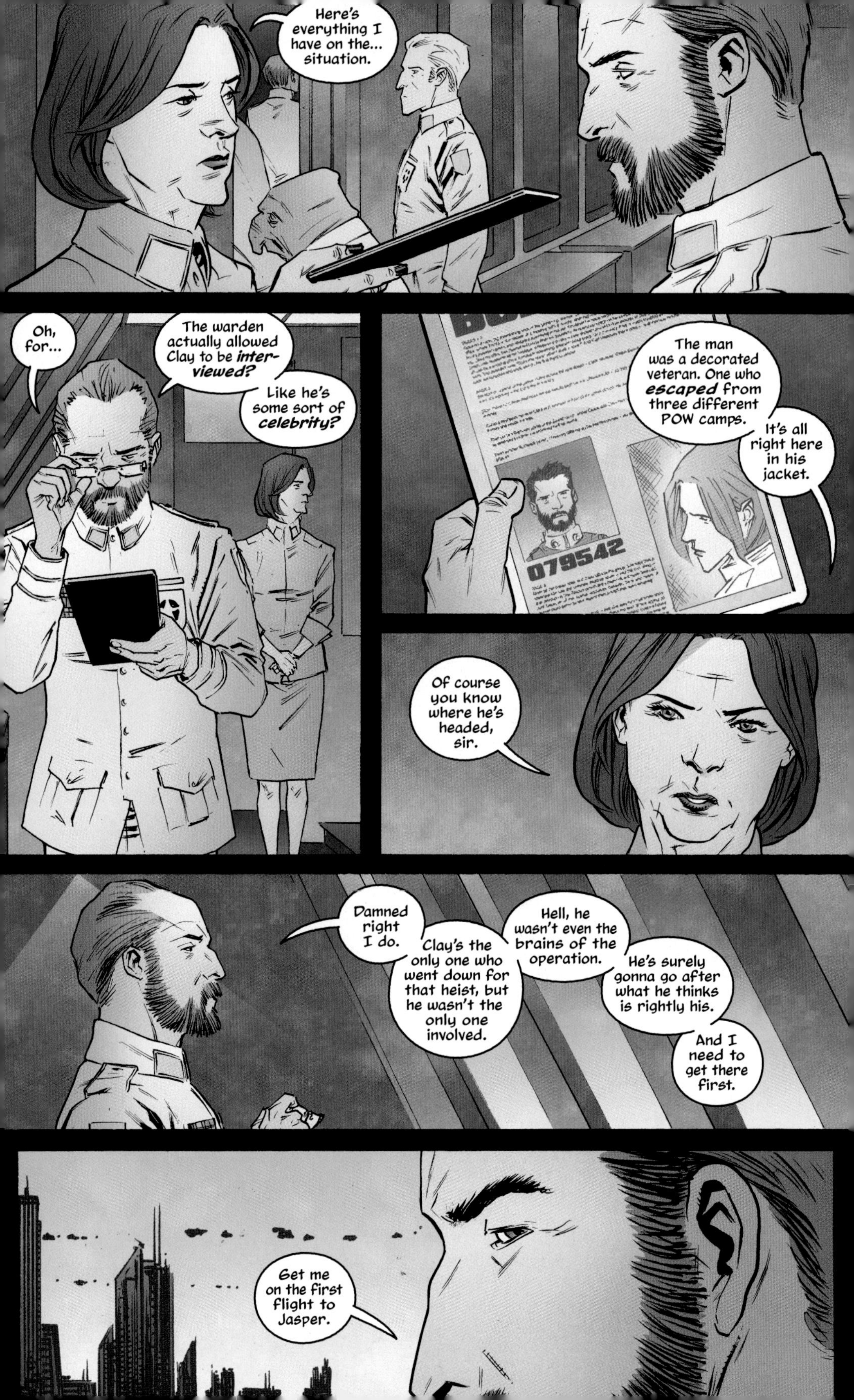
Here's everything I have on the... situation.
Oh, for...
The warden actually allowed Clay to be ***inter-viewed?***
Like he's some sort of ***celebrity?***
079542
The man was a decorated veteran. One who ***escaped*** from three different POW camps.
It's all right here in his jacket.
Of course you know where he's headed, sir.
Damned right I do.
Clay's the only one who went down for that heist, but he wasn't the only one involved.
Hell, he wasn't even the brains of the operation.
He's surely gonna go after what he thinks is rightly his.
And I need to get there first.
Get me on the first flight to Jasper.

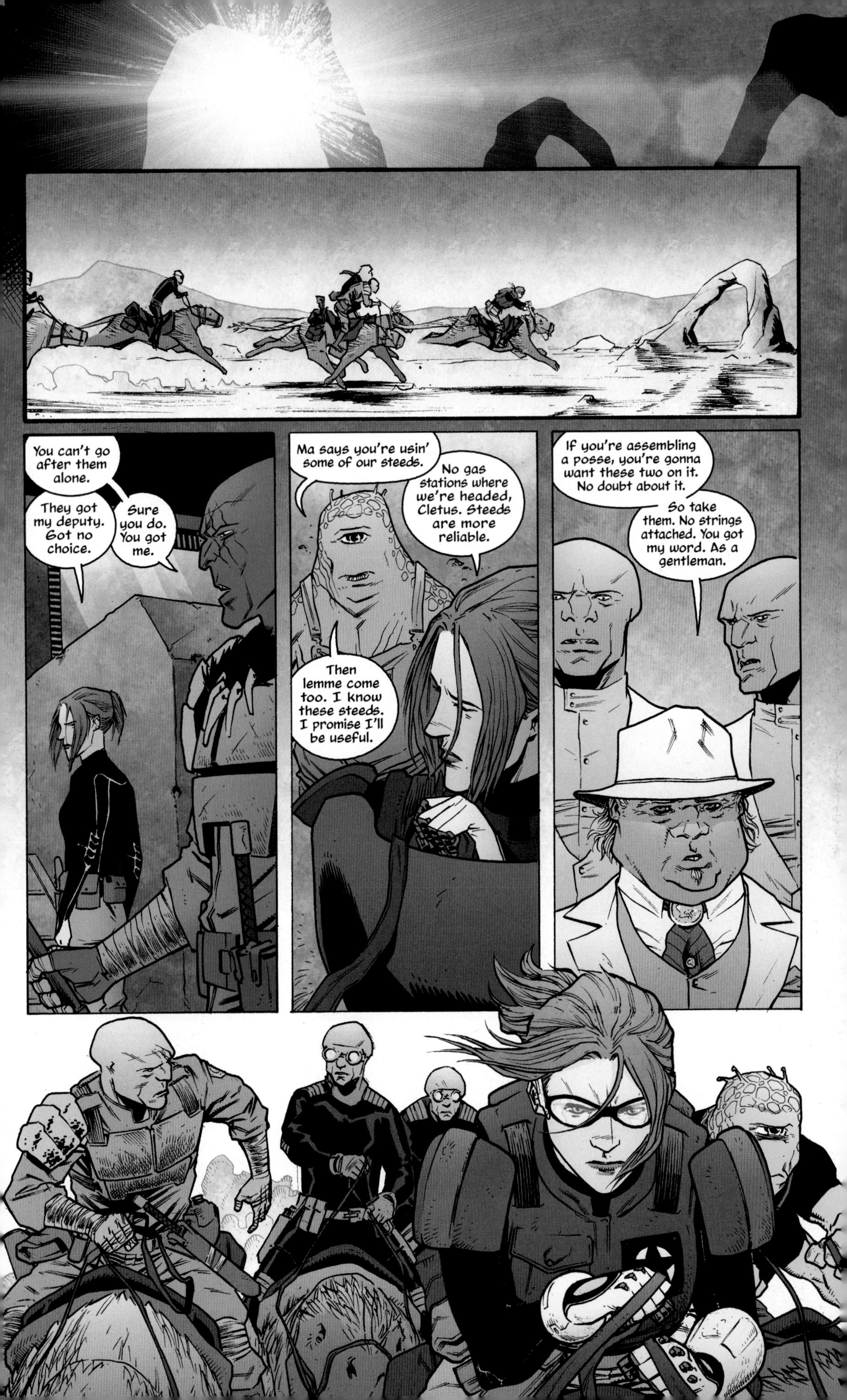
You can't go after them alone.
They got my deputy. Got no choice.
Sure you do. You got me.
Ma says you're usin' some of our steeds.
No gas stations where we're headed, Cletus. Steeds are more reliable.
Then lemme come too. I know these steeds. I promise I'll be useful.
If you're assembling a posse, you're gonna want these two on it. No doubt about it.
So take them. No strings attached. You got my word. As a gentleman.

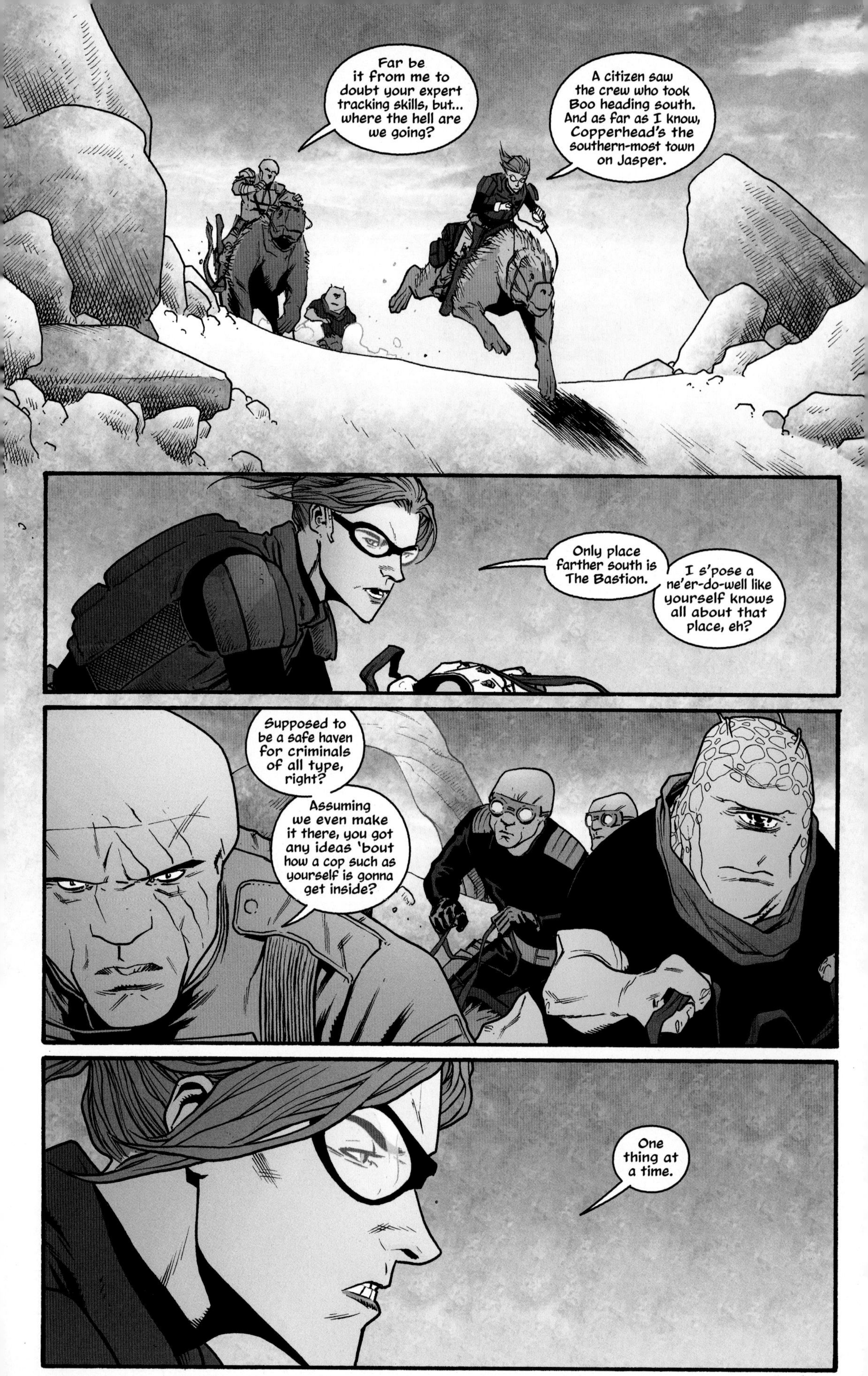
Far be it from me to doubt your expert tracking skills, but... where the hell are we going?
A citizen saw the crew who took Boo heading south. And as far as I know, Copperhead's the southern-most town on Jasper.
Only place farther south is The Bastion.
I s'pose a ne'er-do-well like yourself knows all about that place, eh?
Supposed to be a safe haven for criminals of all type, right?
Assuming we even make it there, you got any ideas 'bout how a cop such as yourself is gonna get inside?
One thing at a time.

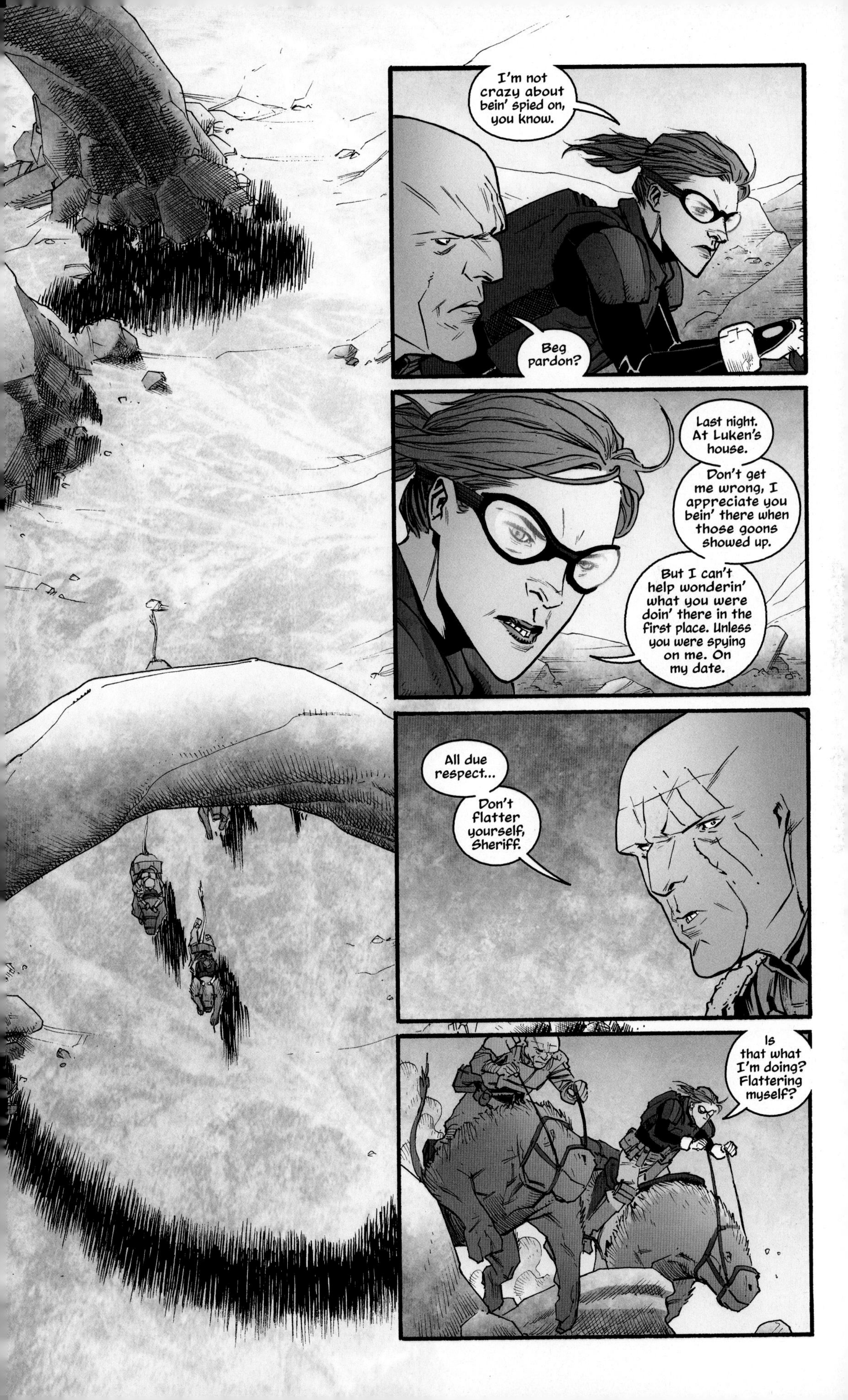
I'm not crazy about bein' spied on, you know.
Beg pardon?
Last night. At Luken's house.
Don't get me wrong, I appreciate you bein' there when those goons showed up.
But I can't help wonderin' what you were doin' there in the first place. Unless you were spying on me. On my date.
All due respect...
Don't flatter yourself, Sheriff.
Is that what I'm doing? Flattering myself?

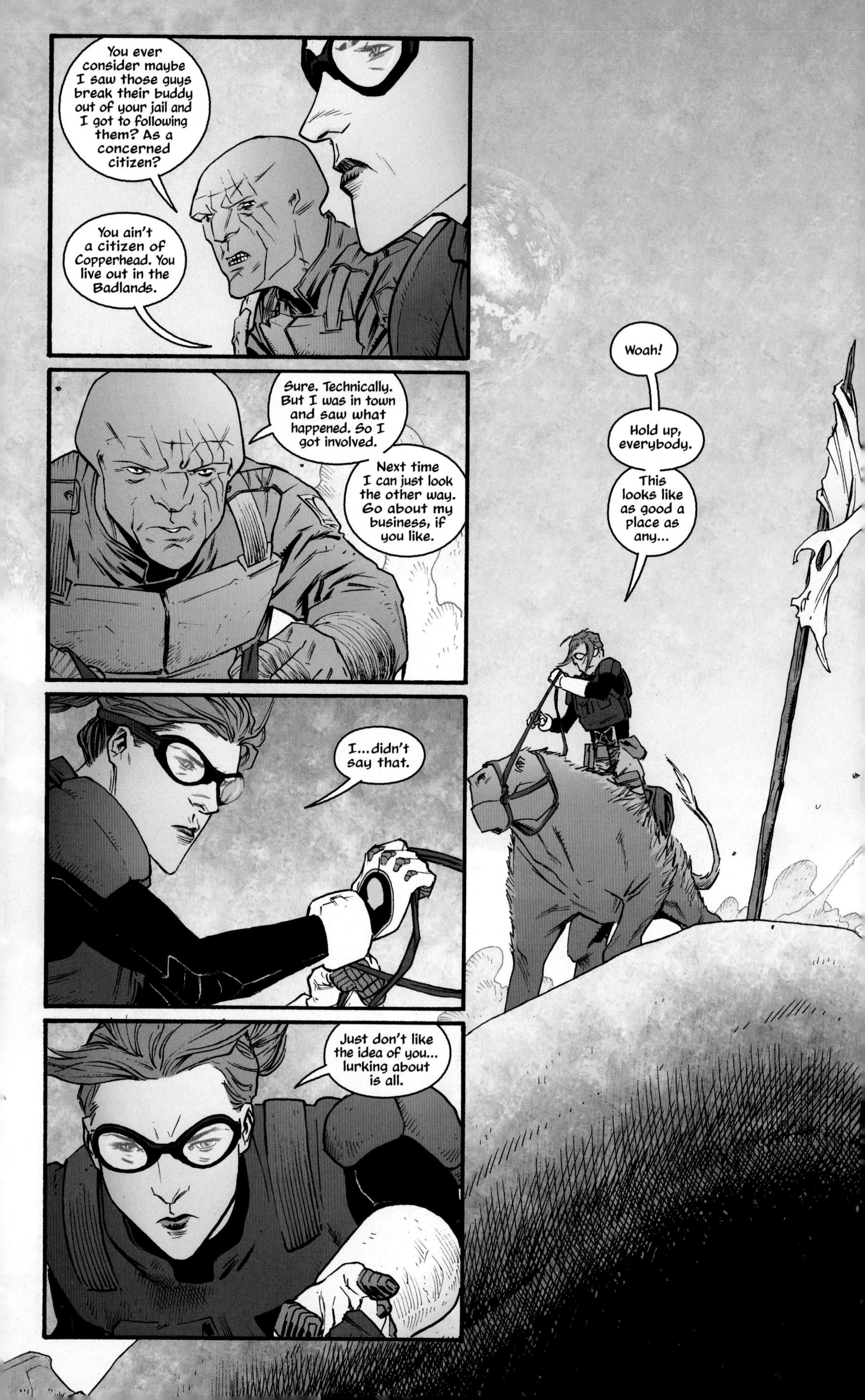
You ever consider maybe I saw those guys break their buddy out of your jail and I got to following them? As a concerned citizen?
You ain't a citizen of Copperhead. You live out in the Badlands.
Sure. Technically. But I was in town and saw what happened. So I got involved.
Next time I can just look the other way. Go about my business, if you like.
I...didn't say that.
Just don't like the idea of you... lurking about is all.
Woah!
Hold up, everybody.
This looks like as good a place as any...

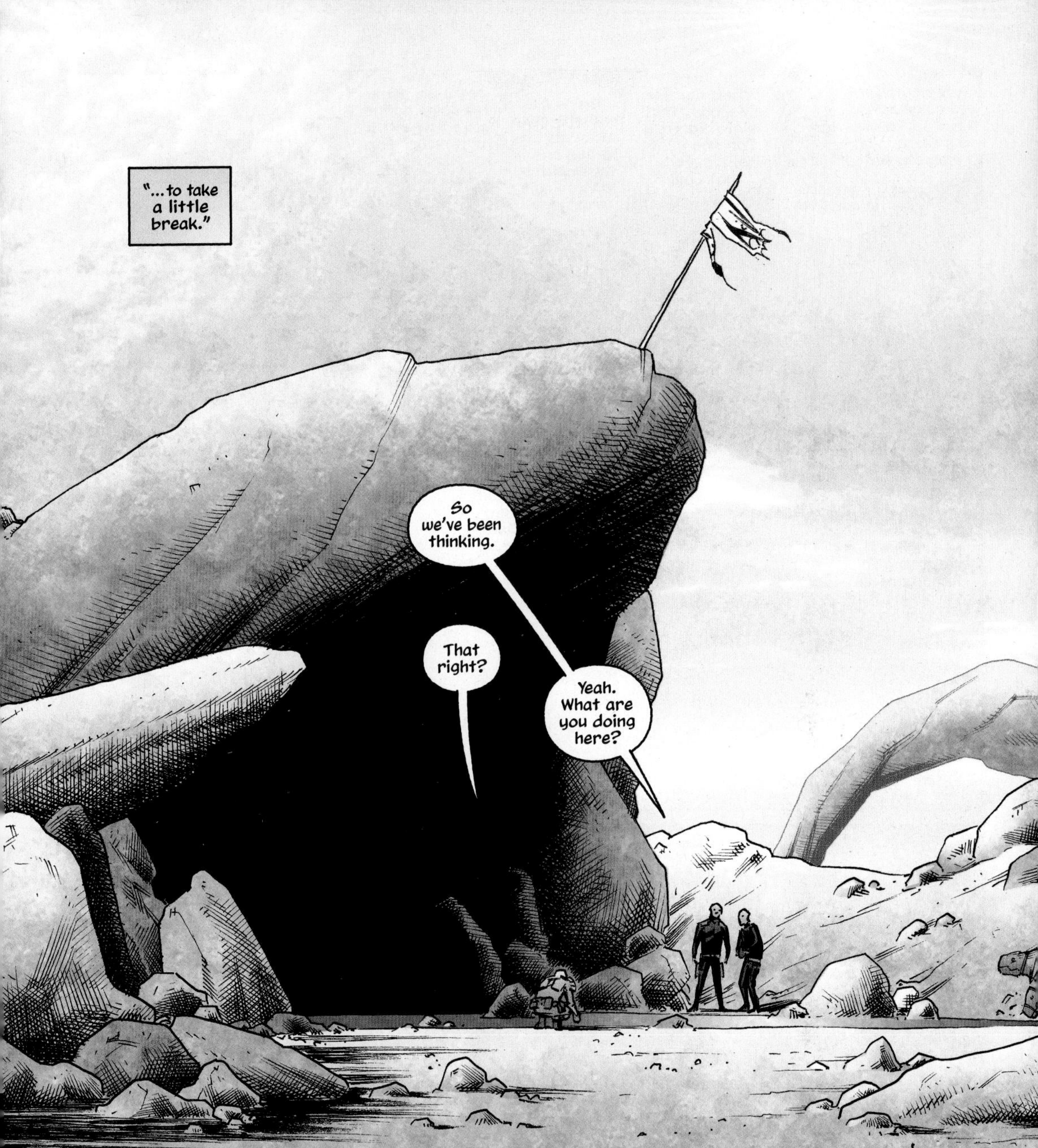
"...to take a little break."
So we've been thinking.
That right?
Yeah. What are you doing here?

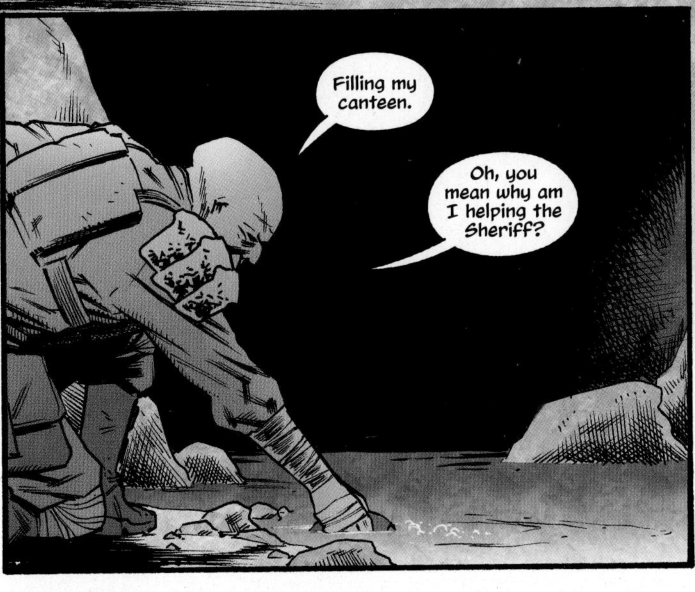
Filling my canteen.
Oh, you mean why am I helping the Sheriff?

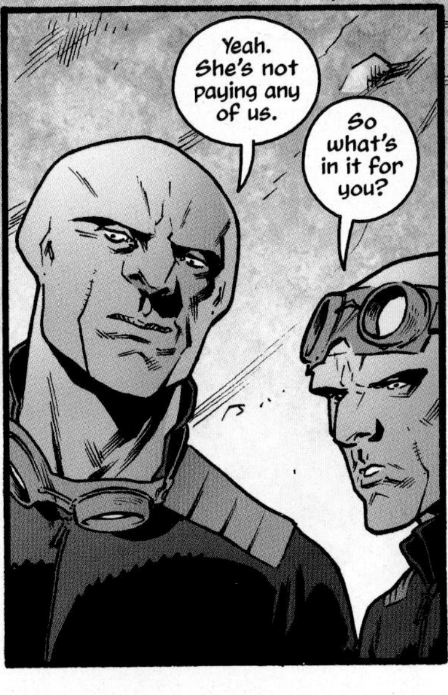
Yeah. She's not paying any of us.
So what's in it for you?

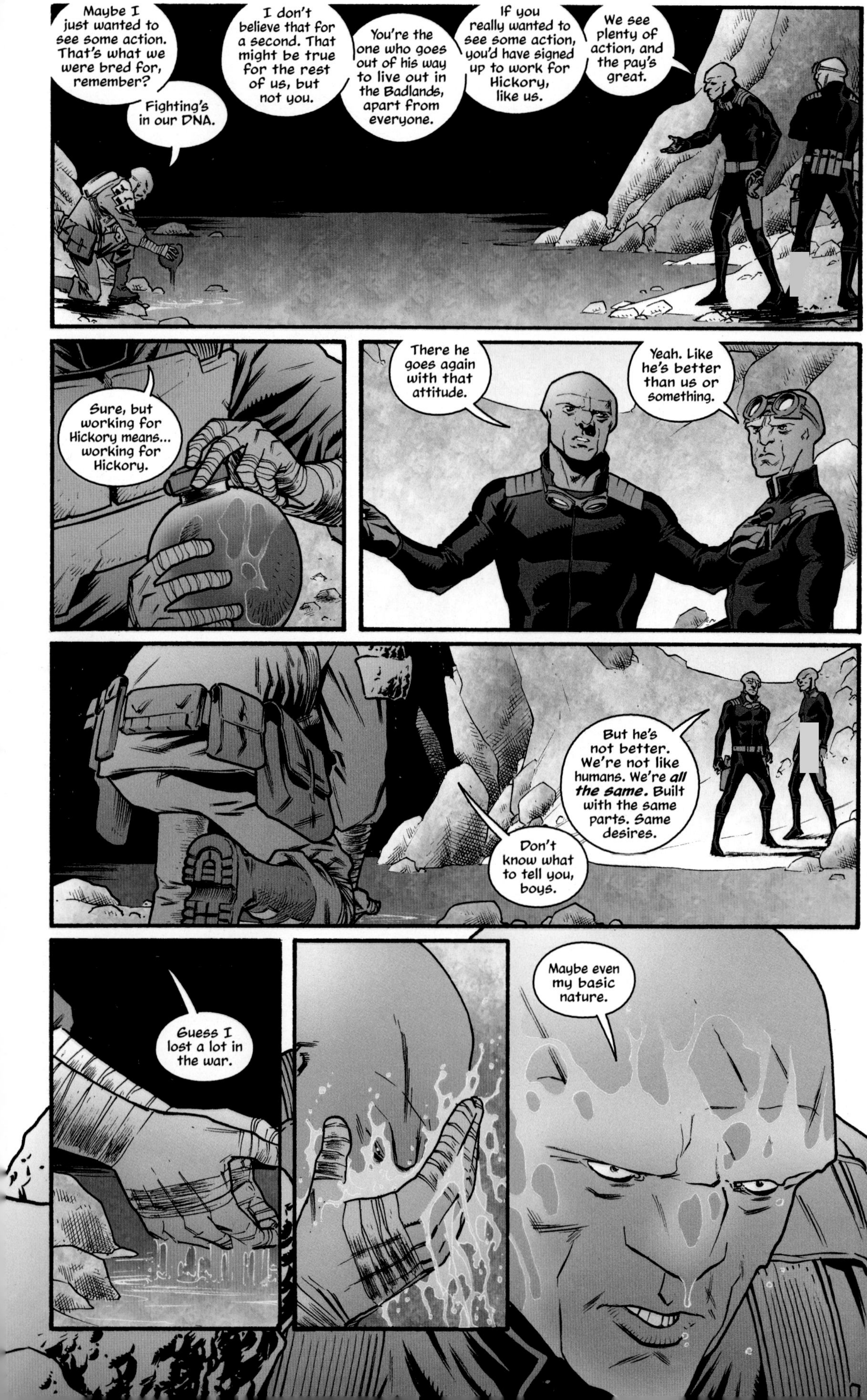
Maybe I just wanted to see some action. That's what we were bred for, remember?
Fighting's in our DNA.
I don't believe that for a second. That might be true for the rest of us, but not you.
You're the one who goes out of his way to live out in the Badlands, apart from everyone.
If you really wanted to see some action, you'd have signed up to work for Hickory, like us.
We see plenty of action, and the pay's great.
Sure, but working for Hickory means... working for Hickory.
There he goes again with that attitude.
Yeah. Like he's better than us or something.
But he's not better. We're not like humans. We're *all the same.* Built with the same parts. Same desires.
Don't know what to tell you, boys.
Guess I lost a lot in the war.
Maybe even my basic nature.

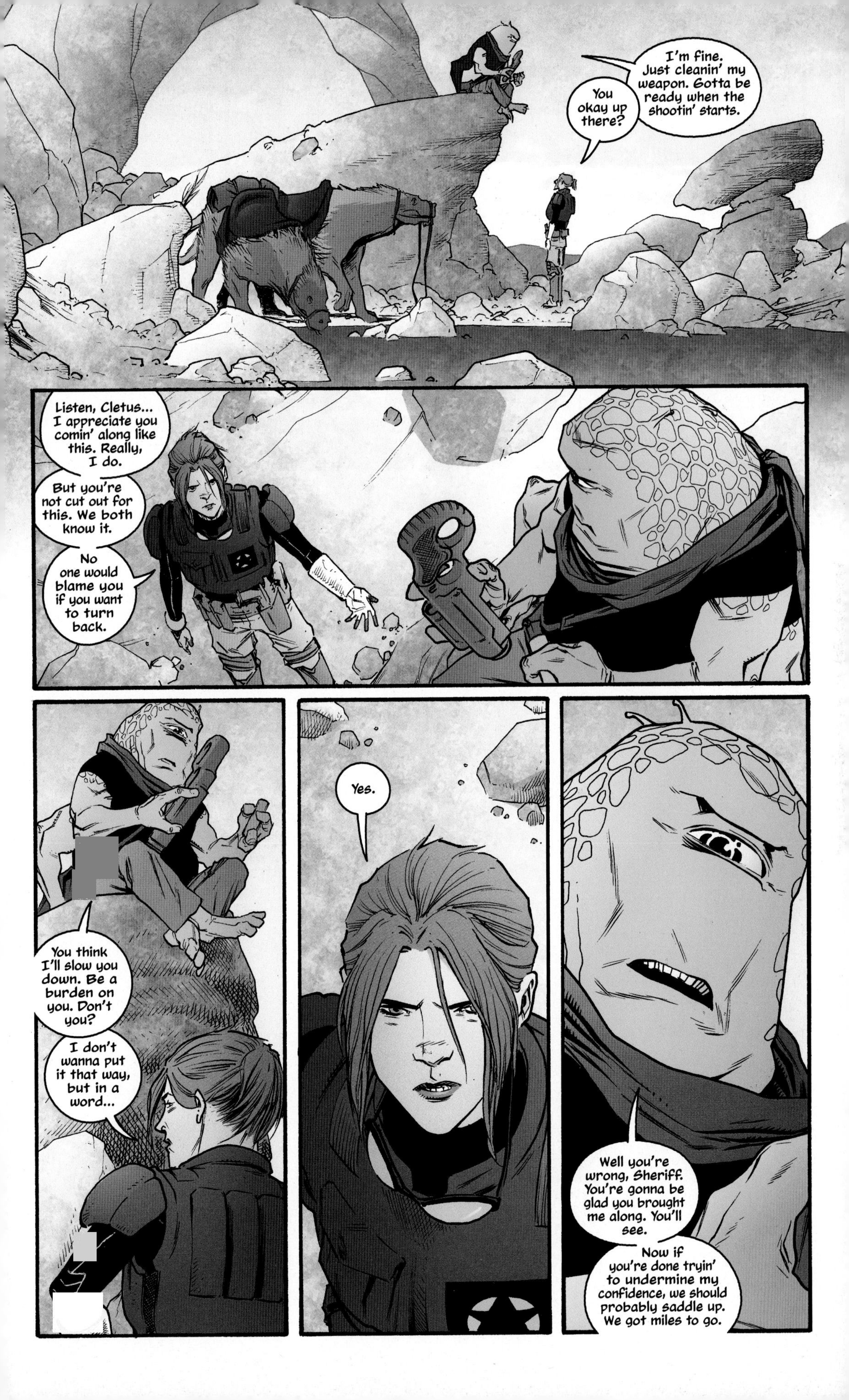
You okay up there?
I'm fine. Just cleanin' my weapon. Gotta be ready when the shootin' starts.
Listen, Cletus... I appreciate you comin' along like this. Really, I do.
But you're not cut out for this. We both know it.
No one would blame you if you want to turn back.
You think I'll slow you down. Be a burden on you. Don't you?
I don't wanna put it that way, but in a word...
Yes.
Well you're wrong, Sheriff. You're gonna be glad you brought me along. You'll see.
Now if you're done tryin' to undermine my confidence, we should probably saddle up. We got miles to go.

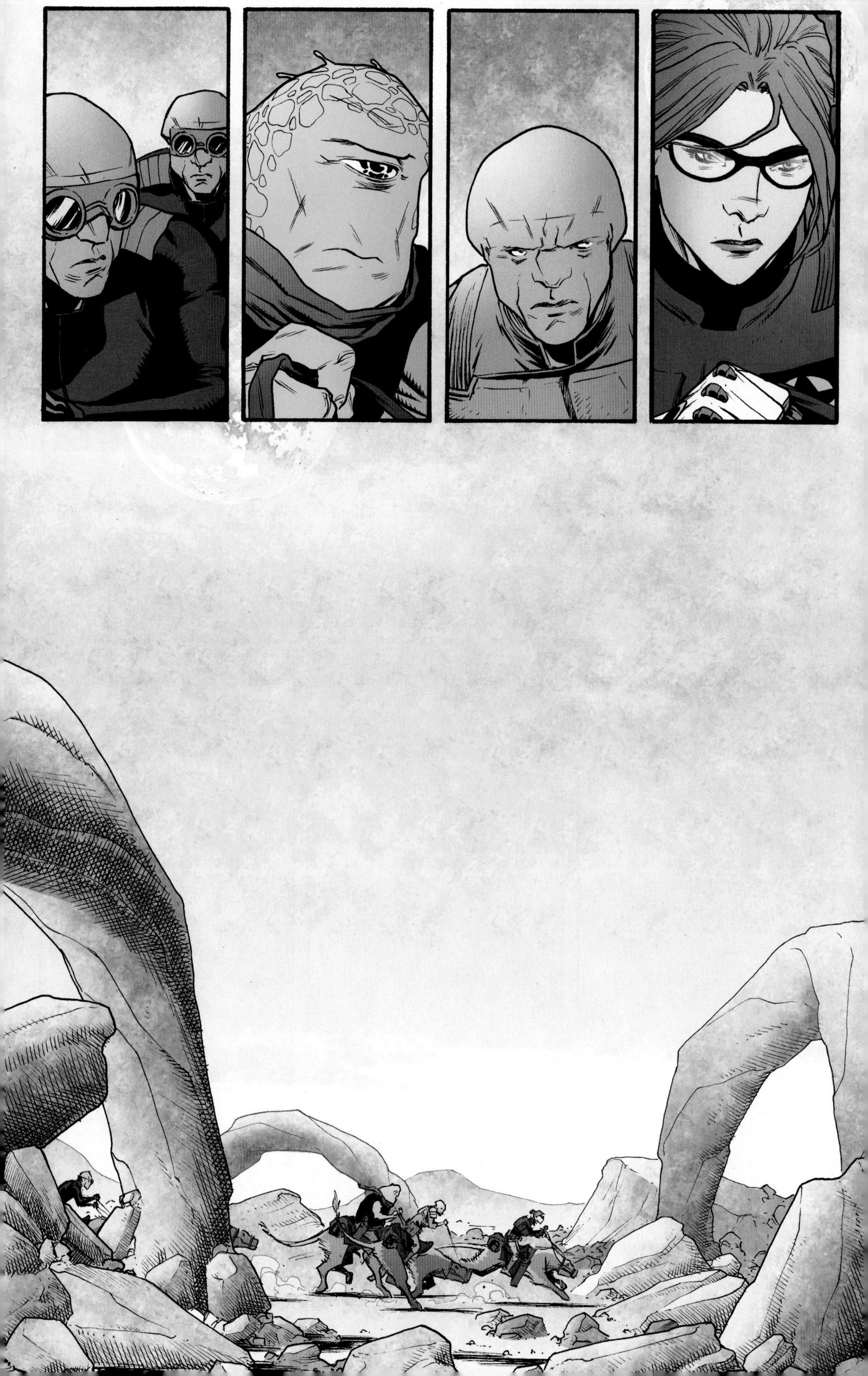

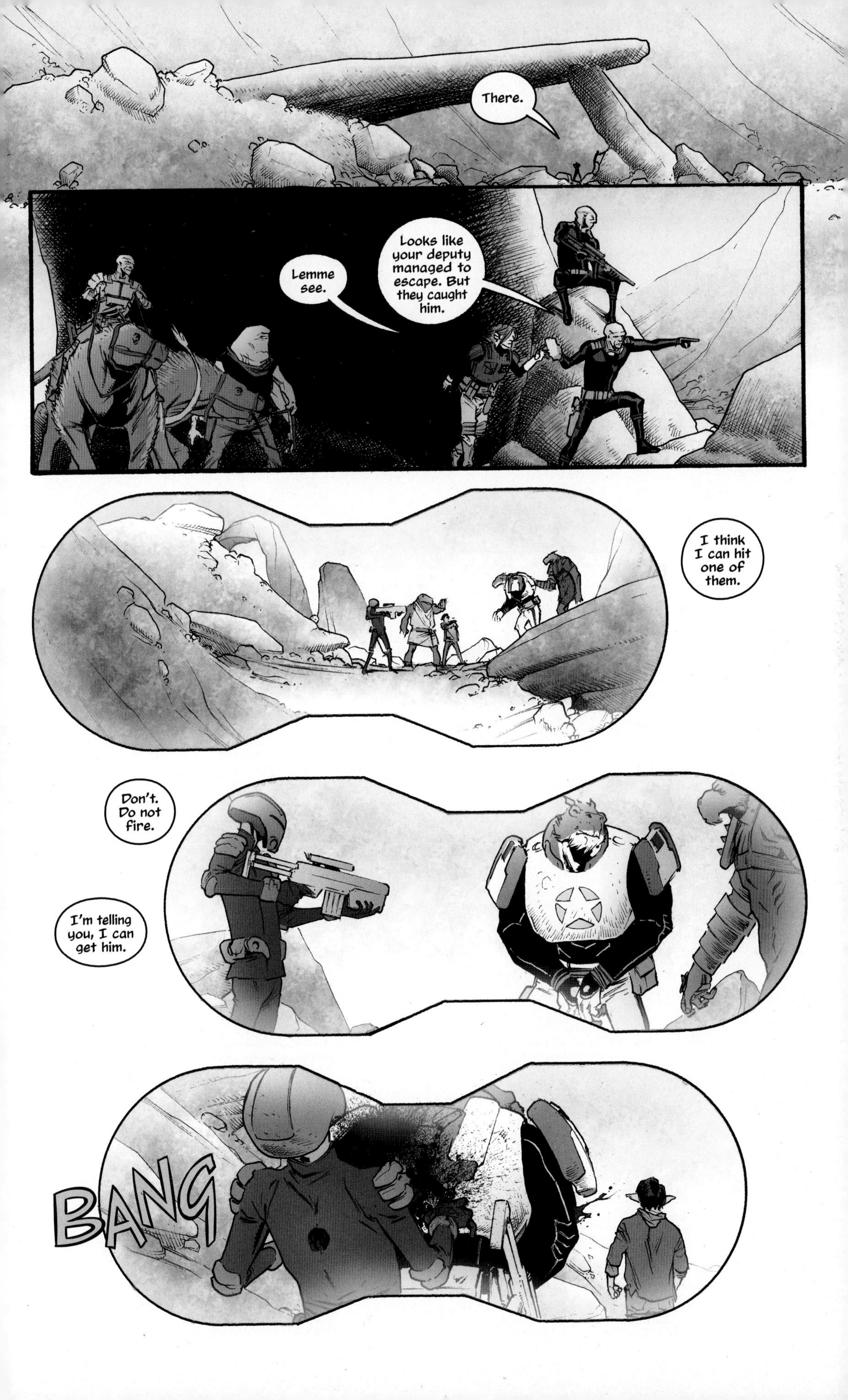
There.
Lemme see.
Looks like your deputy managed to escape. But they caught him.
I think I can hit one of them.
Don't. Do not fire.
I'm telling you, I can get him.
BANG

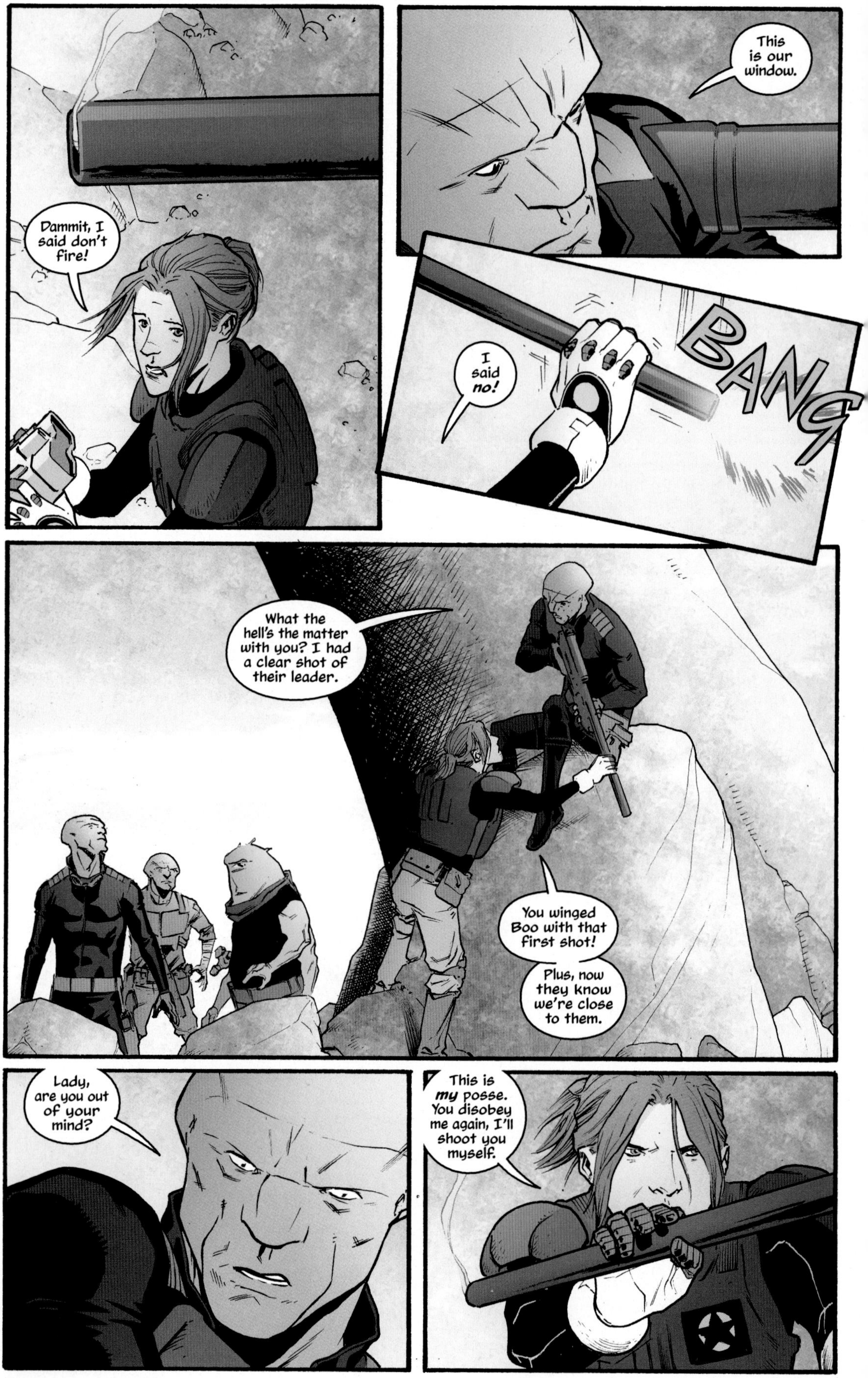

Dammit, I said don't fire!
This is our window.
I said no!
BANG
What the hell's the matter with you? I had a clear shot of their leader.
You winged Boo with that first shot!
Plus, now they know we're close to them.
Lady, are you out of your mind?
This is my posse. You disobey me again, I'll shoot you myself.

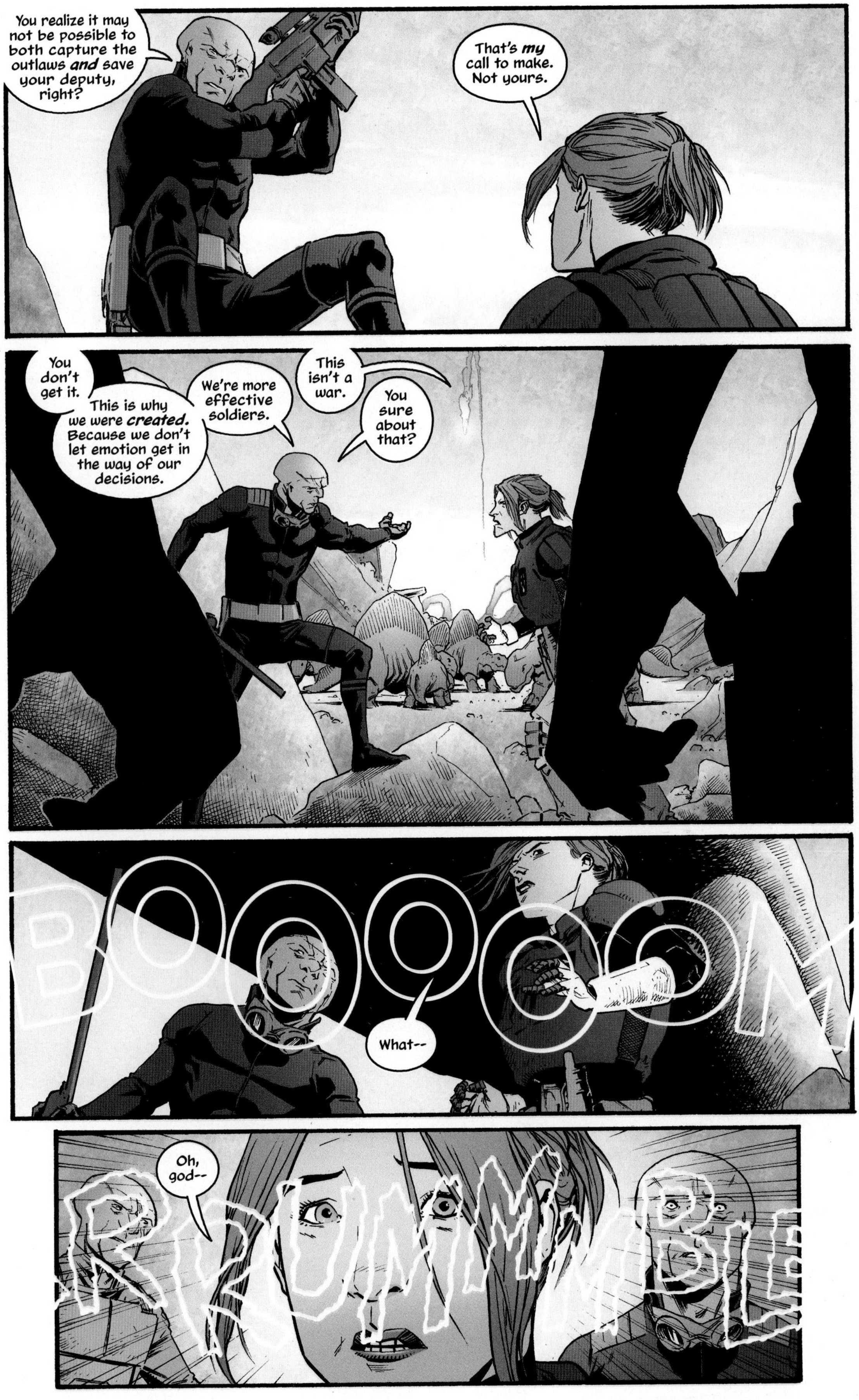
You realize it may not be possible to both capture the outlaws *and* save your deputy, right?
That's *my* call to make. Not yours.
You don't get it.
This is why we were *created.* Because we don't let emotion get in the way of our decisions.
We're more effective soldiers.
This isn't a war.
You sure about that?
BOOOOOM
What--
Oh, god--
RRUMMBLE

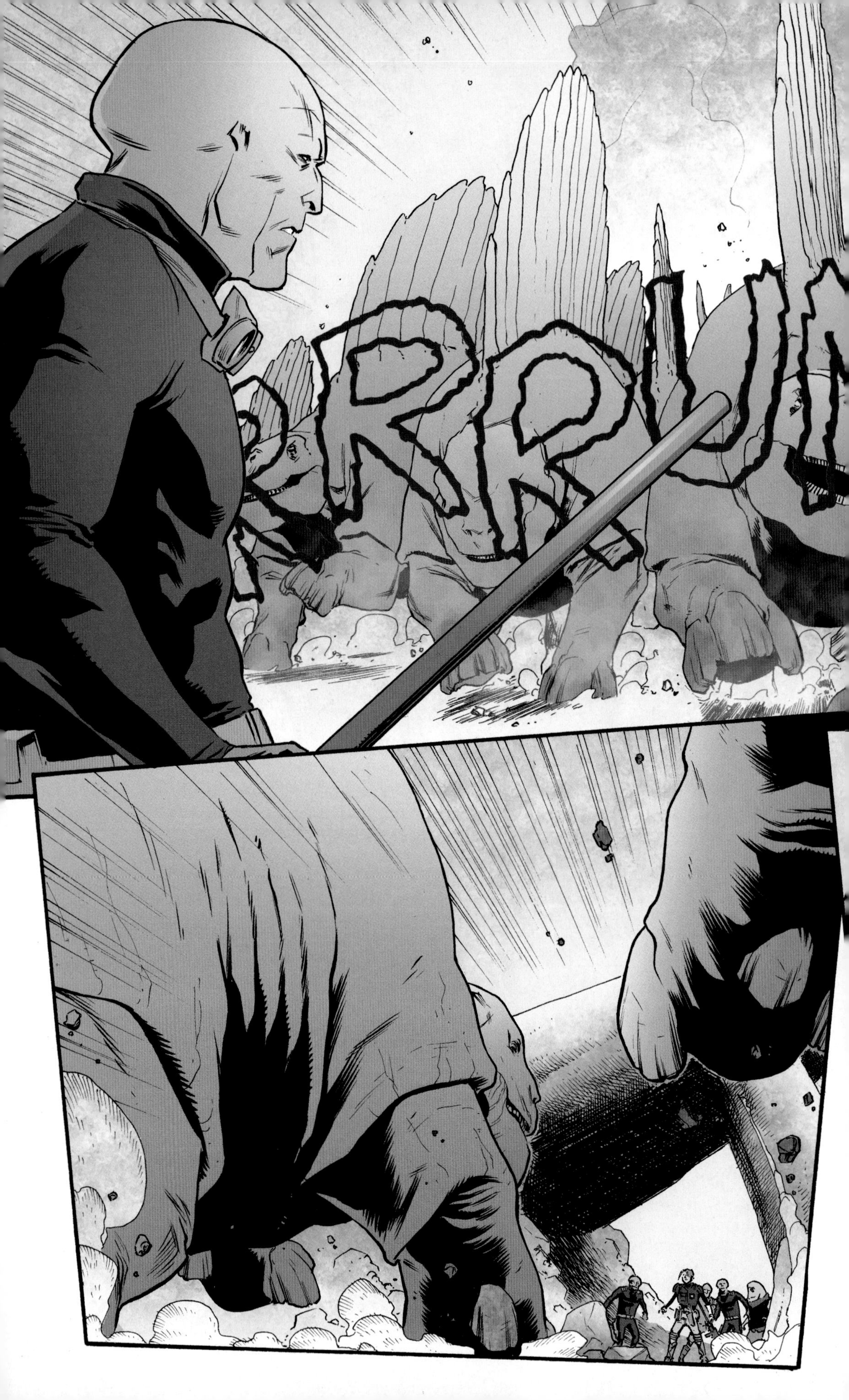
RRRUM

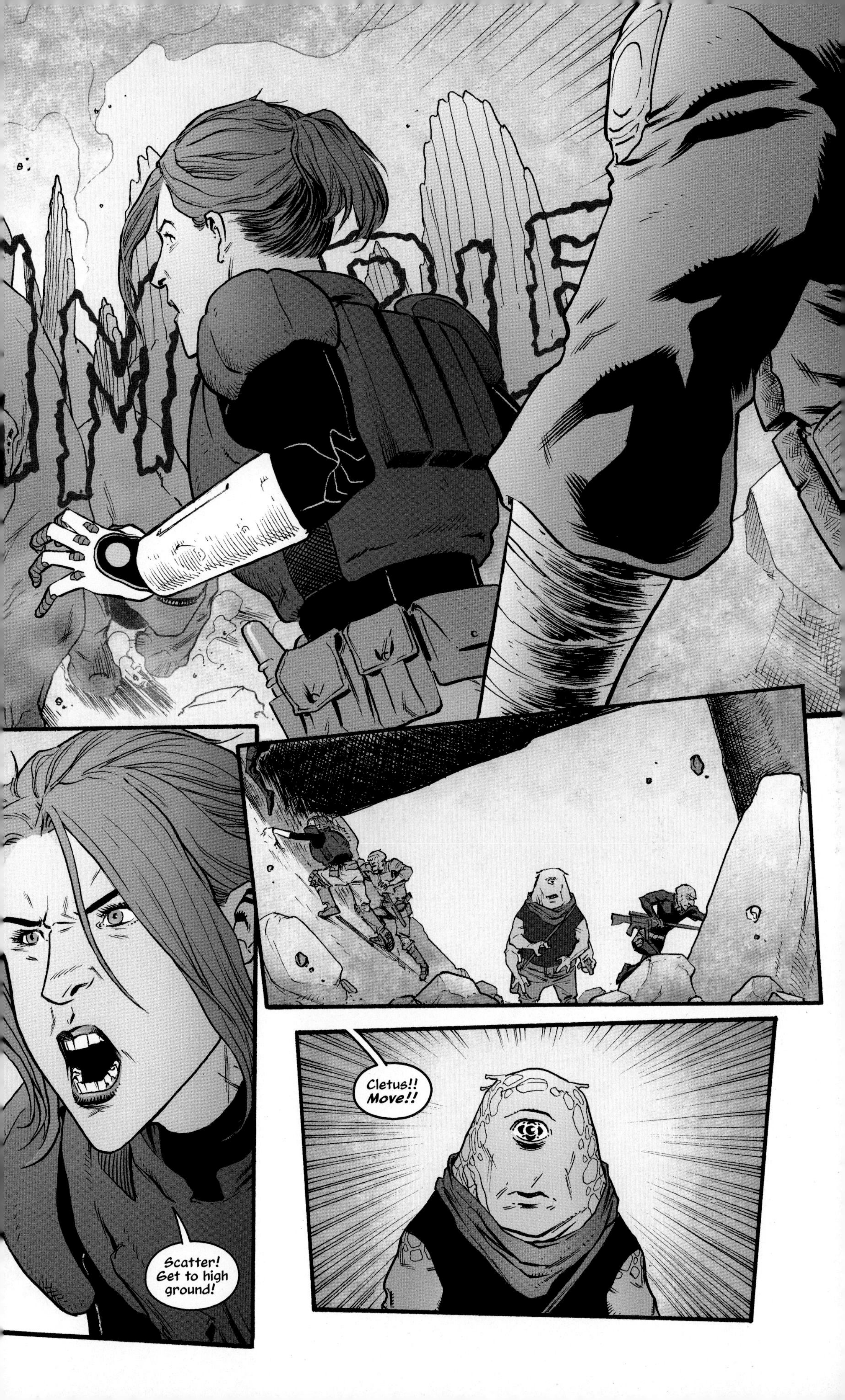
Scatter! Get to high ground!
Cletus!! Move!!

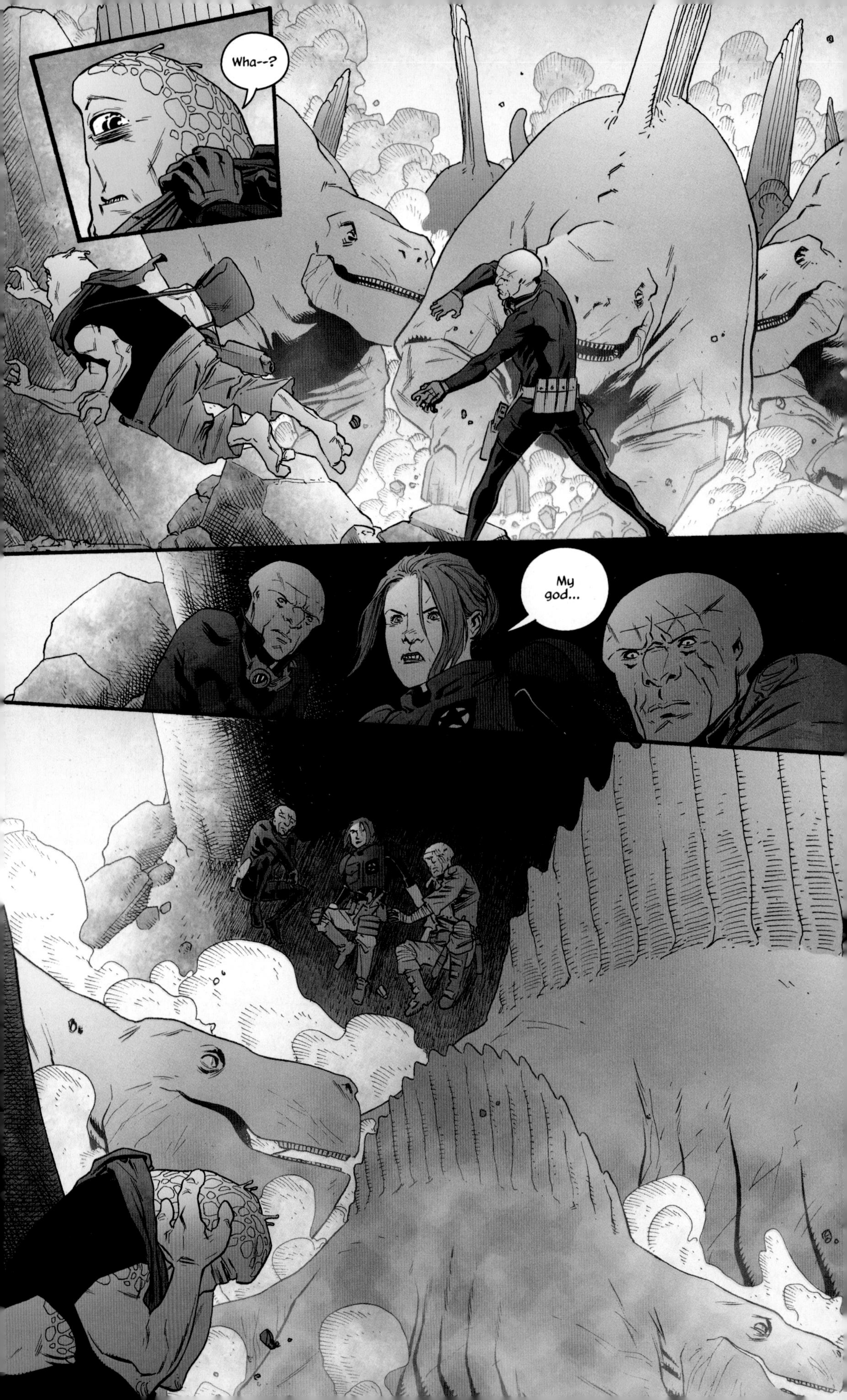
Wha--?
My god...

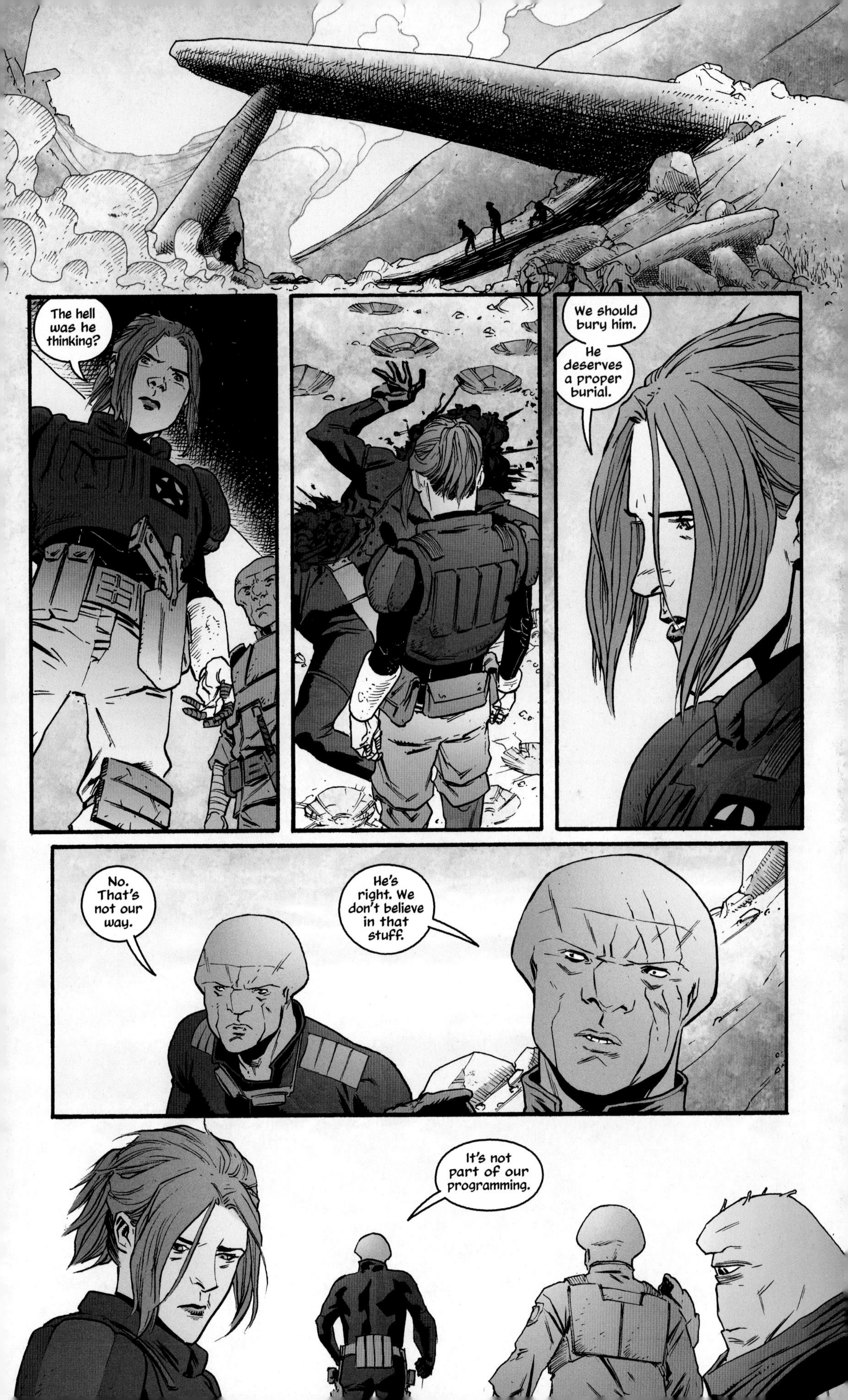
The hell was he thinking?
We should bury him.
He deserves a proper burial.
No. That's not our way.
He's right. We don't believe in that stuff.
It's not part of our programming.

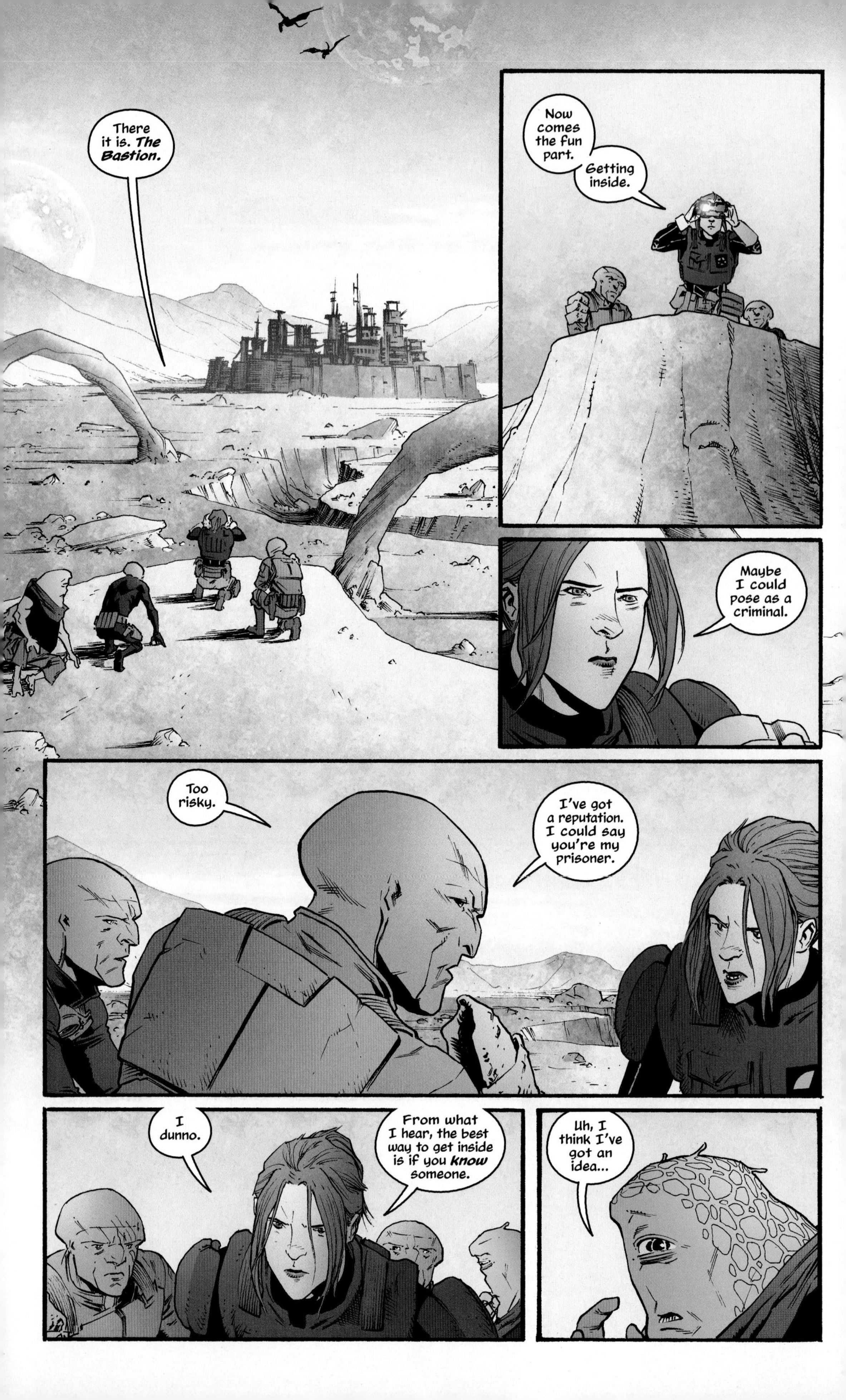

There it is. *The Bastion.*
Now comes the fun part.
Getting inside.
Maybe I could pose as a criminal.
Too risky.
I've got a reputation. I could say you're my prisoner.
I dunno.
From what I hear, the best way to get inside is if you *know* someone.
Uh, I think I've got an idea...

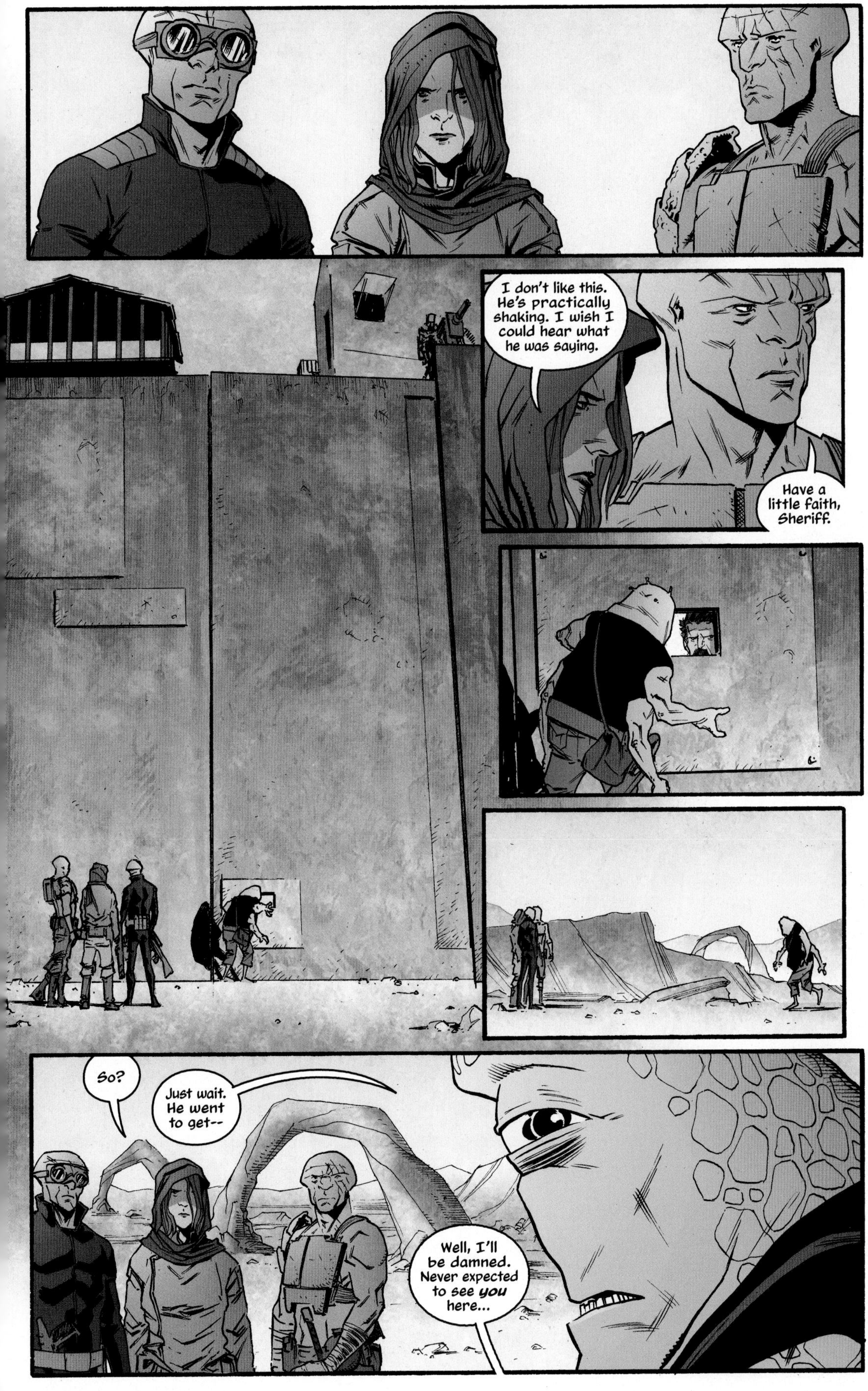
I don't like this. He's practically shaking. I wish I could hear what he was saying.
Have a little faith, Sheriff.
So?
Just wait. He went to get--
Well, I'll be damned. Never expected to see *you* here...

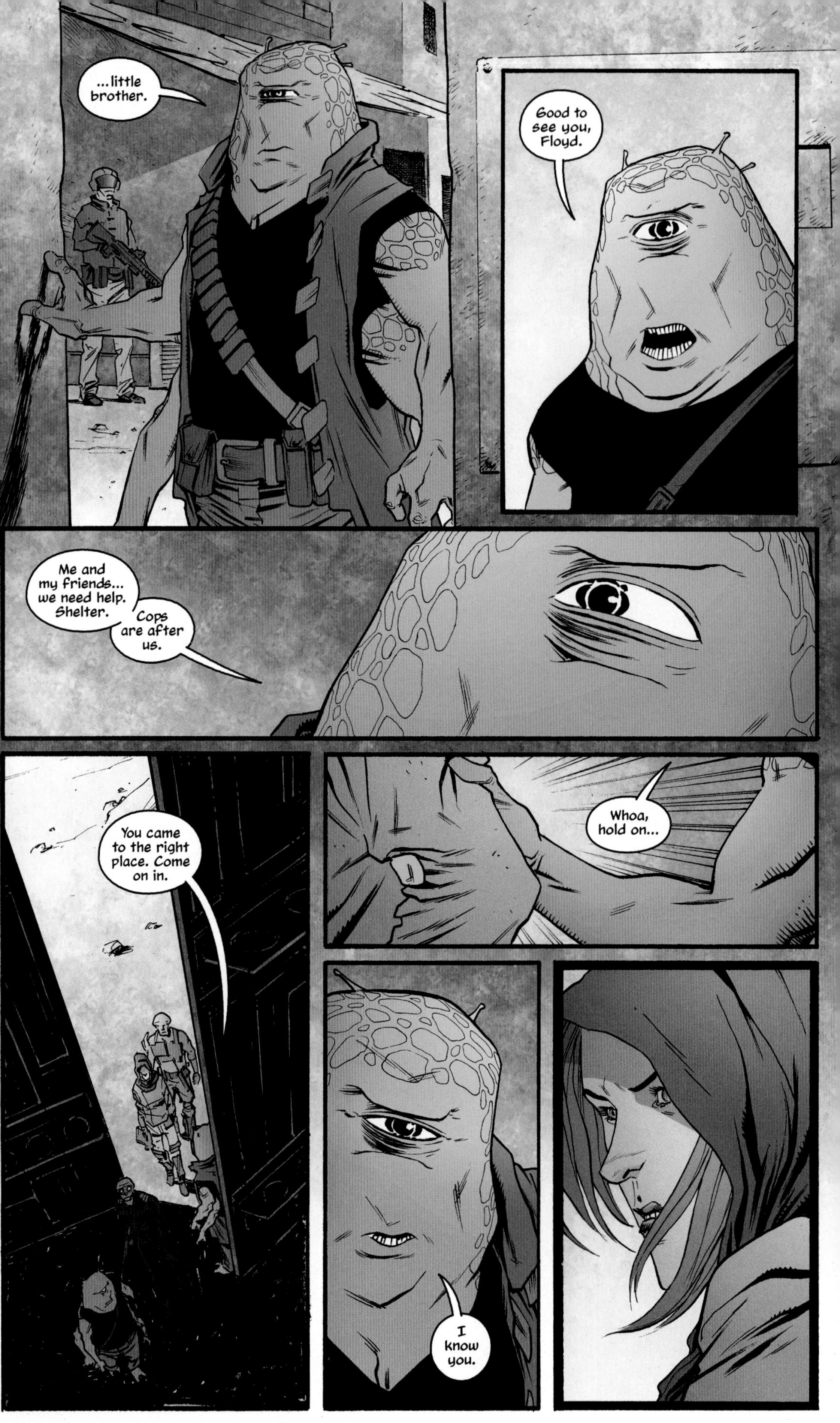
...little brother.
Good to see you, Floyd.
Me and my friends... we need help. Shelter.
Cops are after us.
You came to the right place. Come on in.
Whoa, hold on...
I know you.

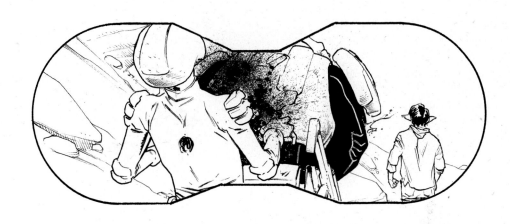

CHAPTER V

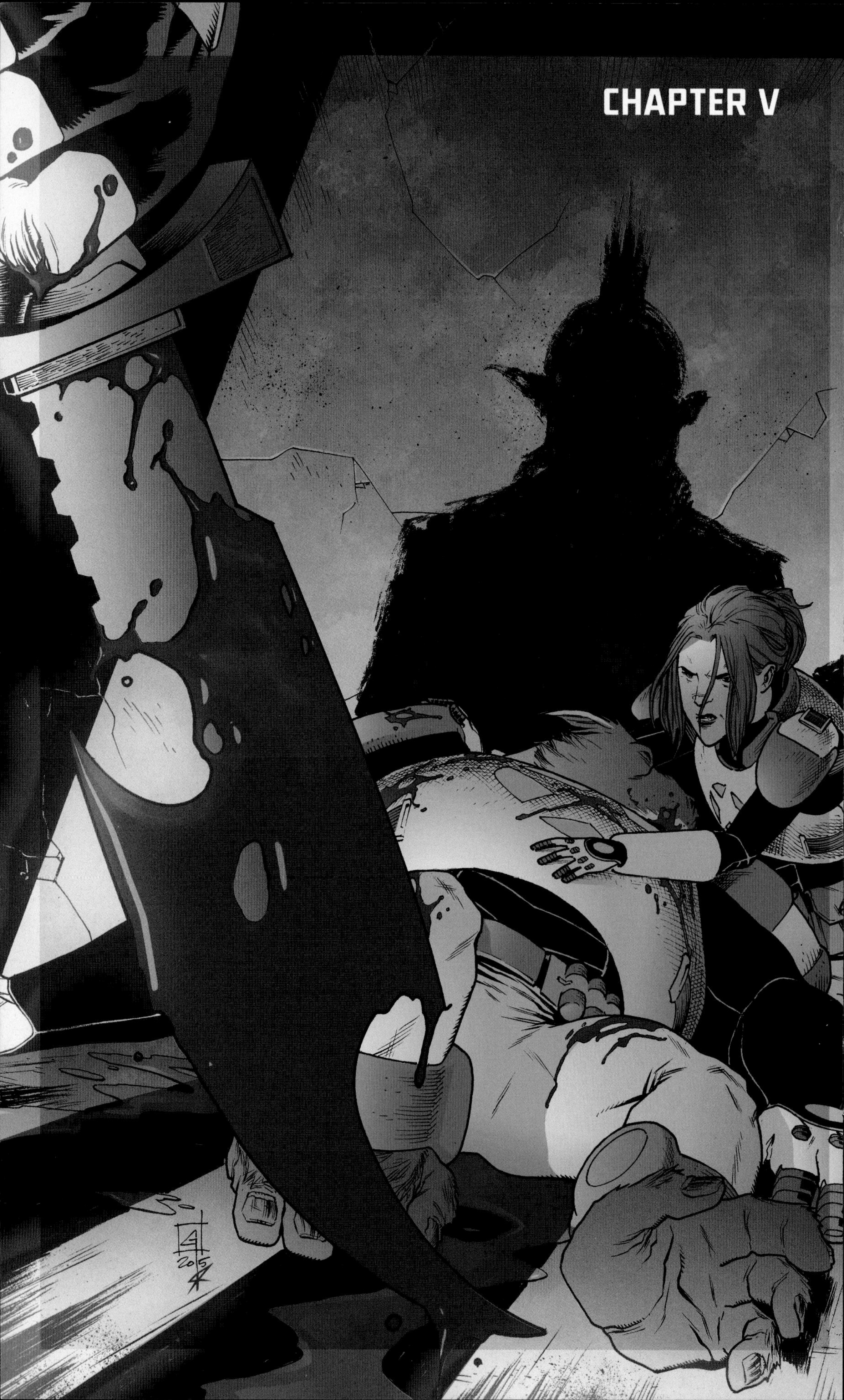

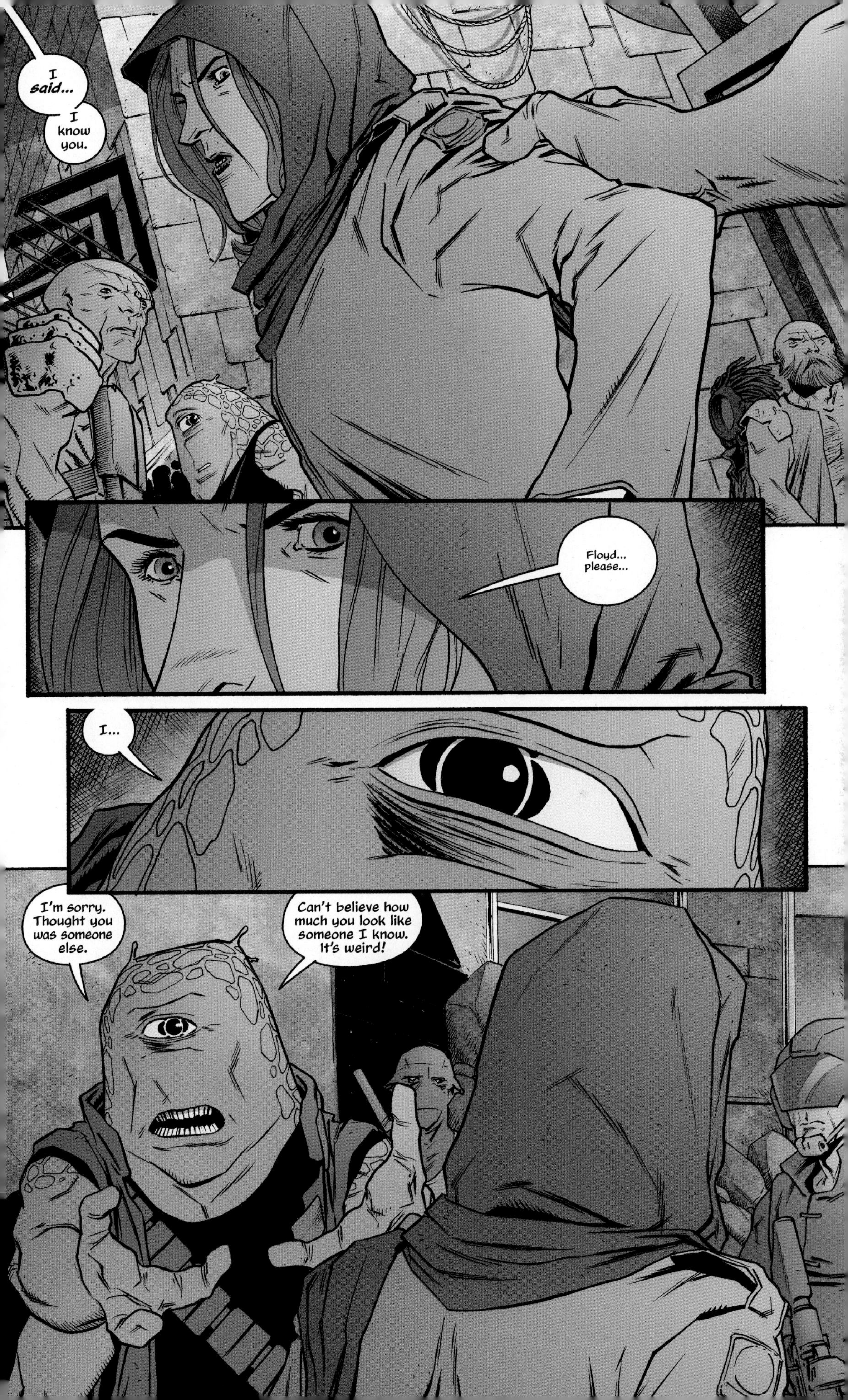
I said... I know you.
Floyd... please...
I...
I'm sorry. Thought you was someone else.
Can't believe how much you look like someone I know. It's weird!

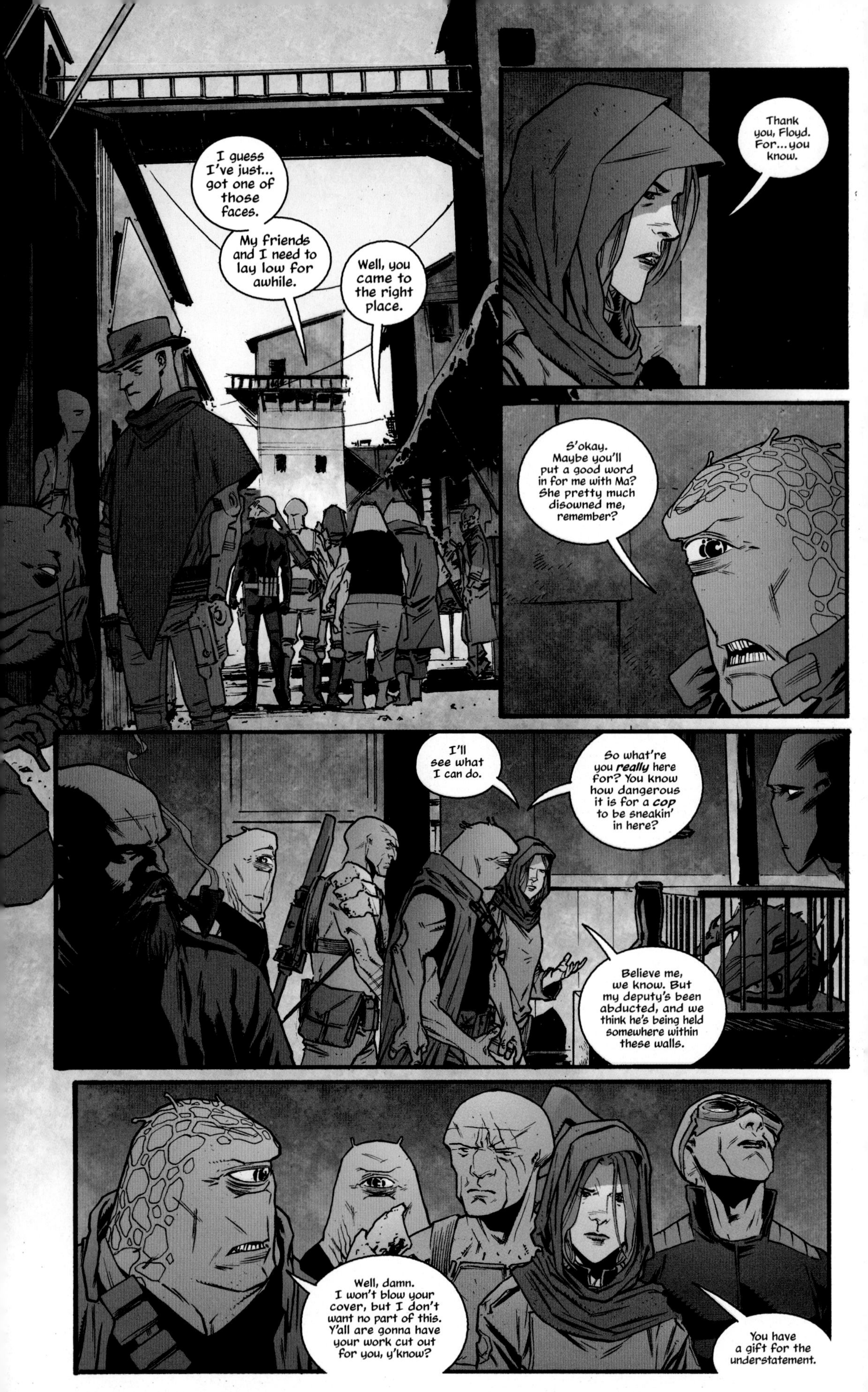
I guess I've just... got one of those faces.
My friends and I need to lay low for awhile.
Well, you came to the right place.
Thank you, Floyd. For... you know.
S'okay. Maybe you'll put a good word in for me with Ma? She pretty much disowned me, remember?
I'll see what I can do.
So what're you *really* here for? You know how dangerous it is for a *cop* to be sneakin' in here?
Believe me, we know. But my deputy's been abducted, and we think he's being held somewhere within these walls.
Well, damn. I won't blow your cover, but I don't want no part of this. Y'all are gonna have your work cut out for you, y'know?
You have a gift for the understatement.

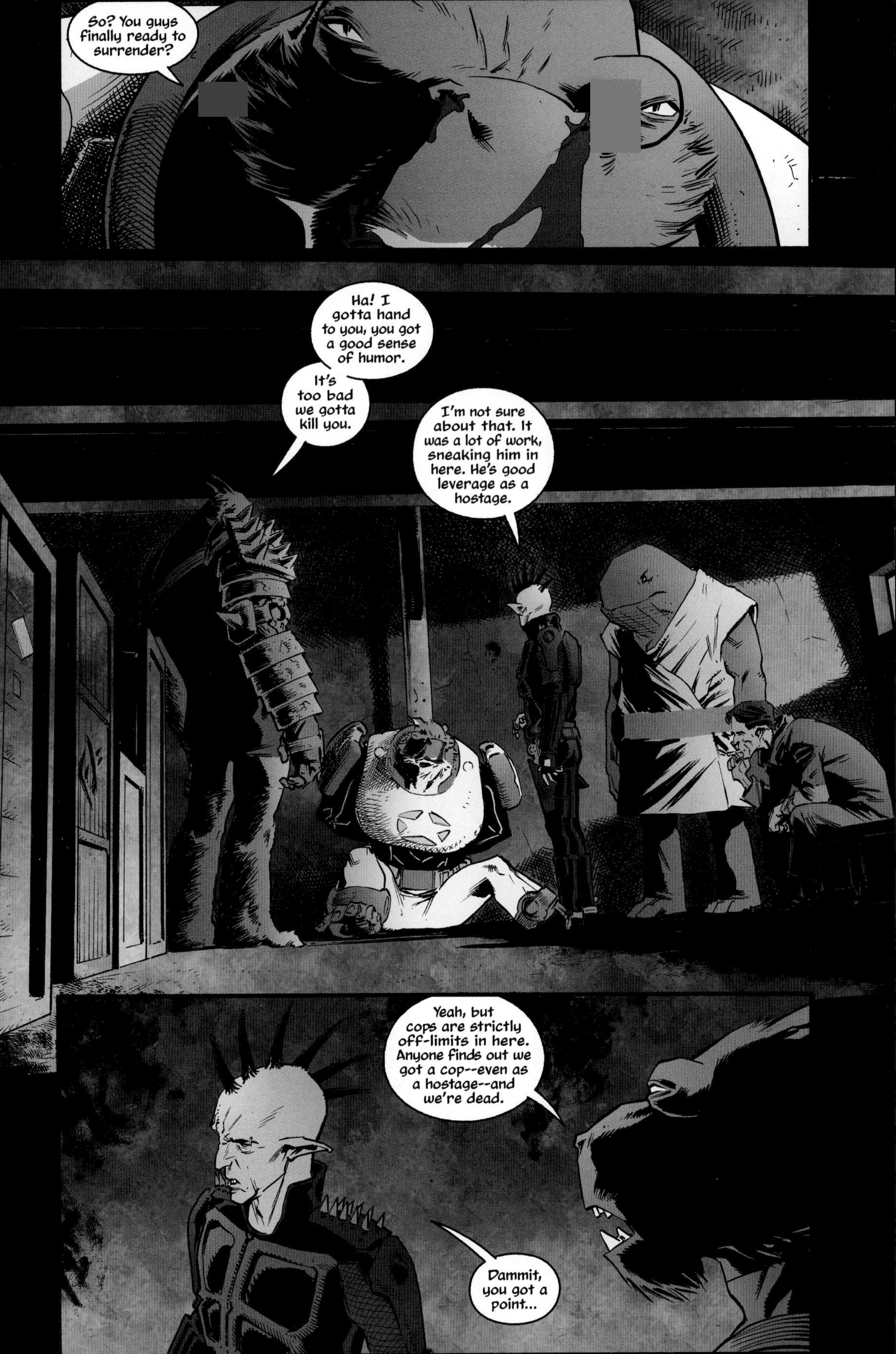
So? You guys finally ready to surrender?
Ha! I gotta hand to you, you got a good sense of humor.
It's too bad we gotta kill you.
I'm not sure about that. It was a lot of work, sneaking him in here. He's good leverage as a hostage.
Yeah, but cops are strictly off-limits in here. Anyone finds out we got a cop--even as a hostage--and we're dead.
Dammit, you got a point...

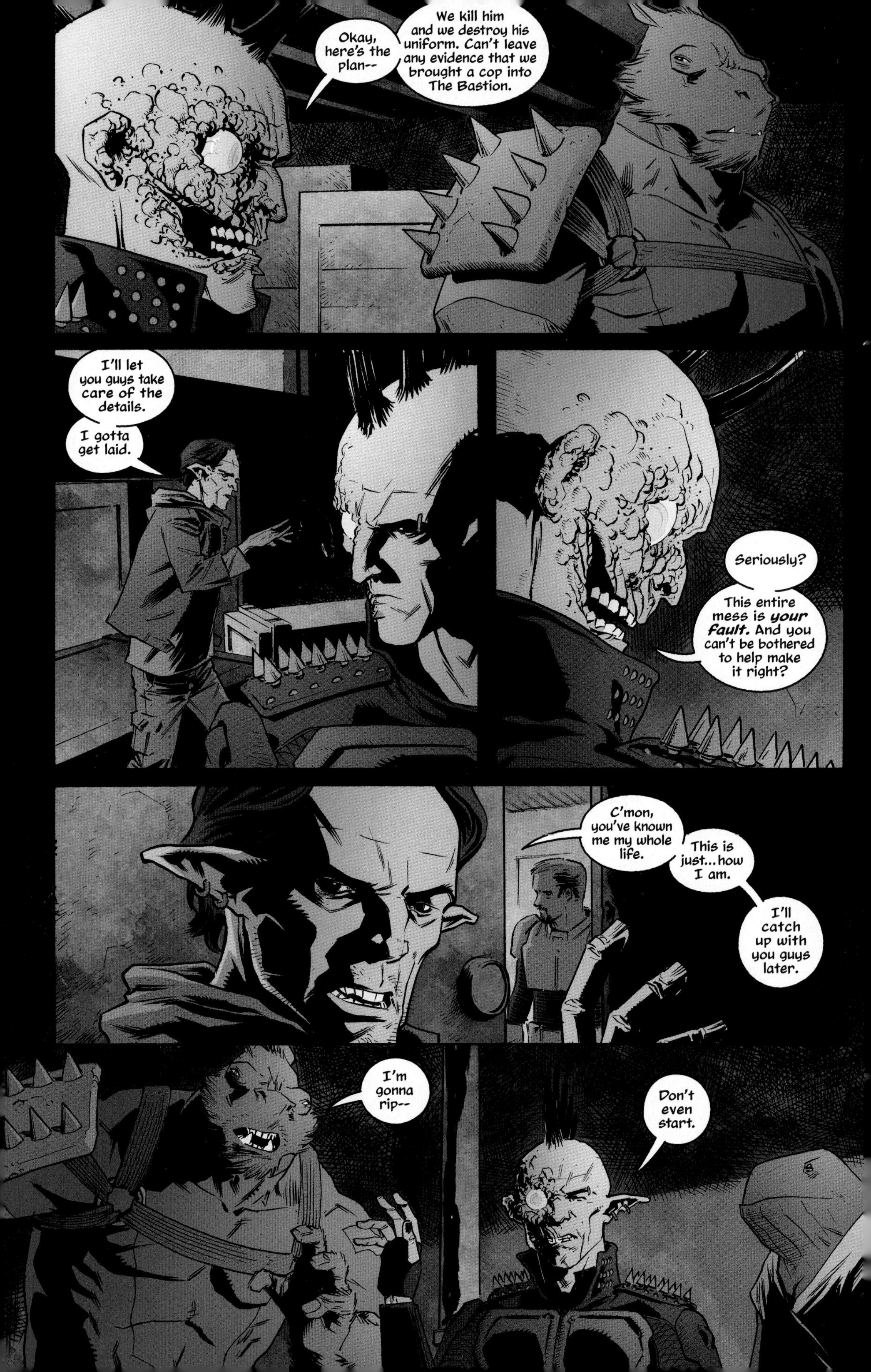
Okay, here's the plan--
We kill him and we destroy his uniform. Can't leave any evidence that we brought a cop into The Bastion.
I'll let you guys take care of the details.
I gotta get laid.
Seriously?
This entire mess is *your fault.* And you can't be bothered to help make it right?
C'mon, you've known me my whole life.
This is just...how I am.
I'll catch up with you guys later.
I'm gonna rip--
Don't even start.

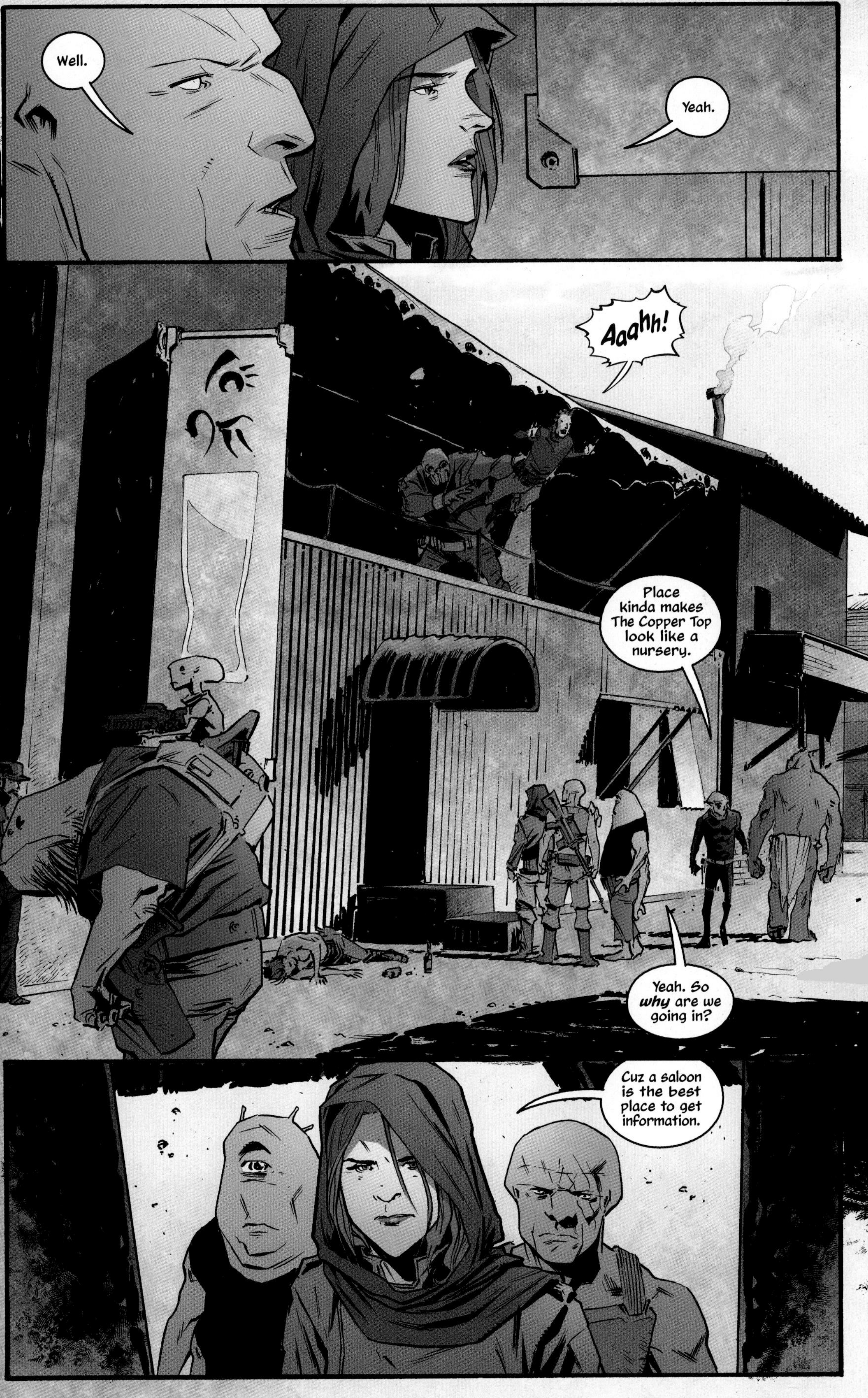
Well.
Yeah.
Aaahh!
Place kinda makes The Copper Top look like a nursery.
Yeah. So *why* are we going in?
Cuz a saloon is the best place to get information.

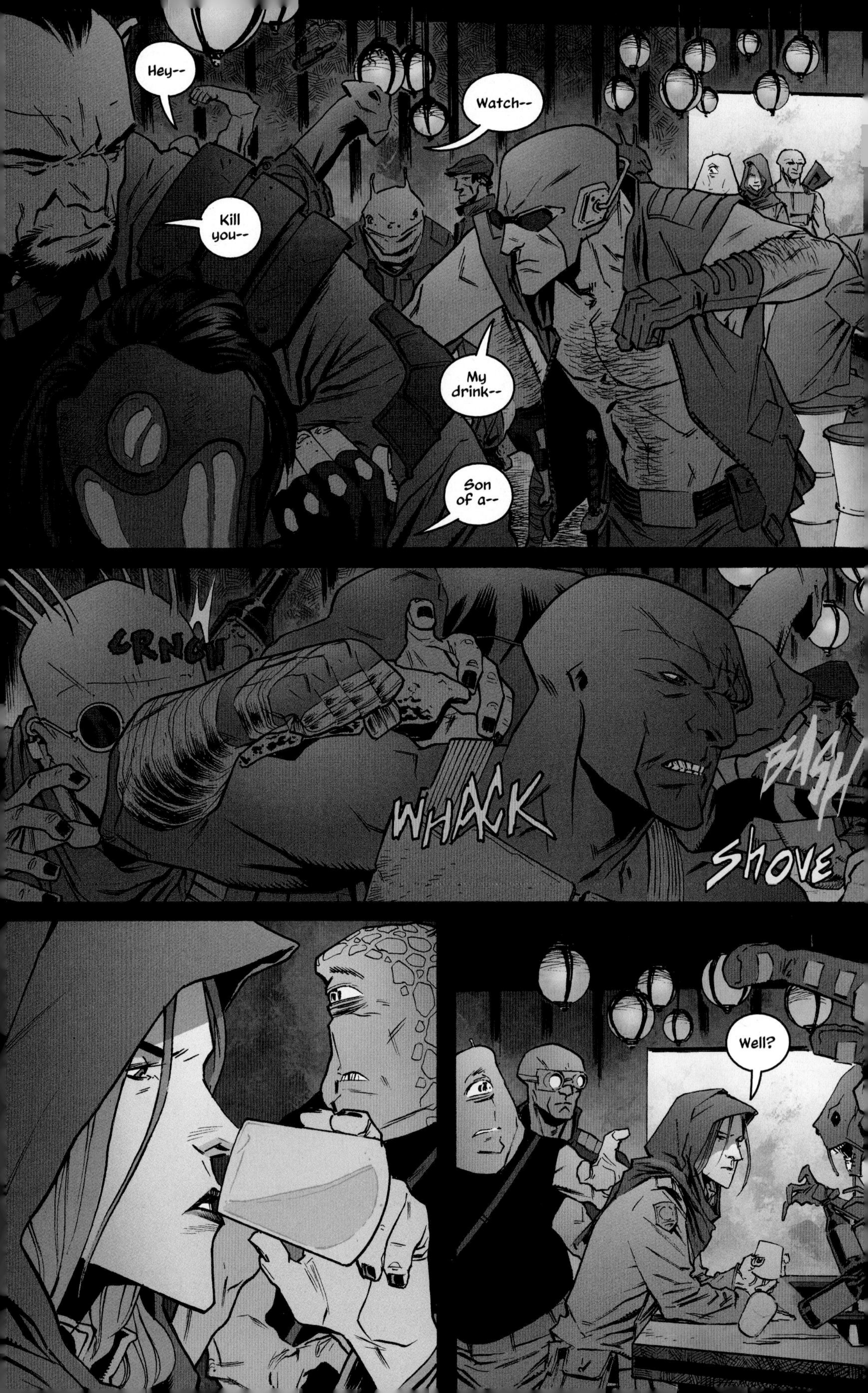
Hey--
Watch--
Kill you--
My drink--
Son of a--
CRNCH
WHACK
BASH
SHOVE
Well?

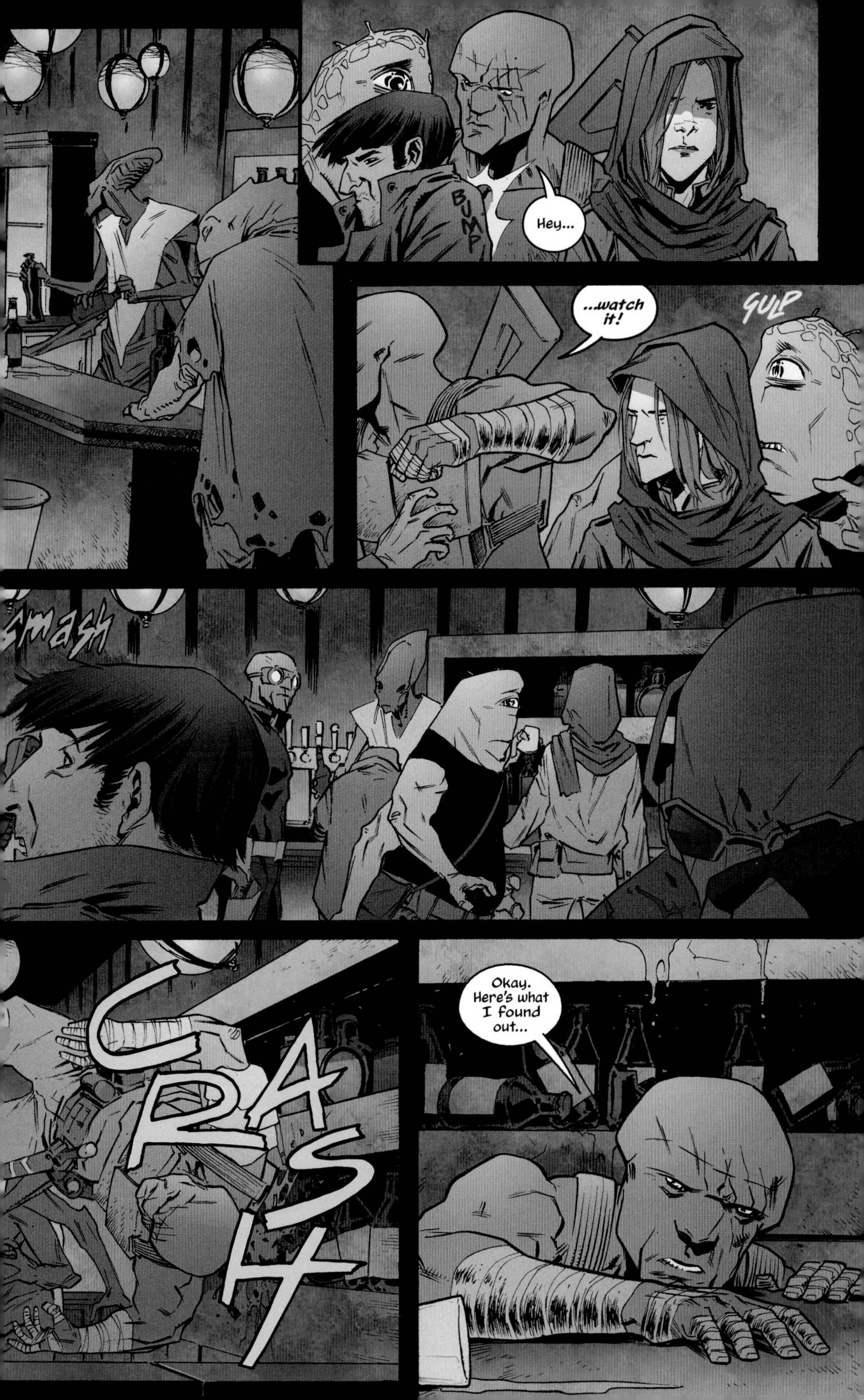
BUMP
Hey...
...watch it!
GULP
SMASH
CRASH
Okay. Here's what I found out...

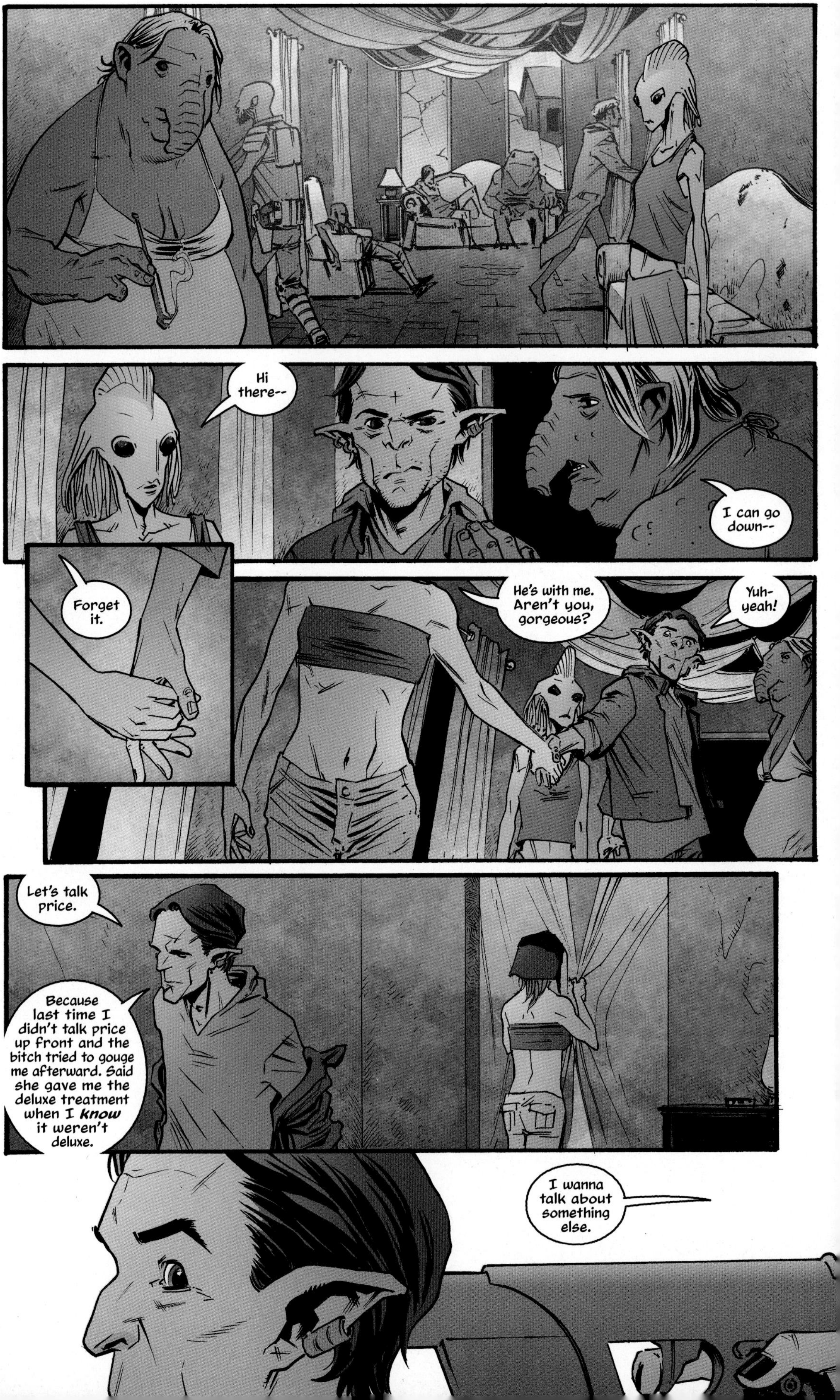
Hi there--
I can go down--
Forget it.
He's with me. Aren't you, gorgeous?
Yuh-yeah!
Let's talk price.
Because last time I didn't talk price up front and the bitch tried to gouge me afterward. Said she gave me the deluxe treatment when I *know* it weren't deluxe.
I wanna talk about something else.

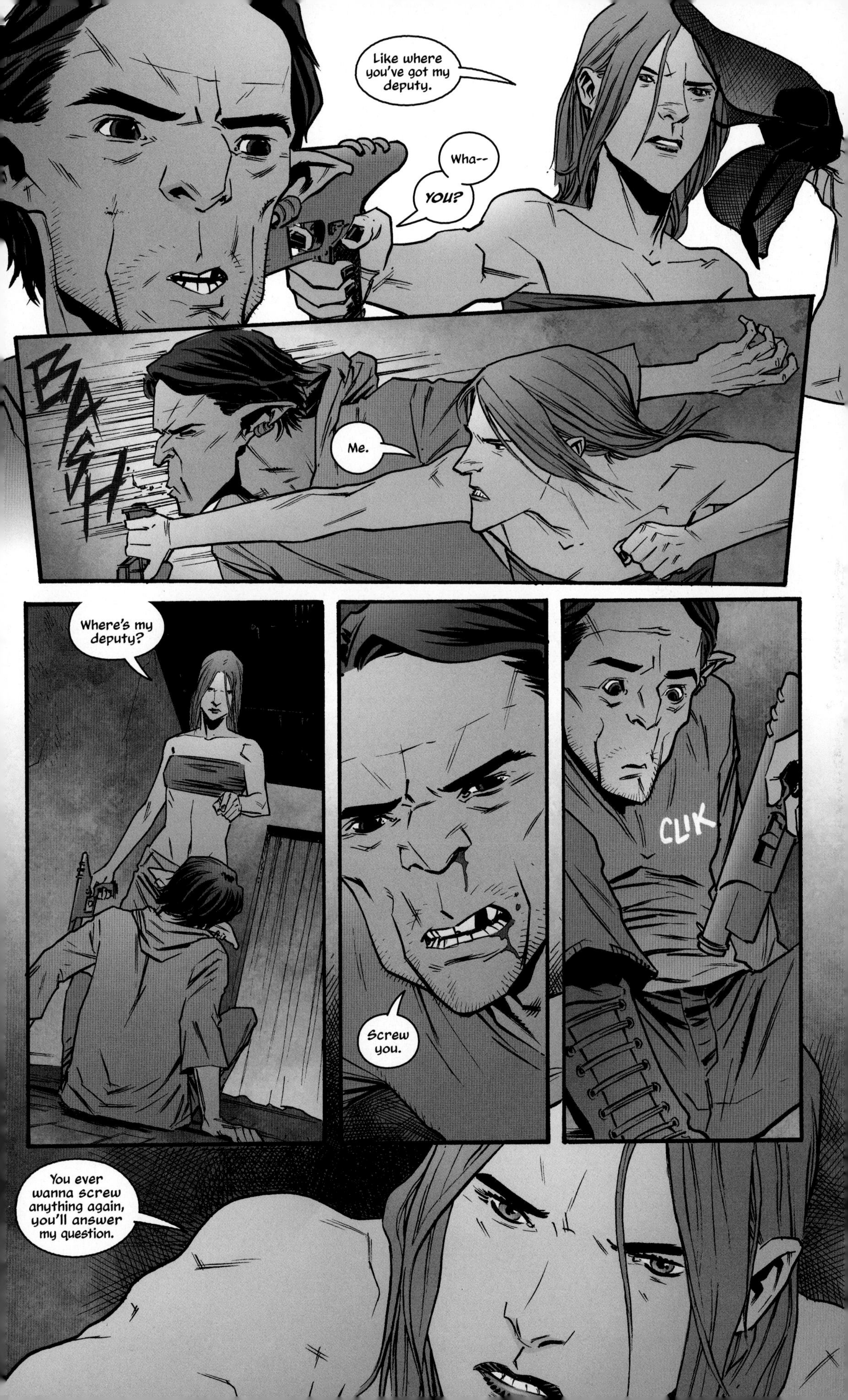
Like where you've got my deputy.
Wha--
YOU?
BASH
Me.
Where's my deputy?
Screw you.
CLIK
You ever wanna screw anything again, you'll answer my question.

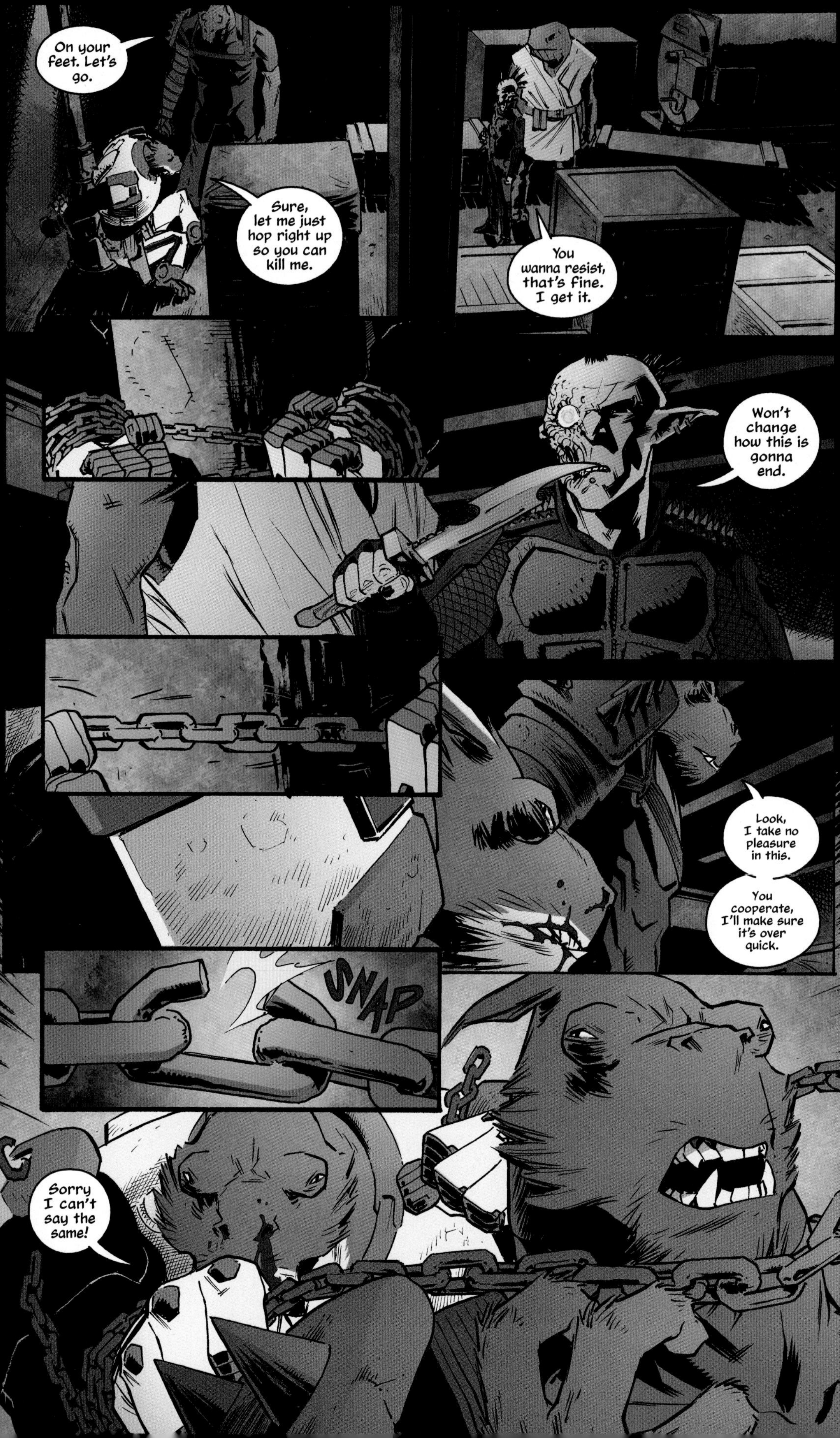
On your feet. Let's go.
Sure, let me just hop right up so you can kill me.
You wanna resist, that's fine. I get it.
Won't change how this is gonna end.
Look, I take no pleasure in this.
You cooperate, I'll make sure it's over quick.
SNAP
Sorry I can't say the same!

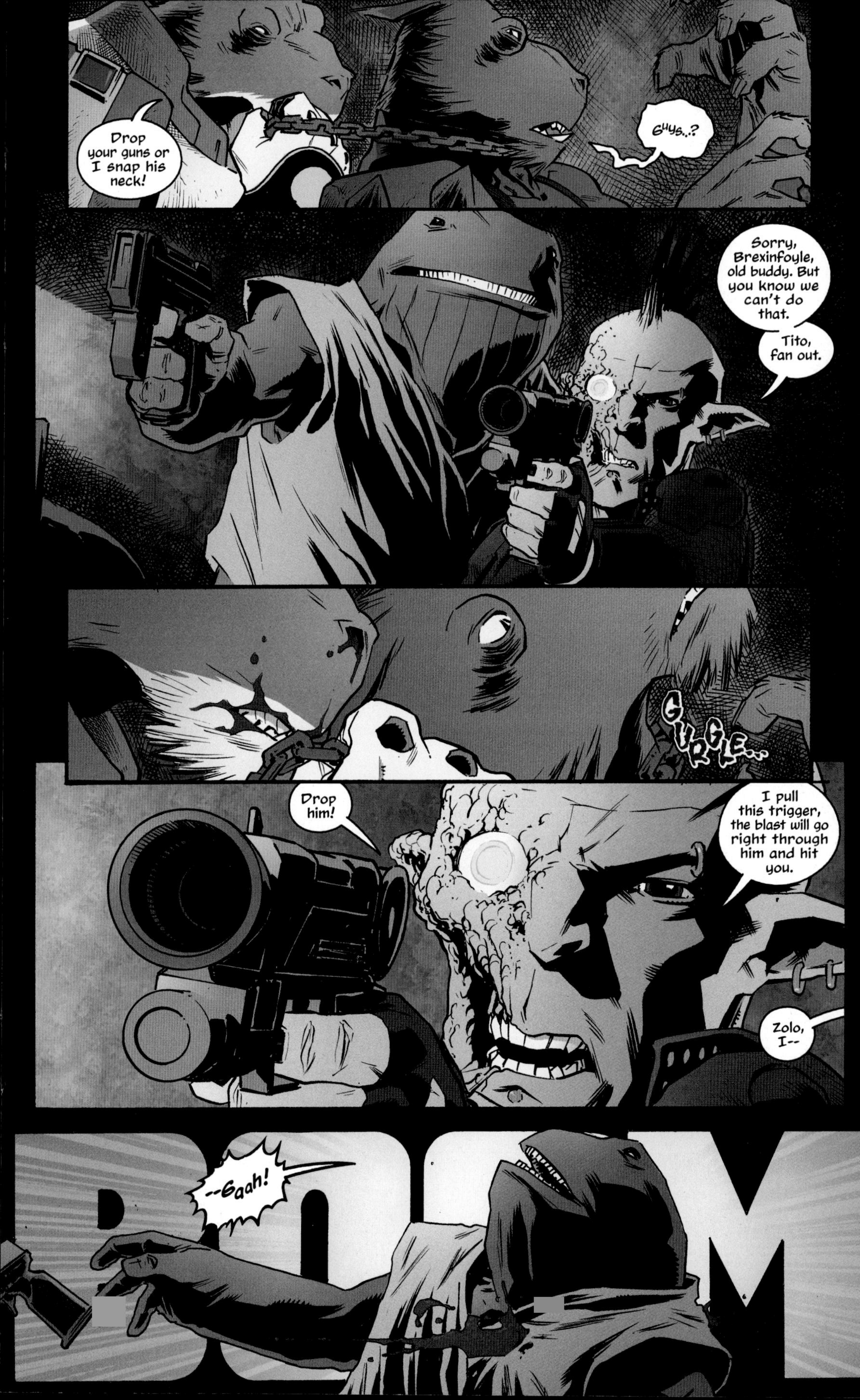
Drop your guns or I snap his neck!
Guys..?
Sorry, Brexinfoyle, old buddy. But you know we can't do that.
Tito, fan out.
GURGLE...
Drop him!
I pull this trigger, the blast will go right through him and hit you.
Zolo, I--
--Gaah!

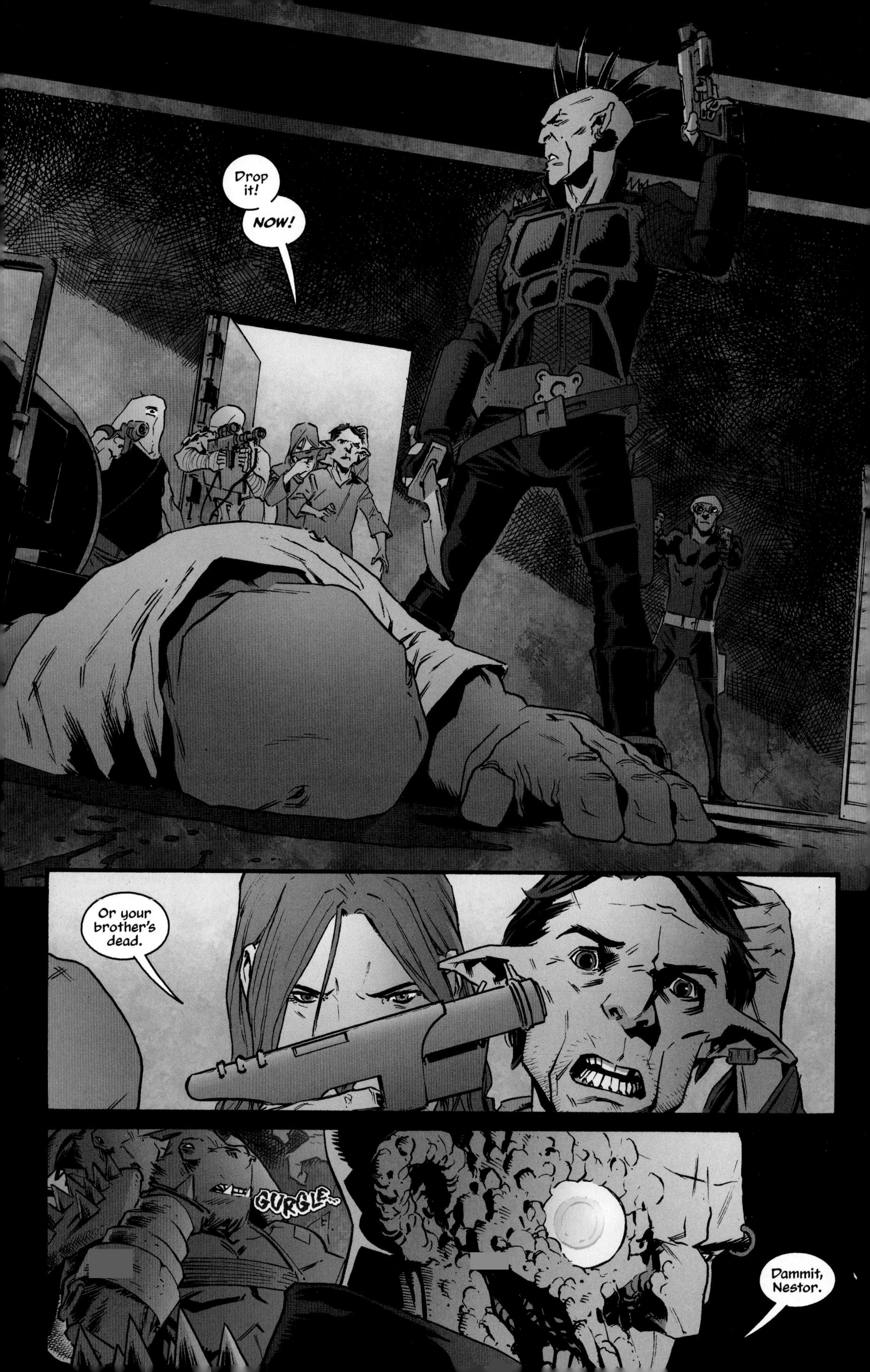
Drop it!
NOW!
Or your brother's dead.
GURGLE...
Dammit, Nestor.

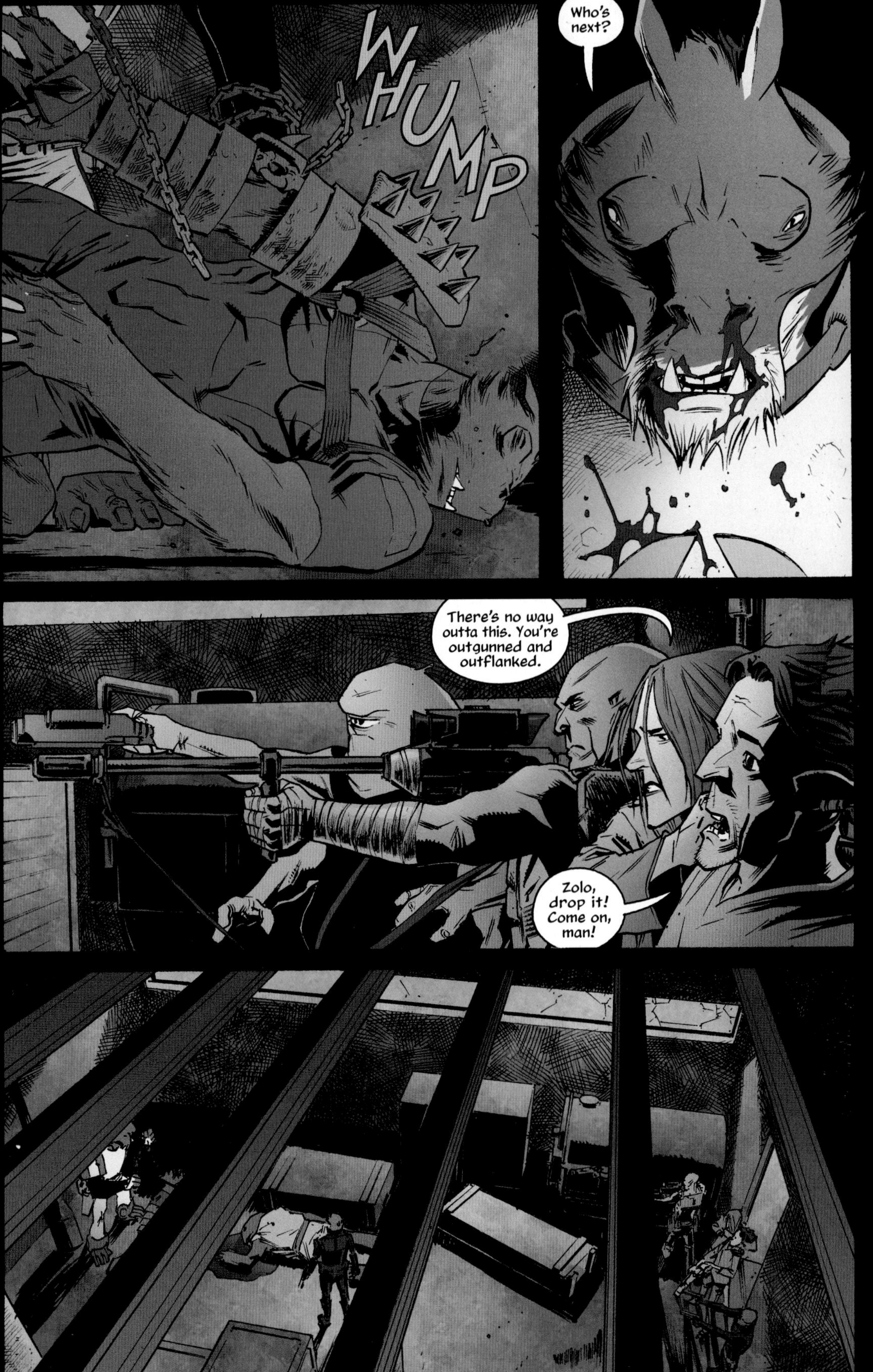
WHUMP
Who's next?
There's no way outta this. You're outgunned and outflanked.
Zolo, drop it! Come on, man!

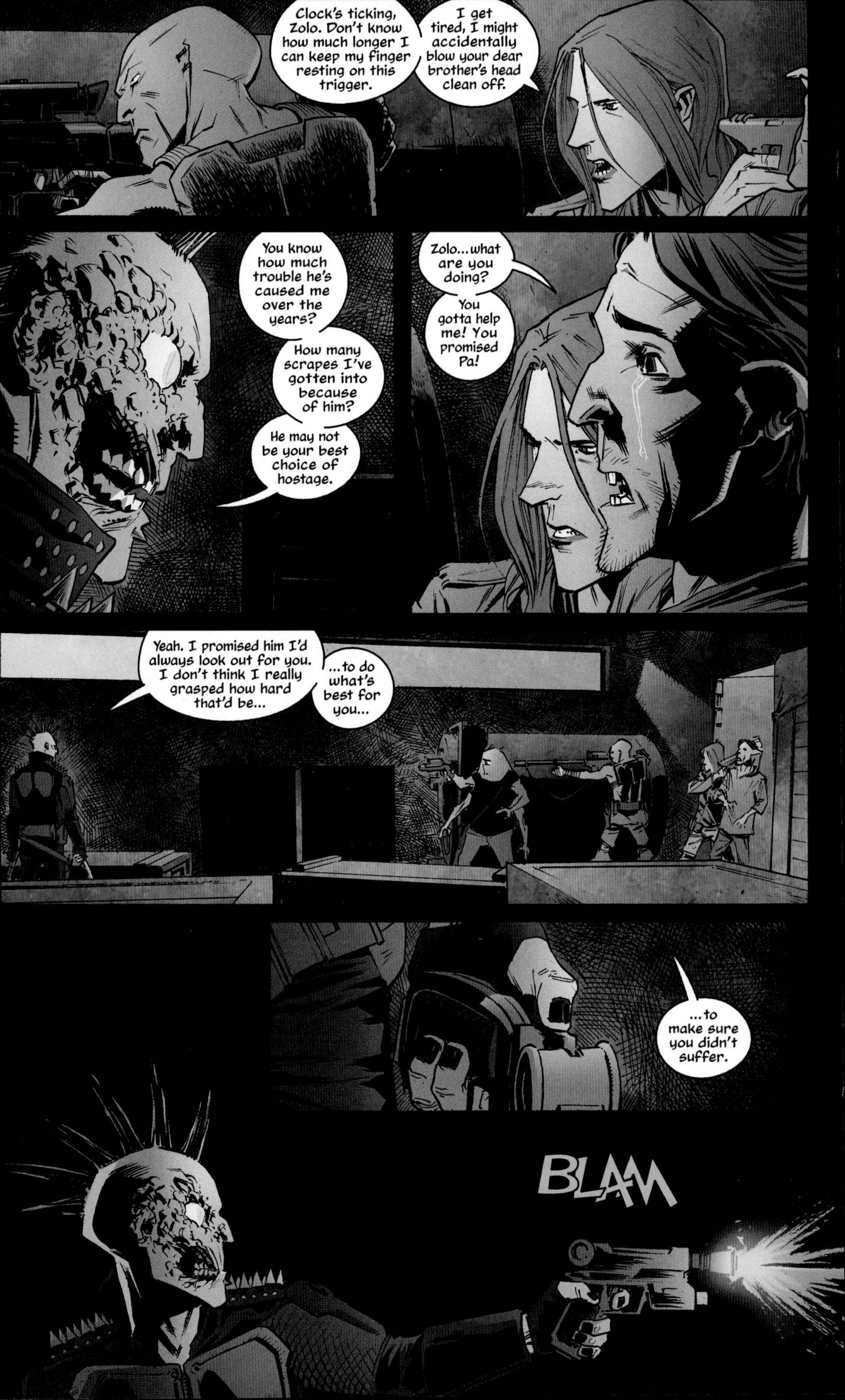
Clock's ticking, Zolo. Don't know how much longer I can keep my finger resting on this trigger.
I get tired, I might accidentally blow your dear brother's head clean off.
You know how much trouble he's caused me over the years?
How many scrapes I've gotten into because of him?
He may not be your best choice of hostage.
Zolo...what are you doing?
You gotta help me! You promised Pa!
Yeah. I promised him I'd always look out for you. I don't think I really grasped how hard that'd be...
...to do what's best for you...
...to make sure you didn't suffer.
BLAM

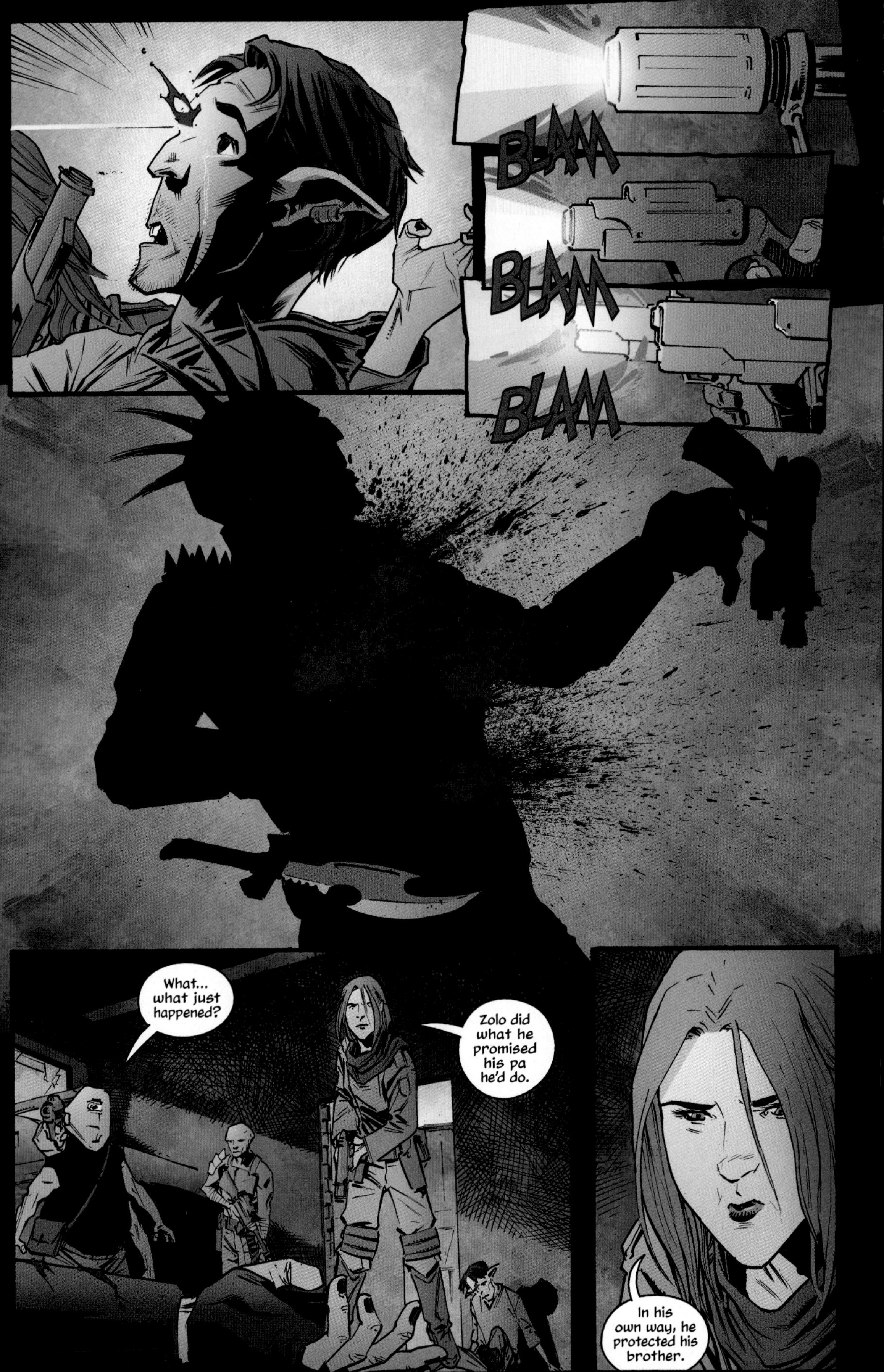
BLAM
BLAM
BLAM
What... what just happened?
Zolo did what he promised his pa he'd do.
In his own way, he protected his brother.

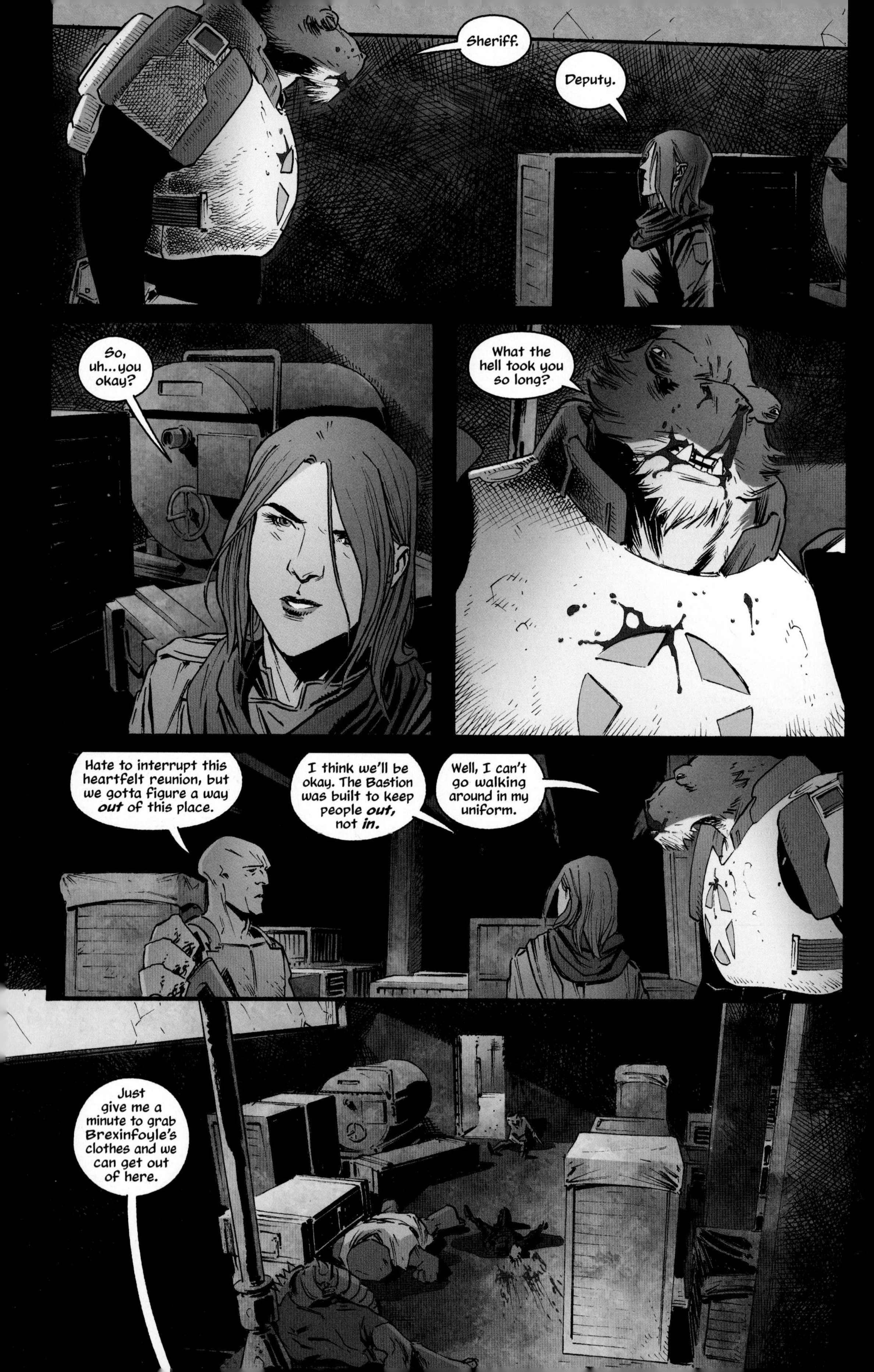
Sheriff.
Deputy.
So, uh...you okay?
What the hell took you so long?
Hate to interrupt this heartfelt reunion, but we gotta figure a way out of this place.
I think we'll be okay. The Bastion was built to keep people out, not in.
Well, I can't go walking around in my uniform.
Just give me a minute to grab Brexinfoyle's clothes and we can get out of here.

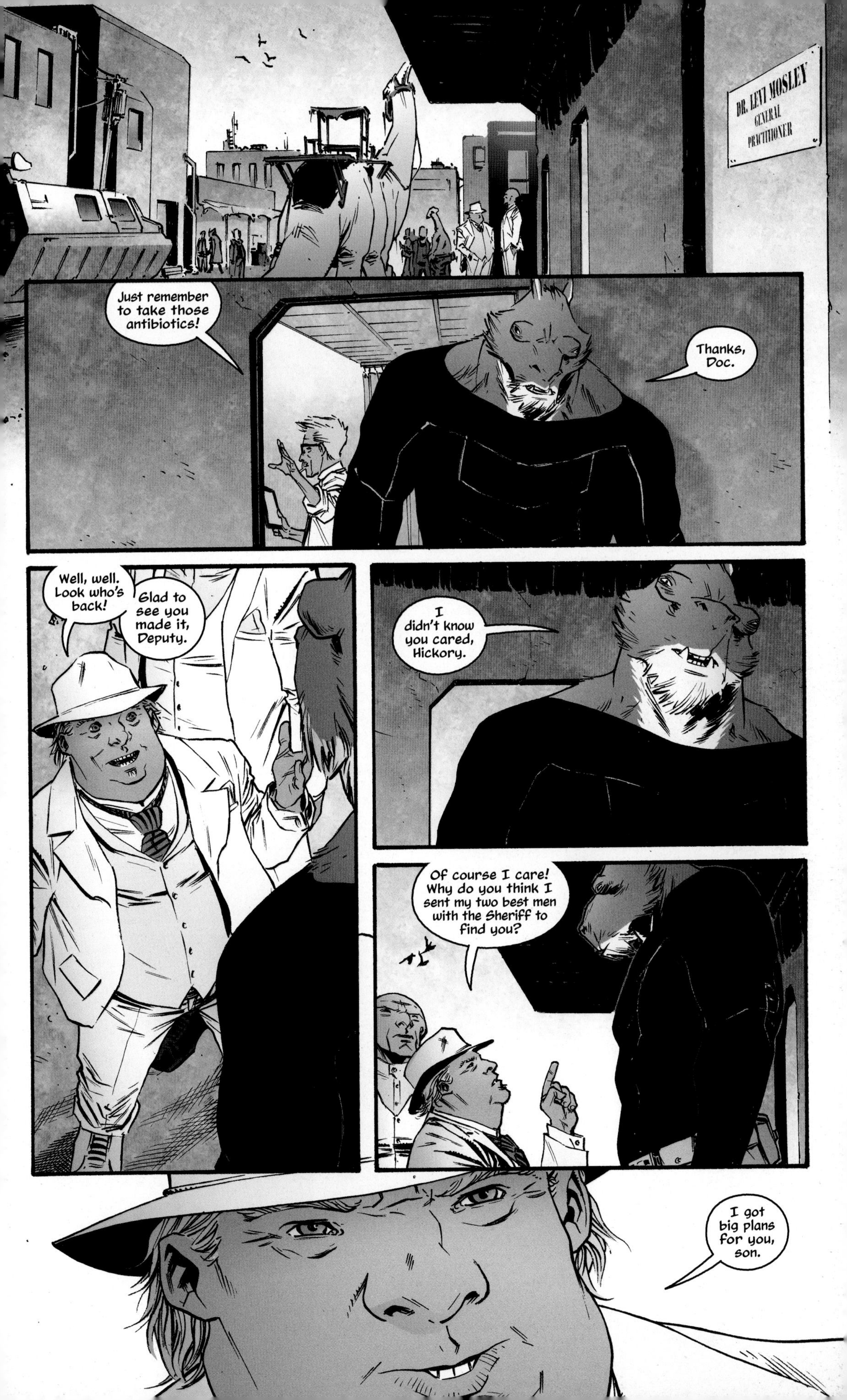
DR. LEVI MOSLEY
GENERAL
PRACTITIONER
Just remember to take those antibiotics!
Thanks, Doc.
Well, well. Look who's back!
Glad to see you made it, Deputy.
I didn't know you cared, Hickory.
Of course I care! Why do you think I sent my two best men with the Sheriff to find you?
I got big plans for you, son.

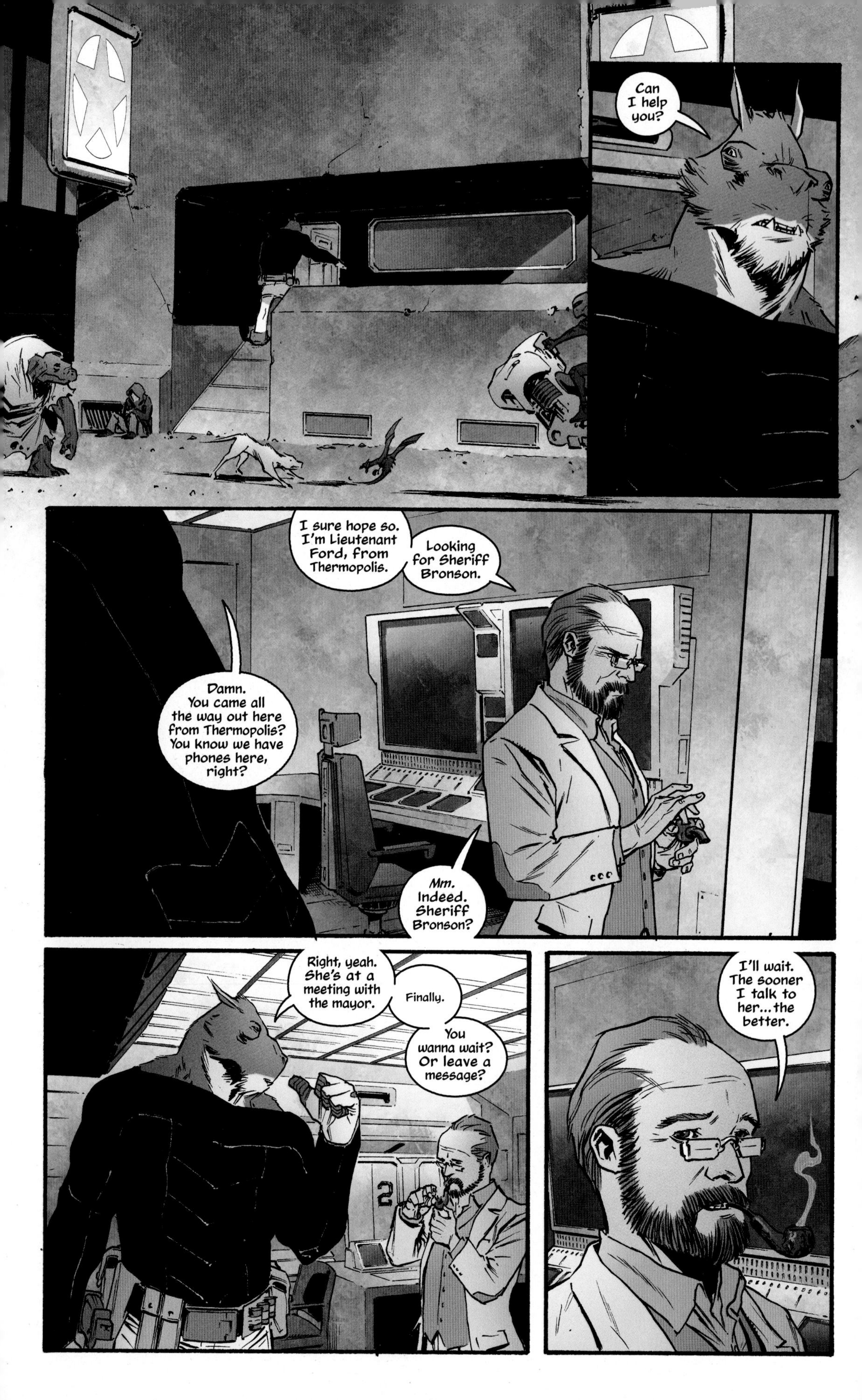
Can I help you?
I sure hope so. I'm Lieutenant Ford, from Thermopolis.
Looking for Sheriff Bronson.
Damn. You came all the way out here from Thermopolis? You know we have phones here, right?
Mm. Indeed. Sheriff Bronson?
Right, yeah. She's at a meeting with the mayor.
Finally.
You wanna wait? Or leave a message?
I'll wait. The sooner I talk to her...the better.

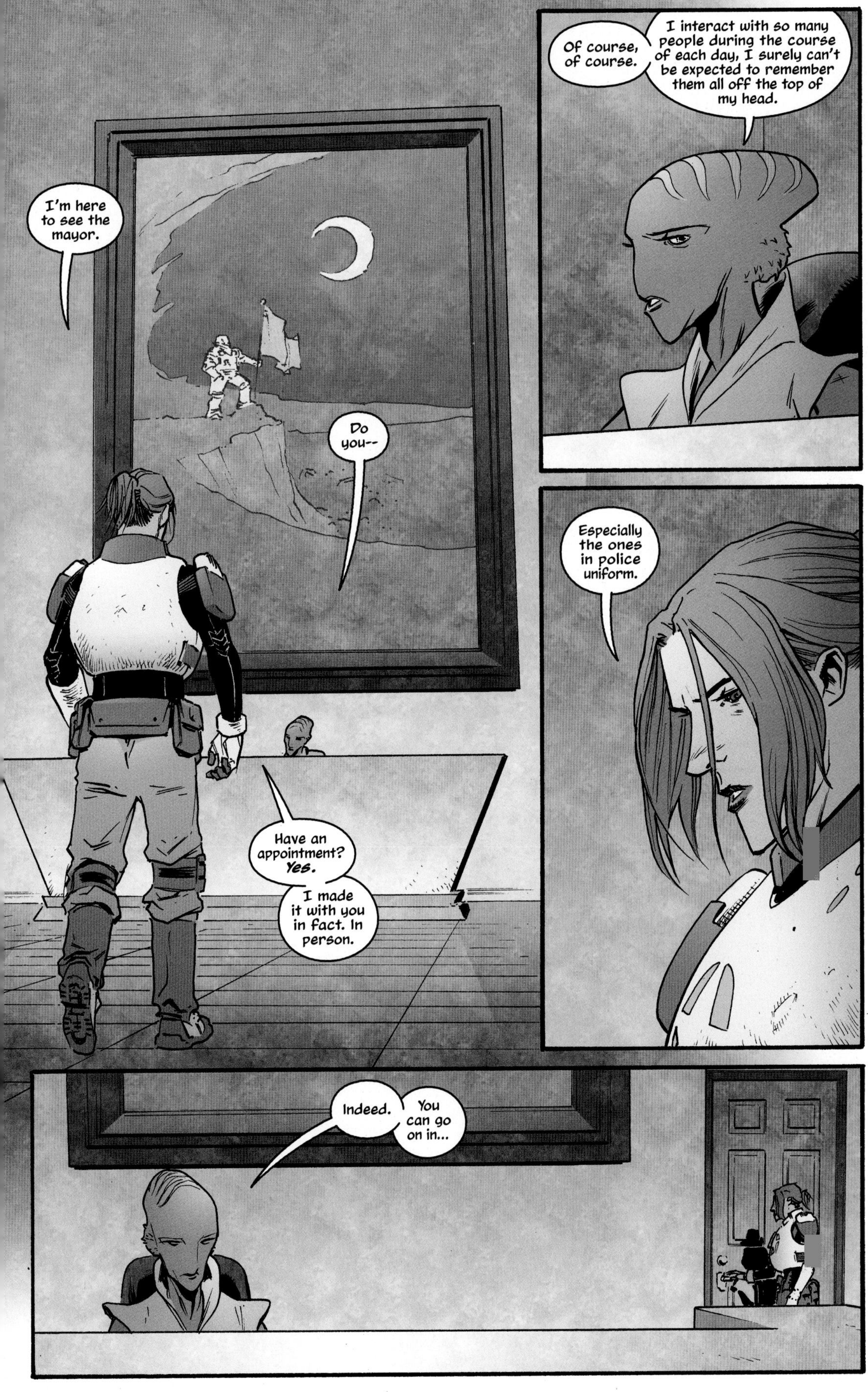
I'm here to see the mayor.
Do you--
Have an appointment? Yes.
I made it with you in fact. In person.
Of course, of course.
I interact with so many people during the course of each day, I surely can't be expected to remember them all off the top of my head.
Especially the ones in police uniform.
Indeed.
You can go on in...

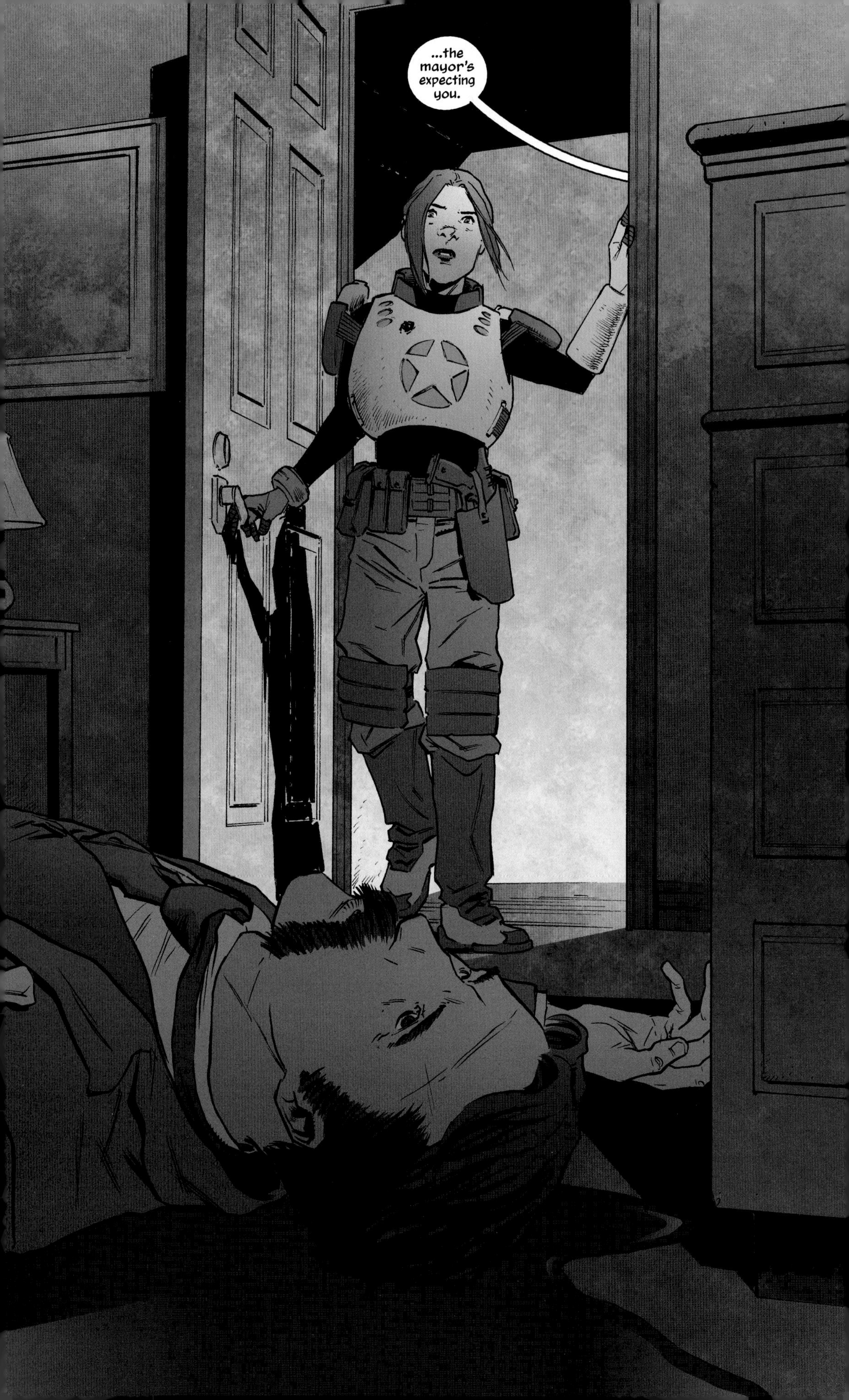
...the mayor's expecting you.

TO BE
CONTINUED

BONUS CONTENT

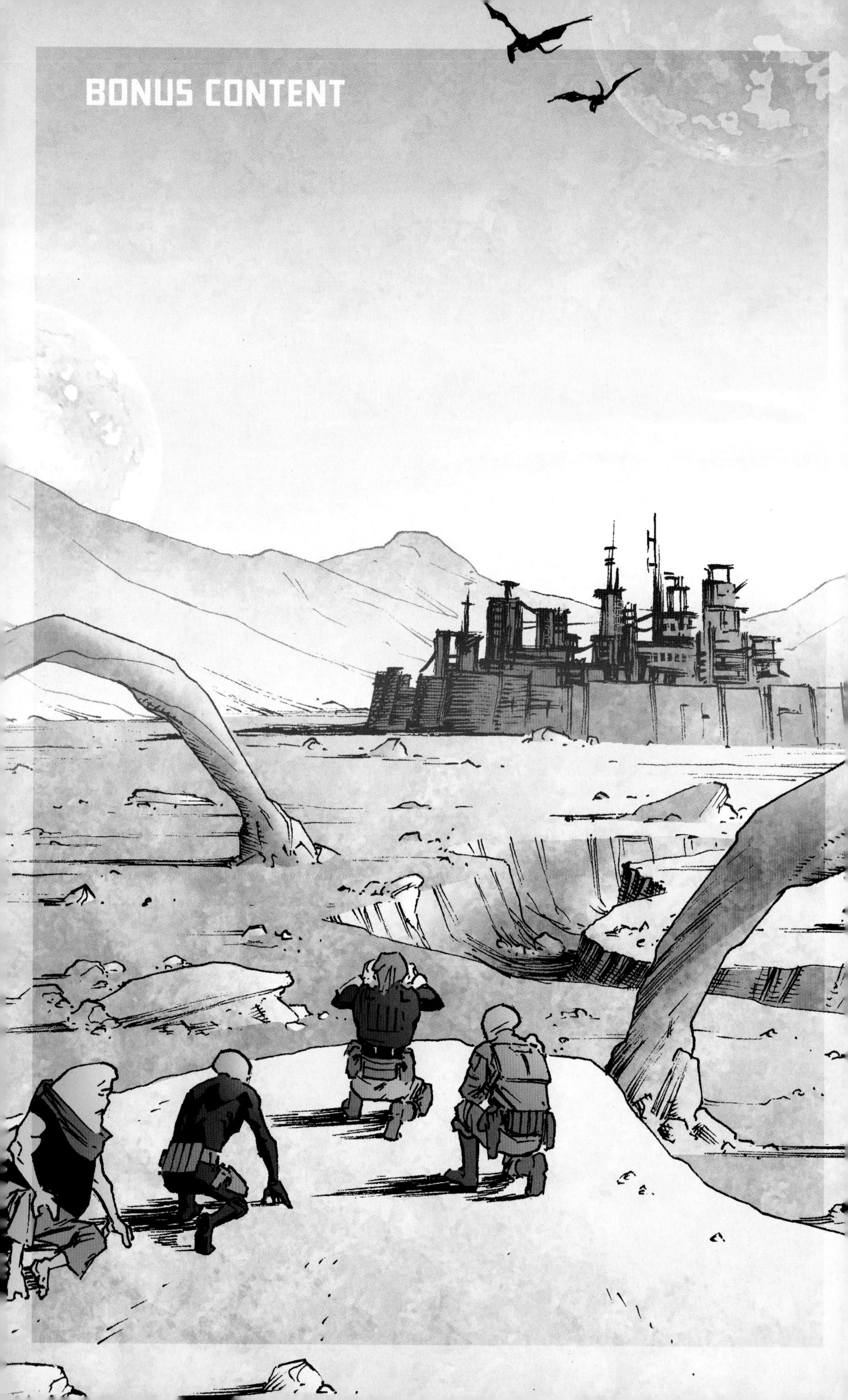

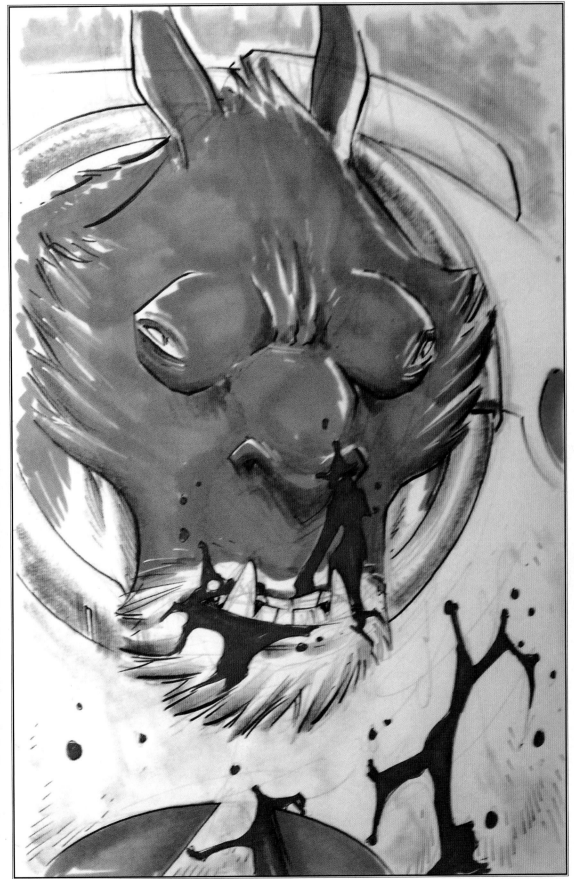

by Scott Godlewski (first shown on social media)

THE MAKING OF ISSUE 10's FIRST PANEL

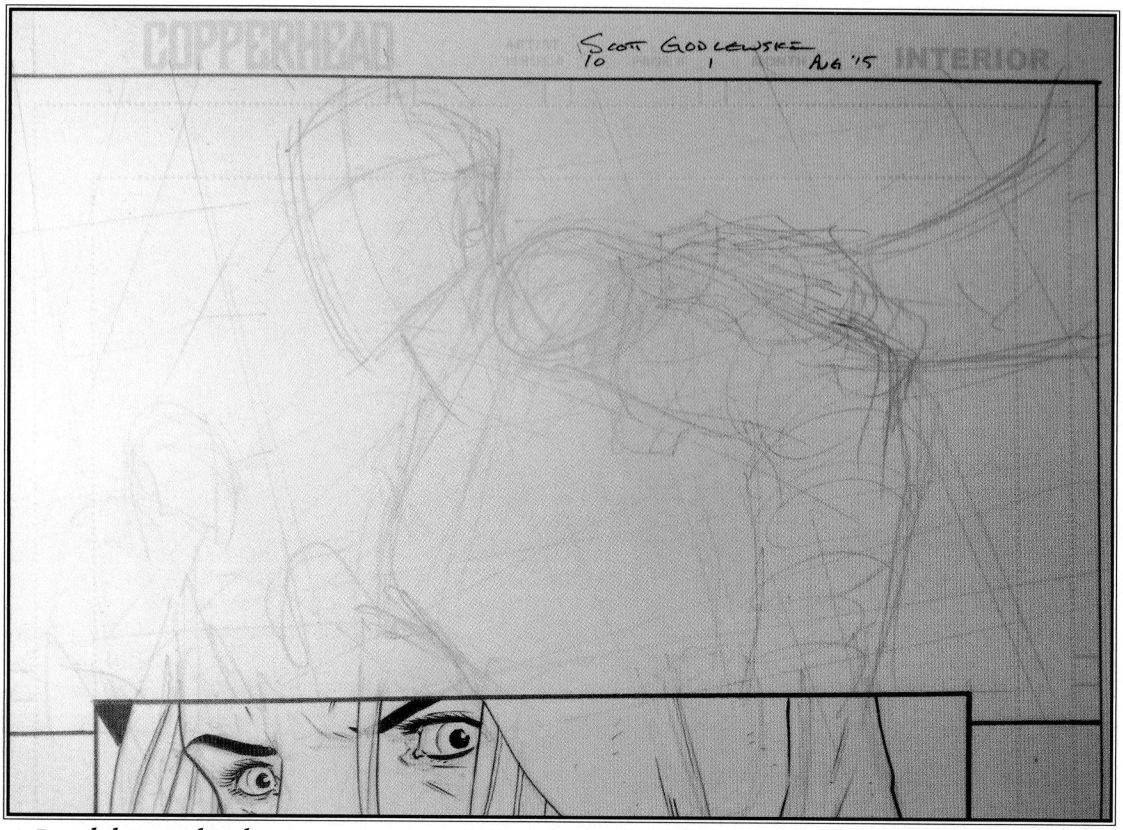
COPPERHEAD
SCOTT GODLEWSKI
10
1
AUG '15
INTERIOR

Rough layout sketch

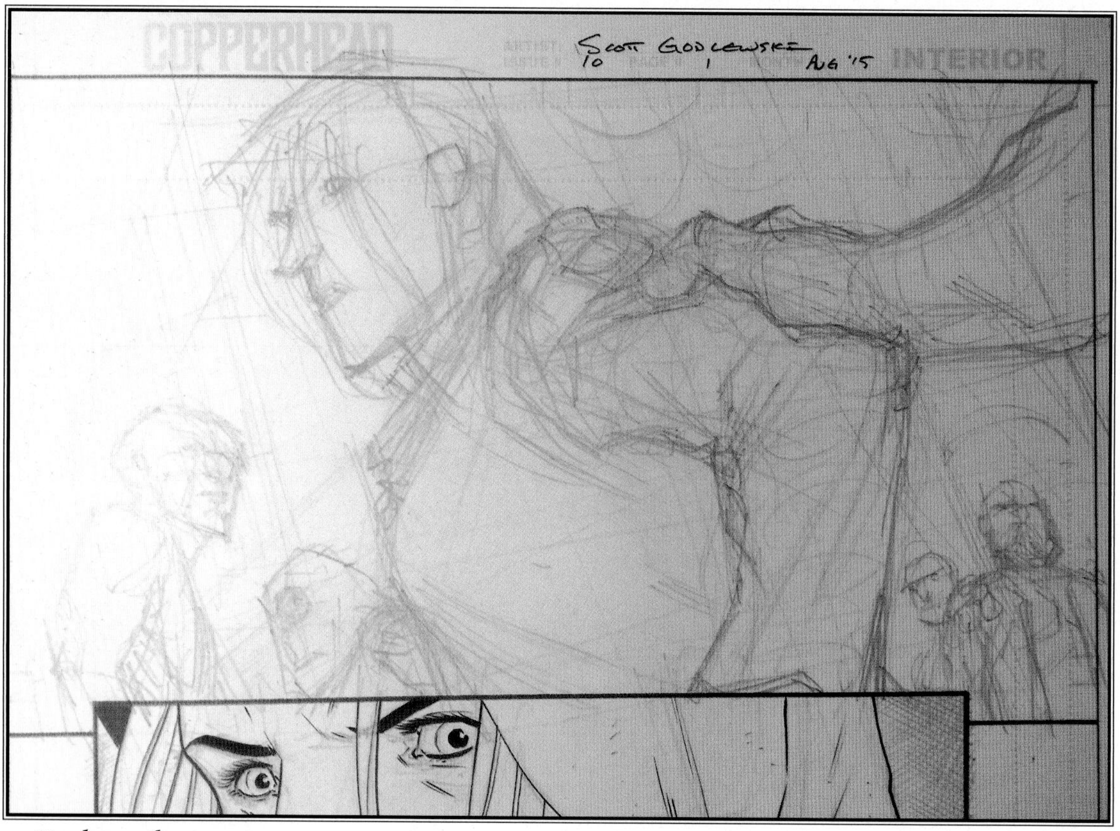
COPPERHEAD
SCOTT GODLEWSKI
10
1
AUG '15
INTERIOR

Final pencils

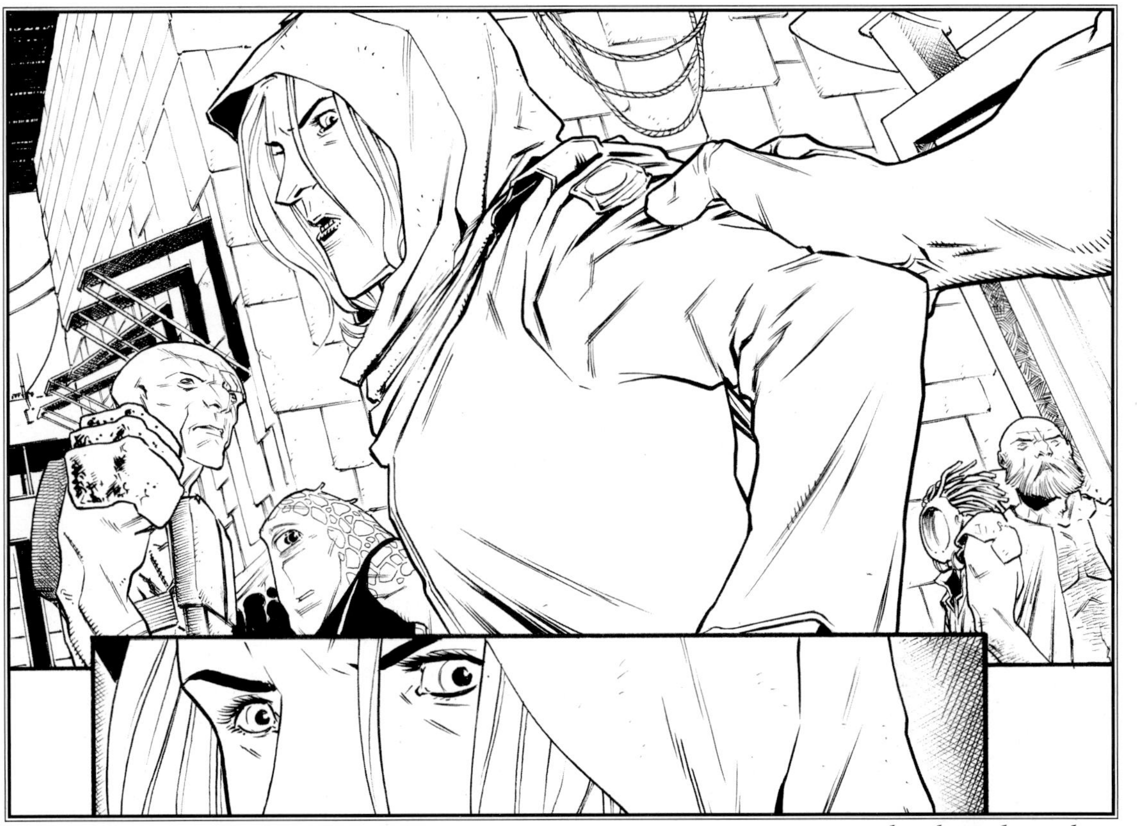

Scanned & cleaned up inks

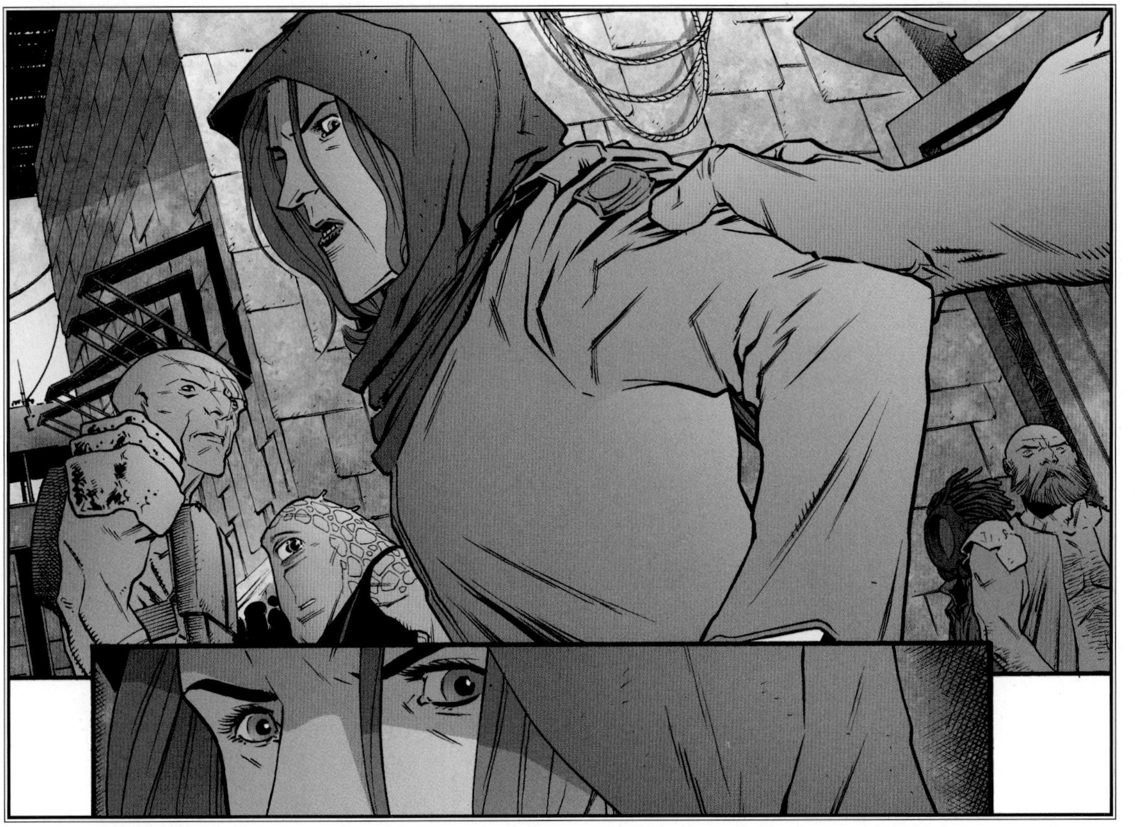

Colors

ZOLO THE GANG LEADER

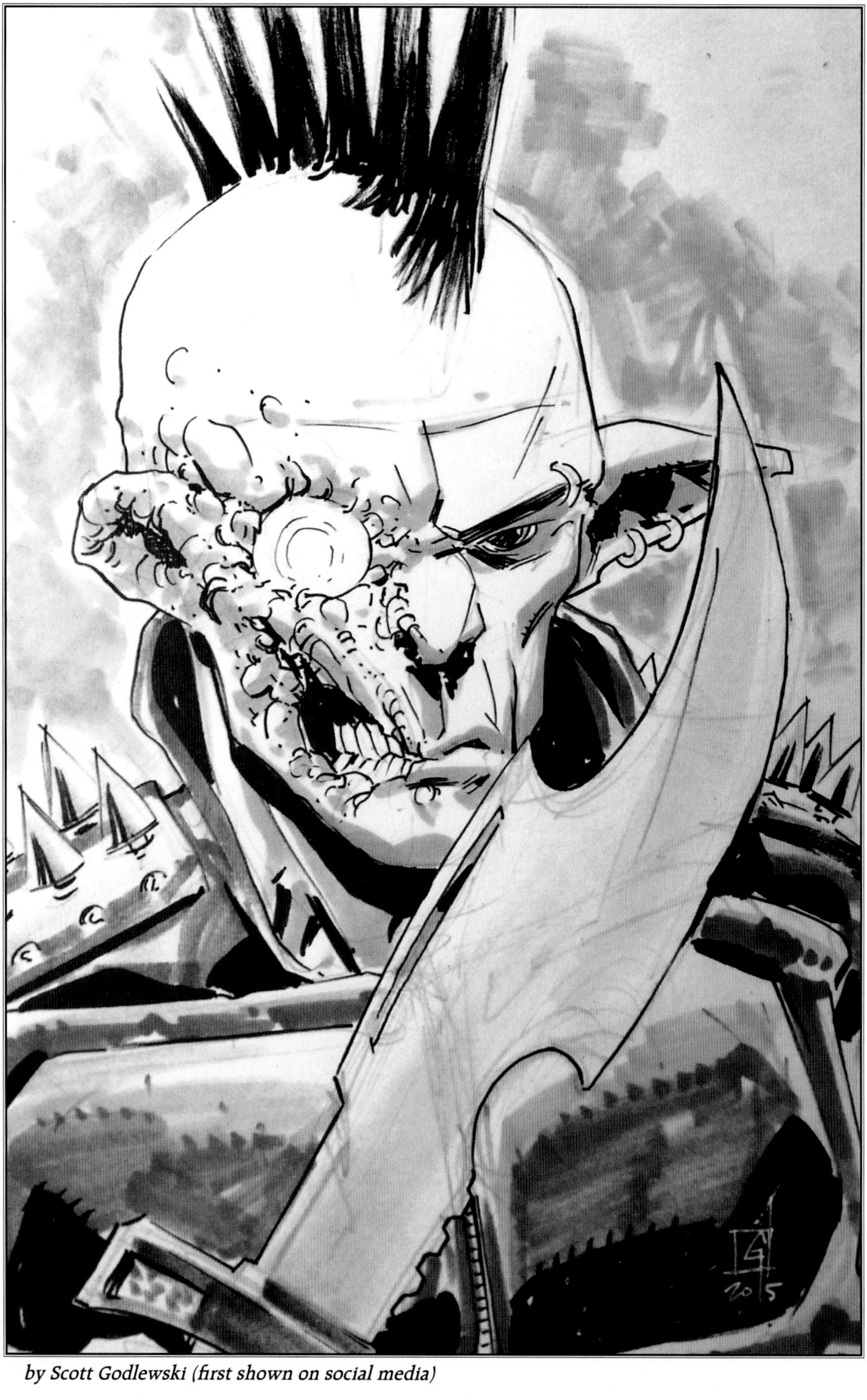

by Scott Godlewski (first shown on social media)

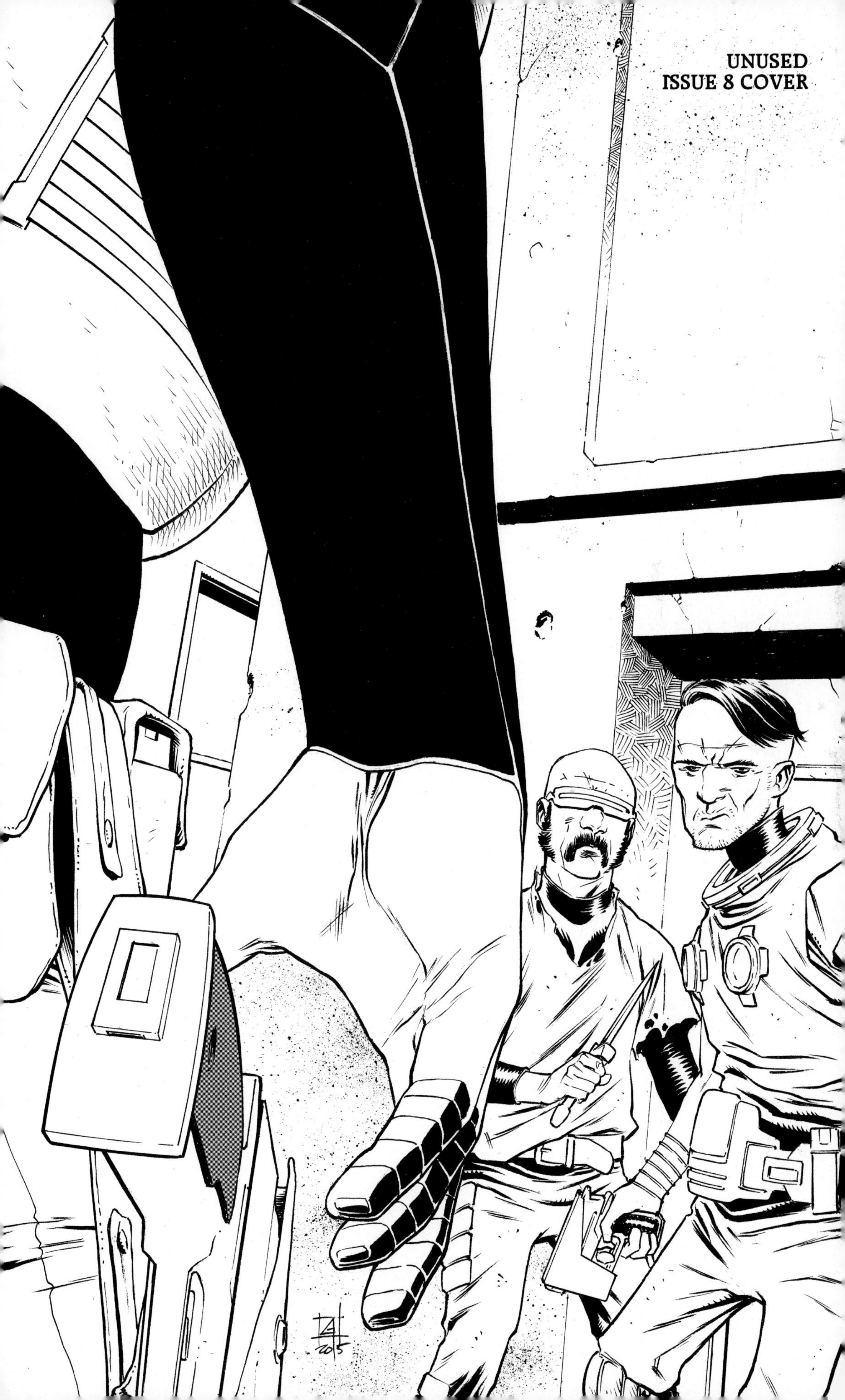

UNUSED
ISSUE 8 COVER

ISSUE 8 COVER PENCILS

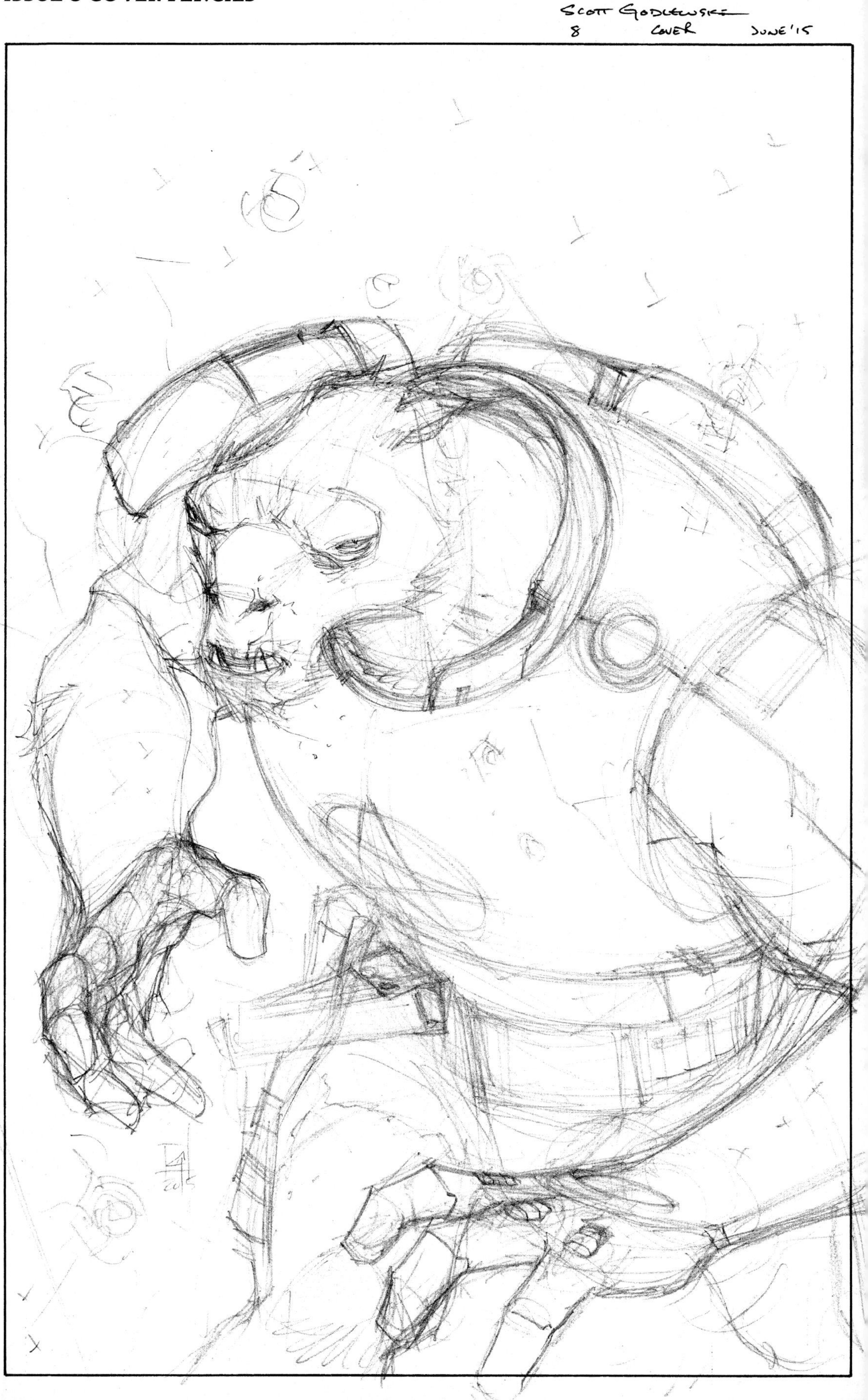
Scott Godlewski
8 Cover June '15

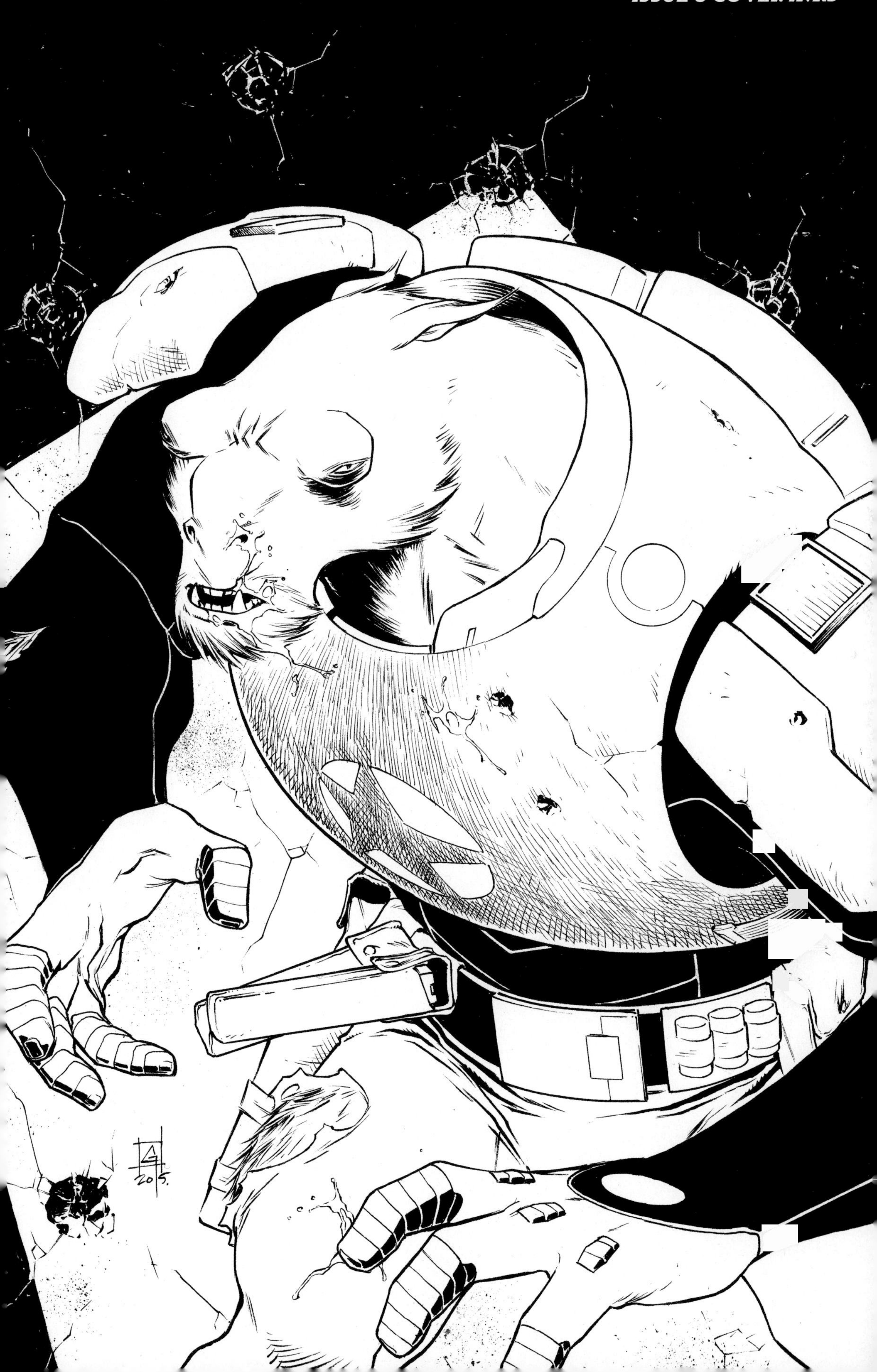

ISHMAEL

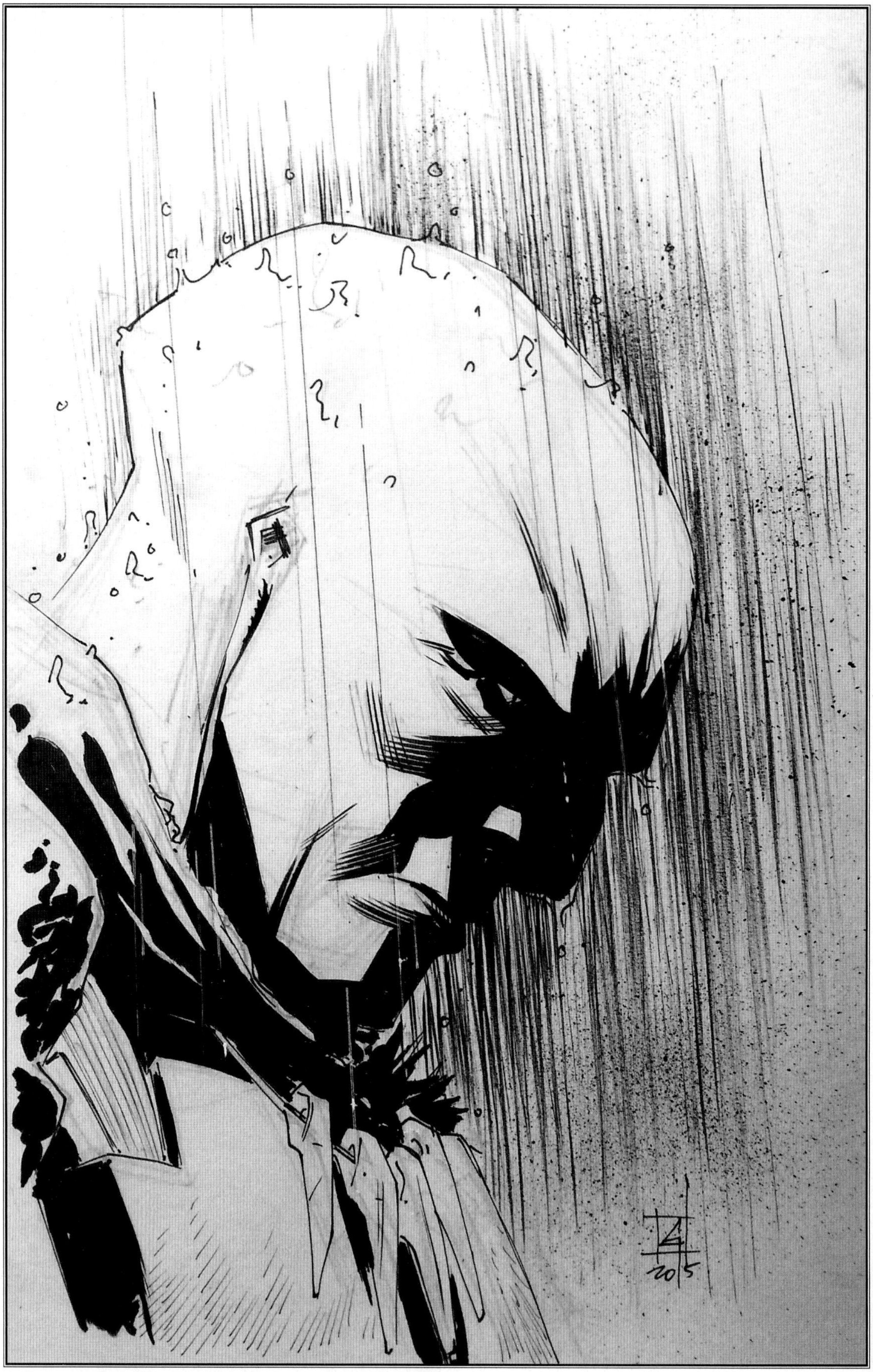

by Scott Godlewski (first shown on social media)

FROM IDEA TO FINAL COLORS — ISSUE 10 COVER PROCESS

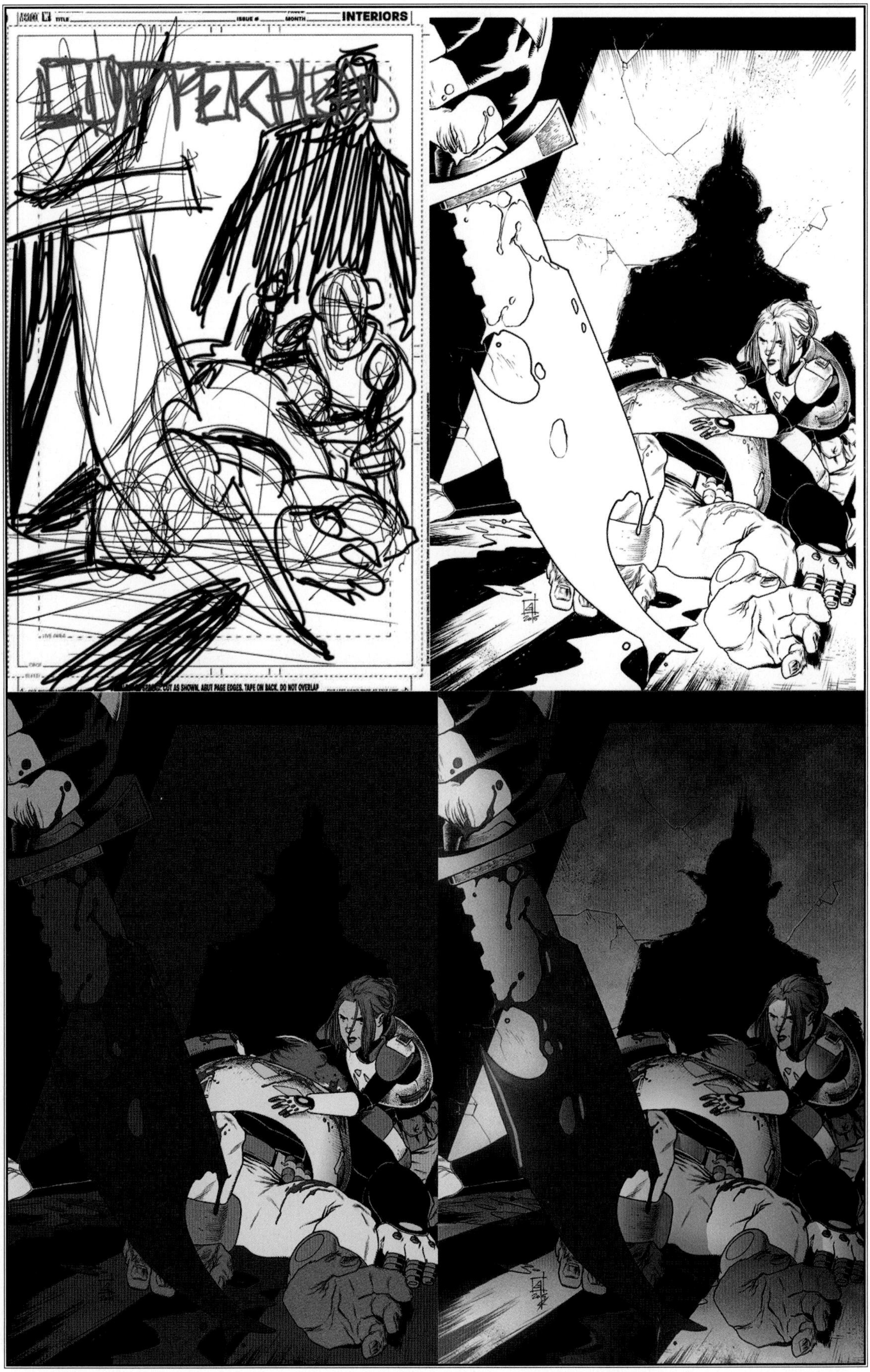
TITLE
ISSUE #
MONTH
INTERIORS
CUT AS SHOWN, ABUT PAGE EDGES, TAPE ON BACK, DO NOT OVERLAP

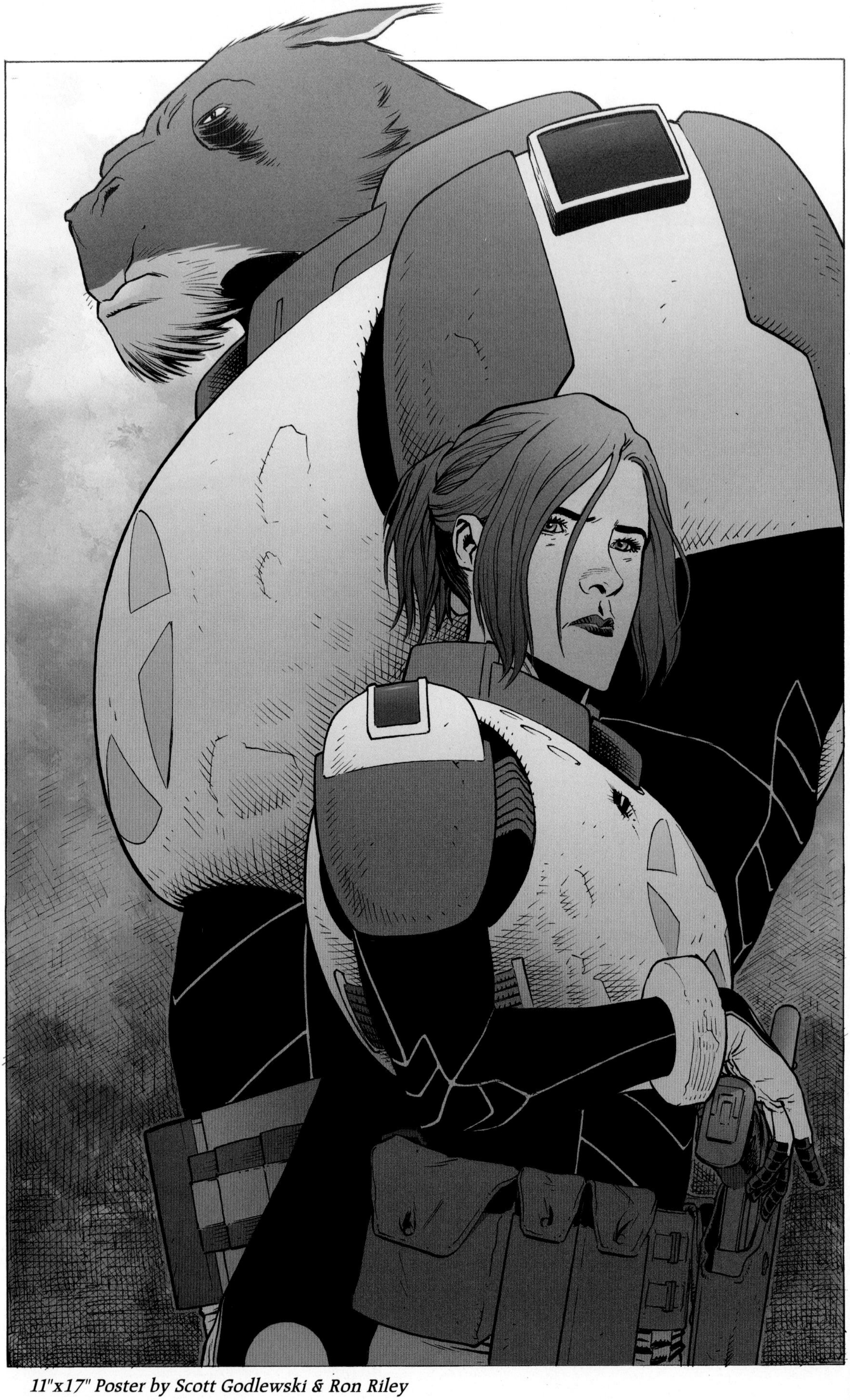

11"x17" Poster by Scott Godlewski & Ron Riley

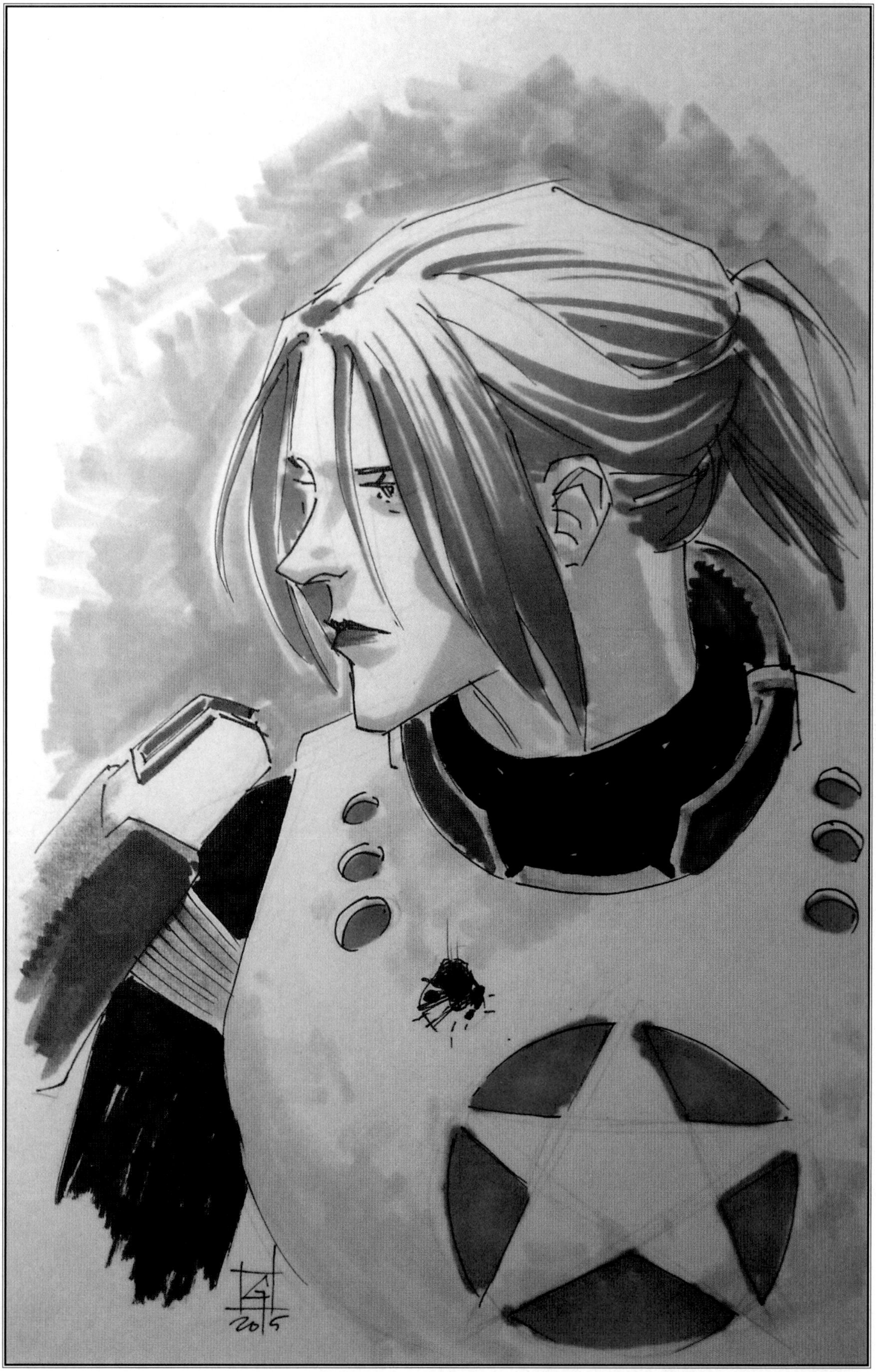

by Scott Godlewski (first shown on social media)